The Glass Eel

The Glass Eel

A NOVEL

J. J. VIERTEL

THE MYSTERIOUS PRESS
NEW YORK

THE GLASS EEL

Mysterious Press
An Imprint of Penzler Publishers
58 Warren Street
New York, N.Y. 10007

Copyright © 2025 by J. J. Viertel

Illustrations © 2025 John Wyatt Greenlee, Surprised Eel Mapping

First Mysterious Press edition

Interior design by Lia Kantrowitz

All rights reserved. No part of this book may be reproduced in whole or in part without written permission from the publisher, except by reviewers who may quote brief excerpts in connection with a review in a newspaper, magazine, or electronic publication; nor may any part of this book be reproduced, stored in a retrieval system, or transmitted in any form or by any means electronic, mechanical, photocopying, recording, or other, or used to train generative artificial intelligence (AI) technologies, without written permission from the publisher.

Library of Congress Control Number: 2025935472

ISBN: 978-1-61316-680-2
eBook ISBN: 978-1-61316-681-9

10 9 8 7 6 5 4 3 2 1

Printed in the United States of America

To Gabriel, who may one day write a book with *his* father.

CHAPTER ONE

Just after four fifteen on a Thursday morning in late April, Jeanette King was awakened from a dream by the insistent thrumming of a boat engine out on the reach. The whining drone was bouncing off the water, making it much louder than the boat's distance might suggest, but at this hour there was no way to know; it was still wet and dark outside, an unforgiving fog covering the ground and creating an impenetrable barrier between the water and the stars. There had been a thrumming sound in her dream as well, but although she had only just awakened, she couldn't remember what had caused it.

She flipped the switch of the lamp on the bedside table and knocked over the half-empty water glass she used to take her evening meds. Only water, she thought. It can dry by itself. The noise of the boat was constant but rising and lowering in volume and pitch as if the boat itself was circling something. Still a half hour until sunrise, she thought. Who the hell is out there?

Jeanette King lived on the reach, a mile-wide stretch of water that separated Caterpillar Island from the mainland; it opened at both ends into the Atlantic Ocean. Most of her friends in the community maintained old saltbox houses up by the road. Those houses had been built by lobstermen, who saw quite enough of the water every day. People from away built along the reach. She had moved into this place eight years earlier when the couple building it as a vacation home blew up their marriage just before the interior walls of the place had gone in. Building a house can do that to a marriage, she knew, though her own had imploded for its own reasons. Some nights she still missed it, but after it all fell apart, she found she couldn't stay in the home where they had lived together as a family—it was too painful. In any case, this house was a bargain, and she had finished the cabinets and kitchen counters herself. She was used to doing things for herself. She threw on a sweatshirt and jeans, located a headlamp hanging in the mudroom, and pulled on a parka with a broken zipper. I should just call the cops, she thought, but by the time the local Caterpillar Island police wake up someone at the Coast Guard, whoever is out there could perish in the dark water. Anyhow, if you want things done right . . .

She shook her head, pulled on her mud boots, and clambered along the hall, catching herself in the mirror of the coatrack by the side door. Her short hair was tousled helter-skelter by the parka hood, a little more gray in it than she might have liked, framing a round face and large, gray eyes that still attracted the lobstermen on the island, but she'd had enough of lobstermen. The sweatshirt and the unzippable parka bulked around the rest of her, obscuring a slender frame she remained moderately proud of. But not dressed like this. You look like a walking hedgehog, she thought.

She let herself out and made her way down to the dock, which had taken three years to get permitted. The fog was merciless, and the unmown grass slippery, but she made it without falling, guided by the light she had posted at the end of the dock. She walked the length of the wooden planks, down the ladderlike stairway to the floating platform that rose and fell with the tide, and got herself into her dinghy. Once her own outboard started, she knew it would be harder to distinguish the location of the boat out on the water, if not impossible. She cast off and turned on the headlamp, which made her feel like a wayward coal miner lost at sea, casting her gaze from side to side. A miasma of gray-white sea smoke moved over the surface as if it were on its way somewhere; it obscured the inky water out ahead. Reluctantly, she cursed and shut off the engine, the better to hear and track the location of whatever was out there. She began to row toward the sound. It was never easy. Once they take your lymph nodes, she thought, you don't want to be pulling oars anymore. But there wasn't a lot of choice. Any sane woman, she thought, would have gone back to bed.

Then, just as light was beginning to dawn over the hills, she saw it. Even through the haze, even at a good distance, she saw it: a lobster boat turning away from her in a lazy arc and flashing its backside with its name painted in red: *Jeanette*. It was her own damn boat—or had been for as long as she'd been a married woman.

"Well," she said to herself softly, "sign me up for an asshole."

She kicked her engine into action again and began to chase the boat that she once co-owned with a man whom, she had to admit, she still cared about on her better days. If that man was on that boat, what was he doing plowing an endless circle in one hundred feet of water that was a notoriously bad fishing ground for lobsters? No one laid traps on this stretch of the reach. And if he wasn't . . . she felt a knot in her belly start to tighten. Nothing to do but find out.

Less than a month earlier another lobster boat had been found derelict off Northport, with a respected fisherman named Tom Hinchcliffe trapped in the rigging of his own haul lines. He had been dead for a couple days, and it was likely mere chance that the boat had turned back to the harbor—he'd gone off to pull traps in deep water offshore. Speculation was that he'd either had a heart attack and, in collapsing, gotten hung up in his own lines, or that the attack had been brought on by the struggle to free himself once some mishap had thrust him into the rig as it brought up a trap. He had been on the ocean all his life, which might have explained his foolhardiness in heading out into deep water without a sternman to assist him.

This memory was stirring in Jeanette as she approached, but as the light began to brighten, she could see that the rigging was clean. The boat was clean—cleaner than it had been kept back in the day. She doubted she would find her ex-husband on board; he would not have stayed below while the boat turned an aimless, lazy circle through the chop. Still, she called for him as she approached.

"Simon, goddammit, if you're on that boat, get up here and tell me what's going on. You know I hate to miss my sleep."

There was no response. She navigated through the fog and when she got close enough, she tossed the anchor line over the gunwale of the *Jeanette*, pulled the dinghy up close, and clambered from one boat to the other, tying up the dinghy in the process. Her heart was thumping uncharacteristically, but she couldn't tell if it was exertion or fear that was driving it.

The boat was unmanned, the steering wheel tied off so that it would turn endlessly in a proscribed circle. She untied it and killed the engine. The sudden quiet was so profound that for a moment she just stood there. The birds weren't even up yet. Then she looked around. The sight of the boat always triggered memories, but she fought them off, armed with the likely possibility that her ex-husband was dead or missing or had met with some kind of foul play and was in danger. It was not exactly a moment for agitating memories of a life that was long gone. Even blissful ones down in the hold. Where the hell was he? There was no sign of a note, or anything that might have indicated a violent struggle. The damn boat was just empty, rocking gently in the current. She examined the rigging, which seemed in place. The chrome-plated winch handles were accounted for, and none of them showed signs of blood or hair or any other human grotesquerie of the kind that are always present on TV when someone is bludgeoned with a winch handle. No one's head had been beaten in.

As she surveyed the deck, she became aware of the soft humming of the saltwater pump that fed the live well. The large rectangular tank that served as a holding pen for the day's haul was directly in the center of the boat's open deck and could hold about seven hundred fifty pounds of lobsters, kept alive and fresh by movement of the water that was pumped through it continuously from under the boat. Why would it be running before first light, when nothing would be in it?

She moved to the well and took hold of the lid. She began to lift it but the hydraulics took over and it rose and tilted toward the stern on its own. If she was lucky, she thought, she'd see nothing but water in the live well. Less lucky would be the presence of a human body, broken, folded, and crammed into the only space on the boat big enough to hide one. The lid, assisted by the little hydraulic cylinder at each corner, glided open at a tilt. She gasped, leaped backward, and snagged her foot in the anchor line. She grabbed onto the boat's rail to keep from going over and stared down into the well. It was alive, but not with lobsters.

Thousands of baby eels swarmed and boiled in chaos in front of her, an aquatic perpetual motion machine, ugly and gasping and seeking—what? Escape? Food? Oxygen? Some kind of return to the open water? She stared down at them, each only a few inches long, translucent, and no thicker than a matchstick. They pulsed with the urge to survive and grow. They were repellent, but so fascinating in their passion for movement that she stood and stared, mesmerized. Elvers. What were they doing here, in a boat with no skipper? Curiosity quickly overcame her shock, and she dipped a finger into the water to try to pick one up. The tiny creatures slithered past, flattening up against it as a cat might against your calf—if you had a cat. She had no use for pets. She pulled her hand away and wiped the unctuous slime from her finger on the parka.

"God, I hate cats," she said aloud to no one. But something shut her up and she cocked her head to the water. The grinding of an outboard motor. She looked up into the coming dawn to see a small Boston Whaler slapping its way across the water, heading directly for the *Jeanette*. She pushed down the top of the live well. There was enough light now to chase some of the fog, and she could make out a scruffy-looking young man at the wheel, wearing a brimmed and battered Red Sox cap. He was tearing through the water directly at her.

Now, for the first time, she felt fear in a profound sort of way that momentary panic does not approach. There was a lot she didn't understand, but an able-bodied young man approaching the boat with purpose was likely to mean any number of bad things for a forty-nine-year-old woman who had no idea how the boat had gotten there, where its proper skipper was, and why anyone would have moved thousands of baby eels into the reach from whatever creeks they had been fished out of.

The young man pulled alongside and looked at her, tipping his head in a way that suggested uncertainty, but not fear.

"Mrs. King?" he said, betraying some confusion.

"Joey?" she asked in return. "Joey Pizio?"

It had been a long time. But the sight of him struck a melancholy chord. He had been one of Liam's playmates, a long time ago—the lovable underdog who got everything wrong. She hadn't seen him since Liam's funeral almost a decade earlier, when he looked like a typical shaggy-haired high school kid in an ill-fitting Sunday church suit. But something had happened to him. He was sallow, his eyes unfocused, his body gaunt. And what was he doing here?

"You and Simon back together?" he asked, blinking.

"I wouldn't go that far," she said, not wanting to give anything away. There was nothing to be gained by answering questions until she had more answers herself. Just act like it's your boat; it even has your name on it. Chase every other thought away, and especially the dark ones. "How are you, Joey?"

He tied the Whaler to a cleat on the port side of the *Jeanette* and tossed a cheap plastic tackle box onto the deck of the bigger boat.

"Can't complain," he said. "Who'd listen?"

He pulled himself aboard with too much effort for so young a man.

"You're looking good," he said. "Been a long time."

"Maybe since the funeral," she said. "I haven't kept up with any of the boys."

"Yes ma'am," he said, nodding slowly. "Can't say I blame you for that. I still miss him sometimes myself. Hard times. That, and then the cancer—I heard about that."

"Thank you, Joey. I beat the cancer. I guess the other thing never goes away."

For a moment they stood facing each other with nothing to say. Then he flipped the lid on the live well, looked at the elvers and closed it again.

"I didn't know you were working for Simon," she said.

"Working *with* him more like. I'd a thought he would have told you," Joey said, "seeing as you're out here, I mean."

"Well, you know Simon," she said after taking a breath. "The strong, silent type."

"Don't talk much if he don't have to," Joey agreed.

"Have you seen him around?" she asked as casually as she could.

"Thought I'd see him here. But here you are instead. It'll be light soon—you should probably scoot. I'll take it from here."

"Where exactly?" she asked. His face clouded over with suspicion.

"Just pick 'em up and drop 'em off," he said, giving up nothing. "That's all I know. And all we're supposed to know."

She looked at him critically for a moment. Bleary dark eyes, pupils a little dilated, mud-colored hair that was still too long and unruly to stay inside the baseball cap, about a week's worth of facial hair. Joey Pizio had gotten older, but didn't seem to have grown up. She could still see a hint of the sweet, troubled kid he had once been.

"I hardly recognized you," she lied, looking for an opening of some kind. "You've changed."

Come on, Joey, she thought, hoping if she kept him talking, he'd share something that might explain what they were doing out there, bobbing in the reach.

"I don't feel changed," he said. "Course I'd be the last one to find out. Just doing my job. Earn a living not working too hard. Not in school anymore, if that's what you mean."

"I mean, what have you been up to?"

"Doing what I'm doing now." He looked around uneasily, like he didn't want to be there much longer. "Mrs. King, it's getting light soon. You need to let me go with the boat now. You know how it works."

He pointed to her dinghy. She had no idea how anything worked. But Joey seemed to have his orders. Dutifully, Jeanette climbed over the side of the boat that had been named for her and into her much smaller one.

He untied her, handed her the anchor line she had used to hook the dinghy to the *Jeanette*, and then reached down to the deck for the tackle box, which he pitched into the dinghy.

"Simon'll be expecting that," he said.

"A tackle box?"

But Joey had already hit the starter on the big lobster boat, and it roared to life. He gunned it, plowing away to the south, dragging his Whaler behind, leaving her drifting in the reach.

For a few minutes Jeanette just sat as the little boat rolled in the chop. Joey Pizio. It seemed he hadn't turned out well. But no one had ever thought he would. She had held out some hope.

Then she started her outboard and motored back to the dock.

Inside the house, she shed her gear, put on a robe and slippers, and took the tackle box into the kitchen, where the overhead light was strong. It was still early enough so that the house remained otherwise dark. She put the box on the counter and flipped open the latch. It was a cheap plastic item, bright red, and without a lock. The top two trays contained light tackle—soft plastic jigs, split-shot sinkers in a plastic dispenser, and some hooks in a plastic sleeve—weekend flounder fisherman stuff from the Walmart, not the type of thing that would ever be used by anyone in the business. She lifted the two trays out and set them on the counter. Worthless junk. There hadn't been any flounder in the reach since the 1980s. At the bottom of the box was a red leatherette pouch with a zipper running along one side. She unzipped it. Inside the pouch were four packets of twenty-dollar bills. Three were untouched; the band was torn on the last. Eight thousand, seven hundred dollars in crisp new twenty-dollar bills, and a fifty that looked to have been around for a while.

Jeanette King had never seen that much cash in one place at one time. The divorce had allowed her to buy the house, with a hefty mortgage, but it had been an uphill battle since the day she moved in. The alimony payments came and went but hiring a lawyer to look into it when they didn't come was out of reach. She spent the better part of each week picking crabmeat and packing it in half-pint plastic tubs to sell to New York chefs and the local stores patronized by summer people. She built the crab shack too. It was up across the street on a spoon-shaped piece of land that had come with the house. The revenue barely covered the payments on the construction loan. On weekends she cut hair at a beauty salon called Bea's Hive of Beauty in Brockton. When the summer people came, she waitressed at the Mariner's Grille, dishing out lobster rolls and haddock-and-chips baskets to whatever tourist families made it this far north. The tips were good, and the waitress job had allowed her to buy a beaten-down Mister Softee ice cream truck at auction. She'd had it refurbished so that she could deliver the refrigerated crabmeat as well as product from other local shacks to Bangor International, where it was shipped to New York.

The work on the truck had been done by a jack-of-all-trades named Keith Fulbright, who was also building the house next door for some new summer people. He painted *The Crab Lady* in canary yellow across the side of the truck, so that was the name of the company. She was in debt to Keith too. Some days it seemed like she didn't own anything outright but her clothes. Still, she was managing about as well as a lot of locals on the island, and better than many.

Now, sitting on the counter was enough cash to stop the overdue notices from arriving weekly. Not enough to get her whole—not nearly enough for that—but enough to stanch the bleeding. She dreamed of paying up and getting out, beginning something new, but she was never sure what. Probably nothing. In any case, there was nothing here but a down payment on what she already owed.

Something, though, moved down her spine as she stacked the bills back up again—an icy small voice that told her not to use it, not without thinking about it more. Most of it was too new. And then there were the eels. She shuddered at the memory of them—freakish, their outsized eyes, their bodies like molten glass, the slime of them that remained along her index finger when she tried to pick one up. Glass eels, some called them. She'd heard of the elver trade in Maine but had never been close to it. People talked about elvers in the same hushed voices they used to talk about black-market pain pills. And now it seemed her ex-husband, always a schemer, might be caught up in yet another bad idea.

Typical Simon. She put the money back in the leather pouch, turned on the coffee maker, which she always set up the night before, sat down, and called Simon on her cell phone. Straight to voicemail. She put the phone down and waited.

CHAPTER TWO

The most notable characteristic of the crab shack was the stench of long-dead seafood that saturated the air and was apparently impossible to purge. The women who worked there seemed inured to it and the place was otherwise clean and unremarkable. Four clapboard walls held a set of metal apron hooks, each of them marked by a trickle of rust on the white paint where the water got in during the winter. At one narrow end were stacked crates of whole cooked crabs, at the other were two oversize refrigerators: one for the whole crabs to be stored in, the other for the processed crabmeat. When both hummed with power simultaneously, the lights over the long steel table in the middle of the room would dim slightly, making the work slower. Next to a slop sink was a saltwater tank that could hold a mass of live crabs waiting for the steamer, which was out back. The table held a tower of half-pint-sized plastic tubs and lids that grew and fell as the workday went on. Three women were seated there, working silently when Jeanette walked in. She'd been up since the boat had awakened her and carried the bone-deep ache of sleeplessness through her whole body. No one commented on her late arrival—she owned the place.

She had started picking crabs after she and Simon had finalized the divorce, and she had gone into business for herself a year later, just about the time the market heated up. Maine rock crabs, which were prehistoric, were suddenly newly minted as peekytoes by some food industry genius and became the perfect protein for twenty-eight-dollar crab salads in Manhattan and for even more expensive mille-feuilles. Mainers were mystified but grateful. They had been calling the crabs *picket toes* for as far back as anyone could remember because of the small spike between each of their claws, but the name change had transformed them from an annoying nuisance that lobstermen pitched back into the sea into a gourmet delight. Not one diner in a hundred could taste the difference between a peekytoe and any other kind of crab, but the rechristening was a testament to the genius of marketing, even marketing that was not all that ingenious.

The pickers—mostly the wives of lobstermen—suffered from backaches and an array of tiny cuts on their hands, but they gossiped and labored, heads down, like factory workers, tearing apart the little bastards up and down the coast. Two of the women who worked alongside Jeanette were married to lobstermen. Patsy Hinchcliffe, a large, thick-fingered woman, could still pick faster than anyone on the island, and cleaner too. She was Jeanette's first hire, and still the best. Patsy had been asked by a top-line New York chef to sign her personal tubs of crabmeat so that he could be sure of having the cleanest ones with the most fully preserved lumps of claw meat. This left her satisfied that she had achieved all that could be achieved. Amelia Boyer was older than Jeanette by twenty-five years, but she was still a beauty. Her white hair was cut short, and she had high cheekbones, blue eyes, and pale, unmarked skin. Her husband was still out on the water, even though he was looking at seventy-five. He had installed indoor plumbing to celebrate their tenth anniversary. She'd shared the story with the ladies on approaching their fiftieth.

"That must have been such a nice upgrade when it happened," Jeanette said.

"Heavens no! It was disgusting. Having a bowel movement in a room next to the kitchen! Can you imagine? But it's like anything." Amelia sighed. "You get used to it."

Patsy and Amelia were compelled by certain desires that their husbands either couldn't afford to satisfy or had no interest in—a Caribbean cruise, money for their kids' college tuition, a comfortable retirement. Their men didn't seem to understand any of these things. They understood trucks and boats, chain saws and deer rifles.

Jeanette had found the third woman a few months ago, smoking a cigarette in front of Bea's Hive of Beauty. Lottie Pride was tiny and dark haired with olive skin and a voice that had something shrill behind it; she never raised her voice, but Jeanette thought she always seemed ready for an argument. She worked two days a week in an otherwise vacant office above the hair salon, which seemed to have no name or announced purpose. The rest of the week she'd been unemployed, living on food stamps and gumption. Jeanette liked her, liked her disagreeability and her deadly earnestness, and her unapologetic need for smoking breaks. She had absolutely no sense of humor, which was somehow endearing. She looked to be in her thirties and claimed to be Passamaquoddy. Jeanette was just glad to have played a role in getting her off government assistance.

Jeanette lifted a mound of crabs from a corner of the room with a metal snow shovel and dumped them onto the table. Then she took her seat with the other three, placing her cell phone on the table, face up. Ring, you bastard, she thought.

"Jeanette, you seen my knife?" Patsy asked. They used short, curved knives, shaped like a bird's beak, with white plastic handles to pick the crabmeat. Patsy preferred one that had been sharpened so many times it had become wire thin. The handle had been partially melted when it had been left too close to the coil on the electric stove. She was partial to it.

"Just use one of the ones in the drawer. I just got some more. They're all the same, Patsy."

"You know that's my lucky knife," Patsy said, looking emotionally struck. Then she looked up from her work long enough to take in Jeanette. "You look like you been on a bender," she said. "You all right?"

"Cramps," Jeanette lied. "You know. Kept me up all night."

"Thank God those days are over," said Amelia Boyer. "Three M's. First the monthlies, then the menopause. Don't pay to be a woman."

"That's two," Patsy said.

"Morgue comes next. Some folks don't want to grow old—I'm just grateful I'm past the first two." She went back to work.

"I can't wait," said Lottie.

"You don't know," said Patsy.

"I'm ready to be done with this part," Lottie replied evenly. "I'm not making babies in this world anyway. There's plenty too many already. No more cramps every month and having to sit in the moon tent during the sweat. You all don't have to do that."

"Nobody said you had to either," Patsy said, winking at Jeanette.

"I say so."

"The change," Patsy said grimly, looking back down at the carapace in her hands. "Something else to look forward to."

"Oh, it's grand," said Amelia. "And just when you think you had your last time, you get one standing in the checkout line at the Walmart, you have to deal with it, and you feel like you're thirteen again. And then one day it really is done, and no man ever looks at you again. That's the part I don't like."

Jeanette stayed silent, regretting bringing up the topic. She was facing fifty, and not happy about it. Any of it. But that's how conversation ran in the crab shack. She cracked the claws off a crab, plunged her razor-sharp paring knife between the crab's eyes, and pried the head and abdomen away from the rest. Then she asked, as innocently as she could manage, "Any of you ladies know anything about the eel trade? I was reading an article . . ." She let her voice trail off. It was a carefully rehearsed speech, brief as it was.

"Elvers? You should know—you're in the seafood business," Amelia Boyer said. "We're already halfway through the season."

"I do crabs. I don't do eels," Jeanette responded, a little defensively.

"Elvers," said Lottie. "Just another fishery that should be ours."

"Here we go," Patsy replied, looking to heaven.

"Native people would run a sustainable fishery. And with everybody craving sushi—you think there's money in lobsters? The real money is in elvers."

"How's that?" Jeanette asked.

"Don't encourage her," Patsy said. Amelia Boyer sucked in her perfect cheeks and snapped the lid on a tub of crabmeat.

"Twenty-five hundred dollars a pound," Lottie continued, "and there are about fifteen hundred of them in a pound . . ."

Jeanette glanced down at the cell phone; $2,500 a pound of anything would certainly be of interest to Simon.

"Worth a fortune, sure," Patsy chimed in. "But creepy looking—like a million see-through snakes in a barrel."

"I never saw them," Jeanette lied again, hoping it wouldn't come back to haunt her.

"And you think eels are ugly," Patsy said. "The men who trap them are worse. That's some unsavory types. Monsters, really."

Jeanette blanched. *Monsters.*

"They do a good business though," Lottie said, "killing the fishery."

"The ones that survive and grow up are okay eating if you don't have to look at them. My dad used to catch them with worms in the Bagaduce," Patsy said. "They got no balls, I hear, nor wombs neither. No one knows how they get born."

"Show me a fish with balls," Lottie responded. "All we know is when it comes time to breed, have a big orgy in the Sargasso Sea and then die. Four thousand miles from here. The current brings the babies back to us."

Patsy Hinchcliffe snorted. "Long way to go to get laid."

Amelia Boyer laughed out loud, a sound Jeanette wasn't sure she had ever heard before. "I do not like talking about the change of life." She snorted. "But eel sex is worse."

"How do you know all this?" Jeanette asked Lottie.

Patsy Hinchcliffe sighed, and signed the top of a crab tub, sliding it down to Jeanette's end of the table.

"I'm an advocate for indigenous fishing rights," Lottie said. "I have to know everything. White people fish for them, Koreans buy and grow them, but the Creator knows it is our fishery."

Jeanette was on point of asking for more, but a quick scowl from Patsy Hinchcliffe silenced her. Just pick crab. She looked down at the table where her cell phone lay inert among the dead crab bodies. Ring, she commanded in her head once more, but the phone refused to cooperate. Bad phone service in the shack, she thought. Maybe there'll be a message.

The tubs of crabmeat piled up and Jeanette carried them to the refrigerator. Eleven dollars each, wholesale. And elvers were $2,500 a pound.

THE CRAB

Where the stony creek met the reach it was edged with a mat of tangled seaweed, and the hollow heads of it bobbed on the surface, following the tide up, up toward its fully extended breaking point, skate eggs clinging, larval shrimp snapping here and there, sleeping life waiting to be dispersed into a ready-made nursery of nooks and crannies, protection from those larger, and, at the same time, food for those that could find a way in.

A crab scuttled across the pebbled bottom, hovering, grabbing, and pulling itself along. The seaweed slid past its shell, while small shrimp flipped themselves out of its path. Its suspicious pendulum eyes, like the burnt end of a short piece of fishing line, reached to see in every direction. With the legs of a dancer, it seemed to steer its own shell along, always level, its face folded, tucked in, as though waiting to stretch out when the time was right. It was never right.

For a moment the crab rested. A herring swam too close; claws snapped open, the body tilted back, and the claws traced the path of the herring like an antiaircraft gun following the path of a plane. The herring veered into deeper water and disappeared into the shadowy haze of the creek, which, as the tide rose, flowed upstream. For a long moment the crab remained still. Then the claws relaxed, the shell tilted back down, and the eyes extended and looked about. The crab resumed its march.

The sharp edges of the shadows on the seafloor began to soften, as if a cloud was passing between the water and the sun. The crab slowed. Then, at once, the shadow was all around—the crab tipped back again, jabbing its open claws upward. But there was nothing to aim at. It was surrounded by blackness. A cloud of wriggling eels, each skinnier than one of the crab's legs, and not much longer, snaked up the creek. They seemed a never-ending wave. The water was so thick with them, they blackened the crab's sky. The crab turned to one side, then the other, jabbing and snapping. There were too many to see any one of them. A little eel, its eye almost as big as its head, brushed against the crab's shell as it flashed by, followed by another, and another. The crab spun left and right, pointing defiant claws at the endless swarm until one side of it slipped off a piece of blue stone, and it flipped over entirely, coming to rest where the stone met the gravel bottom. It was upside down.

It tucked its crab claws into its body, and lay there, still, like an hors d'oeuvre. Only its eyes, peering on their awestruck sticks, moved, watching the river of eels flow above it. And then, as quickly as they had arrived, they were gone, up the stream with the rising tide, toward slower waters, undercut banks, pools, and an unseen lily pond at the head of the creek. Those that found a still spot would call it home, at least for a time, and for the luckiest of them, for the better part of a decade. Once they had passed, light shone on the bottom again, and on the crab's bright belly. It waved its legs, reaching for something to pull itself over. Its front leg caught a piece of the blue stone and slowly the crab levered its way over and settled upright.

It paused and looked in all directions before tiptoeing out of the water onto the dry sand. On land, newly bound by gravity, its hovering ceased. The crab marched sideways, looking around, at first in a rush, then more tentatively. Being on land was dangerous. A double-dashed track in the sand spread behind it and melted away where it met the water.

The crab picked its way along the base of a blue stone ledge, which rose sharply out of the sand. Its eyestalks searched the open area in front. When it passed under a shadow, the crab paused.

The shadow shifted suddenly, and the crab flinched, but that was all it had time to do. A man's shoe came down hard on the crab. The carapace broke into three pieces; greasy brown intestines and feathery gray gills smeared into the sand.

Its legs twitched, its claws extended upward and pinched three times, first quickly, then slowly. And then they closed, and they did not pinch anymore.

The shoe was a wingtip made of burnished full-grain leather with leather soles. The man wearing the shoe also wore a tweed suit and a blue oxford shirt. He was modest in height but fit looking—an athletically built man. He had been sitting on the rock ledge surveying the creek bed when he noticed the crab leaving the water. When he saw the crab work its way toward him along the edge of the stone, the man had slowly raised his leg, and waited, motionless, holding his foot suspended.

The skin on the man's face was pulled taut, like a mask made of scar tissue. His eyes peered out as though from behind the face. After the man stopped holding his foot suspended, when he heard the crack and the squish, he smiled, and breathed out satisfaction, as though a deep need had been met. But it was not a normal smile. His facial muscles were functional, but their effect was somehow blunted, so the smile appeared only half accomplished. Still, in his eyes, the man looked happy.

But when the man examined his shoe and saw the crab's hepatopancreas smeared, mustard yellow, on the deep brown leather, the smile disappeared, and he cursed quietly. He kicked some sand onto the crab carcass in disgust and took a long drink of watery iced coffee from a plastic Dunkin' Donuts cup through a straw, until it gurgled empty. He threw the cup into the creek and began walking up the bank. He stopped and wiped his shoe on a clump of sea lavender until he was satisfied that the mustard taint was mostly gone. He shook his head as he walked.

There were two cars and an old ice cream truck that had been repainted in the little parking area. All three had license plates with images of lobsters on them. The man passed them by and ambled down the road for fifty yards or so, where a turnout provided good cover for his own car. He unlocked it with an electric key fob, opened the door, and pulled a wet nap out of a dispenser on the dashboard. He balanced himself on one leg, leaning against the side of the car as he wiped the remains of the crab's insides from his shoe. The license plate on the car had a little red barn on it, not a lobster. Instead of *Vacationland*, it read *America's Dairyland*. A plastic shopping bag with a Home Depot logo sat on the passenger seat. He got into the car, fastened his seat belt, and drove away.

On the bank of the creek, two flies buzzed over the crab, and a gull approached, with its head cocked to the side, holding one foot up, then the other. Its beak tugged at the torn carcass of the crab. A breeze blew the clear plastic cup with the pink and orange letters into the water, where it bobbed slowly inland and caught on a branch. The sea lavender's leaves were torn and bruised dark, with bits of yellow smeared on them. They quivered in the breeze.

The tide continued to rise.

CHAPTER THREE

The women finished the day's allotment at four, cleaned up the place until almost five, hosing down everything, which helped with the smell. They carried contractor bags of shells and guts to the side of the road to be picked up by the organic farm on Cape Herrington to use as fertilizer and said their goodbyes.

Caterpillar Island was shaped like its namesake, twenty-eight miles long and about five miles across in the widest spots, but the road Jeanette was driving on ran by a dozen inlets and coves that usually slowed her down as she took time to gaze out at the smaller rock islands that dotted the water, the boats and the landscape—clamming beaches at low tide that all but disappeared when high water came in, and sea grapes and beach peas tangling with each other along the side of the road above the gravel on the beach. Now that it was almost May they'd be starting to bud out, but spring crawled along at a snail's pace this far north. You could watch it inch forward day by day. She looked forward to it, the stately tempo of it.

The place had never been densely populated, but here and there she noticed new construction; the increase in out-of-staters, people from away, was relatively recent. Now that southern Maine had begun to seem like a suburb of Boston, second-home people were beginning to turn up with increasing frequency, like the couple building next door. The second-home people had money to burn, though where they got it from was a mystery. For people on the island, work was work. If a job wasn't in the Bible—fisherman, carpenter, farmer—it wasn't really a job. An investment banker, folks supposed, must be like a moneylender. But a management consultant? Must be some sort of prostitute. Those were in the Bible too.

Usually it took Jeanette a half hour to drive from the crab shack to the lobster co-op where Simon's boat was moored, but today she raced, her Subaru wagon keeping pace with her unquiet mind.

Simon. The man who had insisted that she was an artist and brought home whatever flotsam and jetsam he could collect when he was out pulling traps—lobster buoys that had come loose from their traplines, busted Styrofoam coolers that had fallen from some tourist cruise—surely she could paint them up with little island scenes and sell them to the increasing number of "citiots," as he called them. Pull in some extra cash in the process. She didn't know whether to be flattered or humiliated and was both. Simon, who had invented the lobster skylight—something for the wealthiest and most exclusive new homes: put a skylight aquarium in your living room and fill it with live lobsters so you could watch them as you enjoyed your martinis or whatever it was you drank at cocktail time. He had even built one, as a model, hoisted it up to the roof of their home, and watched as the lobsters gradually baked in the sunlight until they all floated upside down and began to stink. He was not a practical man. But he had a million entertaining ideas, and most often she was grateful to be married to a lobsterman who was actually interested in having fun, crazy as the ideas often were.

His disdain for his actual profession—his father had been a lobsterman and what else was he supposed to do—and his dreams of glory had made him an endearing husband, at least for a time.

At five forty-five P.M., Jeanette stared down at the moorings surrounding the lobster co-op from a bluff above the harbor. She stood by the driver's seat of the Subaru, trying to find the *Jeanette*. It was not at its mooring. She got back in the car, slipped it into gear, and headed down to the dock. That idiot Billy Willig, the wide-eyed dockmaster, was no help.

"Dunno," he said in response to her question about when the boat had last come in. "She's not here now, then sometimes she is. Yesterday, maybe. If Simon was here today, I sure didn't see him."

"What about your brother Kenny?" she asked. "Wasn't he Simon's sternman?"

"Simon fired him. Said he couldn't see paying a sternman seventeen cents on the dollar when he could do the work himself."

"That's Simon," Jeanette replied. "Thinks he's being strategic when he's just being cheap."

"It's you who said it," Billy replied.

Back in the car she headed off to the west, homeward bound, growing progressively unnerved. And it annoyed her that the idea of seeing the boat, the hope of seeing it, fired a flash of memory from the days when she was young. She had sometimes served as her husband's volunteer sternman.

"Well, you've got the stern for the job," he said sometimes. Then he would slap her gently on the ass and off they'd go. Corny but sweet. A vanished world. What had he ever done in the end but break her heart, steal away their only child, and escape into the silence of guilt? She was ready for an end to the nostalgia and the deep sadness it always brought with it as an unwelcome guest.

She inhaled deeply and turned off the road—the turn she had made for so many years—and made her way to the house she and Simon had shared from the day they married. It had been Simon's parents' house before that—a nondescript Maine saltbox with a flower garden she had kept in front and an inflatable swimming pool in the backyard during the short summer season. The pool had come down in the fall before Liam died and never been seen again—she had no idea what Simon had done with it. The end of good times.

The place looked abandoned. But she stopped to look at the yard. Simon's lobster traps were neatly stacked on the lawn four high. They should have been on the ocean bottom baited with bags of bunker and herring. He was not lobstering.

Nor was he at home. The house was locked up and the shades drawn. She walked around to the back but that door, too, was dead bolted. No lights were on and it was coming on dusk. Rattled, she returned to the car and headed home.

∗∗

As she turned into her driveway, she saw that a bright red Ford Mustang had beaten her to the only real parking space in front of her porch, so she stopped the car by the side of the road and got out.

Two men were seated on a little rusted wrought iron bench that ran along the porch wall outside her front door. One she recognized instantly—it was Joey Pizio. The man next to him was older, more broadly built, with a neatly trimmed beard and wraparound polarized shades. She had seen him before, around the lobster co-op, where he had started working a few years before, but she had never met him. He stood as she climbed the three steps to the porch. Joey stayed where he was.

"Jeanette King?" he said. "I believe you have something that belongs to us." His voice was lacquered.

Jeanette took a breath. Her heart began to pound again, and her mouth was suddenly dry. She had managed to keep her composure with Joey on the boat, but now there were two of them.

The older one held out his hand.

"Bennett Tyson," he said. "May we?" He gestured to the front door.

"I don't think so," she said. It was barely a croak. Who knew if he was armed or simply far stronger than she was. Beating up women was hardly an unknown phenomenon in her world, but generally it was a domestic matter. This was something different. Maybe he understood that, maybe not. He had introduced himself freely, which made it seem that he was looking for results, but perhaps not trouble.

"Bennett Tyson," she said, letting him know that she'd heard the name clearly. "That doesn't give me much to go on. Not the chicken family?"

Tyson smiled. "I'm a friend of your ex-husband," he said. "And I think you know my associate, Joey."

"I've known Joey since he was four. I hadn't seen him in a while." Joey looked down at his feet and squirmed. She wanted to help him. But she was in no position to, with his boss leaning on her. Maybe Joey was the only thing keeping her safe right now. She assessed the situation. Bennett wanted the money, but it seemed persuasion was his first line of attack. For now. Just put your hand up and ask, she told herself, like school. What can you lose?

"And what subject are we discussing?" There was a little more timbre in her voice and a little less open breath.

"Joey here made a mistake," Tyson said smoothly. "Simple mistake. He was supposed to meet your husband early this morning, but he met you instead, that's all. Then he made a couple assumptions he shouldn't have made, and the result is—well, you know what the result is. Joey's young, and sometimes things happen."

Joey looked at his feet, staring down hard as if something might crawl out of his shoes. What kind of a mess had he gotten himself into? He was off-balance and waiting for this to be over. She was waiting for the same thing. But not by giving back the money. Not now.

"Let's just say mistakes were made," she said. "I might be the beneficiary."

Bennett Tyson opened his mouth to speak, but Jeanette wasn't finished. She suspected that he thought her an innocent bystander in whatever game he was playing, and likely to be a compliant and uninformed one. But it didn't have to be that way. It was her front porch.

"Here's my question," she said. "If you're using my ex-husband's boat, how are you using my ex-husband?"

Tyson looked at her silently.

"What business is it of yours? Who says I'm using him for anything?" Tyson's voice had a new edge. He took a step toward her.

"Don't talk to her that way," said Joey, still seated, looking down. Just this side of sulking.

"You can look at me, Joey. We've known each other a long time."

Joey reluctantly looked up, shoulders slumped, his face holding a blank stare. Shame or resentment? Maybe both.

"The boat has my name on it," she said to Tyson. "And the man owes me lots of back alimony. Good enough?"

"That's between you and him. But we pay him, not you. What he does with it is his business."

Against her better judgment, Jeanette was beginning to enjoy herself. "I pick crabs," she said. "That's my business. But I'm not a fool. There wasn't but eight thousand, seven hundred and fifty dollars in the tackle box, and there must have been over ten pounds of elvers in the live well. Eighty-seven fifty makes my ex-husband some kind of delivery boy or something."

"Ten K," Tyson said. "There was ten."

"Not the way I counted it," Jeanette said.

Tyson took a deep breath, calculating. Then he turned to Joey, who had shrunk back into the decaying back support of the bench.

"That's interesting," he said to Joey.

Joey waited as long as he could.

"They's gonna repossess my truck," he said bleakly. "It was a short-term thing, I swear. A week. Two at the most. It was between me and Simon."

Jeanette's heart sank to her feet. Joey was in enough trouble without her volunteering how much money was in the tackle box. She'd just made it worse and for no reason.

"Hell," said Tyson. "I don't know what made you think you could keep up payments on that truck to begin with. Ma'am, can we go in the house and get the money? What's left of it, I mean."

Jeanette shook her head sadly, like Bennett was a little boy who'd peed in his pants.

"Men don't understand," she said. "They think a house is someplace you sleep, someplace you eat. Women don't see it that way. To a woman—at least to this woman—a house is a fortress to be guarded. It's the definition of who I am. The walls, the wallpaper, every chair and table, every dinner plate, the hooked rugs—it's not to be violated. I am my house."

Bennett Tyson looked befuddled and took a half step back—just far enough for her to lift the front door latch, turn, and slip inside—the door was never locked. Now she secured the dead bolt from the inside, leaving Bennett Tyson standing outdoors, with Joey slumping beside him. She stood still, barely breathing. She couldn't imagine why she had said any of what she said, what had compelled her. That it allowed her to get inside and safely lock the door seemed even stranger. Then her brain, the part of it that was used to being in charge, came unfrozen. She ran to the side door that led out to the creek and dead bolted it as well. She looked through the glass panel in the door but there was no sign that Bennett Tyson had scrambled to the other entrance of the house.

She moved quickly back to the front door, feeling more trapped by her house than safe in it. Looking out the window she saw Tyson and Joey Pizio at the side of the red Mustang. Tyson shoved Joey against the side of the car, leaned down, and said something, but she couldn't hear what it was. Then he pushed Joey away. Hard. Joey stumbled a few steps, seemed like he would fall, and then caught his balance. Tyson got into the car, slammed the door, and revved the engine. The Mustang screeched as it sped up the driveway, spitting pebbles and sand at Joey from its rear wheels.

Joey started walking up the drive. Jeanette opened the door.

"Joey, wait." He waved her off and kept walking. She took a step toward him, but something stopped her. "Jesus, Joey," she said softly. "Get away from that guy."

She went to the kitchen. The leather pouch and the tackle box were sitting on the counter where she'd left them. She reached inside the pouch; it was empty. The money was already gone.

CHAPTER FOUR

She stood, dumbfounded, staring into the empty pouch. Who? But there was no time to think. There were two additional doors to the house including a sloped steel cellar door in the basement. Jeanette poured a quick Beefeater and tonic to calm her nerves and circled the perimeter of the ground floor, rechecking the back and side doors, and then descended to the basement. She was closing the hasp on the padlock that would keep the cellar door secure when it occurred to her that she was not actually sure where the keys were located. It had been years since she'd needed them. As she climbed the unfinished cellar stairs the doorbell rang. She froze.

Feeling her pulse rate rise, she edged up to the front door. But neither of the men had come back. Instead, Lottie Pride stood outside, smoking.

Jeanette fumbled with the lock and finally opened the door. Lottie flicked at the glowing end of the cigarette with her thumb and forefinger, sending it onto the grass, where it fizzled out. She placed the remaining half carefully in the pocket of her flannel shirt.

"All locked up?" she asked. "Can we talk?"

"You could have smoked," Jeanette said, letting her in. "Or have a drink? There's only gin and tonic."

"Alcohol hasn't been good to the tribes," Lottie said. She reached into the pocket and pulled out the remains of the cigarette, which she re-lit from Jeanette's gas stove.

"I saw the two men," she said.

Jeanette moved to the counter and poured herself another gin and tonic, sweeping aside the pouch and tackle box as casually as possible. Her head was just beginning to buzz from the first drink, which seemed to have gone down quickly.

"They were here for a while, waiting for you," Lottie said. "I saw them from the crab shack. You come in this morning looking like a sleepless night, you ask about the elver trade, and then there's a red Mustang in your driveway. Then the two men. I got worried for you."

"I appreciate it," said Jeanette, motioning them into a couple chairs. "I don't really have that—someone to worry for me."

"You got me off relief," Lottie said. "It's the least I owe you. Ashtray?"

Jeanette rose quickly and brought Lottie a chipped saucer.

"It's just the eels," Lottie said. "It's a bad business, and you don't want to get mixed up in it."

"What makes you think I'm mixed up in it?" Jeanette asked, realizing, as she said it, that she was surely mixed up in it, though she didn't know how.

"I don't know. The Mustang—I know who that guy is—he's an aggregator. Without a license."

"What does that mean?" Jeanette asked. "An aggregator?"

"Look," Lottie said, "there's a legally licensed elver business here. A guy named Tommy B. Donovan basically runs it—all the licensed eelers work for him. They call him the Eel King. He aggregates their catch. But then there's all these unlicensed guys on the margins. Eeling in small creeks, keeping out of sight, selling a few ounces here and there—it's a job for pill junkies and the unemployable. The guy in the Mustang buys their catch—aggregates all these little bits and pieces—ships it off to Korea."

"Ah," Jeanette said. "So that's it. In springtime, people make a mess in my creek. And if I see lights down there, I go and throw them out. They always just seem like they're drinking beer and catching bait. They leave a hell of a lot of garbage on the banks of the creek. Sometimes I even clean it up."

"Small-time guys," Lottie said, "They get forty or fifty, maybe a few hundred, sell 'em to an aggregator. He buys them for cash, bundles them, and handles the business end. Used to be a free-for-all. It's regulated now since the new governor. Maybe that'll change things. I doubt it."

"I worked on her campaign," Jeanette said. "To get rid of Lester Birdwell. He was ruining the state and lining his pockets. The worst governor ever."

Lottie stabbed out the cigarette.

"Let's not overdo it," she said. "We've had two governors who only lasted a day each. I'm no fan of this new one either. She hasn't even returned our calls. The settlers—the white people—are grandfathered in. And the black market takes the rest."

Jeanette looked at her, amused.

"So you're telling me to stay out of the elver business, but you should go into it," she said.

"Not me personally. It's just that with all these new regulations and changes you'd think she'd recognize the tribes. I mean, every time there's a transaction you have to swipe a card and let the state know about it. You're supposed to have limits, only fish in season. Some people do—the big-time guys. We would if they'd give Native folks licenses. But not to this guy with the Mustang. He's a bad guy. A black market guy. I'd stay away."

"I didn't go looking for him," Jeanette said.

"None of my business," Lottie said. "I just felt like I should give you a heads-up."

Jeanette nodded, and for a moment they sat in silence.

"You're sure I can't get you anything?" Jeanette asked. Lottie shook her head and reached for her pocket, extracting another half-smoked cigarette.

"Menthol," she said. "The worst there is. All I need. Thanks for letting me smoke indoors."

She got up and went to the kitchen stove to light up, leaving Jeanette sitting.

"Listen," Jeanette said, as Lottie returned, "you seem to know a lot about this, so can you tell me why? Why is the price so high? How does that make sense?"

Lottie settled back in the chair and inhaled deeply. She looked at the cigarette and frowned.

"This one's old," she said, but made no move to extinguish it in the saucer. "Elvers are shipped out of Bangor."

"To Korea, you said."

"And China. And sometimes Japan. By the time they're grown over there in Asia they weigh about eight pounds each. Before they know what's happening to them, they're unagi sushi. Sold by the serving—eight bucks, ten bucks? It's a threatened species, but when some guy picks up sushi at the JetBlue terminal at JFK, he's probably eating what you saw, just fully grown—and chopped to pieces. The state of Maine exports about twenty million dollars in elvers a year. Legally. Illegally, who the hell knows? That's a cash business."

"Jesus," said Jeanette, thinking about Simon and how easily he could be charmed by fast money. Her stomach tightened.

"Puts a gleam in your eye, right?" Lottie asked. "Retail, once they're grown, it's a billion-dollar industry."

"I can't even start to count that high."

"It's better than casinos. And the coastal Wabanaki would run a sustainable fishery, put the money to good use. At the moment the legal stuff around goes from Tommy B. to a guy called Sung Ho Han. Gentleman. The kind of guy who'd rob you with a pen, not a gun. But the guy in the Mustang? Be careful."

When Lottie was gone, Jeanette went back to the counter and rechecked the leatherette pouch. Still empty. Old habits die hard, she thought. She hadn't locked her front door for years. For a moment, she couldn't breathe. At least whoever took the money hadn't ransacked the place—money on the counter, no need. Whoever took it knew what they were looking for. Lottie's words echoed in her head: *Be careful.* But aside from locking her door going forward, Jeanette wasn't sure she even knew how.

She looked out the window, wondering who was out there, but now it was dark. All she could see was her own reflection in the glass, looking back at her.

***

Jeanette Hatcher was born and raised in Maine's north woods in the town of Fort Kent. She met Simon King when she was a scholarship student studying marine biology at the College of the Atlantic in Bar Harbor, where she had gotten her scuba instructor's license and saved up enough to purchase her own wet suit. Simon was not a college student; he was a man of the world, handsome in a rugged sort of way, ten years older than she was. Working in the lobster fleet, he made more money in a year than her parents made in five. She married him when she was still a junior, dropped out, and moved across the bridge to the island. It was a romantic place to live. In the beginning.

Their first winter they took their earnings and drove south, out of the weather. They went to stock car races in North Carolina and spent a day on the Blue Ridge Scenic Railway. Simon was determined to prove that the same Route 1 that took them through Camden and Portland was still in business when they hit the Florida Keys.

"A hell of a long road," he said as they crossed the seven-mile bridge.

When they arrived in Key West, they spent an afternoon at Jack Strudwick's shipwreck museum with its tales of sunken treasure, and she managed to get Simon to put a scuba tank on his back. But, somehow, they had given up traveling.

Once Liam came, she had let something else take over. A vision of home, where children would be loved and listened to, and never slapped down for having an original thought. And eventually, grandchildren. Family weddings in the garden. Holidays. A closet full of toys that would get used by at least two more generations she would come to know before she was gone. She was still young; she believed one could make a life.

She learned that one could also take a life. Liam, who had loved pirates, and had always chosen rum raisin ice cream because he thought it would be their favorite flavor too. Pirates liked rum. Liam had moved from pirates to pilots on the day he saw a seaplane touch down in the reach, make a U-turn in the water and zoom aloft again; he then dreamed of nothing but getting a pilot's license. Jeanette encouraged him. Any passion of Liam's, even though he was not yet an adolescent, was worth supporting for however long it lasted. He was a popular kid, and the house was always full of rambunctious noise and action, especially on birthdays. Jeanette could not have been happier. But Liam didn't have enough birthdays. Liam: gone in one awful night.

He had been invited by his father to go ice fishing on Long Pond for his sixteenth birthday. He was buried three days later. Accidents happen. Especially when mothers don't listen to their gut. Fathers love an adventure. Liam wanted to go anyway, and she was tired of being the parent who said no. Simon had never been ice fishing himself, but it was something new to try. He'd watched some YouTube, bought some equipment, so what difference would it make if she were to speak her mind? All the difference in the world, as it turned out. But she hadn't done it. A boy who wanted more than anything to go up in the air had gone under the ice. And then it was all gone. A preliminary inquest, a funeral, a casket that she closed the lid on herself. So much else closed with it. Then her grief and sorrow and rage. Her losing battle to forgive. It simply took over.

The marriage was doomed from the day Liam was lost under the ice, but it unraveled as slowly as spring came to the island. It took four years for divorce papers to be signed. And all during that time Simon worked aboard the *Jeanette*, came home silent and detached, ate his dinner, and settled down in front of the TV. He watched others go on wild adventures as he nursed one Allen's Coffee Brandy after another. He grew fond of a TV series hosted by Jack Strudwick—the same man whose museum they had visited on their one trip to Florida. It was about underwater treasure seekers finding Spanish galleons and nineteenth-century schooners wrecked against coral reefs. It fed his fantasy of sudden riches and, for all she knew, his need for an escape to somewhere—anywhere. Even when lobster went to six dollars a pound, hauling them off the bottom of the chilly waters of the Maine coast was never going to make him a rich or happy man. But he persisted.

When she turned from him in bed he never complained, beyond a grunt of acceptance. Simon's first affair was something that had to happen. She had let it happen, maybe even caused it to happen. And in some ways, she could hardly blame him even while she raged at him for it. There was nothing left now to protect.

She gave all the toys to Goodwill in Brockton.

And then one day he was gone for good. But the dream of something out there for her never quite died. One day she'd have to go out and find it on her own. But she hadn't. And now she was looking at fifty.

Instead, she survived. On the corkboard in the kitchen, she had pinned a picture she had taken of Simon and Liam. They were in the backyard of the old house. Liam was sitting on his father's shoulders, holding a plastic model airplane that he appeared to be zooming through the air with his left hand. She looked at it at least once a day, and sometimes she bid it good night.

Now, ten years on, she still worried for Simon. She had always worried for him, but especially now that she wasn't able to provide any kind of course correction. What was it now—elvers? What else could it be?

Whatever it was, it was not supposed to be her problem, and it wasn't, until Joey Pizio had thrust that tackle box into her hands and made off with the *Jeanette*, leaving her to bob in the early morning chop and wonder. She worried for Joey too.

CHAPTER FIVE

A decent night's sleep was out of the question. She kept checking her phone for a reply from Simon that might put her mind to rest, or at least explain some things, but none came. She texted three times, to no avail. She made coffee at sunrise and waited for the Bread & Butter Mart to open at seven. Returning home with a jar of Marshmallow Fluff, a loaf of Country Pride white bread and a jar of Jif smooth peanut butter, she set to work making a fluffernutter sandwich. At this hour the smell of the gummy marshmallow paste was vaguely nauseating. As she cut off the crust, she remembered how her roommate in college had kept a jar on hand to stick posters to the wall. The sandwich came out handsomely enough and she sealed it in plastic wrap and put it in a paper bag.

At a little after ten A.M. she got in the car. She passed the bridge to the mainland and made her way out toward the eastern side of the island, the less populated side, navigating by imperfect memory. It took a couple wrong turns and retracings to locate Joey Pizio's house—the old double-wide mobile home where he had grown up and where he had remained since his parents had been killed by a drunk driver. She hadn't been there in years, not since the days when she drove the school carpool. The mud-brown siding was in need of paint, and the yard hadn't been tended in a very long time. The place sat on a cinder block foundation, just down the road from a tumbledown fisherman's house that had, to the best of her memory, been vacant since she came to the island almost three decades earlier. A spruce tree grew through the roof. What was keeping it from total collapse she could not imagine.

Picking her way across the lawn with the paper bag firmly gripped in her hand and a purse slung over her shoulder, she reached the two steps leading to the front door and pushed the doorbell. She could hear its angry buzz inside, more a warning than an announcement of company. There was a lurch of movement inside and a voice—Joey's, she thought—asking "What?"

"Jeanette," she said, and tried the doorknob. The door gave inward, creaking on its cheap aluminum hinges. Joey was slumped in an easy chair upholstered in pea-green vinyl, from which cotton batting escaped every corner. He wore a ragged Coldplay T-shirt and faded plaid boxers, nothing else. His feet were bare. His eyes, unfocused and dead, looked up at her.

"Hey," he said, making no move to rise. Jeanette looked around. The front room was in chaos, and who knew what more lived behind the bedroom door. A stained-black glass coffee carafe sat on the stove in the kitchenette and an open carton of orange juice graced an otherwise empty table. Jeanette looked at Joey and saw, beside him, a collection of pill bottles.

"Joey," she said. "You okay?"

"Never better," Joey said, still not moving. It was about all he could manage. Then he raised his right hand above him in stoned exultation and added, "Day off." The hand dropped slowly to his lap, and he appeared to nod off. She watched him breathing evenly in an oxycodone haze.

"Joey," she said again. "I came to apologize. I didn't mean to get you in trouble. I brought you something—your favorite."

But he was not in a place to have a conversation. Or even a sandwich. His chest rose and fell evenly, and a small bubble appeared at the corner of his mouth and exploded gently as he exhaled. Jeanette sighed and looked around at the disorder of a disordered life. She saw a brown paper bag by Joey's feet and approached to look inside. There were four empty beer cans—Pabst Blue Ribbon, always the same. She lifted the bag. Joey did not stir.

Removing the cans and placing them on the kitchen table, she stowed the orange juice in a softly humming acid-green fridge that almost matched Joey's easy chair. Then she tore off a panel of the bag and took a pen from her purse.

> *Joey,*
> *I brought you a treat. Your favorite. Please get in touch. We have to talk about Simon and the money. Enjoy the sandwich.*
> *Jeanette*

She left the note under the paper bag containing the sandwich on the kitchen table. Then she watched him for a few minutes. His breathing was regular, and from time to time he stretched unconsciously. She contemplated calling an ambulance but thought better of it. She'd gotten him in enough trouble already. This would certainly mean more—jail time, probably. What else was there to do, she wondered. She took a moment, then turned back to the kitchen. She washed the dishes in the sink and put them away, gathered the dirty clothes on the floor into a neat pile, and emptied the ashtrays. The place looked better. Then she reapproached and took his hand, which didn't wake him. As gingerly as she could, she put a thumb and forefinger on his wrist and looked at her watch for fifteen seconds. Eighty-four beats a minute.

"Okay," she said aloud, certain that he was up somewhere circling the moon. He was high, but not dying. She placed his hand back in his lap and walked quickly back to the car.

***

Sung Ho Han, the northeast regional director for the Korean company Bando, had made his fortune in eels. He lived in a home at the top of a long and winding driveway on the mainland in Compton Harbor. It was not near the water, but majestically positioned high above it, so that from the living room one could look out to both the east and west—a panoramic view of the ocean and the islands in the bay. It was a turn-of-the-century cottage, as these mansions were quaintly called; they had long served as summer homes for a certain class of people. He was hated by all his blue-blood neighbors, descendants of wealthy nineteenth-century WASP bankers, industrialists, and carpetbaggers. They couldn't imagine how or why the house had been sold to a man from outside their circle—an Asian man. A Jewish person would have been one thing, but this was not even a white man. Beyond that, Sung Ho was beginning to suspect that trouble of another sort was on the way. And he suspected the ex-governor was at the center of it, which was why he hadn't been surprised by the man's request to visit his hilltop home.

Sung Ho's houseboy, a very blond high school dropout named Blake, who ran Sung Ho's boats and traveled with him everywhere, welcomed Lester Birdwell, leading him to an overstuffed chair in the living room. Birdwell, silver haired and jowly, his face pink and smooth with too much barbering, or perhaps high blood pressure, walked with an elegant cane. He awkwardly settled himself into the chair and waited.

Sung Ho let the ex-governor sit and stew for a few minutes, hoping he was impressed by the surroundings, then entered down the stairs from his bedroom. He was a slender, elegant man in pressed L.L. Bean blue jeans and a boatneck top with horizontal stripes. It was his uniform. He was all in for Maine.

"Governor," he said. "I'm sorry to keep you waiting."

"Not at all," said Birdwell, successfully heaving himself back into a standing position. "Thank you for making the time." His voice was a politician's baritone betraying not an ounce of a Down East accent.

"It's an honor, really, to have you in my home."

"Don't be honored, just be helpful," the ex-governor replied. "That's what I tell everybody. That's what makes for a great state and a great country. Don't be honored, just be helpful."

This speech, which Sung Ho had heard twice before, always reinforced in him the conviction that the ex-governor took him for a fool, and it was hard not to express annoyance. But he gestured for Birdwell to sit again, which he saw was more difficult for the large man than it should have been. This, at least, gave him some pleasure.

The houseboy Blake appeared at that moment with a tray on which were perched two cans of Moxie next to frosty glass beer steins full of ice. He set the tray down between the men and retreated silently. Beads of condensation dripped down the sides of the cans.

"Thank you for rolling out the red carpet," Birdwell said to Sung Ho, looking at the soda pop with some disdain. "Moxie," he said, as though reading the can.

Sung Ho couldn't detect a note of sarcasm in Birdwell's voice, but suspected it was there someplace.

"Moxie, as I'm sure you know," said Sung Ho, "is the official soft drink of Maine. Since 2005. I've always believed that when in Rome, one should do as the Romans do."

"Those were some ancient Romans," Birdwell said. "The modern ones drink beer, mostly."

"It is also an expression of cross-cultural appreciation," Sung Ho said. "It is said to contain gentian root extract, which we use in Korea for herbal medicine. So you see, there is a connection, a commonality between our cultures. Also, I believe Mr. E. B. White once said that because Moxie contained gentian root, it was the path to the good life."

"Don't think I know who you're talking about," said Birdwell.

"I believe he lived in Maine for quite a time. He wrote an influential book about a pig and a spider."

Birdwell grunted softly, leaving the can untouched.

"In any case," Sung Ho said, choosing his words, "to what do I owe the opportunity of being helpful?"

"I'll get right to the point," Birdwell said. "It's a matter of money."

"So I suspected," said Sung Ho.

"It's hardly a surprise. I left the office, and my remittances stopped coming, and I assume are now being delivered to that woman who took my job."

"Surprisingly," Sung Ho said, "the new governor is not interested in remittances from the elver industry. She's keeping her environmental bona fides pure for the moment."

Sung Ho Han's business was a simple one. He bought from the eelers at a wholesale price and arranged delivery of the whole catch to an aquafarm outside Seoul. He also ran the trucking company that took the elvers, still swimming in tanks, by refrigerated truck to Bangor International, where they were flown to Korea. Bando took care of growing them to adulthood and selling them back to the world.

For the whole of the ex-governor's term in office Sung Ho had also been a sort of bagman, taking 10 percent of what the eelers were supposed to get and putting it into Birdwell's hands, in return for which the then-governor blocked any and all regulations having to do with elver fishing. He vetoed the swipe-card legislation twice. Making fishermen register and record their catch with swipe cards was government overreach. Pure and simple. Bad for business. He turned the regulatory system for overseeing quotas into an understaffed shambles, claiming he was merely creating efficiencies that would save the taxpayers money.

When Birdwell lost his reelection campaign, Sung Ho had mixed feelings. He was relieved to stop the payments, but under the new governor's leadership quotas quickly shrunk, hurting Bando's profitability. It cut deeply into Sung Ho's bonus, though not nearly as deeply as it cut into the ex-governor's payments, which went to zero. Sung Ho could see what was coming.

"We've always worked well together," Birdwell began. "Our previous arrangement was very good for you, for me, your company, and for the eelers. Why should a little election get in the way of all that history?"

"I do not understand," said Sung Ho.

"The new governor fancies herself an environmentalist, which is bad for you, and you've already told me she's not asking for your campaign contributions, up on her high horse as she is. But I don't see why I should stop receiving them. I do plan to make a comeback, and, in the meantime, I remain influential in political circles. And a reelected Governor Birdwell would be good for Bando."

"Then let's talk once your new campaign launches," Sung Ho said. "There is no way to justify paying you to be the former governor."

"Of course not! You would be paying me as a consultant."

"And what might you be 'consulting' about?"

"Well, deregulation efforts, of course. And, also, I would offer you valuable advice about how to ensure the former governor"—he gestured to himself grandly—"does not write a letter to Bando about the remittances you previously paid."

"Ah, I see," said Sung Ho, grimacing, as he tried a sip of Moxie. "You are diversifying, from just bribery to bribery and blackmail."

"'Bribery,' 'blackmail,' those are very strong words, old friend. Very strong. It is a consultancy that simply keeps me on retainer, so our ducks are in a row when the time comes. And in the meantime, I can keep you from finding yourself in any trouble back home."

"Governor Birdwell, my company already knows about our arrangement, and, though they might deny it publicly, I have what I believe is called tacit approval. Do you have the same from your district attorney? I am told the American legal system is a very wide and deep black hole once you fall into it."

"There's no reason to get excited, sir." The ex-governor reddened, beginning to backtrack. "We're only speaking theoretically."

"You will not be paid to do nothing, and I will not be threatened."

"Heaven forbid. Please, accept my apology for any misunderstanding. I'm simply offering you an opportunity to further explore working with the highly respected ex-governor of one of the most beloved of all fifty states. Maine. Proud birthplace of Heebie White. Also, there is another matter in which I could perhaps be useful."

Sung Ho raised his eyebrows.

"We both know that there are many, many elvers being taken by what you might call independent fishermen."

"Poachers," Sung Ho said, nodding. "I believe you call them 'scofflaws' here."

"We do? Anyway, they don't follow quotas, they're like wildcat oil drillers. And it is a damn shame. But the bigger shame is that all those elvers aren't landing in your live wells, going to your farms in Korea. I believe that I might be able to coordinate their efforts, and the benefit would go to you."

"Have you learned nothing, Mr. Birdwell?" Sung Ho asked. "Discretion is a core principle of the company and has been the foundation of Bando's international success. The notion that we would begin illicitly trading in eels that are illegally fished, contravening the current regulations of the state of Maine, all coordinated by a recently deposed leader who has a penchant for bribery and blackmail and no experience running such an operation . . . I hardly know what to say. It will never happen."

"Never say never."

"I just said it. Perhaps it is time to finish up your Moxie and go."

Birdwell sighed, heaved himself out of the chair and held out his hand—a born politician's natural instinct. Sung Ho took it half-heartedly.

"Well," Birdwell said, smiling, "I feel you should be interested. I know things are hard for you and Bando now. I'd hate like hell for them to get worse when they could get better. Promise me you'll think about it."

CHAPTER SIX

Jeanette had spent the day anxiously waiting for a call from Joey—or Simon—and fearing a second visit from Bennett Tyson, demanding the money that she no longer had. But neither Simon nor Joey ever called and there was no second visit. She wanted to assume that the money had been found, and no one had any further business with her. But she didn't believe it. Someone had slipped into her kitchen and taken something, even if the thing taken wasn't rightly hers. She had told Bennett Tyson that she was her house, and now it had been violated.

She had checked with the folks she knew who were still friendly with Simon—Billy Willig again, the people at the Bread & Butter Mart, even Keith Fulbright, the housebuilder who had no real reason to know. He did not know. After leaving Simon two more messages and sending a text, Jeanette sat at the dining room table in front of her laptop trying to find new articles on the elver business. She had a rocks glass with two ice cubes and two fingers of Beefeater on the table. It was full dark now. The glass was halfway to her lips when a beam of light came through the window on the creek side of the house and lit the wall behind her. Not a car on the road—just a single beam.

Flashlight, she thought. Deadbeats on the creek. Tonight, of all nights. She looked skyward and spoke to the God she did not believe in.

"Jesus Christ," she said. "You sure know how to make a girl feel good."

She flipped down the lid of the laptop as the beam came again, sweeping across the window. Nothing to be done. She pulled the cardigan tight across her body and rose from the table.

"You are really gonna get a piece of my mind this time," she shouted at the window. "I'm sick and tired of this."

Grabbing the headlamp and a pair of gardening gloves she hurried to the side door in fur-lined slippers, swapped them for her muck boots, and, buttoning her sweater as she went, stepped outside. The grass was already wet with dew. Still, the sky was clear and a gibbous moon overhead to the west put the foliage in silhouette but allowed her to find her way. She turned on the light anyhow and began to stride to the creek.

"I don't want to see you," she said into the shadows. "Just take your junk with you when you go. I'm no trash collector."

The response was silence. Then the beam from the flashlight swept across one more time and pointed straight up into the spruce trees above the creek. She shook her head in frustration. The roots of the spruce and tamarack trees had created a floor that was hard to navigate after dark. In between the roots, swampy puddles were disguised by wild overgrown grasses, and it was impossible to discern how far one could slip or sink with a single misstep. By the time she reached the top of the creek bank she was cold, wet, and there was a large spatter of mud across her right cheek. She had no idea how it had gotten there. She was ready to give these littering poachers a piece of her mind. Below her there was the light, the beam of a flashlight, now still, pointing out toward the reach. She could not see what, if anything, held it.

"Hey!" she shouted. "Private property. It's the middle of the damn night. Get gone!" No one answered. Her heart quickened. From the top of the bank, it was a short, unpredictable drop down to the water's edge. She reached for a cedar sapling to steady herself and felt both feet go out from under her as she lost her grip on the young tree. And then she was falling, though it felt like flying. She was not sure if any part of her was in contact with the earth. She threw her arms around her head in fear of rocks that could do some permanent damage and tried to curl her body into a fetal position, but her foot hooked around the elevated root of a tree on the bank, springing the muck boot off and twisting her leg. A sharp agonizing pain shot through her from the knee upward and she screamed. Then the rest of her body hit what should have been the water. But it was not the water. Instead, her back landed in the slanting mud of the bank as the foot of her uninjured leg thumped against something soft and meaty below, something that rolled away from her by a few inches until she slid further down the bank and her foot landed on it again as it came to a stop. Even in excruciating pain she sensed it was not earth, or a rock, or any kind of living animal. Whatever it was, the flashlight lying atop it rolled into the water, briefly illuminating the creek bed before its light was extinguished.

For a moment she lay on her back, feeling for all the world like a crab that had been flipped onto its shell. Her knee throbbed. The headlamp had flown from her head and was lying a few feet away, illuminating the edge of the water. Something sharp, a root or snapped-off branch, was digging into the space between her shoulder blades. The wind was knocked out of her, and it took her a few moments to breathe at all.

Finally, when the world felt like it had perhaps come to rest, she took a couple shallow breaths, all she could manage, and felt around her body to try to assess the damage. The leg wouldn't move on its own and just trying to lift it sent an electric surge through her body. Using her arms to pull herself along in the mud, she reached for the headlamp and fixed it back on her head. She turned to get a look at whatever it was that had prevented her total immersion in the creek. The lamp shone down on a wet, lumpy mass of flannel and wool. She stared at it for a moment trying to catch her breath.

She turned the light to the water's surface; inches away staring up at her were two dead eyes, wide-open and startled. She pulled away from the face, a puffy face, slightly blue, but entirely recognizable.

"Joey," she gasped, her voice strangulated by fear and shortness of breath. Joey Pizio lay motionless against a large rock, his body half on land and half submerged. She froze. "Joey," she said again, sounding guttural and hoarse. Her blood raced and she tried to back away using her arms but slipped again in the mud. Now she was almost on top of him.

She slapped his face once, twice, and opened his mouth to see if there was breath. It was filled with creek water. He was gone. She began to hyperventilate. The leg pain would not let up. She realized she was whining, like a wounded animal.

What was he doing here? Was that him signaling with the light? What if she had come down sooner? And then, she understood, it couldn't have been him. Someone else is out here. Trembling, she forced herself into a sitting position and turned her head upstream toward the woods. Light from her headlamp flashed through the trees.

Long shadows and tangled branches. No one breathing, no twigs breaking, no sign of anyone else. Which didn't mean they were not there. She wanted to get Joey's body out of the creek, take care of him, call an ambulance. But she couldn't even stand.

As she lowered her head, the headlamp's beam landed on a red-and-white Playmate cooler just above where Joey lay. It had to be his. She pushed herself over to it, her knee screaming. She pressed the buttons on the side of the cooler and slid the top down. She found what she thought she'd find: a small swarm of elvers moved in a lazy circle in a gallon or two of water. They moved without the energy or frantic pace of the ones she had seen in the live well of the *Jeanette*. They've been here for a while, she thought. Too late for Joey, but save what you can. She pushed the cooler to the water's edge, tipping the contents back into the creek. She saw the elvers just for a moment in the beam of the headlamp as they darted into the darkness with ease. Within a half second there was no sign of them at all, though she could see clear to the creek bottom with the beam of the headlamp. Someone—whoever had flashed the light up at her house—was still here. If I can't see him, she thought, I'll be damned if I let him see me. She turned off her headlamp.

"This was a good decision."

The voice, low and without affect, burned her ears from somewhere nearby. Now her heart jumped again, but she did not move.

"A good decision. To release the living and leave the dead be. A principled response to a difficult situation."

A match was struck just off to her right and lit a candle. Terrified, Jeanette turned her head toward the light. The candle, in an old-fashioned glass lantern, was being held in the large hand of a tall, thin man dressed in black, with a wide, flat face framed by shoulder-length black hair. The light, flickering in the slight breeze, caught his eyes, which were a deep brown and very large. He was the definition of stillness. She had never seen him before.

"Always release the living," he said. "The innocent living, I should have said."

"Jesus," Jeanette said. "Don't kill me."

He took a sure-footed step toward her.

"No. No no no," she begged.

"I need to get a look at that leg," he said calmly. "Or you're not going anywhere."

"Don't touch me!" she snarled. "Don't come near me!"

In two swift steps he was by her side and kneeled down to her.

"Please," she begged. She looked up into his dark face, just beginning to be creased with the lines of age. Not a kid, she thought—perhaps thirty or thirty-five with a distinct scar on the left side of his neck. As she shrunk from him, his hands reached out and moved along her leg from the mid-thigh down toward to her knee. Even their light touch caused a radiating stab that landed somewhere in her gut. But he was delicate, like a good surgeon.

"You dislocated your patella," he said. "Your kneecap is in the wrong place."

"How would you know?" she asked.

"Close your eyes and think of Christmas," he said. "Or whatever your favorite moment of the year is."

"I hate Christmas," she said.

He smiled. "Already we have something in common."

Before she could ask him what he was talking about he had placed the thumbs of both hands on one side of her leg, his forefingers on the other, and she could feel the bone sliding inside of her.

She shrieked, and then it was over. The leg throbbed, but the excruciating pain that had seemed to be pulsing through every part of her body was suddenly gone. And she could move the leg. A little.

"Thank you?" she said, uncertainly.

The man gripped her upper arm, put it around his neck and raised her to a standing position.

"How did you do that?" Jeanette asked. "Who are you?"

"Patellas hurt like hell," he said, "but they heal quicker than a sprain."

He helped her up the bank, located her stray boot, and gently placed it back on her foot.

"Come for a ride with me," he said.

"Thank you for fixing my knee. But not in a million years," she said.

"You want to go back to the house? Alone? With a corpse in the creek? It's safer you come with me. And we should really talk."

CHAPTER SEVEN

The man said his name was Jesse Ed Davis.

"I don't care what your name is," she sputtered. "I've got to call the police."

"Do not call the police," he said. "Come with me."

Looking at the size of him and the strength of his grip, she realized that, if he wanted to just overpower her, he could have, would have already, but he was giving her a choice. The rational part of her brain screamed caution but going with him felt safer than going back to her house alone. And how would she explain this all to the police anyway?

He helped her through the woods to a red Chevy Silverado pickup, held the passenger door open, and hoisted her in.

"Jesse Ed Davis," she said. "That doesn't sound like a name from here."

"I'm named for a very good Native guitar player. Forgotten now and gone, like a lot of Native people."

"So it's not your real name," Jeanette countered. Talking to someone actually eased her panic.

"What do you mean by 'real name'?" Jesse Ed Davis said. "The Europeans came to this country, changed their own names, and when they got through with that, they changed everyone else's. The ones they left alive. Brutal place. Made-up identities. Lots of descendants wandering around with no idea who their ancestors were. Natives, Europeans, Africans, Asians . . ."

"So you're a lunatic *and* a historian," she said.

He laughed, as if he might not disagree with her, and started the engine. She was not comforted by his low chuckle.

"Where are you taking me?"

"Where we can talk a little and get something to drink and eat," he said.

"But . . ." Jeanette said, nearly choking on the words, "there's a dead boy back there."

"Not at my hands," said Jesse Ed Davis. "Or yours. I was just coming to clean up the trash. Because I do, most nights anyhow. I got to the creek and there was considerably more than trash. So I waited. Let the people building the house next door find him.

"The Framers," Jeanette said.

"Lynne." Jesse said with some distaste. "And Barton."

"You know them?"

"They should be here in the morning to talk to Keith about the kitchen cabinets in the house."

"You know Keith."

Jesse didn't respond. Jeanette sat in the truck for a long moment. She looked Jesse Ed Davis—or whoever he was—in the eye and he didn't look away. He didn't speak, and he didn't force the issue.

"If I get out of this truck and limp back to my house you won't follow me?" she asked.

"I will not," he said.

She nodded and stayed where she was. The pain was increasing. She didn't think she could make it up a flight of stairs on her own.

"Okay," she said. Jesse put the truck in gear and pulled out. She sat silently for a few minutes as Jesse Ed Davis raced the truck down a straightaway. Finally, she spoke, but her stomach was unsettled now, and the words came out in short, uncertain bursts.

"You know the Framers," she said. "You know Keith Fulbright. There's a dead boy at the creek and you were what—watching over him? You call yourself after some dead Indian—I'm sorry, I mean Native. Native rock guitar player."

"Blues, mostly," said Jesse Ed Davis. "First-rate slide player. Did you fasten your seat belt?"

"Of course."

"Hold tight." He slammed on the brakes. White, noxious smoke rose up all around them as he spun the truck into a 360-degree turn, pulling the passenger-side tires off the road entirely, and then sent the truck back down the straightaway in a series of bursts and sudden screeching stops, swinging wildly from side to side. Twice more he spun out, neatly avoiding the gravel at the side of the road and lifting the wheels. Then he drew to a stop, made a wide, slow turn, and flipped the lights to bright. Stretched out in front of where the truck had been was a series of swooping, visually balanced tire tracks where the rubber had remained on the road. In the truck's headlights it looked like a huge, abstract black-and-gray mural, alarming and meaningless, but impressive. Jeanette, who was holding her throat to try to keep from vomiting, simply stared, breathing very deliberately through her nose.

"I've been meaning to hit this patch," Jesse Ed Davis said. "Just haven't had the chance."

"So that's you too," said Jeanette. "The burner." There were many such asphalt and rubber tire artworks in the surrounding area. No one knew who or how many people made them or why. Or at least Jeanette hadn't known. They seemed like suicide missions.

"Is this your version of Native art?"

"It's interesting you would ask me that." He smiled. "People are prone to make assumptions based on stereotypes. I've sometimes been asked if I weave baskets. I have never woven a basket. I wouldn't know where to start."

They crossed the bridge to the mainland. When they reached the end of historic Main Street, the outer edge of the quaint part of Brockton, the truck turned right, onto one of those commercial strips dominated by fast-food franchises, from the Burger King to the Dairy Queen. It was a four-lane highway where an enterprising shopper could get a burrito, a new muffler, a discount mattress, and a tank of gas and still be home by cocktail time. About halfway to the Walmart there was a rental storage place, one even less attractive than most of the burger joints and competing big-box stores. It was tucked up a driveway to the north, toward the Clammett Harbor Airport, where the billionaires landed their small private planes. Jesse Ed Davis spun the truck into the driveway and pulled around back. By now Jeanette had begun to trust that this more than eccentric person was unlikely to hurt her—he'd had too many opportunities that he hadn't taken. Even so, her pulse raced, and her back was beginning to throb from the fall she'd taken down the creek bed. Her knee hurt like hell.

"You're not thinking I'm going to follow you into a storage unit," she said as he killed the lights of the Chevy. "I've seen this movie."

"Wait," he said. "It's perfectly safe. I'll show you."

He turned the lights back on and spun the truck forty-five degrees until it illuminated the door of one of the larger units. Then he got out of the truck and left her belted in the passenger seat. He walked to the corrugated metal door, which was as wide as a two-car garage, took a key from his pocket, popped the lock, and rolled up the door. The lights of the truck revealed a home. There was a bed, dresser, sofa, and coffee table. The tin walls were hung with pictures. There was a TV on a small folding table sitting kitty-corner facing the bed. And a mini fridge. As far as she could see, there was nothing to cook with and nowhere to relieve oneself. Other than that, it looked entirely livable.

Jesse returned to the truck and opened the passenger door. He gestured for her to get out and follow him.

Jeanette did not move.

"Looks aren't everything," she said.

"Come in, I'll wrap your leg, give you a couple Advil. And have a drink at least. I bought Beefeater and tonic especially for you. You might need one."

She sat for another full minute, fear, suspicion, and curiosity each taking a turn in her mind. He had gin and tonic? How could he have known to do that? He waited without moving. There was something eerie about his ability to be still. All kinds of clichés ran through her head—stereotypes, admirable and demeaning characterizations of every sort. Noble, stealthy, bloodthirsty, wise . . . still. She sat for another moment. If I'm murdered for trying to prove to myself that I'm not a racist, she thought, you can blame it on John Wayne. But she couldn't manage to make a move. Jesse Ed Davis stood beside the passenger-side door and offered her an arm.

***

He not only had Beefeater and tonic—he had ice and lime. He was prepared. She let herself gingerly into a folding chair and removed the lime from her glass.

"Never use it," she said apologetically, "but it's nice of you to have thought of it."

He nodded, reached into the minibar-sized fridge by his side and pulled out a Lone Pine IPA. He knocked the cap off on the side of the fridge.

"So, explain," she said.

"First, let's do this," he said. He reached into an old dome-topped trunk strapped with dark wooden stripping—the kind she had seen in pirate movies. He lifted out an army-green first aid kit and extracted a bottle of ibuprofen, a bandage roll, and a pair of scissors.

"Lift the leg," he said. "The best you can."

"Why the scissors?"

"I need to cut up the leg of your pants."

"I paid twenty-eight fifty at the L.L. Bean outlet for these and they've served me for a decade," she said.

She gently pulled the left leg of the jeans up past her calf and then even more delicately over the knee. She winced. But the jeans remained intact. He grasped the back of her ankle in his large hand but the touch, once again, was light. He lifted her leg into his lap. Then, moving with a sure but careful hand, he wrapped the bandage from mid-calf to just above the knee, and replaced her foot on the floor. He took a long slug of his beer while she popped four Advil.

"You were saying?" he asked.

"I was asking for some kind of an explanation, as in, what am I doing here? What were you doing there? That kind of thing. And why I'm not at the police station. They'd be interested."

"Too interested," he said. "You report a body, they want to know how you found it, what you were doing there, exactly when you found it. And then you're a person of interest, and you don't need that. Especially because there's no other person of interest."

"Unless I tell them about you," she said.

He toasted her with his beer bottle. "I'm no one. I have no traceable connection to this. You, though—it's your creek. And that young man."

"He was working for my ex-husband."

Jesse nodded. "And the story they will tell, if you don't go, is that it was an overdose. Because that is a short, straight line, one they like because it's simple, the media won't care, and it will never come back on you."

"Won't they see where I slid down the bank?"

"It will be more confusing than anything else. They'll think he slid down the bank. Wind is blowing in the rain now. Pray for a real downpour before morning. Covers your tracks. They don't know how to read the tracks anyhow, even without rain."

"What about the cooler? Joey's cooler?" she asked.

"You were wearing gloves," Jesse said. "No fingerprints. And those elvers would have been dead by morning. Now they live. At least for now."

Jeanette drained the dregs of her drink

Jesse reached for her empty glass and went to fix her a refill. Then, he put down the empty Lone Pine bottle and reopened the mini fridge. From its tiny freezer compartment, he extracted a single-serve cup of

Ben & Jerry's ice cream that had a little wooden stick-spoon taped to the cap.

"Cherry Garcia," he said. "It's good. You want one?"

She held up her hand.

"Not with gin and tonic," she said.

He reached back into the trunk and drew out a white envelope, which he handed to her. "Eight thousand, seven hundred and fifty dollars," he said. "You shouldn't leave things lying around."

Jeanette looked at him, incredulous.

"It was lying around on *my* kitchen counter, in *my* house. And what were you doing there? I mean a gin and tonic and an Ace bandage, all very nice, but what the hell were you doing in my house?"

"I thought you were a smuggler," he said.

"And what gave you that idea?"

"I watch things. Your ex-husband, his boat, your boat, the tackle box."

"You were out there at four in the morning, watching?"

"I rise early. If there's something to learn, I try to learn it. But then you released those eels and I realized I was mistaken. Maybe we're on the same side. Maybe for different reasons."

Jeanette took this in for a moment and had a sip of her drink. "It's not even my money."

"It's yours now. Someone gave it to you. That someone's dead."

"He wasn't someone. His name was Joey Pizio. I knew him from when he was a kid."

"Give me a minute," Jesse Ed Davis said.

He plopped the last blob of ice cream into his mouth. Then he held up a finger, excused himself, and left the room, wandering out into the night. She assumed he was relieving himself and took a moment to take in her surroundings. Nothing out of the ordinary except for a milk crate at the foot of the bed. It had a bumper sticker on it, which read *No Compromise in Defense of Mother Earth*. The crate was full of neatly bundled steel spikes. On top of the spikes was an antique tool, the sort used for boring holes in wood before power drills were invented. Before she could draw any conclusions he was back, with a full Lone Pine bottle, which he placed outside the rolling door before closing it.

"Modest inconvenience," he said once he had settled himself down on the bed. "I'll dispose of it tomorrow in an appropriate place. Humans ought not to pee against the sides of buildings. Other animals I can understand."

"I didn't ask," she said.

"I thought you might be curious anyhow," he said. "You know, some species shit in their own drinking water. Some don't. But only one species has invented a contraption designed specifically to facilitate shitting in its own drinking water. And then engineered infrastructure to clean that same water. A sane person might ask why we don't stop fouling our water in the first place. Instead, we use it as the first measure of progress and then create an industry to . . ." he trailed off, noticing that Jeanette was no longer listening.

"I'm sorry," he said. "You were telling me about that boy."

She nodded. "I hadn't seen Joey Pizio in a few years, but I remember him," she said. "Especially as a kid. I went on one of those class field trips, you know? Like you do when you're a parent with a young kid."

"You have a child?" Jesse asked.

"Had," Jeanette said. "He'd be younger than you, but not too much. If he'd lived. You?"

"No. But I hate to hear you lost yours."

"Goddamned ice fishing."

"I'm sorry."

Jeanette shrugged. "I'm sorry every day," she said. She took a sip, and looked down at the floor.

"He and Joey weren't really close," she went on. "I don't think Joey had friends. But on this field trip, up Cedar Hill he just lagged behind, lagged behind like he didn't want to be there. Head down, wouldn't talk. Finally, he just stopped when we hit a steep patch. He said, 'I'm not going up there.' I picked him up in my arms and carried him up the rock face until it flattened out. He didn't say anything, just started walking again. To this day I don't know why I didn't try to talk to him. I just couldn't abide how miserable he was on a beautiful spring day. Broke my heart—a little doomed kid like that. I asked his teacher about it, and she said there was trouble at home. 'Trouble at home,' that's all I ever knew. Hell, who didn't have trouble at home?"

She was looking around Jesse's tidy living quarters and thinking about Joey Pizio's. What if she had called an ambulance when she found him in the double-wide? It would have been rough, but he'd be alive.

"That poor boy." She saw his face, his mouth full of creek water. "His eyes. Even when he was alive, his eyes . . ."

"He had a drug problem?" Jesse asked.

"The last time I saw him he was really out of it. I should have done something then." She looked down, remembering the note and wondering if Joey had even seen it.

Jesse Ed Davis nodded and stayed quiet for a moment. Then he spoke.

"I've been watching the elver trappers on all the local creeks for about four years now," he said. "Every spring. I've even seen you toss some of them off yours. I enjoyed your performance."

"You've watched me?" Jeanette closed her eyes and shook her head. "I didn't even know what they were up to."

"Now you do. I've scared a few of them away myself."

"You've seen Joey there?"

"I've never seen him on your creek or any other. I've never seen him trapping. Not at all. But I've seen him meet your husband on the boat."

"Why are you sneaking around my creek scaring away elver fishermen?"

"I'm a concerned citizen, that's all. An industry disruptor."

"An ecoterrorist?"

"The elvers have no agency. I mean, they might be willful when they grow up, but these little ones go where the water takes them."

"Like little kids," Jeanette said.

"Little orphans," Jesse responded, "They're like a million orphans and most of them get kidnapped. Or die. Like Joey Pizio. Or your son. I don't have much faith in people. But the eels—maybe I can do something for them."

Jeanette nodded, considering his explanation.

Then she pointed to the milk crate at the foot of the bed.

"And those spikes?" she asked.

"Those can be inserted into trees. The brace-and-bit drills quietly. It doesn't hurt the trees. But it hurts the sawmill when the band saw finds a spike. You spike the trees, then write a letter to the timber companies when the rights are getting auctioned. Slows down timber sales."

"So you are an ecoterrorist."

"I'm a concerned citizen," he repeated.

CHAPTER EIGHT

The macabre shrieks of a woman in panic came just after nine A.M., as Jeanette was folding her newly cleaned clothes from the previous night. The load had gone into the machine off the kitchen as soon as she'd returned home. Jesse Ed Davis had given her a walking stick to keep her upright, and she had spent the night on the living room sofa. A little after five A.M. she had moved the clothes to the dryer and lain back down, listening to them thump nearby. The unquiet mind was not an orderly thing. Each time she closed her eyes it was something different—Why had she not called an ambulance to Joey's mobile home instead of leaving that idiotic note? And a sandwich. The kid was obviously in trouble. And would the police search his house? Would they find her note? An uneaten sandwich? Would Liam still be here if she had stood up to Simon and kept him from going ice fishing? Joey under the water, Liam under the ice, swarms of elvers pulsing against the edges of live wells and coolers, trying to get out—stark images and unanswerable questions circled around her brain, each one like a hungry shark. Circling. As she rolled over and flipped the pillow, hoping for a cooler surface on the other side, she felt tangled in the afghan she had thrown over herself. Listening to the rain beating down on the roof above, she had finally fallen back into a fitful sleep.

She was up but groggy when the scream came. Then a few minutes later she heard sirens and the arrival of a police car pulling into the unfinished gravel driveway on the other side of the creek.

She prepared to go outside and meet them; she dreaded seeing Joey's body again and regretted the choices she had made the night before. At the same time, they seemed to her to be the only choices. There was Simon to think of, angry as she was at him. And her own involvement. The money was back in the tackle box, which she had carefully wiped down with rubbing alcohol and tucked behind the furnace in the basement.

She bundled up in a wool jacket and jeans. She put on her muck boots, her knee aching as she bent. Seeing mud clinging to them, she took them off again, resolved to clean them later, and replaced them with the cracked leather, lace-up hiking boots she had owned since college. Before she stepped out, she took a look in the mirror. Normally she took a moment to put her hair together, to try to look as appealing as possible. Instead, she mussed it, hoping to seem harmless and a little older than she was. It pained her.

She took up her walking stick. Good prop, she thought. She carefully chose a different route to the creek, feeling guilty with every hobbling step.

As Jesse Ed Davis had predicted, there had been a drenching rain, but now the clouds had all blown away and it was beginning to look like a beautiful day was in store for the living. She clutched her wool jacket at the neckline and stared down from her side of the bank.

She forced herself not to look down into the creek, and instead focused on the two cops who were standing on either side of a woman who could only be the new homeowner. Dressed in a pleated skirt and white silk blouse, she wore three rings on her left hand, including a wedding band, and two on her right. Turquoise. She had taken a different approach than Jeanette to her middle years. Streaked yellow highlights in her dirty blond hair, an overgenerous application of powder and eyeliner, especially for island life. Keith Fulbright stood a few steps away holding a T square in one hand, wearing his inevitable green plaid flannel shirt and canvas overalls, keeping his thoughts to himself. It was one of his best qualities, Jeanette thought. He looked like an aging lumberjack, the type who, in his younger days, would have turned up on the labels of maple syrup jugs, or advertising extra-absorbent paper towels.

There weren't a lot of cops on the island and Jeanette was relieved to know the two who were facing her across the creek. Bert Gantry was from off island, but he had been around for a few years and seemed nice enough. She had known Toland Bates since he was a little boy, in school with Liam and Joey. There was only one school on Caterpillar Island. His mother had been the town clerk, until cancer took her quickly. Glioblastoma. Brain cancer.

"Morning, Toland, Bert. What happened?" Jeanette asked in as timorous a voice as she could manage with people she knew.

The summer lady pointed down at the creek. Jeanette looked and saw what she had already seen. The corpse seemed hyperrealistic in the morning sunlight. As she was about to turn and look away a gray squirrel scrambled down the bank to the creek, scampered across Joey's face, and, using the bridge of the nose as a springboard for its hind legs, made a short leap to the low overhanging branch of a nearby spruce tree on the other side. Jeanette felt her stomach heave, but she inhaled firmly and stayed in control. She put her hand to her chest, and forced out an "Oh, my." But the squirrel, only going about its business, had broken her heart all over again.

She turned toward Toland Bates and asked, "Is that Joey Pizio?"

He nodded slowly. "Yes, ma'am."

When Joey Pizio had been covered, placed on a stretcher, and hauled up the bank and into a waiting ambulance, she thought, Poor kid—he never made it up a hill on his own. As the ambulance set off for the coroner's headquarters in Brockton, Bert asked the woman from away if she wouldn't mind coming down to the police station to make a statement.

"Me?" she asked, sounding terrified, then offended. She pointed at Keith, who was still standing with his T square looking across at Jeanette.

"Why don't you take him? He knows what's happening on this godforsaken island. Or is it because he never talks?" Bert and Toland exchanged glances. Keith kept looking straight ahead.

"You found the body and we got the call," Bert responded.

"But—"

"Go with them, honey," Jeanette called across the little creek. "They're good guys. I'm Jeanette, by the way. The crab lady. I'll be your neighbor, you ever get this thing built. Go with the police. They won't hurt you."

Bert and Toland waved at Jeanette and escorted their witness into the police car. Jeanette climbed back up to the house and put on coffee, wondering what she was going to do with the $8,750. Obviously, she couldn't put it in the local bank. One of the tellers was dating Bert Gantry, one of the cops. It was just like that in these coastal towns.

* * *

At a little after noon there was a knock on the door and Jeanette's new neighbor, looking pale and exhausted, asked if she might come in. She said her name was Lynne Framer, and she'd been through hell. Jeanette let her in, settled her in the living room, and offered her a coffee or tea.

"Got anything stronger?" Lynne Framer asked. "I know it's on the early side."

"Ah," said Jeanette. She went to make drinks.

"Were the police okay?" she asked as she returned.

"Fine, I guess," said Lynne, who had added a blocky gold necklace to her ensemble. "I'd just never . . . you know. I was a little panic-stricken. I mean, seeing that body, and then the sirens and everything. I felt like I was on TV."

"That's the first thing I thought of," said Jeanette. "When I got out there it was *Law and Order* in the woods. It's a hell of a way to meet someone."

"Barton will get to the bottom of it," Lynne said. "He'll be here late tonight. They had no right to question me without a lawyer. They should have taken in Keith Half-bright. That's what Barton calls him."

Jeanette frowned. "Fulbright," she said. "He might be the smartest guy on the island. Can Barton build a house, *and* rebuild the motor of a thirty-five-year-old ice cream truck?"

Lynne Framer ignored the comment.

"He was hiding inside the construction trailer when I drove in and saw the body," she said.

"Working," Jeanette said. "Probably since before first light."

"Maybe. I didn't even know he was there. I took out my phone to call Bart—he's in Kansas City on a case. I couldn't get through."

"You've probably got Verizon. The only place you'll get any service is standing on that rock in the reach," Jeanette said, gesturing to a seaweed-covered boulder jutting out of the water. A seagull was perched on it, pecking at a broken mussel shell. "You can only get there at low tide."

"Well anyhow, I couldn't get through," Lynne Framer said. "And I'm the one they took in for questioning. I was in a state. I mean—I have no idea what I said. I don't *know* anything. Anyhow, I called him from the back of the police car and left a message. He's chartering a plane from JFK when he gets in."

Barton Framer was an attorney who specialized in environmental litigation on behalf of various activist groups, including the Natural Resources Defense Council and the Sierra Club. Jeanette found this interesting, especially given the private airplane charter.

"And you're building a second home," she said, in as nonaccusatory a voice as she could.

"Third, actually," Lynne said. "We have a place in Saint John for the cold months."

"Good that you drive a Tesla."

"You have to do what you can," Lynne said. "We have two. Barton calls them the Teslae."

"Sweet. And this house looks like a big one. You'll burn a lot of oil in the winter."

"Too deep in the woods to do solar," Lynne said. "We asked. Listen, do you have a sandwich or something?"

She made Lynne Framer a bologna and Swiss on white bread. The fridge was stuffed with fresh crabmeat, but women who picked crab could seldom afford to eat it. It was overflow awaiting shipment. Besides, she didn't really like this woman enough to chop up celery and make her a crab roll.

Lynne seemed let down by the quality of the lunch but kept quiet about it, for which Jeanette was grateful. Jeanette watched her wipe a dab of mustard off her lower lip.

"You're really called the crab lady?" Lynne asked. "What does that even mean?"

Jeanette was tempted to say something about how her body transformed at midnight when the moon was full, but just shrugged.

"It's on the side of my truck," she said.

THE EEL

In her long journey from the creek to the Sargasso Sea she had been deep. But not this deep. For almost two months, like a sine curve, she descended and ascended, weaving, up and down, a needle threading the deep ocean together with the shallows; down in the day, up at night. Fifty-seven times rising. Fifty-seven times falling.

Early in her journey, she would spend the nights, body undulating, propelled forward, at about one hundred fifty feet, cruising south and east. Before dawn, before the bluefin tuna began to hunt, she would drop deeper, to seven or eight hundred feet. Sometimes even a thousand feet. The porbeagle sharks hunted all day, well above her, as she cruised forward, always east. Always south. At dusk, after the tuna's last rush, she would rise back up. By her twentieth day, acclimated to the pressure, she was dropping deeper still.

She was under pressure that would have destroyed many living things, but that would keep her safe from predation. She did not stop.

Her eyes had become blue to absorb what little light could be appreciated. She hadn't eaten since she began her journey. Her digestive tract had dissolved and been replaced by roe. Eggs. Somewhere, undulating up and down, another eel's digestive tract had been replaced by milt. Sperm. They moved toward a common place in the middle of the ocean. The Sargasso Sea.

She had lived in a slow pool on a tiny unnamed tributary of Maine's Bagaduce River for twelve years, growing larger, scavenging and hunting at night by smell, with no reproductive organs, and no sex yet. Then, for no reason that could be explained, on a rainy, flooded, dark October night, she set off downstream, accompanied by cohorts from the river. As they journeyed to the ocean, they transformed. Brown eyes turned blue. Her sex defined itself; she was drawn by a new urge, and by destiny.

Fifty-seven days and 1,750 miles later, her journey was complete. But she was tattered. Her stored fat had burned away, even her muscles had begun to consume themselves to propel her forward. Her flesh and skin hung loose, seemed on the verge of slipping off her skeleton. She was spent. Expelling the roe that had filled her belly, she deflated. She kept undulating, as though to move forward, but the movement did not propel her as it once had. Her rate of fall overtook her forward progress, and at a lazy angle, she sank deeper. Down. Down.

At two thousand feet her movements slowed. At three thousand feet they ceased. She became still, a silvery blue skin, drifting downward in the dark. Spread around her, for a mile in each direction, scattered here and there, were other silver-blue slivers, twisting, and falling, finally still. They disappeared.

Above this graveyard, milt clouded the water, surrounding a sea of roe. A small percentage of the eggs were found by sperm, and an even smaller percentage of the sperm found an egg. Nine days later, spread over several square miles of ocean, a sparse cloud of translucent willow leaves with little black eyes hung suspended. Leptocephali. They were no more than two millimeters long. If you looked into the ocean, you would not know they were there. If you dragged a fine-mesh net for miles and miles, you might find one. As they drifted north in the current, they ate plankton, and they grew. Some grew more slowly than others.

In a year, the willow leaves had reached three centimeters, and instead of simply growing larger, they, like their ancestors, began to change. Their bodies became thin and elongated, still transparent, but with a black thread running down their center. Their black eyes grew in what now formed a head at the end of a glassy thread. They became glass eels. Elvers. And their destiny was no longer to merely go where the current flowed. They were weak swimmers, but they congregated into a school. They made a collective decision. Turn left. To America.

They swam west, and they rode the current north, to the coast of Maine.

Most of the eggs had not been fertilized. Of those that were fertilized, most had been eaten before they managed to become leptocephali. Of those that were spared and managed to become translucent willow leaves, most had been eaten before they grew into elvers. Of those elvers that were not eaten in the Sargasso Sea itself, most were eaten on the journey north and west, well before they reached the coast. They fed mackerel, bonito, false albacore, juvenile dorado, giant filter feeding whales, and basking sharks. By the time the clouds of glass eels approached the land, the population was well under one percent of the eggs that had been spent in the open sea. Still, at the right place, at the right time, there was an illusion of abundance. Clouds of little eyes and glass threads stained the water.

CHAPTER NINE

Jeanette had spent much of the winter teaching Zach the barman at the Clamdigger how to make a proper martini. He was on work release from Bolduc Correctional Facility after a botched armed robbery in Bangor and mainly knew how to draw beer from a tap and pour straight whiskey into shot glasses, which was all that was usually required. Jeanette had introduced him to the martini glass, even brought one from home. She felt it was her mission to give him a chance at a better life one day—in a better bar at least.

The Clamdigger was the only real bar on the island. This allowed it to maintain a low standard. It had once been a car repair place, and to enter you still had to move past two chest-high concrete bumpers through a double door as wide as a one-car garage, into a room that had once had hydraulic lifts on either side. Now there was a wooden bar made from old boat planking painted black, and a set of stools with circular tops, upholstered in cracked red vinyl. Across from the bar were a set of unmatched tables and chairs that had been pulled out of various derelict farmhouses over the years. Its one concession to professional bar-dom was a flat screen TV.

Jeanette carried the drink to a corner table, still sporting a slight limp, greeting the folks who were out relaxing; casually, she knew them all and they all knew her. And what they don't know, she thought, won't hurt them. She had told anyone who asked that she had twisted her knee getting out of the car and stepping on a root on her own driveway. Now she sat alone at a corner table, nursing her drink and looking back over the day.

In the crab shack she had cut herself three times on the hook-beaked blade. She'd been distracted and slow, haunted still by the sight of Joey Pizio's body, washed by the creek. Unsurprisingly, it was the only matter being discussed among the women.

"That boy," Amelia Boyer had said, clicking her tongue against her teeth. "Seen a lot like 'em lately."

"It's the money," Patsy had replied. "They make a pile during the summer hauling traps, and then the winter comes. No place to spend it except with the pill man. You can only rebuild your truck engine so many times. Pills is a hobby that never gets old."

"Speaking of money," said Amelia, "buy some more knives. We're getting low again."

"I'll order more," Jeanette replied. "Just quit taking them home."

After they'd closed the crab shack for the day, Lottie hung back.

"I'm scared for you," she said, as Jeanette packed away her tools. "That boy wasn't in a creek, he was in *your* creek. And after those two men came to talk to you about whatever they wanted. Are you in this?"

"Not even a little, Lottie. I can't even stand the sight of those little critters."

"That boy. He was one of them, wasn't he? One of the two who came to your door?"

"How do you know that?"

"Someone posted his picture on Instagram. I'm not gonna tell anyone, if that's what you're thinking. I'm not that type. But it feels like you're awful close to this. I just have a bad feeling. And I want you to know that I'm here if you need me."

"I appreciate it," Jeanette said. "Really, I do. Can I ask you a question?"

"Fire away," Lottie said.

"Do you know a Native guy named Jesse Ed Davis? Tall, sort of aloof?"

Lottie's eyes narrowed. She seemed to be thinking. "I don't." she said. "Why do you ask?"

"I don't know. I just met him. Seems like an odd one."

"What makes you think all Native folks know each other?"

"Sorry, stupid, I know," Jeanette backed off.

"It's okay. But listen, anything happens to you, I'll be right back on relief. I don't want that. Don't put yourself in the crosshairs—for both of our sakes."

Crosshairs. It was the sense of being in the crosshairs that had driven her from her house to the Clamdigger. The house was quiet, surrounded by darkness, and suffused with Lottie's cautionary voice. She took a sip of her drink and looked up at the TV above the bar, but the weather was being featured with motion graphs in lurid colors. She took another sip. Then she stopped. There was a hand on her shoulder. "Evening."

She looked up. Keith Fulbright was standing by her table with a glass of beer.

"Keith," she said. "Take a seat."

"Not if you're thinking," he said. "Never like to interrupt somebody's thinking."

"Please," she said.

He nodded and settled in at the table.

"You know a man named Jesse Ed Davis?" she asked. "Native, I think. He says he knows you."

Keith rubbed his chin for a moment. "Don't believe I do," he said. "And I thought I pretty much knew everyone. So. Watcha thinking?"

"Just thinking about life," she said. No point in going into detail.

"I wouldn't do that," he said. "Not overly. You had a shock with that kid. Wanted to let you know I'm sorry."

"Thanks," she said. "Actually, I was thinking about what might be out there for me next. A change, you know? You ever get tired of building houses?"

Keith took a sip of his beer and wiped his mouth on the sleeve of his green plaid flannel shirt. Jeanette smiled. She was wondering if he had more than one. He wore it like a uniform.

"I like building houses," Keith said. "If I didn't, I'd stop. You don't like what you're doin'?"

"I'm a crab-picking, hairdressing waitress, Keith," she said.

He nodded.

"Could be time for a change," he said. "You got your freedom."

Jeanette laughed and tossed back the rest of the martini.

"Just another word for nothing left to lose," she said.

"How's that?"

"It's a song," Jeanette said. "Freedom's just another word for nothing left to lose."

"Sounds like a bad song," Keith said. "Maybe you're just lookin' through the wrong end of the telescope."

"I don't have a telescope," she said.

"Everybody's got a telescope," he said. "My mother used to tell me. You look through the wrong end, everything gets smaller and farther away. Flip it around and see what happens." She had never heard him utter so many words in one sitting. He looked down awkwardly, unaccustomed to it, tipped his lumberyard cap, got up, and went to the bar. A few minutes later, Zach placed another martini in front of her.

"From Mr. Fulbright, over there," Zach said. "Said you weren't done thinking."

Jeanette raised her glass, nodded to Keith, and took a sip. She looked over to a table where Amelia Boyer and her husband each had a meatloaf plate in front of them.

There they are, she thought. Amelia and her husband. He'd pulled his suspenders from his shoulders, and they drooped around the side of his chair, his generous belly unhitched from its tethers. His hair, white and wispy, had apparently been left uncombed when he had removed his hat. He shoveled food into his mouth with a tablespoon while Amelia picked at hers with a fork, as if looking for something in particular. Her husband paused, took a long pull from a bottle of Miller High Life, and went back to his tablespoon. High life indeed, Jeanette thought. Don't send me there. Amelia and her husband ate in silence.

She gazed around the bar. She knew everyone in the room, had known their parents, knew their kids. But one person who wasn't there—who was never there—was Bennett Tyson. All she knew about him was what Lottie had told her, and what she had seen. Any man who slams a kid like Joey up against a car might be willing to do much worse. He certainly didn't want to be seen casually hanging out chatting with folks at the Clamdigger. She took another sip of the second icy martini and wondered where he had come from, and why, on such a small island, she had never met him, or even heard about him before the day he turned up on her front porch. She was going to have to get to know a lot more about Bennett Tyson. Turn the telescope around. She felt a hand on her shoulder again; Keith was back.

"How about that?" he said, pointing to the TV above the bar.

Jeanette raised her eyes to find a video image of a refrigerator truck, with the words *Bando International* painted brightly on its side; it was billowing smoke from its rear end.

Flames were licking at the paint on the side panels. At the bottom of the screen, she could read the words *Chemical fire causes elver transport mishap*.

Jeanette watched the fire, mesmerized, until the video switched to a shot of the contents of the truck with the doors swung open—containers of chemically smoked dead seafood and a large cache of lobsters lying belly up in blackened seawater.

"Blown-out compressor lines?" she asked.

Keith nodded. "Just plain carelessness." She watched the TV until the video switched to an interview with Sung Ho Han, Bando's regional director, who was issuing a statement about the burning truck. But with the sound turned down, there was no way to know what he was saying. Keith put his hand on her shoulder.

"Won't happen to your truck," he said with some pride. "Unless someone breaks it on purpose."

***

Assistant Fishery Resources Commissioner Gary Kell left his office in Augusta telling the receptionist that he was headed out for lunch. She expressed not the slightest interest—didn't even look up at him, for which he was grateful. He was not headed out for lunch.

Gary Kell's post as assistant commissioner was designed to be at the heart of a bureaucrat's comfort zone. At just under 5'8", he looked the part—his sandy hair thinning although he had yet to see forty, rimless spectacles, and a slight stoop that would no doubt grow more pronounced with age, as if he wanted his head closer to the ground in case anyone knocked him over. This did not mean, however, that he was without ambition or connections. Gary Kell saw himself as a cautious and clever man, a political chess player, with a future that was far brighter than his present. His greatest desire was to make friends in the right places, though he was aware that, if the opportunity ever presented itself, which so far it had not, certain ethical compromises would be almost inevitable in achieving that goal. Today excited him. He was, at this moment, on his way to meet a man who he knew could do things for him, although he didn't have a clue about the purpose of this visit. He had been summoned that morning and was not about to miss the opportunity.

He was ushered into Lester Birdwell's oak-paneled office in Augusta by an executive assistant in high heels whose hair was pulled tight in a neat bun, and whose blouse was silk, pale green, and open by one button too many. Gary Kell was impressed and a little stirred in a non-business fashion. No one at the state office looked like this.

She led Gary Kell to an overstuffed chair at a coffee table some distance from the impressive but empty desk in the office and offered him a coffee, which he declined with thanks.

Birdwell's office walls were lined with photographs of the governor with celebrities, politicians, and athletes. There was even one with the president. And more impressive than that, with football hero Tom Brady. Those were hard to get. There was a box of cigars on the desk and mounted on the wall behind was an impressive stuffed sailfish, which had seen better days. Someone had placed one of the cigars between its stiff plaster lips. Gary Kell wondered who. The governor was famously devoid of a sense of humor.

Birdwell entered with his hand out. "Lester Birdwell," he said as Gary Kell shot out of his chair and took the ex-governor's hand. "I'm pleased to meet you, and thank you for coming on short notice."

"It's an honor," said Gary Kell.

"Don't be honored, just be helpful," the ex-governor replied. "That's what I tell everybody."

"How can I be?" asked Kell.

"Everything all right over there at the Resources Commission? You doing fine?"

Kell acknowledged that he felt quite well.

"I wanted to see you," Birdwell explained, "because you, well, of course, you take an interest in the environment, as do I."

This somewhat puzzled Gary Kell, who vividly remembered standing by helplessly as the then-Governor Birdwell eagerly tore down every environmental regulation he could get his hands on.

"We've got a situation," Birdwell continued. "Unsafe refrigerator trucks. Now don't get me wrong, I think everyone is entitled to make a living, an honorable living in the state of Maine. Maine is open for business, and I'm a free enterprise man. But do you know how many eels and lobsters we lost in one badly maintained truck yesterday? Not to mention hundreds of crabs whose lives were sacrificed in vain, so to speak. It makes Maine look like we don't care. Did you hear about this?"

Kell allowed that he had heard.

"Man named Sung Ho Han owns that trucking company, buys and sells eels, you know, a foreigner, not that there's anything wrong with that, but not one of us at all, a man with different interests, and I fear he's become a careless businessman. Now what I want to know, Mr. Kell, is this."

Gary Kell looked up expectantly.

"If the wisest thing to do under the circumstances was to shut down this particular trucking line until a proper investigation could be arranged, and all the trucks inspected and repaired, would that be a rule you could impose in your role as the resources commissioner?"

"I'm the assistant," Gary Kell said, but Birdwell did not seem to be listening.

"It seems to me," he went on, "that the health of the fishery, the wildlife in general, the sanctity of the animal kingdom, which includes you and me *and* the eels and lobsters and crabs for heaven's sake, would benefit from some serious attention here. There's no point in hunting and trapping sea life just to burn it up in an electrical fire."

The idea appealed enormously to Gary Kell. And his boss was at a conference in Denver. This was timely, a virtual emergency, and what was a good assistant for, after all?

"I'd be honored to be helpful," Kell said, conflating the ex-governor's two options together. Clever, he thought.

"Excellent," said Birdwell. "I've been looking for a man like you."

"Thank you, sir," said Kell, trying not to say more than he had to. He was beginning to feel beads of sweat breaking out on his high forehead. Was this a golden opportunity or a slippery slope? Or both?

The ex-governor had to have an angle, but Kell could not for the life of him figure out what it was. He wasn't sure he wanted to know. At that moment, Birdwell looked to him like a great big golden door through which he was being invited to pass.

"What we'd want," said Birdwell, "is a spokesperson from within. Someone who had the authority to try and stop this Sung Ho fellow from allowing all this slipshod business behavior."

"But it would be a temporary thing, right? I mean, the eelers will be adversely affected."

"The thing is," Birdwell said, "we'd want to do this with a passionate voice. With some moral force behind it. A major environmental statement from someone who is known to care deeply. I have to repeat . . . deeply. It's a role I can't play. But it's a role I can see you in. You see, the long-term interests of the eel fishermen will be improved with better shipping, even if they are temporarily inconvenienced."

"I'm flattered," said Gary Kell, feeling a bit overwhelmed. "Of course, I wouldn't want to be the cause of pain to the fishermen without preparing a response—they don't brook interference easily. If there's no way to ship, there's no point in netting eels, right? And there goes the economy. I mean temporarily, of course. There are things to consider. I'd want to weigh . . ."

"The risks versus the rewards," said Birdwell.

"I'm not sure that was what I was about to say."

"Well, you didn't say what you were about to say, now did you?" Birdwell asked. "So let me tell you. The rewards will outweigh the risks. In a very dramatic fashion. And soon. Trust me."

CHAPTER TEN

Jeanette was in her living room on her laptop trying to find information on the Bando truck fire when she saw a police car pull into her driveway. She was not surprised and had done her best to prepare herself for the inevitable visit. She was not comfortable telling lies, and particularly not to people she cared about. And here was Toland Bates walking up the steps with Bert Gantry.

Years earlier, Jeanette had given Toland a tight hug after his mother's funeral, wondering at the irrationality of it all. She'd felt like she might be hugging her own lost son, while holding someone who had lost his mother. She'd had a soft spot for him since the days when she hosted a co-op playgroup while Simon was out on the water. The girls, generally speaking, were well-behaved and played quietly, while the boys slammed around the house like three-year-olds playing ice hockey. But Toland Bates was a quiet one. He made buildings out of blocks and stuck them together with Play-Doh. Then he would wait for Jeanette to come over and admire them. Whenever it was time to go from one place to another, he would reach up to her and say, "I need a hand." He had been an awkward but irresistible boy, and close to Liam. Now, here on business, some elements of the boy still shone through.

"You want to grill me here, or do you want me at the station house?" she asked, pretending indifference. But her palms were sweating. Had they found her note—the note about the sandwich, the money, Simon? She'd find out soon enough.

"It's nothing like that," Toland said. "We just want to know more about what you saw. We don't need an Alpha David or anything."

Jeanette and Bert exchanged confused looks. There was a pause.

"Like a statement you sign or something? Here is fine," said Toland.

"Especially if you got any pound cake or anything like that," Bert Gantry added. He was a little older than Toland Bates and already going to fat. It befitted his senior rank, Jeanette thought.

Jeanette set out some Sara Lee, a coffeepot, and two mugs.

"So," she said. "Grill." But it took some gumption to say it so casually. She was about to tell a series of lies to a young man she liked and felt a kinship with, and she hated to do it. She was beginning to resent Jesse Ed Davis and his plan to keep her off to the side of all this.

"We just want to know what you know," said Gantry. "Don't suspect it's much."

Jeanette swallowed hard. "I heard that Framer woman screaming. I thought maybe there was a rafter of turkeys strutting around on the hood of her Tesla scratching the paint or something."

"A rafter?" asked Gantry. He was taking notes.

"A flock, most people say," said Jeanette. "With turkeys it's properly known as a rafter."

"If you say so," said Gantry.

"Then I heard sirens, and I figured I better go out there and see if everything was okay. And when I got out there, I see you two. And the Framer woman all shook up, and Keith. And I saw the body in the creek, and I thought, 'Is that Joey Pizio?'"

"We were in school together. All the way from grade school," Toland said. "You remembered him—from Liam . . ." He trailed off.

"Of course I remembered him," Jeanette cut him off. "I carried him halfway up Cedar Hill once."

"I'm sorry, Jeanette," said Toland. "I don't mean to bring up Liam."

His earnest feeling for her was starting to kill her. She felt it stabbing at her stomach, where it usually did. But she simply nodded.

"It's all right," she said.

Toland turned to Gantry, who was dunking a piece of cake in his coffee.

"What killed him?" asked Jeanette.

"We're supposed to be asking the questions," said Gantry.

"Then what's the cake and coffee for?"

Toland shrugged.

"Overdose is the usual cause," he said. "But not the usual kind. It looks like someone spiked something. The coroner's dealing with it."

"What?" Jeanette asked. "How spiked?"

Gantry looked up from his cake.

"That's police business," he said, giving Toland a look. Toland shrugged.

Toland. He wasn't going to keep anything from her.

Jeanette felt her stomach fall. Had someone actually killed the boy? She remembered Bennett Tyson shoving him against the red Mustang. She opened her mouth to speak but retreated into silence. Don't talk if you can listen, she thought. But an awful silence descended on the three of them.

"Coroner. What an awful job that is," she finally said. "Does that make it—what—murder?"

"Homicide's the proper term at the moment," Toland said. "If it proves out."

"Oh my God," she said. "That poor, poor boy."

"We don't know all the facts," Gantry said. "Don't jump to conclusions."

"He died in her creek, Bert," said Toland. "And she knew him from when he was a kid. She's entitled to whatever we know."

"It'll play out as a standard-issue overdose," Gantry said tersely. "That's how the chief sees it."

Jeanette knew he was right. The chief was a weak-chinned veteran with thinning hair named Otis Sumlin Jr. Everyone on the island referred to him as Little Otis, but never to his face.

His father, Big Otis, was the town supervisor, from one of the oldest families on the island. Big Otis, who dressed like a poor man, owned about a mile and a third of shorefront property on the island's east coast, looking out to the small islands and the open ocean. The views were breathtaking. Big Otis believed that when the summer people finally began to come this far north in numbers, his fortune would be made. He'd even sneaked through an approved subdivision while no one on the town council was paying attention. He was pushing eighty and it was likely that Little Otis would end up with the property one day. He was not a police chief who was looking for disruptions to the bucolic promise of a Maine summer home for the millionaires from away who would one day come flocking. It had never really mattered to her before. But now . . .

"Jesus," she said. "Joey. He was an orphan, no?"

"An only child," said Toland. "Peggy and Joe—those were the parents—killed in a car wreck. One of those crazy burners smacked into them trying to blacken up the road. Must have been ten years ago."

Jeanette felt her stomach tighten more. Killed by a burner. By Jesse Ed Davis? She was remembering her terrifying ride as he laid down a double strip of black rubber on the road, spinning wildly in all directions.

"Joey didn't have no luck," Gantry said.

"And nothing else neither," Toland added. "I guess he just couldn't make it. He wasn't much of a student. Or a ballplayer, to tell the truth, but I kind of liked him. Harmless type of a guy."

"Who was the burner?" Jeanette asked, finding her voice.

"I don't remember the guy's name," said Toland. "He spent a year or two at Bolduc. Vehicular manslaughter."

"Any idea what Joey might have been doing down there?" Gantry asked, his pencil poised.

"Eels in the creek," Jeanette said. "I just assumed that's what Joey was doing there."

"Elvers is a good business for those who can do it," said Gantry, putting down the pencil long enough to take a stab at the cake with his fork. "Till your truck blows up, I s'pose."

"I saw that," Jeanette said. "On TV."

"Now they shut the whole operation down," Gantry went on. "You see that on TV?"

"They what?"

"The DEP," said Toland. "Took all the trucks off the road. Inspect and repair. The whole business is stood still."

***

When the two men had left the house and the black-and-white had pulled out of sight, Jeanette donned a light sweater and went to her own car. It took her half an hour to drive to the storage place in Brockton where she had spent an unsettling time with the man who called himself Jesse Ed Davis, who, she had convinced herself, was a good candidate for the death of Joey Pizio's parents. She turned in the driveway and moved to the parking space opposite the unit she was sure was his. There was an orange sign on the door with the word AVAILABLE in block capital letters written across it, hand-lettered, just off-center. Beneath was a phone number, less formally scrawled. She moved to the unit and was about to try the garage-sized door when she saw the hasp and the padlock.

Returning to the car, she dialed the number on the sign. A man answered after the second ring.

"Self storage," the voice said. It was a scratching, unsteady sound, even in two words. Cigarettes, Jeanette thought. Too many cigarettes.

"I'm calling about the vacant unit here in Brockton," she said.

"Un-hunh," the man said. "One eighty a month, first month free."

"Let me ask you something. Was there a man living in this unit before? Just recently, I mean?"

"Friend of yours?" the man asked. The voice curled into something that suggested there was a smile on his lips.

"No. Yes, well, I knew him. Do you have any idea where he might have gone?"

"You can't live in one of these places," the man said.

"Yes, but do you know—"

"I don't know how he managed it as long as he did. I told him I'd call the cops. He was gone the next day."

"So you don't have any idea—"

"Place isn't zoned for residential living," the man said. "I don't even know where he went to pee. You want the place?"

Jeanette paused for a moment, deciding quickly that this was all the information she was going to get.

"I'll have to think," she said. "Thanks."

"It'll go quick," the man said. "I'd take one sixty."

"I'll let you know," Jeanette said.

***

The next morning Toland Bates found himself standing by the side of the road, staring at a boulder on which were painted the first names of this year's high school seniors, all of whom were getting ready to graduate. There were two Emmas and a Spike, a Brian, a Joey, and one Melissa. There was Dave A. and Dave M. and a dozen more. It looked like each of them had taken a turn with the paint brush. The boulder was covered with names. Bert pulled his cruiser up by the rock and got out.

"Partner," he said.

Toland turned around and looked at the older, softer policeman with a bewildered stare, as if he was awakening from a dream.

"You missed our shift time," Bert said. "I been out looking for you. Hell are you doing at the rock? Jesus, you look like you seen a ghost."

"Sorry," Toland said. "I guess I sorta did get spooked. Let's go."

"Get in the car," Bert said. "No need to go any place so quick. I don't want to ride with a man's been put under a spell."

They climbed in.

"You mind telling me?" Bert asked.

"Haven't slept," Toland said. "I don't know why, but this thing's got me."

"Any special thing? You mean that kid in the creek?"

For a long time Toland sat in silence. Bert Gantry thought he might start to cry, which Bert hoped to avoid at all costs. A crying man was not something he wanted to have to handle without some special training. It was bad enough when Laureen, his bank teller girlfriend cried. She cried every time she watched *Titanic*, and always at the same spot, when that girl says goodbye to her boyfriend while he gets taken by the hypothermia. Bert didn't like cold water. But he liked it better than watching *Titanic* with Laureen.

"They buried him," Toland said, finally. "I followed the casket. Nobody else did. Except Jeanette King."

"Joey Pizio had a funeral? And the crab lady was there?"

"She knew all of us back in the day. I haven't slept in the couple nights since. Thinking about him, you know?"

"You guys wasn't close, I thought."

"I guess he coulda been me is all. Only thing is, he couldn't have been. He was always this one, not that one."

"Please boy, try to make a little sense," Bert said. "Just for my sake."

"I'm sorry," Toland said. "It's all coming out in spits and farts. What I've been thinking about—back then, in sixth grade, he was Mr. Big League Chew."

"The what? You mean the bubble gum? Comes in a pouch?"

"Like tobacco. Like real men chewed. His father worked at the general store in Hamilton. Joey said he could get it for seventy-five cents—it cost a dollar at the counter. So we all gave him our three quarters, week after week. For a minute, he was important to us. We called him Big League. He loved it. Turned out his dad was stealing it and giving it to him for free. Make him feel like a big man. His dad was stealing all sorts of stuff. He got canned from the store. When we found out we just sort of never treated him the same after that. Some of us had paid for gum we didn't get. We tried to get our money back, but he said he had spent it. He probably gave the quarters to his dad. We started calling him Little League. Felt mean. It was sad. All I know is I haven't slept since I saw his body go in the ground, and there's something wrong about it."

"You were a kid. Kid fucks up or his dad does something stupid, other kids tease him, maybe even beat the shit out of him. He's lucky that way. That kinda thing's been happening since the Bible got written."

Toland blew a long, low whistle through his lips.

"He stood on my shoulders right here at the rock," he said. "No one else would let him. Right in the middle of the night so he could paint his name higher than mine. That's what he wanted. And I said fine. Maybe he looked up to me, kind of, despite everything. But he also wanted to be on top of where I was. I don't know. Wasn't that long ago. My mom had just got the diagnosis. We knew she wasn't gonna survive. My dad was starting to live on Allen's Coffee Brandy. The big bottles. And here I was out in the dark with Joey Pizio sitting on my shoulders, dripping paint onto my head. You ever seen a guy like that—that you knew like that—seen his casket right down into the ground?"

"Can't say that I have."

"It'll stick to your ribs," Toland said.

* * *

Jeanette paced back and forth on the bluff above the lobster co-op, looking at the mooring where the *Jeanette* should have been. Her head was filled with warring senses of possibility and danger. Was the truck fire an accident? It seemed unlikely. And it seemed like an opportunity. Her heart was leaping a little. She put her hand to her chest and felt her breastbone, but there was nothing there. Forty-four was a lousy age to get breast cancer. Not fair—not that any cancer was fair. Or maybe all of them were. For cancer, one body was as good as another.

She got back into the Subaru, put it into gear, turned onto 172, and turned down the hill toward the lobster co-op.

A black sedan with Wisconsin plates was tucked behind a small stand of birches just off the road. From the driver's seat a man had watched her arrive and was now watching her leave—watching her through a pair of apparently dead eyes peering from a waxwork face so impassive that it would have been impossible to know what was going on behind it.

* * *

Jeanette arrived at the lobster co-op and was greeted by the cashier, an unsmiling little woman whose natural gray curls Jeanette colored auburn once a month at Bea's Hive of Beauty. When Jeanette asked about Bennett, she learned that he was the co-op's bookkeeper, with an office on the second floor. "I don't know if he's in or not," the cashier said dismissively. "He don't show up for work as often as all that. He's always up to something." Jeanette was not surprised. She viewed the stairs on the exterior of the building with trepidation. Her knee was not fully healed, and she was far from sure she wanted to come face-to-face with the man again.

The co-op shipped about four tons of lobster a day, moving it mainly to New York and Boston. Below the office was a tank eighty feet long and twenty-five feet wide enclosed in a prefab metal structure that was a temporary home to as many as twenty thousand lobsters at a time. Sometimes they lived there for weeks. Eighteen-foot-high pumps pulled seawater from the bay, pushed it through the tank at one end, and expelled it from the other. Fluorescent lighting illuminated the place but was normally turned off. The lobsters didn't like light. They were not fed, in order to purge their intestinal tracts; though no misleading claim was ever made about what was contained in the thin dark tube running down the center of a lobster's tail, it was in everyone's best interests to have it be as empty as possible to keep consumers from pondering too much. The lobsters remained alert but famished.

Today Tyson was in, but apparently not expecting a visitor. He pushed his desk chair back eight inches when Jeanette knocked on his door and opened it. He looked up at her. It was the first time she had seen him without sunglasses on. His eyes were piercing and strange. It took her a moment to discover the reason: one was brown and the other green. They shone oddly in the bright fluorescent light of the office.

"Well, look who's come to pay a debt," he said.

"Too late for that, I'm afraid," she replied. "The mortgage, the insurance, the taxes—you know how it goes."

The tackle box, in truth, was still securely lodged behind the furnace.

"So?" Bennett Tyson asked.

"I felt maybe I could keep earning it," she said.

"I don't follow," said Bennet Tyson tersely.

"It's pretty simple," Jeanette said.

As she spoke, she glanced around the office, taking note of whatever she could. Cheap metal three-drawer file cabinet. A pile of labels on his desk in both English and some Asian language. Dead bolt on the door. A cardboard box of spiral-bound notebooks next to the desk. Like kids use in school. No lock on the file cabinet. Might be empty. Or not.

"Earn it how?" Tyson asked. "A simple hint about where the hell your ex has gone off to would be a step in the right direction."

"Can't help you there," she said. "I was hoping you could keep better track of him than I have. Looks like we're both out of luck."

"He was my best man," Tyson said.

"But not your only man," she surmised. "I just want to help. Especially since you lost poor Joey Pizio. That was unfortunate."

"Sad," said Bennett Tyson, shaking his head. "Very sad. And right in your creek too."

"I've had to deal with the police and my side yard is a crime scene, complete with yellow plastic tape. But I want you to know, I decided not to talk to them about you and Joey coming to visit me. I did you a favor. I didn't have to do that."

"I'm supposed to say thank you? That kid gave you ten K in cash, with his fingerprints all over it, and then he shows up dead in your creek. I think you've got a lot of reasons not to talk to the police, and concern for my well-being is low on that list."

Jeanette felt a familiar sharp pain in her stomach. Soldier on, she told herself. She shrugged. "I only came to help," she said.

"If you don't know where Simon's gone off to—"

"You still have the catch," she said. "The licensed eelers have stopped. You don't have to. You should invite me to sit down."

Tyson sighed unhappily and put his hands flat on the desk as if he might get up and leave the room.

"So . . . what?" he asked.

"I'm assuming you were transporting your elvers on Bando's trucks, paying off the drivers."

"I wouldn't assume anything," Tyson said.

"But the trucks are gone, you have elvers to move," she said, "and you've got no way to move them. I have my own refrigerator truck, and it is already making legal, aboveboard crabmeat deliveries to Bangor International twice a week. Elvers don't take up much space. It's not a pretty vehicle, but it will haul your product while everyone with elver licenses sits and stews."

Bennett cocked his head to the side. He was listening.

"Now ask me to sit down."

CHAPTER ELEVEN

There was not a lot of light left in the sky when Jeanette pulled into her driveway, but there was a sedan blocking the way and Toland Bates, by himself this time, was down by the creek.

"Toland," she said. "What're you doing here?"

"Taking samples," he said.

"Soil samples?"

He straightened up and walked up the bank, carrying a plastic bag full of soil and decaying leaves with him.

"I'm a mess," he said. He wore a white zippered jumpsuit streaked with creek mud and spattered with dead, wet leaves.

"Here," she said, beckoning him in. "Come get cleaned up."

"I don't mean this," he said, rubbing his hands on his clothing. "It's just—we were in high school together. He tried to teach me to smoke cigarettes, but I never could get the hang of it. Dead in a creek bed at twenty-six? I know it doesn't compare to—" He broke off.

Jeanette nodded. Liam was never far-off. "So you took an interest."

"Couldn't help myself. I'm still here, he's gone."

"Survivor's guilt."

Toland's eyes narrowed.

"Never heard of that," he said.

She sighed. She was sure he hadn't.

"Come in the house and have some coffee."

"Gimme a minute," he replied. He stripped off the jumpsuit and dragged it over his boots. Flipping the trunk of his car, he rolled the jumpsuit up and tucked it in between a fly rod tube and a compound hunting bow.

She led him in by the side door, where he shed his boots. She put on coffee and opened a fresh Sara Lee.

"Survivor's guilt," she said, "is . . . I have it with your mom. We drank a lot of coffee together when we were raising you kids, and she was there for me after Liam. But it was more than that."

"Because?"

"Because," Jeanette said, "she was there to listen. I owed her a lot for that. Then she got sick. I beat it. She never had a chance. No one knows why that happens. People just leave you."

"Don't I know it," Toland said.

"When Liam died," Jeanette said, "I was grateful to get to know you. You weren't mine, but you were here. I just feel bad that it came at such a terrible bad time for you."

"It was hard," Toland said quietly. He took a bite of cake as she went to get him a cup of coffee.

"Thing is," he said, making sure to chew and swallow first, "I shouldn't be coming to you. It's police business."

He took a larger bite of cake. She waited. That woman, she thought, God bless her, she taught him not to talk with his mouth full. Finally, he couldn't stall any longer.

"I don't think he died here," he said.

"What? What do you mean?"

He sighed heavily.

"I called the coroner. I was having a tough day. Joey Pizio died of organ failure due to the ingestion of glyphosate," he said. "Maybe in a form that he thought was oxycodone, which was a problem of his. Or maybe injected somehow, or something. This stuff will kill you pretty fast if it's concentrated enough. Or if you ingest enough of it."

"What is—what did you call it?"

"It's the active ingredient in Roundup. The weed killer. Mixed in a percoption.

"A what?"

"Percoption. You know, that's half prescription, half concoction. You never heard of that?"

Jeanette shook her head. "You mean like Valium and tonic?" she asked.

"Why not? Course, glyphosate is not your usual bar beverage."

"Good Christ," Jeanette said. "Weed killer?"

"That's what the coroner found in him," said Toland. "It's a preliminary report. But dollars for donuts it'll never come out. None of the big guns on Caterpillar want a murder on their hands. Bad for property values. Overdose is easier on them."

"So what's with the soil samples?"

"The thing is, the doc thinks he would have vomited quite a lot while he was going. I'm just wondering."

Jeanette thought about the night she had fallen into Joey's body, when Jesse Ed Davis was waiting in the dark. The air had that clean woodland smell that you get with spring rain. Nothing unusual. Nothing unpleasant. But she held her tongue. She had not even been there, as far as the police were concerned. A pang of guilt ran through her like ice water dripping down her back.

"Well, there's this thing I do, you know?" he went on. "With my bow when I get a little spare time. I stand about six feet from a target and shoot with my eyes closed. It makes you more accurate, though you might think just the opposite. You get so that you release the string so smooth it surprises you each time. Like it isn't even on purpose. That way you don't anticipate the release and flinch. You just let it slip away . . ."

"I'm not following," Jeanette said.

"Well, when I heard that, I just had to be by myself, so I went to practice. That's when I realized I couldn't relax at all. I missed the damn target standing right in front of it. And I realized, what I was thinking about, standing there with my eyes closed, was if there was any sign of human vomit in the vicinity of where that Framer woman found him."

Jeanette nodded.

"Because if there isn't, and I'm betting there isn't, then he didn't die here. Someone put him here."

Jeanette took this in silently, but her gut turned over. Her stomach hadn't been treating her well anyhow, not for years, but this was worse.

"Poisoned him?" she asked. "Who would do a thing like that?"

"It's just that Bert pulled over a guy speeding," Toland said in what appeared to be a complete non sequitur. "But it's police business."

She waited. Mainers could be so enigmatic, she thought, realizing that she was, of course, one of them. Which meant she knew enough to keep silent and wait.

"Guy from away. Just a speeding ticket. But it was the night before you found Joey in the creek. Bert told me all about it after we questioned the Framer woman—he was pretty proud to catch up with a guy going that speed on the bridge—guy was doing about seventy-five. I didn't think much of it at the time."

"And?" From Jeanette.

"After I visited the coroner, I thought back to it, remembered the one thing Bert said except about how fast the guy was going. Said he looked like a city guy, out-of-state guy from Wisconsin, said the whole car smelled like weed killer. Said the guy's gonna have the devil's own time getting that smell gone. He said he bets he loses his rental deposit."

"And you think Joey might have been . . . ?"

"Could be," Toland said. "One other thing, Bert told me the guy he gave the citation to's got an odd face. Like his face doesn't move, only his eyes and his lips. Spooked him pretty good. Like the guy had a mask, except it wasn't a mask."

"A mask?" asked Jeanette

"But not. Out-of-state tags. So, I did a little research. Couldn't help myself—I'm like a dog with a bird about some things."

He let the information out like it was being squeezed from an almost empty toothpaste tube.

"Name's Thurston Harney. He done a stretch for manslaughter a while ago."

"Manslaughter?"

"I don't know more than that about it," Toland said. "I'm working on it. It don't make me comfortable."

She took this in and was silent for a moment.

"You liked Joey," she said finally.

"Big League, we called him. He was a harmless one, harmless enough," Toland said. "No reason for him to die like that. I gotta find out what I can. You know? Sometimes you just gotta."

"So you're doing it on your own?"

"They're not gonna look for what they don't want to find. I'm learning a lot about shorefront property and how to protect the value. You gotta have peace and quiet, even when there isn't any. I swore an oath to serve and protect. I didn't mean serve the chief and protect his daddy's real estate investments. Joey deserves more than that. He deserves the truth."

"The truth," Jeanette said, and the words sprung something inside of her. She paused before going on. "Well then, I should tell you, Toland. The Framer woman wasn't the first to find him. I was." It just came out.

"Beg pardon?" Toland said.

So she told him. Meeting Joey on the *Jeanette*, the visit from Bennett and Joey, the flashing light, her unexpected tumble down the creek bed into Joey's body, the fear, the horror of recognizing the corpse, and then Jesse—the ride in the truck, and everything that followed.

He began to fidget as she spoke, clenching and unclenching his fists. By the time she had described the cooler with the elvers in it, the mysterious visit to Jesse's storage unit, his face had reddened, and his breath came short.

"You broke a lot of laws," he said coldly. "Let me get this right. You found the body. Not the Framer woman." His voice remained even and slow.

"That's right," Jeanette said.

"And lied to me and Bert about it."

"That's right."

Jeanette sensed a seething hurt underneath the anger.

"It was my choice not to call the police," Jeanette said. "I was scared. It wasn't just Joey—the boat, the money, Simon being gone, it felt like the police might make it worse. I just couldn't bring myself to tell you—"

Toland looked in her eyes unflinchingly. "I came to you, and I told you all kinds of things—confidential things—because I trusted you. All the time you were a POI."

"A what?" Jeanette asked.

"Person of Interest," Toland said.

"You don't think I killed Joey Pizio?" Jeanette said. "I hauled that boy up a mountain on a field trip once."

"Of course not." Toland looked wounded. "But what about the guy who was there, standing there over the body? He's suspect number one."

"His name is Jesse Ed Davis, and I don't know much about him really, but I don't believe he killed Joey."

"Because why?"

"Because why would he still be there? And if Joey's body was moved, even more so. He'd be as far away as he could get. Not calling attention to himself."

"Fair enough, I think," Toland said. "Still. What was he doing there?"

"I wish I had the slightest idea. And he's a burner. For all I know he could have killed Joey's mother and father. And I went back to his place this morning—he's disappeared without a trace."

"I don't know, Jeanette. You put me in a terrible spot."

"I'm sorry," Jeanette said. "I really am. I felt awful about it."

Toland put his fork down and pushed his coffee mug away.

"Go on and book me," she concluded. "For whatever. Cuff me if you need to. I made a mistake."

He looked at Jeanette as if she were a specimen of some sort, as if he might learn something by observing this particular type of human being.

"You've got a hell of a poker face," he said, finally. "All that stuff about a raft of turkeys and coming out of the house when you heard the Framer woman screaming—Bert wrote it all down too." He laughed a little.

"I don't know what to tell you," Jeanette said. "I was just spooked. Nothing like this ever happened to me."

Toland nodded. "I get that. But still. If we'd dragged you down to the station and took an Alpha David under oath, what then?"

"I don't know, Toland. I just don't know what would have happened. I was just glad you didn't."

"I had to talk Bert out of it. That was my first mistake, I guess. I wasn't gonna put my mother's best friend in an interrogation room, even if we had one, which we don't."

"I'm grateful," Jeanette said. She reached her hand across the table and placed her hand on his. The back of his hand was soft, like a child's. He did not pull away. "I didn't know where Simon had gone. And I still don't. And I was scared they'd think I was involved."

"Well, you were."

"But not like that."

His fingers drummed a tattoo on the table under her palm.

"Toland?"

He drained the coffee mug and took his hand back. "Nobody knows that the body was moved from some other location," he said. "And nobody knows that you were the one who found him."

"Nobody but us," Jeanette said. "And Jesse Ed Davis."

"Who has disappeared," Toland said. "And nobody but us wants to hear about it. Or make it right. They're just gonna pretend he OD'd."

"I can't let that stand," Jeanette said.

"So?" Toland asked.

"I don't know," Jeanette said, looking back into Toland's eyes. "But whoever killed that boy is gonna be good and goddamn sorry."

CHAPTER TWELVE

Aggregating baby eels from a dozen or so pill junkies, meth heads, deadbeats, and fading alcoholic senior citizens was a damn sight more trouble than Bennett Tyson had imagined it would be, and not the way he had planned to spend the prime of his life. But he had done a small stretch for kiting checks in his twenties and a longer one for ripping off small-time investors in what could have become a decent Ponzi scheme if he had ever gotten it off the ground. When he got out of prison for the second time, he was sporting a virtually perfect replica of a Maine driver's license with a new name that one of his cellblock mates at Waupun had provided for a modest fee, and the phone number of another block mate, who had promised him a job tending bar in Lewiston, Maine, and helping out with a burgeoning business selling prescription painkillers.

He first heard of the elver business from one of the black-market eelers who was supporting an oxy habit. He soon discovered that there was an enormous quantity of cash being generated by small-time poachers, and Bennett Tyson sensed an opportunity—the need for an entrepreneur like himself, who could form a commune of workers from a sorry lot of miscreants. If he could collect the catch from each of these small-time eelers and get the crop into the hands of professionals before it died, there was decent money to be made. It took time, making a deal with the Bando truck drivers to let the eels hitch a ride to the airport, and then another with Bando's much smaller competitor Kang Brothers in Changwon, who were happy to get whatever supply wasn't already committed to Bando. They had designs on one day overtaking Bando, positioning themselves as "artisanal providers." It was a term that they didn't understand, but it was gaining currency in the US, as Tyson explained. Smaller could be better, at least until you got to be bigger.

With hard work and ingenuity, he had forged a real black-market business. Now the money was pretty good. He was four years in when the trucks were taken off the road, and the big-time eelers were forced to stop eeling. But his men, unlicensed and beneath the radar, were still working, and all he needed was a truck.

Now he had one.

***

Jeanette made the usual trip between the island and Bangor International the next morning, but it was her first one carrying contraband elvers. She had stopped to get gas and taken the opportunity to take a cell phone photo of the labels on the cargo. Kang Brothers. Not Bando. That was all she could glean.

The international freight delivery area was south of the roadway that led to the passenger terminal, and she was told to expect two men in orange T-shirts to meet her at the curb by the intake double doors. They were waiting when she got there and off-loaded the elvers, who were swimming in a customized 250-liter Yeti cooler that pumped air through the brackish water like a motor in a homestyle aquarium. The baby eels could survive for about twelve hours out of water if you kept them cold, but Bennett Tyson had invested in the coolers just in case. The men took the cargo, and handed her an envelope containing $450, a more than decent price for a round trip to the airport.

"Bill of lading?" she asked.

"Right here," said the taller of the two, removing a rumpled sheet from his shirt pocket and handing it to the other.

There had to be a bill of lading, and it had to go back to Bennett Tyson's office. With any luck he wouldn't be there, and she'd get a chance to poke around a bit, leaving the documentation of the shipment on his desk.

The shorter man took the paper, leaned against the side of the Mister Softee truck, signed it, and handed it to her.

"All right and proper," he said. His cigarette never left his mouth and smoke curled across her face. She thanked them, moved the truck down the roadway about a quarter of a mile to the domestic freight delivery area, off-loaded her crabmeat, which was packed in ice in a less elaborate cooler, and headed back to the island.

She climbed the outdoor stairs at the co-op, let herself in, and moved to Tyson's office. It was now late afternoon, and no one seemed to be around. She tried the door, but it was locked. For a moment she stood motionless, considering her options. The bill of lading was in her straw purse along with her wallet. She vaguely recalled a scene in a movie where an experienced thief had opened a locked door with a credit card, slipping it between the doorjamb and the door and smoothly pushing the triangular door latch out of the way. Could this be done by amateurs? she wondered.

Taking a quick look around, she reached into her wallet searching for the most flexible card she had—a Walgreens membership card. She slid the card along the face of the door and forced it into the sliver of space between the jamb and the door just next to the knob. It turned the corner, and she could feel the edge of it meet the latch. But there it stopped. She pushed delicately and then with some force, but nothing gave. Gingerly, she got down on her knees, placing herself at eye level with the doorknob. Maybe that would help.

"Help you?" The voice came from behind her.

Christ, she thought. And at her age she couldn't even stand up quickly to turn and see who had busted her.

"Jeanette?"

She gripped the doorknob and hoisted herself to her feet, turning to find herself face-to-face with Billy Willig, the idiot dockmaster.

"Billy," she said, her mind racing.

"What're you doing on the floor, for heaven's sake? Are you okay?"

"I . . . it's just that . . ." She glanced at the purse and spied the bill of lading rolled up there. "I'm supposed to get these papers to Mr. Tyson. I thought his door would be open but then . . . well . . . then I thought I'd slip them under the door. You don't happen to have a key?"

"I'll take 'em," Billy said. "You can't hardly believe that guy—got a dead-bolt lock with his own key plus the ones we keep on the board downstairs. Don't know what the heck he thinks is in there that's so valuable."

Jeanette took a moment. Her heart was still racing.

"You'd give these to Mr. Tyson?"

"Not a problem."

"You wouldn't mention that you found me on the floor. I wouldn't want him to think . . ." She had no idea what the end of the sentence would be.

"I'll just give him the papers, he ever shows up. He makes himself scarce around this place."

"I appreciate it, Billy."

"Ain't nobody's business who found who on the floor," Billy Willig said. "But you sure did throw a scare into me. I thought you was sick."

As she headed home from the co-op, she spied a red Silverado tailing her and thought she recognized the driver. She accelerated as much as the ice cream truck would let her, but the Silverado's horn blasted as it pulled in front of her, peeled out, and spun into a U-turn up on two wheels, so that it suddenly faced her. She braked hard and Mister Softee sheared left, then right, and came to a stop with its hood facing the red truck's. Jesse Ed Davis stepped out of the truck and looked behind him, admiring a graceful black rubber arc on the road that doubled back on itself—a perfect helix. Jeanette's heart raced as she tried to catch her breath. He's going to kill me, she thought. But why? Jesse walked to her window and tapped on it. She thought for a moment, then rolled it down. He leaned in to speak to her, but just as he opened his mouth, she reached across the steering wheel and slapped his face as hard as she could. He winced, more in surprise than pain. "Shame on you!" she said. "Tearing around on the roads like this. Is this how you killed Joey Pizio's parents? Making your damn art?" He looked at her, completely nonplussed.

"I what?" he asked.

"Did you?" she asked again.

"Not me," he said. "We need to talk, though."

A wholesale seafood truck barreled around the curve in the road and Jesse pressed himself back against the door of Mister Softee. The sixteen-wheeler blasted its horn as it passed, narrowly missing both of their vehicles. Lobsters heading south.

"We can't talk here," Jeanette said. "Follow me home. And no more artwork."

At the house she gave Jesse a glass of water and swallowed one herself.

He paced impatiently, like a lion in a cage. She sensed he didn't like being inside conventional houses. He paused only by the windows.

"You said we should talk," she said. "So, talk."

"Joey Pizio's parents," he said. "You could look it up. That disaster would belong to one of my mentors in the art of burning, an inspired alcoholic reprobate named Shandy Epps."

"I never heard of him," Jeanette said dubiously.

"He never drove sober. He made some beautiful things on the road, but there was always danger. Something was bound to happen. Joey's mother and father. They were on their way home from midnight mass, I believe, praying for forgiveness. Apparently, their God said no. Sometimes worlds collide quite literally."

"Why should I believe you?"

"Joey Pizio lost his parents in 2016," he said, looking Jeanette in the eye. "September. I was in North Dakota fighting the Dakota Access Pipeline with the Sioux at Standing Rock Reservation. Getting torn up by government dogs, if you must know."

He put his hand to his cheek, where the scar seemed to redden on its own. His eyes remained placid.

"I never hurt anyone. At least not by accident. At least not yet. He wasn't a bad man, Shandy Epps—just a danger to himself and everyone around him."

"That sounds like a bad man," she said.

"In the tradition I come from, morality is not simply a matter of deed, but is derived from one's inner world, one's consciousness, one's *intention*. Shandy Epps had no evil intent that I'm aware of. It's rare for a man like that to end up incarcerated, but he was. And then gone. I have no idea where."

Jeanette pondered for a moment, then nodded.

"Okay," she said. "But you almost just killed me. Why?"

"I'm a good driver," he said. "You were safe. I just needed to elevate your heart rate."

"You are insane."

"Me? You're delivering eels now. And you say I'm insane?"

Jeanette sighed. "How do you know?"

"I followed the truck. You told me you had nothing to do with this ring of smugglers, and now I find out you're driving for them?"

"I'm a good driver too," she said. "I see they threw you out of your place."

"Zoning. Another invention of civilization. Explain yourself," he said.

She looked at him and weighed how much to share.

"When the trucks got pulled off the road," she began, "I got Bennett Tyson to hire me. I had a hunch his haul was riding on Bando's trucks—he must have been paying off the drivers."

"So you're participating in a trafficking ring. There are laws about giving comfort to the enemy."

"That's only in a war," Jeanette said. "Can you light in one place? Settle down, will you?"

Jesse looked pained but chose a spot on the sofa where he could watch the water.

"So," he said. You work for this guy now. What happened to the intrepid, morally upright crab lady? I liked her better."

"It's not like that," she snapped. "I took the job to get to the bottom of all this. I've already learned where the eels are going—a firm in Korea called Kang Brothers. Competition for Bando. I tried to break into Tyson's office, but I almost got caught. Luckily by an idiot who didn't realize what was going on and won't do anything about it."

"Billy Willig?"

"Of course you know him."

"You broke into Tyson's office?" Jesse rose from the sofa and got himself more water. Then he began to pace again. Jeanette pointed to the sofa as if he was a recalcitrant dog. Jesse sat.

"I tried."

"That's impressive," Jesse said. "What did you think you'd find?"

"I don't know. Something. Something that would help. For me, Joey, my ex—maybe even the eels. Which I guess means for you. However you want to look at it. And there's something else. I told the police."

"You're full of surprises," Jesse said.

"Toland Bates. He's a policeman, but I've known him all his life. He's hardly more than a kid."

"You told him?" Jesse asked.

"He came clean to me, I had to. Told me things that are supposed to be strictly police business."

"Like what?"

"To start, Joey Pizio was poisoned. By weed killer."

Jesse grimaced. "That's a rough way to go."

"And Toland said Bert pulled a guy over speeding on the bridge. The driver had a face that was all scars and the car reeked of Roundup. Wisconsin plates."

"Wisconsin?" Jesse asked. "America's Dairyland. I've seen that car."

"Of course you have," she sighed.

"Black sedan."

"But Toland doesn't believe Joey died on the creek bank. He thinks the body was put there."

"So they murdered him somewhere else? I wonder where."

"And then moved him to the creek."

"Your creek," Jesse said. "I knew he wasn't poaching elvers. But why *your* creek?"

"Maybe someone's trying to scare me? Bennett Tyson and Joey tried to get into the house, and I managed to keep them out. Maybe Tyson has something to do with Joey dying? I don't know yet. But suddenly the eel fishery is shut down while they fix the trucks and my husband—ex-husband, dammit—and the *Jeanette* have taken off for God knows where. Unless something much worse has happened to him. And I keep thinking . . ."

"I can probably explain that part," Jesse said.

"His running off with the boat?"

"I can't stay on this sofa," Jesse said. He rose and began to pace again. "Let's go out on the dock."

Outdoors, he was suddenly relaxed, almost pleasant. He stared out at the reach for a time and Jeanette waited. Then he turned back toward where she had seated herself at a picnic table she'd owned since Liam was a little boy.

"I've been watching your husband—ex-husband—for a little while," he said. "I do watch things."

"I can see that."

"He's been buying elvers all up and down the coast. Then every Wednesday, at about three thirty in the morning, he heads out into the reach. I followed him in a borrowed boat a couple times. He takes the *Jeanette* out to the same spot and meets this kid Joey in a small Whaler. I figured this is when he hands off everything he's aggregated and gets paid. So this time I got myself onto the Jeanette about two A.M. Hung out below deck—it stinks of oil and bait if I can say so—and stayed still. He motored his dinghy out to the mooring at about three fifteen like always and headed out."

"To right in front of my house.

"That's where he always meets the kid. Joey."

"Odd."

"In any case, I didn't wait for that. As soon as he got about twenty-five yards from his mooring I came up from below and pitched him into the water. It was a short fight. I assumed he could get back home on his own steam, even chilled and wet, even in a little pain."

"Hypothermia. He could have drowned."

"Could," Jesse said. "But I didn't think he would, and I don't think he did. And I knew the eels would be okay."

"So, after I tossed your ex-husband, I motored the boat out to the reach, the usual spot, then a little closer to shore, so the swim would be short. I tied the steering off so that it would move in circles and got ready to release them."

"Closer to shore. That's what woke me up."

"The point is," said Jesse Ed Davis, "before I could get the top off the live well, I heard a different boat headed toward me."

"That would have been me," Jeanette said caustically. "Ruining your plan. I'm so sorry."

Jesse shrugged.

"I jumped overboard. It was a short, cold swim to the shore, and to be fair, after what I'd done to your husband, I had it coming. From there I could watch whatever happened. Not what I expected."

"So, you saw it all."

"I didn't know it was you at first. Till the fog burned off some. You tied your dinghy up to the boat, you got out, and a little after that, Joey Pizio arrived as usual, gave you the tackle box, and took the boat. I didn't know what to think."

Jeanette nodded. "Once you threw him off the boat he must have thought he was in trouble. So, he ran."

"I don't suppose you'd know where to?" Jesse asked.

"I don't have the slightest idea. He had a thing for the Florida Keys. We honeymooned there."

Jesse nodded and sat for a moment, lost in thought.

"A lobster boat is likely to stand out in the Florida Keys."

CHAPTER THIRTEEN

Lester Birdwell's immaculately coiffed assistant, Kat Rutherford, greeted Sung Ho Han on a Wednesday morning and served him a black coffee while he waited for her boss to arrive. She found it highly unusual and possibly interesting for the vice president of the Bando Corporation to make an unscheduled visit.

Kat Rutherford had come from nothing, but with an iron determination to escape. She had taken on an impossible level of debt to put herself through college and gotten her first job in politics by claiming to be the great-great-granddaughter of Rutherford B. Hayes, who was president of the United States back in 1877. As a pitch, it seemed to work like a charm. Had it proved to be true, it would have come as a complete surprise to her. She didn't even know if the arithmetic added up, but apparently no one at the Maine State House, where she was hired as an administrative assistant, had bothered to check.

Given her childhood playing dolls on the oil-stained floor of her father's filling station, she was as surprised to find herself now striding down the corridors of power while simultaneously drowning in student-loan bills. Scrolling through Google in a slow moment in the office, she typed in "pay off college debts fast" and came upon a first-person account of a gay man in San Francisco who had simply typed the word *escort* as his occupation on an instant messaging site and gotten out of debt. The thought had never occurred to her. It took her almost a month of internal struggle and having her credit card turned down at Hannaford's supermarket to make a decision.

Her self-esteem had gained force and blown apart simultaneously. Sitting in on meetings and taking minutes for the Joint Committee on Inland Fisheries and Wildlife made her feel like somebody, but at the same time, she knew she was the least important person in the room. She took comfort knowing that in a few hours, she would be the most important person in a different room.

Her moonlighting took a dramatic turn the night she knocked on the door of room 414 of the Graystone Inn in Bangor and found herself face-to-face with the state's governor, Lester Birdwell. Inevitably, they recognized each other from the Capitol.

It was an awkward moment.

"Oh," he said. "I know you. From the State House." He seemed momentarily frozen in place.

"Hello, Governor," she replied. "No worries—it's just you and me here."

"You could get into a lot of trouble, you know. Ladies like you are security risks," he blustered.

She smiled, in control. "Unless I talk first," she said.

He looked at her, sighed, and gestured her into the room. "No need to argue. But just to be clear—I do know this game better than you. I can move through this machine like a greased rat in a rain gutter. You might be more of a drowned rat."

Over the course of the next few weeks, they struck a deal. She went to work for the governor, who agreed to keep her safe from public disgrace and pay her more than her combined current earnings, plus health care. The debts would soon be paid off, the work was manageable, and despite the poisonous feelings that welled up in her every time she looked the man in the eye, she told herself she had sort of arrived. Or had a pathway to arriving.

Two years went by, and after he was voted out, she found herself working for him in the lobbying business. As the clients streamed in and out of the office, hiring her boss to promote everything from potatoes to pipelines, his increasing ire at not being the current governor made his presence genuinely tiresome. There had to be something better than this. It might be productive, she thought, to know exactly what the old crook was up to in these client meetings. She decided to put the voice memo app on her phone to good use by leaving it behind a vase of flowers that she fussed with each time she ushered a possibly suspicious client in to see the boss. She felt a little like a greased rat herself, just looking for a profitable gutter.

"Sung Ho!" The governor beamed, entering the suite. "Sorry to keep you waiting. Please, come in. I was really sorry to hear about what happened to your truck." Kat Rutherford escorted the two men into the inner sanctum, quickly adjusted the flowers, and went back out front to attend to her nails.

Sung Ho cut him off. "You have now proved your point."

"I don't know what you mean, but I've heard that your trucks will be back on the road tomorrow, which is great news," the ex-governor said.

"They're my trucks," said Sung Ho. "I know when they're going to be driving again. The inspectors were very efficient. All is well."

"Except the damn eelers are hollering bloody murder," Birdwell said. "But I think there's a good way for us to work together to profitably pacify them."

Sung Ho sighed unhappily.

"Why would I want to go into business with a man who arranged to sabotage one of my trucks, and then used that as an excuse to shut down my shipping company? I can now add that to the growing list of impediments."

Birdwell looked at him a minute, his face a model of hurt feelings.

"Me?" he asked. "I had nothing to do with this."

"Let us just say you got my attention."

"I did nothing but wait for you to see how useful I could be to you. Please forget every other thought I presented to you when you were kind enough to host me at your beautiful home. I've had a completely different idea."

"I can hardly contain my enthusiasm," Sung Ho said. His manners were beginning to fray.

Birdwell ignored him.

"I just think that together, we could do a better job. Look, what's the problem we're all facing—you, me, and every licensed eeler in the state of Maine?"

Sung Ho sighed. He was now being lectured to as if he were a high school freshman. "Reduced supply," he said.

"Because the new governor has imposed all these socialistic policies," Birdwell confirmed. "But the state of Maine, in its constitution, has provided a remedy. Have you ever heard of a ballot initiative?"

Sung Ho was silent.

"A ballot initiative, if approved by the voters, is a kind of people's veto. We gather enough signatures, we put a question on the ballot: Shall the elver regulations be rolled back? If the voters say yes, the rules simply go away and we're back where we want to be. But a ballot initiative is expensive—it's a campaign."

This caught Sung Ho off guard. He stirred the coffee Kat Rutherford had brought him and pondered the unlikely possibility that Lester Birdwell had actually had a good idea. I wonder if it's his first, he thought. Then he thought again.

"I don't know," he said. "The environmental community, the local communities around the rivers . . . they could be organized into a very substantial protest movement. Even the respected liberal members of the State House are likely to notice. And then there's the media. Nothing they like better. It's a concern. And if they ever found out it was backed by a foreign corporation—"

"Dammit," Birdwell interrupted, "that's just the cost of doing business. Hell, you don't care about eels any more than I do. You want to live in a fine house, with a fine car, eat good food and drink good wine, and get as much pussy as you want, when you want it. Or whatever it is you want. In short, you're just like everybody else who was ever born. Or is it different with Koreans? I never knew one till you came along."

Sung Ho looked at him for a long time. "I go to Bando," Sung Ho said finally. "I say to them, look, this is an opportunity to quietly set straight a wrong that has been done, and all it will take is a little support.

A little financing. The results will be that the money is returned in expanded profits once regulations are lifted."

"Exactly," said Birdwell. "Discretion assured."

"I don't know," Sung Ho said. "Sometimes I wonder, Governor, could you not live like the lobster? It is the official crustacean of Maine. It is an opportunistic scavenger. It does not scheme. Why not scavenge a living on what you make from other lobbying efforts and, whatever else there is, you can vacuum up. Leaving the rest of us alone?"

"I'm a lot smarter than a lobster," Birdwell replied genially. "Lobsters have claws. I have ideas. If a lobster could come up with a good scheme you can damn well bet it would do it. And, incidentally, I didn't get elected governor of Maine because I liked leaving other people alone."

***

The sunset was just concluding its breathtaking play of colors across the cumulus clouds of early spring when Jesse brought Jeanette to a site she already knew well and had no interest in observing after dark—the town dump.

She had been surprised to find the red Silverado in her driveway just as the light was beginning to fade, but there he was. He had found temporary digs, he explained, in a disused freight car that had once been a lunch place for the tourists, but had long since gone belly-up.

"Sign says it's for sale," he said. "But it was just going to waste. There's even some propane in the tank. Get in."

She had not fought him, but was more than a little surprised by the destination he had in mind. Relatively manageable during the winter months, the dump's stench began to increase as the weather warmed and would reach the limits of tolerability in early August. Now, in April, the smell was merely incubating, making repulsive promises, Jeanette thought. It was maintained by retired fishermen who had worked in industries that predisposed them not to mind strong odors.

He parked the Silverado down the road beyond the gated entrance and led the way to a mountain of discarded and rotting household furniture—old mattresses, busted-down cabinets and dressers, window frames with shards of glass protruding from their sashes. He took her arm and they moved slowly. They looked out on the dumpster that contained the stuff that people threw in day after day—plastic kitchen bags of food waste, milk cartons, cereal boxes, lobster shells, and pork chop bones. The air immediately around the dumpsters was already overripe and the buzz of eager flies and other insects was audible.

"Breathe through your mouth and stay quiet," Jesse said.

They waited and watched. After a quarter of an hour Jesse left her side to survey the household debris nearby, returning with a discarded but still barely functional folding chair. He dug it into the surrounding gravel and gestured for Jeanette to sit. She looked out at the remains of so many lives and sighed.

"Have you ever thought about living in a real house?" she asked.

"Damn, some people have a hard time staying quiet," he said.

He, too, looked around at the mounds of discarded appliances, bent-up aluminum siding, and plastic bottles. "And they really do waste a lot of stuff," he added.

He handed her a thermos he had brought along in his backpack.

"Not thirsty," Jeanette said.

"Drink," Jesse replied. There was gin and tonic in the thermos.

Just as the twilight settled on them, headlights approached and they heard a turbocharged exhaust system. They could make out the outline of a large truck pulling up to the gate. The engine died and then the headlights. It was an impressive truck, reflecting yellow in the flashlights guided by the two men who emerged. They crawled through the gate and approached the small shack where the men who worked the dump in the daytime sat. There was a pair of old beach chairs in front of it and they settled in quietly. One of them carried a baseball bat.

"Big Otis," Jeanette said. "Why?"

Big Otis Sumlin, who was in his eighties, had been town supervisor for as long as anyone could remember. He was as genial as a good life insurance salesman, though he answered to no one. Most of his day was spent on an old John Deere tractor, keeping the growth on the roadside from encroaching on the pavement with a sickle bar mower attachment. No one could seem more harmless. Now here he was with a baseball bat in his hand.

"And Tommy B. Donovan?" Jeanette asked.

Jesse nodded. "The elver king. *Legal* elvers."

"With no trucks to move them," Jeanette whispered. "Come on."

As Big Otis laid the bat against the side of the shack and popped a Twisted Tea, which he gave to Tommy B., Jeanette moved toward them, hoping to hear what they were saying. Jesse reached for her arm, but too late. She settled just behind a stack of old stereo equipment. At least it didn't smell. Jesse followed, but now they were too close to Tommy B. and Big Otis to talk. Jesse merely shook his head at her, impressed, perhaps. Or irritated.

They sat in silence, watching. Tommy B. took a long slug of the hard tea and put the can on the dirt in front of the shack. As the dark began to envelop them, Jeanette could hear the bird cries dying off as the Earth settled down. The shift in time was slow, but palpable. Then there was a rattle at the dumpster, and in the dimness of the last of the day's light, Jeanette saw two rats, each as big as a small house cat, emerge onto the gravel.

In a flash of movement, Tommy B.'s hand came out of his pocket holding a pistol. Two shots broke the air in rapid succession, almost like a ricochet. Jeanette winced, and Jesse grabbed her and motioned to stay silent. One of the rats was lifted into the air and fell flat in the dust. The other was knocked against the dumpster and splattered its insides on the first. They lay motionless except for a few spastic moves of their forelegs, followed by stillness and silence.

"Got 'em clean," Big Otis said.

"What I'd just as soon do to those pen pushers in Augusta that took the trucks off the road," Tommy B. said. "I'm losing my shirt. And the season ends in three weeks." He finished his drink in one long slug.

"Wish I could help you," Big Otis said, handing Tommy B. a second can.

"You don't stick your neck out for nobody," Tommy B. said.

"Can you blame me?"

"Can't say I do," Tommy B. said. "Only satisfaction in all this is that the goddamn poachers got no way to move their stuff either. We'll all starve together, I guess."

Jeanette looked at Jesse's impassive face. She'd seen enough. But having moved in close, there was now no escape. They'd be there as long as Big Otis and Tommy B. wanted to sit.

Over the next half hour, Tommy B. killed four more rats. Big Otis just watched, supplying a third and fourth can of the spiked tea.

In the dark, Tommy B. illuminated a headlamp and cast its beam around the dump's perimeter.

"Only one more thing I want," he said to Big Otis. "Make the night complete. And there it is."

He rose from the chair. Big Otis, without instruction, handed him the baseball bat by the shaft so that the handle landed in Tommy B.'s fist.

"Porky!" he shouted, and he took off toward the dumpster. His headlamp illuminated a lumbering porcupine who seemed not to know which way to turn.

"No," Jeanette gasped under her breath. Jesse tightened his hand on her shoulder.

A porcupine's quills are enough to protect it from anything that dares to come too close. But not from a thrill seeker sporting a Louisville Slugger. Tommy B. took an expert backswing and belted the animal across the dump, where it landed against a pile of bicycle tires and spare parts, still very much alive and chirping in dismay. Now Jeanette grabbed Jessie, her fists balling against his shirt. The porcupine waddled toward the shack, with Tommy B. in clumsy pursuit. Big Otis stood to get a closer look at the action and Tommy B. took one more home run swing at the confused and panicked animal. It lifted off the ground, landed with a thump, and rolled over twice. It came to rest against Big Otis's left shin.

The old man howled in pain and backed away, nearly toppling over backward. Jeanette stayed frozen on the spot.

"Jesus, Tommy, help me!" Big Otis cried, his voice a falsetto whine.

Tommy B. dropped the bat and rushed to his companion, pulling the lamp from his head, and focusing it on Big Otis's shin. Two dozen porcupine quills were embedded in the old man's socks and skin, where his jeans came up just a few inches short.

"Holy God, Otis," Tommy said. "I didn't mean nothing."

"Christ, of course you didn't *mean* nothing." The words squeezed out of Big Otis's lips like a man spitting bile. "It ain't your intention that matters."

"We gotta get you to the emergency room," Tommy B. said. "Can you walk?"

"Gonna have to," Big Otis said. "Ain't I now?"

Jeanette and Jesse watched the limping old man, with an arm around Tommy B.'s shoulder, as the two of them worked their way around the dump gate and into Tommy B.'s truck. The headlights went on and Tommy B. revved the engine. In a moment they were gone.

Jeanette released Jessie's shirt and ran to the porcupine. Its skull was smashed, blood caked with dust. "You didn't deserve that," she said quietly. Then she turned on Jesse angrily.

"That's what you wanted to show me?"

"I needed to warn you."

"You think I need to be educated about men? You took me out to a literal dump to tell me all about how men behave. Jesse, I was married to one. You're better than that. But then, you are a man. Nothing should surprise me."

Jesse looked chastened.

"The porcupine surprised me," he said. "Tommy B. just likes to shoot rats. As far as I know this is the first time he's ever smacked a porcupine into Big Otis."

"I wish it hit Tommy B. on the rebound."

"Instant karma," Jesse said, picking up a quill which had been dislodged. He handed it to her. "They both have it coming." Silently he led her back to the Silverado. When they had gotten far enough from the dump road for the smell to abate, he spoke.

"You just need to know who you're dealing with when you're dealing with elvers."

CHAPTER FOURTEEN

When the Bando trucks went back on the road, Jeanette offered to drop her price to $200 per round trip to the airport to keep the job. She and Tyson were upstairs at the co-op.

"Take a walk with me" was all he said. He stood up from his cluttered desk, which she had now surveyed several times without discovering anything of use, and he motioned her out the door, which he locked behind him, and down the external staircase to the parking lot. The place was not busy except down at the dock, and he took her by the arm, not gently, and guided her out to the road. She moved alongside him apprehensively, wondering what was so confidential that it couldn't be spoken in his office on the near-empty second floor. And then he turned onto Snowman Lane, an obscure dirt path that led nowhere. She felt the muscles in her neck tighten and tried, without success, to free herself from his grip.

"This is a serious business, your husband," he said. She started to correct him but thought better of it. Husband, ex-husband—clearly not the point. "It's bigger than you. I don't know you, I don't trust you, but you're all I've got here, and I wouldn't want anything to happen to you."

"Comforting," she said. The sight of Tommy B. clubbing the porcupine flipped through her brain.

"Now listen to me," he said. "There's people with an interest in where Simon is."

"Such as?"

"That's as much as you need to know. Except this: If anyone knows where he is, you do. And at some point, people might go to some lengths to get that information out of you."

She shrank from him and felt his grip on her arm tighten. Just at the point when it began to hurt, but before it did damage, she jerked free. She took a few steps back from him. Her heart was pounding.

"I actually don't know where he is," she admitted. "I wish I did. I'd tell you. I scoped out his house—which used to be our house—I keep an eye out for the boat, I've got nothing to offer."

"That's too bad," Tyson said. "You don't want anyone to test that proposition."

She was on a forgotten dirt path with a man who stared at her with those two different-colored eyes. A part of her was panicked, needed to escape. She wished he'd worn his shades. But another part of her was watching it all from above. She stopped and looked back into Tyson's eyes. "Putting me in a creek doesn't help you. It's just a matter of time till I get you what you want."

"I don't read you. You're talking in riddles."

"Men are like that," she said. "They don't see around corners. They can't even find the milk and have to ask us where it is when it's the biggest thing in the fridge."

"Start making sense," Tyson said.

"Simon has always wanted me to take him back," she said. "To forgive him, really."

"Forgive him?"

"He took our son ice fishing just to show him what a real man will go through to catch a fish. Our son drowned. The kid didn't even like the cold."

"I'm sorry for your loss," said Tyson. "Where's this getting us?"

"While I was in the hospital with cancer wondering how long I was going to live, Simon came to beg forgiveness every damn day, as if that would make it easier. Or cure me. I loved the guy, but it was too late. For all of it. Nothing brings things into focus like your hair falling out after a double mastectomy."

Men like women's breasts, she knew, but they hate hearing them discussed this way. This was more than Tyson wanted to know, and maybe enough truth to get him off her back. She waited to see if he would react. He shifted his weight from one foot to the other, looked down, and said, "I'm sorry."

"Sorry's not the point," she went on. "I mean—I don't know what he's done, but the point is, he wants to be forgiven. I don't know where he is. But if he knows he's in trouble, he'll get in touch with me. That's what he does. And, generally, I tell him to go to hell. That's what I do, with some reluctance. But this time, I'll forgive him. And he'll come back. And then you can talk to him. We just have to be patient. I'll find your milk carton, but you've gotta wait for it."

"Don't make me wait long," Bennett Tyson said.

*
* *

Jeanette drove to the other end of the island, down a road not unlike Snowman Lane. Simon's sometime girlfriend lived in a prefab that her ex-husband had built. Back in the day she and Simon had flaunted their affair all over the island, alienating a lot of the locals. And for Jeanette it had been a source of continual and awful humiliation. Was it still going on? Her name was Gail Bauer, and she earned her money—a little—by evaporating seawater, mixing the resulting salt with homegrown herbs like lavender and thyme, smoking some of it, and packaging it in what she thought were adorable little hand-labeled bottles. There was a boutique in Brockton that sold it steadily once the summer came: an artisanal Maine phenomenon. Jeanette referred to her as Flower Power Bauer, but not to her face, which she tried to encounter as infrequently as possible.

The sun was setting when she turned in to the woman's driveway. There was no car to be seen. She traversed the lawn, rang the doorbell, and knocked hard at the door, but Gail Bauer was not to be found. Around back there were tubs of salt water under a tented clear tarp, presumably evaporating. But no girlfriend. The herb garden was overgrown and weedy. Jeanette wondered if Gail and Simon might be off together. The place looked deserted. She scrawled a note, stuck it under the door knocker, got back in the car, and turned toward home as the darkness set in.

The roads were unlit, nothing to see, really, until she approached the house. The crab shack, just across the road, was lit up like a Christmas tree. No one worked there after dark. She turned up the short driveway to the parking area and shut off the car. She was struck by the intensity of the light. The door to the place was swinging wide open, and the glow spilling out was illuminating the hillside that led down to the road.

Damn, she thought. Good way to get mice. Or racoons. Any varmint—or vermin—will chase down the smell of old seafood after dark. But it wasn't the animals that made her stomach turn over. Door open, lights on, no cars in the lot. She took a deep breath. She owned the place, after all.

She turned on the high beams, stepped out of the car but left it running. She moved as quietly as she could to the crab shack and peered inside from the front step. Nothing amiss. Long stainless-steel table, four chairs, refrigerators humming. She stepped inside.

There was nothing to see. She circled the table twice, checked the aprons, the coatrack, the slop sinks, and then the drainboard beside it. Next to the kitchen unit was the crab tank. The lid was raised. She peered inside; the aerator was sending up a stream of bubbles, but the crabs were gone. Someone had stolen roughly nine dozen live crabs. There would be nothing to steam tomorrow, nothing to pick, but the women would still expect to be paid. She had heard of junkies stealing copper from summer houses under construction. But crabs? She closed the lid, turned off the light, and shut the door behind her.

Back at the house, she pulled the key from her purse and reached for the front door lock, but the door was already ajar. A bent crab knife was jammed into the lock and had sprung it. She froze, frightened to go into the house. Her own house. She tentatively pushed the door open. As it swung in, a scratching noise struck her ears. Like a mouse in the insulation behind a wall. Flipping on the overhead light she heard something scuttling for cover. She dropped her coat on the floor, turned on the kitchen light, and then she saw it. A living, struggling Maine rock crab was scratching desperately at the bulletin board, impaled by another crab knife. It had been stabbed through the center of its carapace directly into the photo of Simon with Liam on his shoulders.

The crab gripped a menu for Duffy's Pizza with one claw; the other was raised and open. She gasped, ran to the board, grabbed the crab, and pulled out the knife. A line of yellow hepatopancreas goop smeared Simon's face, which was split from forehead to chin. The crab's legs, scraping and clawing, had worn away parts of the glossy photo. There was moist, torn paper where Liam had once held an airplane.

A strange noise came from her throat, guttural, uncontrolled. Liam, gone again. Simon, impaled. The house alive with scuttling noises. She stood still, her mind racing. She relaxed her grip on the injured crab, which took the opportunity to snap its spare claw around her index finger. She yelped, ran to the counter, and shook it loose. It dropped into the stainless-steel sink with a clank and began to scuttle back and forth, still holding the menu. She left it there and turned back to the picture. She unpinned it from the corkboard and looked at it. There was nothing worth saving. Still, she looked at it. In her own stillness she again became aware of the quiet, persistent scratching, clicking, and shuffling. Not just in the sink.

She dropped the photo, which fell to the ground at her feet, and took in the living room. They were everywhere—on the floor, on the sofa, under the dining room table. One pulled at the tassels in the carpet. She stood watching, trying to come back to earth. Was this Bennett Tyson's work? It seemed somehow beyond him. And yet . . . who else? She thought back to Toland's description of the man with weed killer in his car. Fury poured through her, almost like a drug coursing through her veins.

She picked up a crab and felt like hurling it across the room. But it wasn't the crab's fault. She brought it to the sink. Then she retrieved another. She realized she needed a better way. The bushel totes in the crab shack.

She made her way outdoors. It was a cloudless night but there was no moon to see by. No shadows, no visible landmarks. She moved slowly, finding the path up to the road. A pair of headlights appeared down the road, approaching fast. She ducked down to her knees, still feeling the pain in one, as the car squealed past her house. In a moment it was gone, and she began to breathe again. She looked over her shoulders, one way then the other. As though she could see something. She crossed the road and entered the now-darkened crab shack, running the last few steps, and flipped on the light. She tried to control her breathing. Still nothing out of place. She moved quickly to the side of the crab tank and picked up a bushel basket she used for transporting the crabs. She left the lights on and started back to her house.

Inside, she went about the task of collecting the crabs carefully, picking them up from behind by the carapace, handling each one like a piece of live ammunition. Once in the bushel they could not escape. When one tried to climb up, its neighbors reliably pulled it back. It took her three trips back and forth through the dark, holding the bushel against her hip. As far as she could tell, no one was in the yard; no one bothered her. If Tyson or anyone else was watching, she wanted them to see that she wasn't about to be intimidated. She counted ninety-six crabs, including the one that had been stabbed, which she threw into the reach.

The house seemed quiet. She poured a tall brandy and carried it from room to room making a final inspection. No more crabs. But that feeling of violation, that her home had become an open source of danger and warning, wouldn't leave her. Betray her ex-husband or else. Or else what? And even if she wanted to betray him, she didn't know how. It almost seemed that whoever was doing this was enjoying himself. Terrorizing her. I am not helpless, she told herself. But that son of a bitch. I told him about Liam, he found the picture and . . . unless it wasn't Tyson.

She went to the bathroom and tried to stick to the normal routine, brush teeth, brush hair, facial cleansing, nightgown, always the same. Knowing she would not sleep she moved to the bedroom anyway to begin the futile exercise. She pulled back the coverlet. And there they were. A dozen or so, spread across the bedsheets. Two tussled with each other. One made its way over the edge and fell off, pulling the sheet partway off with it. It turned toward her foot, raising and opening both claws. She jumped backward and slammed the bedroom door, not even moving to turn out the light. She stood outside, panting. No tears came, just rage. Even fear was gone. Moving downstairs she again looked out the window into the darkness, seeing nothing but her own reflection. She clenched her jaw, returned to the kitchen, and picked up the pot she used to cook lobsters. It could hold a dozen crabs, maybe fourteen. One more trip. In her nightgown. She hoped someone was watching.

Keith Fulbright changed the locks on the house and the crab shack the next day. He didn't ask questions, and she didn't volunteer information. She was on the road before he had finished. Toland Bates was waiting for her outside the Bread & Butter Mart.

"Get in," she said. He was in street clothes, as she had asked him to be when she set the meeting. They drove across the bridge, away from the island and onto Route 1 as she talked. She told him everything.

Toland listened, his hands folded in his lap. "You're being targeted," he said, finally.

"You think?"

"By a very creative person."

"I wish he'd find another outlet," Jeanette said.

"They decided to scare you, but not hurt you. For now, at least."

"Cold comfort," she said. "Is it the man with weed killer in his car?"

Toland cracked the window and looked out at the blueberry fields, not yet beginning to show green.

"That would be my guess," he said. "I never use weed killer myself," he said finally. "You can't even buy it in Brockton. I guess you can get it from Amazon. Bert's got a lawn, so he knows it by smell."

"This man," Jeanette persisted. "He may have killed Joey, he may be trying to scare me into saying something. Or doing something. Broke into my house, unleashed a hundred crabs, put them in my bed."

"He has his own way of doing things," Toland said.

"Can't you guys go after him?" Jeanette asked.

"Hell, I went right to the chief. I knew he didn't want a murder on the island, even with a coroner's report. But now we had a suspect."

"The chief," Jeanette said. "Big Otis's kid. Little Otis."

"Don't call him that to his face," Toland said. "That's how Connor Stilmore got demoted to dogcatcher."

"So?"

"So Little Otis looked me right in the eye and told me. Said that his old man had taught him this expression a long time ago. Expression he lived by. 'Don't stir it, it'll stink.' He doesn't want this murder."

Jeanette thought for a moment.

"It's the island community," she said. "They like to protect the reputation, but if there's a maniac on the loose—"

"Island community, hell," Toland said. "Little Otis is waiting for the old man to die and leave the real estate to him. Old man's got to be eighty-five if he's a day. Only thing Little Otis doesn't know is—his daddy's never gonna die. He's gonna live forever. Like Methuselah."

Jeanette pulled the Subaru into the parking lot of a Dairy Queen across from the self-storage place that had been Jesse Ed Davis's home until recently.

"Let's go," she said. "I need a chocolate dip."

They sat at a picnic table out back, undisturbed in the slight chill.

"I get it," Toland said. "Murder scares everyone away. I got friends work at the Bread & Butter Mart. Others selling lobsters to the summer people. Then there's people working the farmers' market, the Clamdigger. Murder's bad for everybody's business—not just Big Otis and his damn subdivision."

"Worse for me. I just hope that he went back to Wisconsin," she said.

"You don't happen to have a gun, do you?"

"For God's sake," she said impatiently, "I'm supposed to be the good guy with the gun who kills the bad guy with the gun? I don't even have a food processor."

"I don't care for them either," Toland said. "Guns, I mean. What's a food processor?"

"It's some kind of a blender for summer people."

"Well," Toland said, "I can't interview Tyson now that the case is officially closed. They'd rip my badge off."

"Toland," she said. "Maybe let it go."

"That's not gonna happen," he said. "I took an oath."

*
* *

Jesse Ed Davis stopped at the Bread & Butter mart for a new supply of Ben & Jerry's minis, and he was back on the road when he saw the red lights flashing in his rearview mirror. He checked the speedometer on the truck's dashboard. It read 43. The speed limit was 40. He wondered if he had busted a taillight but didn't think so. He tried hard not to run afoul of the law. Nonetheless, the cruiser was right on his tail, so he found the first wide part of the road and pulled in. The cruiser pulled behind him.

Toland Bates got out of the police car as Jesse rolled down his window with one hand while popping the glove box with the other. Toland approached the car and looked in the window.

"Please step out of the vehicle, sir," he said in his most professional voice.

"Don't you want the license and registration?" Jesse asked.

"Please step out of the vehicle, sir," Toland repeated.

"You don't have to be so officious. You know you lose yourself when you become officious."

"Just step out of the vehicle," Toland demanded, trying not to sound like he was begging.

Jesse sighed, unbelted himself, and climbed out. He was taller, better built, and, he suspected, stronger than Toland Bates, but he wasn't inclined to get into a physical altercation with a police officer.

"What did I do?" he asked as his feet hit the ground.

"Take a few steps with me," Toland said.

He led Jesse away from the road and into a grove of poplar that had yet to leaf out.

"Officer Bates. I don't believe this is typical police procedure. I have a right to know what I'm being accused of."

They had now gotten deep enough into the grove of trees to be all but invisible from the road, although the truck and the cruiser would have been hard to miss. Still, Toland thought, it was better to be unobserved, and no civilian ever stopped beside a police car with its lights flashing.

"This is what I want to know," Toland said. "Jeanette King is a good woman. And important to me. She told me what happened on the night Joey Pizio's body was found. And by the way, he was a dubbah, but he wasn't all bad himself at one time."

"And you know I was there," Jesse said.

"I know everything she told me," Toland replied. "And I believe she's told me everything. It sounds like you gave her some bad advice, which she took, but it also sounds like your intentions were honorable enough. Sounds like."

"It is what it sounds like," Jesse said. "Except for your characterization of the advice."

"You didn't kill that boy, then?" Toland looked straight into Jesse's eyes, and Jesse looked straight back. Neither blinked.

"If I did, would I have stayed there, fixed up Jeanette's knee, shown my face, and then let her walk away?"

"Well, did you?"

"I did not. That is not me. But I'd like to know who did. Unlike your chief."

Toland looked down.

"Can't comment on that. I only know you as a guy with a couple speeding tickets, a ninety-day stretch out west, and I've heard rumors that you're a burner, which is dangerous."

"Surely you can't object to a beautification project," Jesse said. "Especially one that doesn't cost the taxpayers. What is it you want? I have ice cream melting in the truck."

"Like I said, Jeanette King is a good woman, possibly in trouble, and I'm trying to help her. Practically a second mother to me at one time."

"I could have used that," Jesse said. "Or a first one. I mean, a real one."

"It takes a town," Toland responded. "Are you really trying to help her?"

Jesse grunted.

"Her. The eels. Look, you pull me over—I was doing forty-three in a forty zone by the way—and you want to know if I'm in league with Jeanette King?"

"I already know that much. But I don't know who I can trust," Toland said. "I'm a fair judge of horseshit when it comes my way. And I don't like using that word."

"I don't traffic in horseshit," Jesse said.

"I'm inclined to believe that," Toland said. "Still, I want to know what I'm up against."

Jesse nodded. "You're not up against me," he said.

Toland looked at Jesse for a long time. He had apparently said all he was going to say. After a moment, Jesse turned and headed back toward the road.

"Where are you going?" Toland asked.

"This is where you say, 'You may get back in your vehicle, sir.'"

"Wait," Toland said. He reached into his pocket and pulled out a small wad of cash held in a clip with a tiny police badge on it. He peeled off six singles and handed them to Jesse along with a business card. "Call me if I can help. And get some fresh ice cream," he said.

"Thank you, Officer, I think that will cover the damage."

"You may get back in your vehicle, sir," Toland said, smiling for the first time.

THE BOY

Daniel Nearinsky was born in Maine, on his parents' homestead. But he didn't fit in, and he never would. Elena and Sandy Nearinsky were communists and considered themselves revolutionaries. Worse than that, they were vegetarians. The child of communist vegetarians from away could not be a Mainer no matter what. Sandy had a substantial inheritance—even communists sometimes do. He kept quiet about it as he had become famous in intellectual circles for lectures about the need to overthrow capitalism and redistribute wealth. He redistributed a portion of his wealth by buying up a section of Cape Herrington, surrounded on three sides by the Atlantic. The Nearinskys built a small log cabin with help from a friend they met down the road—an all but silent character named Bill Penny—and they established their homestead. A crew of acolytes began to form around them, which meant that they didn't have to do much work themselves.

Much to their surprise, at forty-six, Elena got pregnant. Their son was born on a cloudless August night. They named him Daniel, which,

Sandy recalled from his brief stint in a leftist Hebrew school on the Lower East Side, meant "God is my judge." Neither Sandy nor Elena wanted to carry the weight of being the judge and, even though they did not believe in God, they felt that their son should strive to meet someone's expectations.

They grew and sold highbush blueberries, their cash crop, with help from an endless stream of young people who picked and weeded and mulched in exchange for the aura cast by their mentors. When special guests came, Sandy put on the only record they owned, Taj Mahal's first album. Daniel would put himself to bed, drifting off while listening to the guitar and the harmonica and the grown-ups talk and laugh. The guitar playing he loved the most.

Sandy told his son that the guitar player, Jesse Ed Davis, was a Native American, which probably accounted for the patient, precise way that he built his accompaniments and solos. It was an important moment for the boy. It dawned on him all at once that bias—a word he didn't know yet—could go both ways. His father thought well of what he took to be certain Native traits. He probably thought less well of others. Both ideas seemed to Daniel to be equally ridiculous.

Daniel raised himself in the woods and fields. It was clear to his peers that he was an odd kid. He ate funny food, didn't know anything about football or superheroes, but knew a lot about stuff no one else cared about. He didn't know when to start talking, and when to stop. And his obsession with sugar was unsettling to them. All kids loved sugar, but he loved it with an abandon that led him to reckless behavior and even theft. He developed a reputation.

One day, after having ice cream at a classmate's birthday party, he recognized the empty Ben & Jerry's containers from the trash bin at his home cabin for what they were. These were containers for this extraordinary, godly food. It occurred to him that his parents had been denying him what they themselves enjoyed in secret. They were hypocrites, and he vowed to live true to his values; the main one being that he needed to be better than them. He turned to the only other adult he knew well: Bill Penny.

Bill Penny gradually became a surrogate parent to the boy. With the exception of one Acadian great-grandfather, all of Bill's ancestors were Passamaquoddy. And though he didn't fit in any better than Daniel or Sandy or Elena, the objective truth was that he was as native a Mainer as one could be.

He was friends with Sandy and Elena. He liked their politics, and he liked their style of settling better than the logging companies and the vacation home builders. Still, no matter how many times they started their farm tours by acknowledging that this was stolen Passamaquoddy land, he never lost sight of the fact that, well, it was stolen Passamaquoddy land.

Once, sitting on the porch of the log cabin, he pushed Sandy on this. They were drinking beer.

"Say I stole your Toyota Tacoma, which I would not do, first because I do not steal things, and second because it is two-wheel drive and the frame is prone to rust, which, as I've told you, in my opinion, makes it a foolish truck for the coast of Maine, but say, just for argument's sake, I stole it from you. And then I kept it, I used it, and I benefited greatly from it, while you had to walk everywhere, and cart your stinky crab fertilizer and your seaweed on your back or in a wheelbarrow. Then one day, I was struck with a great awakening, a pang of conscience, and I began to announce to anyone who would listen, 'This is a stolen truck! I stole it from Sandy Nearinsky.' And then after making that announcement, I kept using it, while you kept the wheelbarrow. I would say things like, 'This truck was stolen from Sandy Nearinsky. I am now going to drive it to the store to buy some beer and potato chips.' Would you be grateful to me for acknowledging the theft? Or would you want your truck back?"

Sandy laughed. They both did. Then it got quiet. "I get your point," Sandy said. "This land was stolen. Not by me, but it was stolen. At the time, my ancestors were in Eastern Europe, getting the shit kicked out of them by Cossacks. Now I own it. It was fenced to me, like artwork sold by Nazis who stole it from my ancestors. Fenced goods. I acknowledge it. But then what? I don't know what to do about it."

Bill responded slowly. "I think you might know what to do about it."

Daniel was inside the cabin, listening to them through a window. He loved Bill fiercely. More than he loved his father.

At his junior high school graduation there was a gift exchange between the dozen graduates. Mike Crayton, who had known Daniel since they were both two years old, gave Daniel a five-gallon bucket containing an orange winter hat with a *No Fear* emblem on it, some HotHands chemical hand warmers, a Primos grunt tube to call deer, three chocolate whoopie pies in cellophane wrappers, and a plastic bottle of Moxie soda pop. "This way you can try to be a real Mainer," he said, loud enough so the whole class could hear. The class laughed. It stung. Daniel blushed and looked down. But he stayed quiet. He knew something his classmates didn't. Bill Penny had taught him how to call a deer in with his mouth; he didn't need their plastic grunt tube. He could start a fire with a bent piece of wood and a string to keep his hands warm without their HotHands. And he knew that he could sneak up behind Mike Crayton even through dry leaves on a frozen morning and scare him, or even cut his throat if the urge to do either ever came to him.

After school, he ate the whoopie pies, drank the Moxie, and took the remaining contents of the bucket to ask Bill Penny what to do with it. Daniel knew Bill Penny was more native than the Crayton clan, even if they didn't know it. He knew Bill would have an answer that was well thought-out and not simply vindictive. He didn't want to be vindictive because, as Bill had told him many times, "Your name means that the gods will be your judges."

What he wasn't anticipating was that Bill, having heard the story and examined the contents of the bucket, would decide that the name had been of as much use to Daniel Nearinsky as it ever would be, and that there was something important to be done about it.

"You're about thirteen, aren't you?" he asked.

"I am thirteen," Daniel answered.

"That's when most Jewish boys have a bar mitzvah."

"I'm not doing that."

"No, I didn't expect you were. But in our tradition, we have something else. We have a naming ceremony. I think it is time you chose a name to live with, as a man. What do you think about that?"

"I've never liked being called Danny. I'd like that."

"Good. Think about it. But please, not 'Little Eagle' or 'Running Bear.' Don't pretend to be something you are not. Just a name that maybe pushes you to be a good settler."

Daniel thought for a moment, trying to piece together what name might do that. There was only one he could think of.

"Jesse Ed Davis."

CHAPTER FIFTEEN

The day after Toland Bates had given Jesse Ed Davis the third degree in the woods, Jeanette, looking for anything that would yield new information, set out for Joey Pizio's trailer. She was stopped by black crows. Less than a quarter of a mile from what had been Joey's driveway she saw them—a cluster of them—dead on the road. Others were circling. She looked across the road at a familiar long-abandoned house that had been falling down for decades, its windows now a few random shards of glass, its roof collapsed and patched with gray moss. One wall leaned outward and was propped up by a half-rotten cedar log. One lone red spruce had grown up directly through a dormer on the second floor from inside the place. She'd passed the house a hundred times, but this time it was different. A flock of jet-black crows was flying in and out of the ground floor window frames, shrieking out to others circling in the sky. And there were the dead ones on the road.

Jeanette pulled over and got out of the car. Slowly, she picked her way through the grass and weeds in the front yard, reminding herself that tick season had started and she'd have to check her clothes and body when she got home.

She moved carefully up the rotted porch steps and pushed on the front door, which ripped from its hinges, thudding onto what was left of the floorboards in the front hall. The noise scared the crows, who lifted off a wet humus of dead leaves, pine needles, and mud in front of the tree trunk in unison. They shrieked again and fled through the roof. But not all of them. A dozen or more were lying dead on the floor. The room stank of an unfamiliar rot—not the rot of the forest floor or long-decaying house timbers, but some animal stench. Animal death was all around her.

She lifted her phone from her pocket and turned on the flashlight. The stain on the floor in front of the tree trunk was puddling with something not quite liquid, brown and dirty, flecked with what looked like decaying white bread.

Vomit, she thought.

She called Toland. He picked up on the third ring.

"Get over here," she said. "That tumbledown saltbox just east of Joey's trailer. Bring whatever it is you people use to collect evidence."

She did not wait for a reply but picked her way out of the house to the fresh air and waited. Pale and deep green mosses humped themselves over the tree roots in the yard, making a variegated carpet dotted by tiny pink blossoms. She wondered how so much ugliness could coexist with so much beauty.

Toland pulled up in his own car, his uniform on, ten minutes later. She met him on the street.

"Where?" he asked.

"Inside," she said.

He flipped open the trunk of the car, reached under the compound bow case, and pulled out a box of plastic bags and a small garden trowel.

The crows sat in the branches of the red spruce trees in the yard and watched but did not reenter. When the two of them got inside, she relit the flashlight on the phone, made her way carefully to the mess on the floor, and pointed. Toland squatted near the swampy mess with its stench filling the room, scooped up a trowel's worth, and dumped it into the plastic bag.

They did not speak, but she could see that Toland was breathing through his mouth, and she realized she was too, fearful of what would happen if she breathed through her nose. Toland was sealing the bag when the beam of Jeanette's light caught something else on the floor, a pattern. Three feet out from the base of the tree, the dirt and leaf litter had been pushed and scraped forward in a haphazard semicircle, exposing the rotted wall-to-wall carpet.

Jesus, she thought. Feet. Pushing, kicking. They actually tied him to a tree and made him drink poison. Just like a movie. She pointed to the carpet and touched Toland's shoulder. He looked; he shook his head and spoke softly, as if he might be overheard. "He struggled."

They worked their way out of the house, moving quickly once they hit solid ground. Bolting through the yard in a few steps, Toland went past their cars and crossed the road. She kept pace and made it ten yards or so into the woods before she saw him begin to vomit, putting his hands against two adjacent white birches, careful to keep his head forward so as not to stain his uniform. When he was done, he wiped his lips on a kerchief that he'd pulled from his back pocket. She touched his shoulder, but he only shook his head. He picked up the little plastic bag and headed back to the road. More food for the crows, she thought. At least this time it won't kill them.

They stood by the cars for a moment in silence after Toland had stashed the evidence bag in the trunk. Then he said, "I gotta go home and rinse my mouth out."

"I get it," Jeanette said.

"But thank you. For finding it. And for calling me. I'm gonna take this to the coroner when they open on Monday. Once we have something solid, I'm gonna go back to the chief and tell him he was right."

"How so?"

"Well, I stirred it, and it surely stank."

As Toland drove he kept wondering what the hell did Joey Pizio do to get someone that angry? A sharp feeling of alarm began to overcome him, as he wondered what, if anything, the entire affair might have to do with his sainted mother's second cousin. If Joey's death was about eels, which seemed likely, it was either something that Tommy B. Donovan, the Eel King, would be mad about or glad about. He had never considered the man, a man he avoided at all costs, a potential murderer, but he was as unsavory a character as Toland had ever encountered on the island, and Toland wasn't proud to share the same bloodline.

Tommy B. had a wife who had taken out various protective orders against him until she finally moved out of state with the kids, who were relieved to be shed of him. What he did with his eel money no one knew—he lived like a pauper and dressed worse. His yellow truck was the only shiny thing he owned. There was a loaded pistol in the glove box and the license plate read EELKING.

Toland had only one clear memory of him. At a Thanksgiving dinner when Toland was just a kid, his maiden aunt Debra had snapped off the long end of the wishbone, and Tommy B., who had gotten the short end, grabbed a carving knife from the cutting board and chased her from the dining room through the living room and into the den, where he backed her up against the ancient console TV set. As she screamed in terror, he slammed the knife into the wood veneer case that held the set, missing the old woman's hand by a half inch and snapping off the tip of the knife in the process. Toland's mom had grabbed him away as Aunt Debra wailed that it was only a wishbone for heaven's sake.

"You ain't gettin' your wish," Tommy B. had snarled.

"I already didn't," Aunt Debra shouted. "You're still walking around eating." Tommy B. laughed and went back for seconds.

Toland was too young to know what the word *drunk* meant, but Tommy B. was never invited back. The carving knife with the missing tip stayed in circulation for years and was reminder enough. It outlived his mother, as a matter of fact.

Despite Tommy B.'s behavior, or perhaps because of it, all the licensed eelers in the area knew that they had a protector. A muscle. A man who might threaten violence to keep people in line, but who had also carefully cultivated a relationship with the governor to protect everyone's interests. As he drove into the darkening night, Toland Bates offered a silent prayer to whoever was up there that his mother's cousin Tommy B. was not at the bottom of any of this. He found it difficult to reassure himself without a sign from heaven. None was forthcoming.

***

Tommy B. Donovan had known Governor Birdwell for a long time. Back in the day, when Birdwell was newly elected on a zealous pro-business platform, Tommy B. had approached him about protecting the eelers from any unwarranted regulation, such as limiting the number of eels they could take and when, and Birdwell had agreed, for a small piece of the action, which seemed entirely reasonable to Tommy B.

It wasn't until Birdwell got voted out and replaced by an environmentalist at the governor's mansion that things started to go south. The limits and the swipe cards were a fact of life that Tommy B. didn't know how to undo. So he was happy to receive a call from the now ex-governor and put on his best pair of jeans and a clean flannel shirt to go meet him.

He opened the door without knocking, startling Kat Rutherford.

"Gimme a hug, sister," he said to her. She did a half pirouette to avoid him and led him directly into Birdwell's inner sanctum, not even offering him a coffee. Pigs did not get coffee, except the boss.

"Tommy B.," said the ex-governor. "Thanks for coming in. I've been thinking about you ever since they turned off the spigot."

Tommy B., who never smiled, took a seat unbidden. "We had it pretty good there for a fair while," he said. "First they brought in the damn swipe cards, and then they took the trucks off the road—I'd like to've hung myself."

"I'm glad you didn't do that," said Birdwell. "Because I think we might be able to turn things on again."

"You gonna kill the governor?"

"The walls have ears. I don't think anything like that will be necessary," Birdwell scoffed. "I can work on getting that lovely lady voted out of office, when the time comes, but meanwhile, we do have some influence with a fine young man at the Department of Fisheries and Wildlife named Gary Kell."

"The guy who shut down the trucks? You gotta be kidding me."

"He's an ambitious young man," Birdwell went on. "I believe he would be a willing spokesman for our position. You know, opening things up. Deregulating. And he's known as an environmentalist. We create a ballot initiative. In this state, the voters, God bless them, get to decide. They can undo a law or a regulation just by pulling a lever."

"More government idiocy. So this guy Kell's a hero and a villain," Tommy B. said. "Depending."

"Let's just say he's malleable. And he'd like to get ahead. And I can help in that cause."

Tommy B. nodded. "What do you want from me? I'm no part of this."

"Well, my usual ten percent commission when we succeed," said the ex-governor. "And a certain amount of control. I'd like to bring together the fishermen and create a kind of formal coalition—a kind of . . . what would you call it?"

"A union?"

"Fine. Call it a union. We could start a pension fund, a group health care fund, that kind of thing."

"And you could loot them all," said Tommy B.

Birdwell frowned. Tommy B. shrugged.

"I was only going to suggest," Birdwell said, "that the logical funding source for a ballot initiative, which is expensive to initiate, and would be so beneficial to you and the men would be, well . . . I don't know how to make it any clearer. You. And the men. Say twenty-five, thirty K to start out. And once we get traction, maybe a bit more to finish the effort."

Tommy B. squinted his eyes as though considering the matter. Then he lifted his legs and dropped his muddy boots up on the ex-governor's desk with a thump. Birdwell shot back in his chair reflexively.

"You're looking at the boots," said Tommy B. "You think the boots tell you something important about me. Don't judge a book by the cover, that's all I'm saying. I learned that in school. I went to school, and I wasn't born yesterday."

He took his feet back down and straightened himself up in his chair. The tooled leather desktop was now decorated with small clods of dried dirt and pebbles, surrounded by gravel road dust.

"Was that strictly necessary?" Birdwell asked. He made a vain attempt to sweep the crud off the desk but quit after one swipe. He had just had a manicure.

"I guess it was," Tommy B. said, "You're asking me for ten percent plus whatever else you can grab, a thirty thousand dollar advance, for what? You're talking 'initiative,' but you got none. How you gonna pass it? What if the voters don't like it? I'm supposed to pay for that? Better odds buying a lottery ticket."

"Frankly, I'm surprised," said Birdwell. "We've done very well together in the past; I thought we were better friends."

"Friends? I don't have friends," Tommy B. replied.

"Well," said Birdwell, "perhaps there's nothing more to say."

"Maybe not," said Tommy B. "'Less you want to help me with my own problems."

Birdwell nodded sagely. "I didn't know you had any. Other than regulations. But you know me. Always willing to be helpful. And I *do* have friends. Good ones, in high places."

"I got a guy chasing me. Bastard named Bennett Tyson. He come into the state some years ago, when there wasn't but a handful of amateurs in this, and now he's got big plans. I don't know where he got 'em—he didn't seem to seem to know shit about the business when he started, but he's doing a business with it now."

"How can I help?" asked Birdwell warmly.

Tommy B. shifted in his seat and reached into the pocket of his canvas jacket. He drew out a pistol and dropped it on Birdwell's desktop. It landed with a clunk that made Birdwell jump again. He didn't like to see firearms tossed around. He didn't like them at all. And had rarely seen one close-up.

"Tyson's a bundler," Tommy B. said. "He's got men fishing everywhere. Got a deal with Korea, starting to be a good-as-goddamn threat to the rest of us. I didn't put in all these years to be threatened by some fella from away."

"I see."

"So, you're a powerful man. I can't challenge Tyson personally—that would look like war. We're a peaceful bunch. I can't bring it directly to Big Otis on the island—he'll do anything to keep things smooth as silk for the summer people and the tourists. But you can help do it from here. I hadn't thought of it till now. You take care of Bennett Tyson in a way that keeps me clean, maybe you and I can work together on this other thing after all."

Birdwell stared at the pistol.

"I can't shoot him," he said.

Tommy B. reached onto the desk, casually picked up the gun, and dropped it back in his pocket.

"You can't shoot anybody," Tommy B. said. "Who said anything about that?"

"Well . . ." Birdwell gestured to the desk and the spot where the gun had been.

"Maybe some things I can't do that you can do—find out who he is, that kind of thing. You got friends in high places, like you said. I've been around long enough to know Tyson's not who he says, I can read it on his face. And that shiny red Mustang he drives. So, who the hell is the guy? Why don't you see what you can do about that, and then we can talk. Other than that, I don't need you. And I don't pay men I don't need."

He stood up and walked out of the office without another word. When he reached the outer office he pivoted to Kat Rutherford, who seemed to be engrossed in some paperwork.

"Honeypot," he said to her, "you might want to take the boss a damp rag or paper towel. Something's got all over his desktop. It needs a wipe."

Kat was heading into the boss's office anyhow. She needed to retrieve her phone.

CHAPTER SIXTEEN

Jeanette was on her knees by the sink, cleaning up a stinking mass of dead crab from the toe-kick space where she had discovered it deceased, long after she'd thought she'd found the last one. She had found it while fixing her morning coffee, which she now couldn't imagine drinking. The bell rang at the front door, and she pushed herself up, off her knees. It was Bennett Tyson.

"I came for the milk carton," he said as he pushed himself past her, into the house. She looked at him, uncomprehending. His eerie, flat eyes were on her. Nasty, angry. She remembered the shredded remains of the picture of her ex-husband and her child—the crabs in her house, in her bed. Impulsively she took the wadded-up paper towel with the crab guts and handed it to him. He took it reflexively, then recoiled in disgust, letting it fall to the floor.

"Jesus," he said, wiping his hand on his jacket, "what the hell is that?"

"The remains of a dead crab," she said, looking directly into his mismatched eyes. He met her gaze but looked confused. "It must have wandered in here," she continued, waiting for a response. He shook his head, like he was missing the joke. Not Tyson. Someone acting without him.

"What are you talking about—milk cartons?" she asked.

"You said men couldn't find a milk carton in their own refrigerator. You told me to wait, and you'd lure him in—I've waited about as long as I can."

"You think I can just make him materialize, pull him out of a hat? I'm not a magician. He'll come when he comes."

"Bullshit," Tyson said. "I'm tired of this bullshit. Someone's gonna get to the bottom of this thing and they're not gonna wait long. Someone. Not me."

She looked at him blackly.

"With weed killer?" she asked.

"Weed killer?" He sounded surprised and a little thrown off-balance. "Who said anything about weed killer?" He leaned into her, and asked quietly, "What are you talking about—weed killer? Where did you hear that?"

"You torture me to death, you miss your only chance to find out anything. It's a bad move."

"I never said anything about weed killer."

"You didn't have to."

For a second—maybe less than a second—he looked lost. Then fury took over. He grabbed a blue-and-white china teacup that was sitting on her counter and threw it hard against the fireplace, where it shattered into shards across the floor. It was the last of a set of four that had been a reluctant wedding gift from her parents.

"Find your husband," he hissed. "Your. Goddamn. Husband."

Jeanette reached out to slap him hard, but he grabbed her wrist and pushed it down to her waist.

"I'm telling you, you don't know who you're dealing with." He slammed the door behind him, storming down the porch steps, leaving her alone to stare at the shattered wedding gift.

***

Late that afternoon, Jesse Ed Davis appeared at her door with a paper bag in his hand.

"Jesse," she said in surprise.

"I brought you a gift," he said.

"A gift?" she asked, ushering him in. He reached into the bag and held up a dark brown lump, which he offered her.

"Thank you, I think?" Jeanette asked, with some trepidation.

"It's Chaga."

"Chaga?"

"A fungus that grows on white birch. I saw it down by your creek, so I swung by and pulled it off. Steep it in hot water for tea. Loaded with antioxidants. Anti-inflammatory too. Better than coffee. Or gin, for that matter. And it's a calming influence, that's the main thing."

"I could really use a calming influence," she said, passing the hard lump of Chaga back and forth between her hands. "It looks a lot like bear shit."

"It is not bear shit."

She described her misadventure with the crabs, her discovery in the murk of the tumbledown house near Joey's trailer, and the recent threats from Bennett Tyson. Jesse's face darkened. He took the lump from her and placed it in the saucepan on the stove, which he filled with water and set to boil.

By the time she had brought him up to date, Jesse was pouring two tin mugs of the Chaga tea. He added a splash of half-and-half and a spoonful of maple syrup from a plastic jug he found in Jeanette's refrigerator and placed the mugs on the kitchen counter.

Jeanette leaned in for a whiff and looked at Jesse skeptically.

"It's not bear shit," he said. "Take a sip."

It tasted like some kind of caramel with a little duff from the forest floor. Still, she was skeptical.

"It's good for you," he said. "Finish up and let's go."

"Go?" she asked.

"I want to see this house. Even good cops aren't good enough to read tracks."

"Why are you even interested?" Jeanette asked him. "This has nothing to do with eels or the fishery or any of the things you say you're devoted to."

"In my tradition everything is tied to everything," he said.

"Don't start with me."

"You take me to the spot where Joey Pizio was killed, who knows what else we might find."

***

The copper and gold that the dying daylight cast on the mainland across the reach had come and gone and only a dark shadow remained. She climbed into the truck and belted herself. There was not much light left.

Heading down the island they found themselves behind a big John Deere tractor, running the road at about fifteen miles an hour.

"Big Otis," said Jesse.

The tractor pulled off the road enough to let Jesse get around and Big Otis waved brightly as they slid past. Jesse and Jeanette returned the wave. Everyone on the island knew that Big Otis hated to go home to his wife until he had to. He conducted town meetings once a month and made sure people like the Framers didn't cut down trees too close to the water unless they had a good excuse. But he seemed happiest when he was riding on his tractor, taking down the weeds. Tidying the island.

"Seems the porcupine quills aren't keeping him off the tractor," Jesse observed.

"What do you think?" Jeanette asked. "Him seeing us together. Small island. Gossip."

"You and me?" Jesse asked. "How likely is that gonna seem?"

"Well, they have to talk about something down at the Bread & Butter Mart. Besides who's pregnant and who doesn't know it yet."

"I hope we gave them a new subject," Jesse said. "But do you think he even saw?"

"He doesn't miss much."

They were less than ten minutes away when they first smelled smoke. Not smoke from a barbecue or campfire, but some kind of acrid mix of sparking electrical wire, insulation, rubber, and asphalt.

"Shit," said Jesse. "House on fire."

"The house," Jeanette said grimly.

The sirens started immediately after. As they reached the turn, they heard them louder, and then the trucks passed them. The island had two.

They easily kept pace with the trucks, which took a hard left onto the familiar dirt road just past the only gas station in town. Now they could see the flames lighting up the sky, and the smell grew worse.

"Maybe Joey's trailer," Jesse said. But it was not Joey's trailer that was ablaze, and Jeanette knew it wouldn't be. It was the abandoned wreck of a house down the road. The fire trucks raced past the now-empty mobile home and pulled up in front of the house, which was already collapsing into itself and would be nothing but a heap of smoldering ashes by the time the firemen got themselves organized. Jesse held his truck back, pulling off the road fifty feet or so behind the fire trucks.

"Too late," Jeanette said. "You'll never see it now. Too damn late."

Jesse cut the engine and kept the windows up. No need to breathe more foul air than necessary. The firemen began to pump water toward the house and tried to reach the big red spruce that was aflame at the top. Pickup trucks began to line the road as volunteers from the hose company arrived on the scene.

"That's the tree that used to grow up through the roof when there was a roof," Jesse said. "I went exploring there once. Long time ago."

"That's the tree they tied him to," Jeanette said.

At that moment Jeanette saw the red-and-blue lights of a police car in Jesse's mirror.

"Toland," she said, somehow knowing who it would be.

She slipped off her seat belt and opened the passenger door.

The cop car pulled ahead of them and came to an abrupt halt at the rear bumper of the fire truck. Toland Bates threw open the door and cursed as he jumped from the car.

"Goddammit to hell," he said. She could see the orange flames in his eyes.

THE SQUIRREL AND THE TREE

The house had stood vacant for almost forty years. The roof had begun to sag about the time that Peggy Alton and Joe Pizio Sr. met. The courtship that followed was not easy. On the day the doctor told her she was pregnant she was just plain angry.

She couldn't see how the two of them would ever make it with a baby. His day drinking had stopped being an adventure a while back. Now the doctor was saying she couldn't drink with him. Or smoke.

On an unseasonably warm March day, the spruce trees had dropped their pollen in big yellow clouds. A fleck of it found its way into a crevice in a female cone on a tree next to the abandoned house by their trailer. The burgundy Oldsmobile Cutlass they had gone in on together turned orange from the pollen. He scooped her up and put her on the hood while she pretended to fight him off and said, "You're gonna mess up my jeans," and then he picked her up again, and he pointed to the round marks on the hood and told her, "You leave a damn fine impression."

He led her inside. Six weeks later, she realized she was late.

The baby came early. On the fall morning Peggy gave birth, Joe was there, but between gasps, she wished he wasn't. It was the last day of deer hunting season, and she knew he was waiting to be thanked for missing it to be with her. She would have died first.

By then the cone that had received the pollen fleck contained the very beginning of a seed, smaller than a grain of sand. On the drive back to the trailer, Joe pointed to the old house.

"Roof caved in," he said. She didn't respond.

On the day when Joey Jr. turned three, the grain resting within the spruce cone had grown to a little triangle of genetic information and spruce fat, with a papery wing. So had its housemates. A fat red squirrel that had been eyeing this cone for its whole life sensed that there was as much energy stored in the cone today as there ever would be. Today was the day.

It nibbled till this particular cone fell, followed it down the tree, picked it up, and took it through the broken window of the abandoned house where it had stored hundreds of spruce cones for the winter. The squirrel left through the same window, hopped around the edge of the house, and followed the seam of the grass to the edge of the road. There was an orchard on the other side. Spruce cones were good in the winter, but apples were good now.

The squirrel stepped into the road and hopped halfway across when a looming presence and a roar scared it forward. It bounded hard, reached the other side, and was part way up the embankment when the screeching started. At the last minute, something compelled the squirrel to turn back into the road. The driver swerved, but it was too late.

"Shit!" He pounded the wheel. "Why do they always do that? And once they've got it beat, too! Goddamn suicide!" Suicide. Shandy Epps had thought about it himself one cold and wet fall day when the notion of being the bait man for another winter of sporadic lobstering in freezing wind and frigid water seemed darker to him than just ending his existence. But he stuck around. Not so the squirrel. "Maybe he just don't want to face the winter is all."

Shandy looked behind him and saw the twitching pile of copper fur and red muscle framed by two parallel black lines running down the road, gently curving—the result of his slamming on the brakes. He liked the look of that. I should be one of those guys, he thought. A burner. Something new to try. Maybe something I could get good at. Then he thought vaguely about fate and time.

"Parallel lines. Maybe they meet after a while," he said to himself. He swallowed the last of a can of Narragansett, kept driving, stopped for a fresh six pack at the gas station, and headed home.

With the squirrel gone, the odds for the spruce seed went up. Still, it would be hard to say why any of the fourteen seeds that sprouted did so, and why any of the more than nine hundred that didn't sprout didn't. It is a little less hard to say why, of those fourteen, one grew into a tree.

The one that made it had a lucky root. It twisted and turned between a rotten floor joist and the rotten plate at the top of the foundation, reached outside, and found soil with rotten leaves piled on top. With that umbilical cord to nutrients and a mulch of wall-to-wall carpet preventing competition, it grew unimpeded.

By the time young Joey Pizio was in eleventh grade, the tree had reached above the roofline of the house, and his mom and dad had gotten religion. Joey couldn't understand how this had happened, but somebody got to them, and they became churchgoers. No more alcohol. A last-ditch effort to save the marriage, perhaps, and maybe also to preserve the crockery, which was no longer smashed during tantrums.

It was an austere, almost silent life, but Joey had to admit it seemed a little bit more like a family. Still, it didn't seem fair that his mom was always so mean to his dad. She told Joey he didn't understand. He agreed that he didn't.

It seemed even less fair when the police pulled up to their place and told him they were gone. Killed by a drunk driver named Shandy Epps. A burner. Shit, he thought: eight months ago, *they* were the drunk drivers.

The night they died the tree was twenty-four feet tall. Graceful. Thin, and moving fast for a tree. Up, up, and out. Quietly reaching.

***

It was dark, and Joey was sweating. He could hear the man outside rifling around in his trunk. Through the haze of the oxy he thought: This tree is huge. Growing in a house. How many times have I driven by this house? My whole life, and I never really noticed a big fucking tree growing through it. Now I'm tied to it. And this guy—he's dressed like he's going to the opera. Joey felt the rope twisting into his wrists and the bark scraping at the insides of his arms. The tree stretched his shoulders. The man stepped inside.

***

Eventually, the glyphosate would have killed the tree too. Once Joey's vomit soaked into the ground and the herbicide found its way into the root system, the tree would have a hard time taking in micronutrients. Zinc. Boron. Manganese. Iron. It wouldn't have died overnight. But the vitamin deficiency would leave it unable to fend off pests and disease.

Grubs would get under its bark, and woodpeckers would whack at them, tearing its cambium. The cambium, there to keep nutrition and water flowing, would be broken. And the woodpecker's beak would inoculate the tree with spores. Shelf mushrooms would digest the wood, softening it. The spruce might hang on for another ten years before it collapsed, but eventually, when it fell, you would have been able to trace back the tree's death to the same chemical that killed the man.

The herbicide never got the chance. While the tree stood and the vomit percolated through the rot, the man returned to the house, made a tepee of kiln-dried campfire wood around the base of the tree. He doused the dried wood with lighter fluid. He rolled up a piece of newspaper into a straw and lit the corner with a pink Bic lighter. Once the flames started to eat down toward the center he dropped it onto the camp wood tepee. He watched for a full minute as it flared up fast, and the plastic webbed handles from the campfire wood curled up and blackened. Once he heard the lower branches of the spruce crackling, he stepped outside, started his car, and drove away.

CHAPTER SEVENTEEN

It was a good thirty minutes after the man drove away before the first fire truck got there, and the words were first spoken: "Surround and drown." Each volunteer firefighter remembered when he first heard the phrase. It sounded hopeless and violent. And fun. They all loved to say it. When there was no possibility of saving a structure, and the only goal was to keep fire from spreading, that's what they were trained to do—surround and drown.

Every firefighter had the chance to say it at least once after making his own assessment of the situation. The ones who arrived at the scene first were lucky and got to say it three or four times.

There was a small pond in the apple orchard with a red pipe sticking up. A "dry hydrant" that could pump from below the ice in the winter. All the ponds near houses had them. They hooked up to it, unrolled the hose across the road to the pumper truck, and began to spray. A fire like this was a social event. When no lives were in danger and nothing that mattered was at stake, the men of the Caterpillar Island volunteer fire company comported themselves as though they were tailgating. They sprayed up and around the house toward the tree, trying to reach its burning peak of new spruce cones. But the water could not reach that high. Still, they tried. Eventually, about two-thirds of the way up, the tree burned through. But instead of falling over sideways, as trees are supposed to, the top third of the trunk slid down, parallel to the rest of the tree. Sparks and embers billowed out and two stark black lines stood above what remained of the house, like parallel tire tracks in the sky.

* * *

Toland followed Jesse and Jeanette off the island and up a dirt driveway that led behind an old boxcar on Route 1. It had once been converted into a luncheon place for the tourists but had gone belly-up years ago. There was a ragged *For Sale* sign out front, but the phone number on the bottom had been sheared off.

"Your new place," Jeanette said.

"For the moment."

Toland pulled up behind them and killed the engine. Jesse led them all inside and ignited a Coleman kerosene lantern. There were four folding chairs and a mattress in the place. A long, disused chrome counter ran down the middle of the car, with the remains of a commercial kitchen behind. It was a definite comedown from the storage unit.

"Make yourself at home," Jesse said.

"Not easy to do," said Toland, settling into one of the chairs. Jesse hoisted himself up onto the chrome counter.

"There's only three of us who know what we know," Jesse said.

"I got the evidence all neatly packed away," Toland said. "But I can't use it now."

"What I want to know," Jesse said, "is this: If they tortured Joey Pizio to death in that house and left some evidence—the poor guy's DNA all over the floorboards—why'd they wait so long to burn it?"

"Doesn't make any sense," Toland agreed. "Either you figure there isn't much evidence, and you leave it, because burning it draws attention. Or you figure you better clean up and burn it. But waiting around for a couple weeks and then doing it? Why?"

They stood silently for a moment until Jeanette said quietly, "Damn. It's me."

"What?" Toland said.

"Like I was telling Jesse before we went riding over to the house tonight, Tyson came by my place yesterday, almost beat the hell out of me."

"Jesus," Toland said.

"He was in a bad place when he got there, but he lost it when I mentioned weed killer. Started throwing crockery around. And then the house burns down."

"You said weed killer?" Jesse asked. "You didn't tell me that."

"He showed up at my house, I told him I couldn't make Simon appear out of thin air, and he grabbed me. I said, 'What are you gonna do, make me drink weed killer?' And he got really scary. Broke the last piece of wedding china I had. And then the house burns down tonight."

"You told him?" Toland sounded stunned. "You just told him? I mean, you may be a good crab picker, but you aren't good police."

"Maybe I'm just tired of being threatened and grabbed and pushed around. You might not know what that feels like."

"Well," Jesse interrupted, "now we know there *is* a link to Tyson. Sounds like good police to me."

Toland conceded, after a moment's thought. "Good police. I take it all back."

***

Big Otis Sumlin was more than a bit surprised to receive a call from the ex-governor of the state of Maine, but he betrayed none. He did not know how to express surprise or most other emotions, and, in fact, rarely spoke in words of more than one syllable except when greeting the people from away. Generally, the policy had served him well.

"Lester Birdwell," the ex-governor announced.

"Yes, sir," said Big Otis.

"There's a fella named Bennett Tyson," Birdwell said. "He may not be who he says he is, and he may not be doing your little community any good. I think maybe I could help. I'd like to see his driver's license."

"His driver's license? Why call me?"

"It's kind of a delicate matter. I don't want the state to get involved at this point. Running computer checks, that kind of thing. Just keeping it local. Wondering if you could help—or would be willing to."

"What do you want me to do?" asked Big Otis with a bit of sarcasm in his voice. "Hit his car with my tractor?"

Birdwell paused before answering.

"That's exactly what I had in mind," he said, though he was completely surprised by the suggestion. But it might be the simplest way. He had heard that Big Otis mostly spent the daylight hours nosing down the island's roadways scything down the weeds. The thought of him making a hard turn into the street while on his usual sluggish rounds appealed to him. It was kind of brilliant in its simplicity.

"Would you recognize him?" Birdwell asked.

"I know him," Big Otis said. "Leastways I know his car. Only red Mustang on the island."

"All I want is for you to copy down his license information and get it to me. You can admit fault if you want—not trying to make him mad, just getting some details. There's a thousand dollars in it as a fee."

Big Otis took a long pull on the cigar he had managed to light up one-handed while Birdwell was talking. He waited long enough for Birdwell to understand that the fee would not be adequate.

"Might damage the tractor," he said finally.

"We'll get that fixed up too," Birdwell said. "And any damage you do to Tyson's car. Might even help get you a new tractor."

For the first time, Big Otis took umbrage.

"What do I want with a new tractor?" he asked brusquely. He loved his tractor—a 1977 John Deere—significantly more than he loved his wife or the memory of his parents. He had rebuilt it three times. "I could use twenty-five hundred plus compensation for repairs—his and mine—all in cash."

Birdwell quickly agreed and put down the phone. He then called Tommy B. and set a meeting at which he expected to introduce him to Gary Kell, the new spokesman for the Coalition for a Sustainable Elver Fishery. Kell was already preparing to host town hall meetings across the state to gather signatures for the ballot measure. Birdwell had come up with the name of the organization himself. Having been impressed by monikers like the Clear Skies Act, the Coalition for Sustainable Organics, and No Child Left Behind, he decided that the best way to name something was to call it the exact opposite of what it was until it was too late for anyone to do anything about it.

⁂

Lottie Pride stood in the crab shack by the table, a crab knife in her hand.

"And the finfish, when they come back," she was saying. "They should ask us how to manage them, too. *Passamaquoddy* means 'the people who come from the place where pollack are plentiful.' White people ended the plentiful part, and pretty much ignored the 'people who come from a place' part too. But when the pollack do come back, they'll ignore us again."

"The pollack will definitely ignore you," said Patsy, who had clearly had enough.

"I mean the government will," Lottie said. "We couldn't even vote until 1954."

"I did not know that," Amelia said.

"We're still living it," Lottie said. "If you didn't know, now you know."

"You're not supposed to answer," Patsy said to Amelia. "She's just rehearsing. She's always rehearsing."

She turned her attention to Lottie. "I think you're ready if Augusta calls," she said dryly. Turning back to Amelia she said, "She keeps waiting."

"I'm sorry," said Lottie, who clearly was not.

Jeanette stepped in and let the screen door close behind her.

"She's earned the right," Jeanette said. She'd been listening at the door. "You have, Lottie. I'm contacting the governor's office. I worked like a dog on that campaign. It's the least they can do to listen to me."

The room fell silent.

Jeanette looked around as the three women went back to their jobs. For too long a time, no one said anything. Jeanette moved a crate of whole boiled crabs from the refrigerator to the corner of the room, ready for picking, but the quiet unnerved her. The usual laconic chatter did not begin.

"What'd I miss?" she asked. "I can take it."

For a few more seconds the room's only sound was the quiet *click-clack* of crab knives, and then Patsy, too casually, said, "Mason's thinking of buying a new boat, that's all. A better boat."

"He must be doing good," Jeanette said.

The others remained silent. Patsy looked up at Jeanette, who was standing above her, and put down the crab she was working on, and the pick, and the tiny, razor-sharp knife. Jeanette had never seen her put down a crab in the middle of the process.

"I been worried to ask you this," she said. "It's kinda uncomfortable."

"Just say it," said Lottie Pride, who seemed to be defending Jeanette's dignity. "He wants to buy the *Jeanette*."

Patsy looked wounded and relieved all at once. She rephrased the blunt statement.

"How would you feel about him buying the *Jeanette*? You can say no. It might be a hurtful thing to do, being as it's named after you and all. I been worried sick over it, like I said."

Jeanette just looked at her for a moment. Her mind was whirling. Finally she spoke.

"The *Jeanette*'s for sale? Where? How'd anybody find it?"

"See." Patsy turned to the other women. "I shoulda just told him no. It's a hurtful thing."

"No, no," Jeanette said. "Where? How?"

Patsy's face blushed.

"He saw it listed in *The Boat Trader*, just by mistake. It's someplace in Rhode Island—Wakefield, I think. That's all I know. He was gonna go down there next week and take a look, but I told him I'd have to check with you. She's named after you. I don't want to be doing the wrong thing."

"He sold the damn boat," Jeanette said to no one in particular, suddenly in a hurry to escape the crab house. "Or somebody did."

"Well, it's up for sale at least. Thing is," Patsy said, "it's bad luck to rename a boat. Almost like taking bananas on board. You don't take bananas on a fishing boat, you know."

"Or put your hat on your bed," Amelia added.

"He wouldn't have to rename it," Jeanette said. "I'd be proud to see it back in the water." But she was blathering as her mind raced.

"I didn't know Simon had put it up," Patsy said. "Has he been gone long? I didn't know he stopped fishing. And why is he selling it down there, and not here? I didn't know any of it."

Jeanette had a powerful urge to say *me neither*, but she kept it in. No good could come from it.

"No need to worry," she said instead. "Thank you for asking me. That was kind."

Patsy nodded.

"Tell your husband to go ahead. Tell him I'm glad he found it."

She turned and exited before any more questions could be asked. She stood outside the door for a moment gathering her wits and waiting for conversation to resume, but it was strangely silent in there. After a moment she walked back to the house to wash her hands and change her clothes. She stank of boiled crab. She could afford to take tomorrow off with the delivery payments coming in. Not much more than a day off, but one would be all right. Let the women think she was upset.

***

It was at just about the time when Gary Kell walked into Birdwell's office to meet meet Tommy B. that Big Otis saw Tyson's red Mustang in his side-view mirror, checked his seat belt quickly, and made a hard left into the road, catching the Mustang's right front fender and smashing a headlight. It was skillfully done, though Big Otis had never done anything quite like it before. The tractor was pretty much unscathed. The Mustang left a few tread marks on the road, nothing you could call art, and Bennett Tyson bounded out of it ready for a fight. Big Otis hobbled down from his perch on the tractor seat, an old man with his arms raised, wisps of gray hair rebelling weakly against his John Deere cap. Before Tyson could speak, he began to apologize.

"Geez, Mr. Tyson, I'm so sorry, I don't know what I did. Musta had a little stroke or something—I never done that before. Is she hurt bad?"

Tyson took a moment to calm down. He started with "You could have killed me!"

"I could," Big Otis said. "I hope I didn't even hurt you. Any injury? I can call the police and they'll take you to the emergency room."

"No need for the police," Tyson said. "What the hell happened?"

Big Otis shook his head, seemingly bewildered. "I never done nothing like that before," he repeated. It was about all he was going to say. And at least it was true.

Dutifully they exchanged license and insurance information. The Mustang was still drivable.

"I love this car, you know," Tyson said.

"I know what that feels like," Big Otis said. "I do. Your best body shop is up in Ellsworth, Sully's Autobody. I don't want my insurance to go up, so just get an estimate and I'll give you the cash. I just . . . I never done nothing like that before."

Sully would no doubt give Big Otis a 10 percent kickback in return for the recommendation. He always had.

* * *

Jesse Ed Davis drove inland to the town of Mount Chase to hear former Assistant Fishery Resources Commissioner Gary Kell speak. He wanted to press him on the subject of increased fishing rights for the local tribes and cause at least a bit of a stir, but he was puzzled when he walked in by the sight of a striking blond woman, tasked with keeping notes on how the meeting went. She was too polished to be from the fisheries department or the town clerk's office.

Gary Kell had practiced his speech on behalf of the initiative, which, if it gathered sufficient signatures, would become Maine Question Two on the November ballot. As a seasoned conservation official, he assured the audience that elvers were plentiful, made Maine a bigger part of the international economy, and were a great source of income—and pride—for the fishermen. These fishermen duly paid their taxes, which helped the schools and hospitals across the state, not just on the coast. One eel could lay up to five million eggs. So, limiting the catch was unnecessary ecologically. It was also costly and created a burdensome bureaucracy that ate up those taxes. It was therefore un-American. He had a sympathetic audience.

Jesse looked around at the faces of the assembled thirty or forty who had come as much for a night out as anything else. It all seemed to make sense to them. Jesse asked his question when the time came and got a noncommittal reply. Yes, of course the tribes were entitled to their rights, but not to special rights. They were Americans like everyone else. The audience seemed to breathe a sigh of relief that that part was over.

Jesse didn't follow up. He noticed another apparent outlier, a young man in a white shirt and pressed slacks, holding a thin reporter's notebook in his lap, a Blackwing pencil at the ready. His wire-rim eyewear also set him apart. A young journalist hopeful from central casting. As Jesse took his seat, the young man's hand shot up and he stood.

"Roland Finkle, *Augusta Chronicle*," he said. "I'm curious where the funding for this initiative is coming from."

Gary Kell was clearly taken aback.

"Young man," he said, "this is a public meeting, not a press conference."

"I'm the public," Roland Finkle said. "I'm also a reporter. They're not mutually exclusive."

"I'm sorry," Gary Kell said. "I have no comment at this time."

"But somebody must be paying your salary."

"I'm a volunteer," Gary Kell said. "I believe in the initiative." It was the first time he'd ever lied to a reporter. It was the first time he'd ever met a reporter.

"What about her?" Finkle asked, indicating Kat Rutherford, who was clicking away quickly at her keyboard. She did not look up.

"I have no comment at this time," Gary Kell said. "Are there any questions from local residents?"

When the meeting ended, Jesse watched as Roland Finkle stepped quickly to Kat Ruherford's table and handed her a business card with the *Augusta Chronicle* logo on it.

"Call me," said Finkle. "I cover local and state politics for the paper, and this initiative could be a big story. I'd love to interview you."

"We'll see," said Kat. She dropped the card into her bag and gave Finkle a bright professional smile.

"Do you have a card?" Finkle asked.

"Not tonight," she said. "If you'll excuse me." She stood abruptly and headed toward the back door. Gary Kell stepped into the men's room. Jesse followed Kat out and intercepted her by the door of a black town car. "This initiative is bad for everyone but the people you work for," he said. "And bad for the eels. You must know that. Maybe you would even like to do something about it. Maybe before that reporter from the *Chronicle* catches up with you."

He slipped her a folded piece of paper with his phone number on it.

"If so, I'm your friend in this," he added. "Call me." Before she could respond, he walked quickly to the road, where he had parked the Silverado out of sight.

CHAPTER EIGHTEEN

Jeanette contacted the boatyard and told the man on the phone her name was Lynne Framer, that she was a widow, and that she was helping her eldest son look for a boat. The asking price, $204,000, was not an impediment. It was easy to get a loan for a lobsterman—the lobster business was booming. Besides, her dear departed husband's boat was just an old tub, and her eldest son wanted something better. The man on the phone, whose name was Mickey Keegan, sounded delighted. He owned the boatyard and would be happy to meet with them.

She drove to the disused boxcar and found Jesse packing his things.

"Moving again?" she asked.

"I can't catch a break," Jesse said. "Somebody bought the place. You don't know any place where there's a storage container or an old yurt or something?"

"I can look around," Jeanette said. "But I need you to do me a favor. I need you to be my oldest son. Just for a day."

"I'm too old," Jesse said. "You would have been, what, when you had me? Fifteen?"

"It's been known to happen," Jeanette said. "It won't be a wasted trip. I found the boat."

"That," Jesse said, "sounds interesting. The boat. You want to help me pack? Then we'll go."

Turning south off I-95 onto Route 1 they saw a billboard advertising the place. MICKEY KEEGAN'S MIRACLE BOATS, it said in bold lettering that was made to resemble wooden ship timbers. And in smaller letters beneath: *If It Floats, It's a Miracle.* They arrived in the late afternoon, stopped at McDonald's, much to Jesse's displeasure, and then proceeded to the boatyard. Jeanette instantly knew that the man who introduced himself as Mickey Keegan was not the Mickey Keegan to whom she had spoken on the phone. He was dressed in an expensive getup that made him look like a prosperous yachtsman from another era—white boatneck sweater over a blue-and-white striped polo shirt, seersucker trousers, and an ascot knotted loosely around his neck. But it was the face above the neck that let them know who they were talking to. He had none. The skin stretched over a reconstructed nose and the lips were thin to the point of disappearing. His eyes, dark and recessed, were all that seemed to move. She and Jesse dared not let their eyes meet. Where was the real Mickey Keegan? This one stuck his hand out, genial as any salesman was taught to be.

"You must be Lynne Framer," he said without affect.

He knows just who I am, she thought, and her every instinct told her to turn and flee. But it was too late. I am safer, she thought, if he thinks I have no idea who he is. She shook his hand, thankful to be in the company of someone as imposing as Jesse. Whatever this meant, it would have to play out in real time. Maybe a burn victim, Jeanette thought. His eyelids, when they blinked, seemed to move in slow motion. He shook Jesse's hand and led the way to the boat, which occupied a slip at the far end of the long planking.

"She's here on consignment," the man who now called himself Mickey Keegan explained. "She just went on the market—you're the first to see her."

"How'd she get here?" asked Jeanette, feigning only the slightest curiosity.

"A man from Maine brought her in. I'm not really sure, but his name's on the paperwork. King, I think." She felt his eyes on her as she tried not to meet them. "I wonder who she's named for," he said, too casually. Then he blinked. That slow-motion blink. Jeanette's stomach turned over.

He stared at her for a moment, his dark eyes waiting, as if for a confession, an admission of guilt. She smiled instead. But she was suddenly feeling short-tempered and nervous. She hoped that what she felt in her gut was only alarm, and not the physical thing she feared it was. Please, not here. Not in front of this man.

"You'd have to ask the original owner," said Jeanette, hoping she was just casual enough. She was glad to know that Simon was probably alive, if in danger. Jesse pinched her shoulder as they walked, and she decided she'd better just shut up.

When they reached the boat, Jesse asked if they could explore it alone.

"We know our way around a lobster boat," he said.

"I'm sure you do," said the man, "but it's against company policy."

The three of them climbed on board and began a tour.

As the man described some of the boat's features from a listing paper he was holding in his hand, they went about their business, ignoring him.

"She's got new Bomar windows and a Twin Disc 2.05:1 reverse gear. Twelve-inch SS hauler direct drive, SS dual ram steering, and a two-inch Jabsco washdown pump . . ."

Jesus, Jeanette thought as he droned on. She shot Jesse a look. *This guy doesn't even know that SS means "stainless steel." I know more about boats than he does.*

Simon had left the boat in good condition and the boatyard had undoubtedly given it a thorough going-over before advertising it. For a couple hundred thousand dollars, customers expected a clean boat.

Jesse inspected the engine beneath the floorboards, which also had been power washed, while Jeanette lifted the live well cover. The hydraulics assisted, and she looked long and hard into the empty space, remembering the aggressive swirl of elvers she had encountered there when the boat had been circling in the reach. Now the inside was white, clean, and dry. Then she saw what she'd not noticed before. She blamed the eels—the surprise of finding them there. She pushed the lid downward and let the hydraulics lower it again.

"Let's go down below," she said to Jesse, and the two of them squeezed into the hold. Their eyes met in the semidark, but before Jeanette could speak, he drew his forefinger across his lips. It would have to wait.

She went back up and checked all the winch handles and sat down on the gunwale, suddenly dizzy, while Jesse inspected the winch motor that hauled up the traps. The knot in her stomach gnawed at her.

The well of pain she had begged her body not to spring on her at this particular moment surged suddenly. It came in a wave from her lower abdomen to her lungs. She'd felt it before, and learned to fear it, but it had been nothing like this. She willed her thigh muscles to lurch her into a standing position, which usually caused things to ease off a little bit. Jesse looked at her, quizzically. She held up her hand, index finger in the air. *Give me a minute.* But she couldn't quite speak yet.

"You all right?" Jesse asked, and he was at her side.

Jeanette nodded, her face reddening.

"I'm fine," Jeanette said finally, not sounding it. "I'll be fine."

She took a couple deep breaths as the pain passed and sat down again.

"Stomach trouble," she said. "It happens." Beads of sweat had broken out on her brow.

"McDonald's," Jesse diagnosed.

The man pretending to be Mickey Keegan eyed her with curiosity, and maybe a little pleasure.

"That didn't look small," he said. "Perhaps you should see a doctor."

"I think I'm through with doctors," Jeanette said. "There's not that much of me left for them to pick over. It just happens sometimes." She closed her mouth and pushed down hard on her abdomen with the muscles around her diaphragm. Sometimes that worked.

Then she stood again. But the pain grabbed her, a rising wave.

"Goddammit!" she shouted suddenly. Her body seized up again and she doubled over, frozen on the spot. Then it eased, and she was upright again. "Okay," she wheezed. "I gotta get off this boat."

"Let's go home," said Jesse. "I'll drive."

"So sorry you don't feel well," said the man who was pretending to be Mickey Keegan, without a shred of sincerity. "It's hard to see you leave in such pain. I can show you more another time—we're just getting started."

"Thanks," said Jeanette, not comforted. "We'll just have to think on it."

Jesse looked at her and furrowed his brow. They'd been on the boat for about ten minutes. But she did not seem to see him. He helped her clamber back onto the dock. She thanked the man with no face for his time and said that they might be back, but she just wasn't feeling well.

He watched her the way a scientist might watch a rat participating in an experiment.

"Never rains but it pours," he said to no one in particular. Then he went back inside the office and picked up the phone.

As soon as Jeanette and Jesse had left the parking lot Jesse turned to her and asked, "Are you all right?"

"For the moment," she said. The pain had abated. All that was left was a thin layer of cold sweat on her forehead. She wiped at it with her hand. She kept her eyes on the road as Jesse drove. "It happens. Sour stomach. Disappointment. Stress. Thurston Harney."

Jesse waited for her to elaborate. She did not.

"You're ill," he said.

"Chronically," she said. She held up her hand and waved away whatever his next question might be.

"Wisconsin," Jesse said. "What's he doing here? And how was he not here when you called, but here now?"

"That face," Jeanette said. "He's got to be waiting for Simon. I've got to warn him."

She took her phone from her purse, punched numbers into it, and waited. In a moment a digitized voice informed her that the party she was calling was not available. Then there was the beep and, as calmly as she could, Jeanette said, "Simon, it's me. Do not go back to the boatyard in Wakefield. Whatever you're doing, they're on to it. There's a man there—I think he's waiting to kill you. I don't know why. But please, if you've never listened to anything I've ever said before, listen to this. Do not go back to the boatyard."

She hit the button that ended the call, switched to text mode, and sent the same message. She dropped the phone back in her bag. For a moment or two she just breathed. Jesse let her decompress.

"And there's something wrong with the live well," she said.

"What?"

"It's about half as deep as it's supposed to be."

"Was it like that on the morning when you saw the elvers?"

"I don't know. I couldn't see through to the bottom. But I'd guess so."

"So, the elvers were camouflage," he said.

Jeanette nodded.

"A few pounds of very effective, very active, very valuable camouflage," he continued.

"Something else was on the boat," she said. "Contraband or something."

"The elvers were already contraband. Contraband on contraband."

"There's a whole set of screws around the edge that didn't used to be there. They're holding it in place. Phillips-head screws."

"Does it matter what kind of screws?" Jesse asked.

"It does," said Jeanette. "We'll need a screwdriver."

"Because . . ."

"Because after dark, we're going back. There must be a Home Depot around here somewhere."

"Now you've lost it," Jesse said. "You think there's a murderer at the boatyard, so you want to sneak back in there, in the dark, just to see what's under the live well?"

He reached out and took her forearm in his hand. He looked into her eyes, his face serious.

"I can't let you do that," he reiterated. He did not let go of her arm.

"You don't have to let me do anything," Jeanette said. "You have to help me. The guy's not gonna be there all night. We can outwait him."

Jesse looked at her. Nodded. She stared back into his eyes and saw something there that looked like newfound respect. Or at least that's how she read it. But all he said was "We'll need a tape measure too."

There was a seafood joint featuring a ghastly green neon fish of undetermined species hanging over the door; its layered scales looked like a set of overlapping salad plates. But it was the best-looking place they could find.

Jesse had a Lone Pine, a dozen clams, a dozen oysters, and a shrimp cocktail. Jeanette limited herself to one Beefeater and tonic and looked at the menu with distaste. Jesse broke the silence.

"Can you tell me what was going on back there?"

"That's what we are going to find out."

"No, I mean with your stomach."

"Oh. That."

"Yeah. That."

"It's nothing."

"Can we talk about cancer?"

"That, I beat," Jeanette said.

"But there's something in there you haven't beaten. More than indigestion."

Jeanette sighed. "It's called Crohn's disease," she said. "People live with it. Except I'm not supposed to drink much." She raised her rocks glass and touched the neck of his beer bottle. "Bubbles don't help, and I'm supposed to avoid coffee. And sweets aren't great. And I'm a Sara Lee addict, so there's that. But I'd rather live in pain than starve to death."

"So, it's not cancer,"

"No, it's not cancer, for God's sake! And it probably won't kill me, but something will eventually, and I'd prefer it to be a disease than a hired sadist masquerading as a boat salesman."

Jeanette placed the phone face up on the table, waiting for something from Simon, and ordered the special—scallops in an herb butter sauce. When the server plunked the plate down in front of her, Jesse glanced at it and held up his hand to stop Jeanette from stabbing into it with her fork. He called back the server and gestured to the plate.

"My compliments to the cookie cutter," he said.

"Beg pardon?" the server replied. She looked confused.

"Not scallops," he said. "Some kind of cheap white fish cut into circles. Maybe skate. Old trick but rarely so obvious. They're all exactly the same size."

"I'll get the manager," said the server, whose hands were beginning to shake.

"Ten dollars says there's a big old skate wing back there with a bunch of round holes in it."

"The manager," she repeated and turned to scurry off. Jesse stopped her before she could get far.

"No manager," he said. "Just take that mess away and bring this lady a nice piece of halibut or something, plain, no gloopy sauce, all in one piece. Not your fault. You'll still get a good tip."

The waitress scurried off as Jeanette checked her phone, and then looked up at Jesse.

"Are you trying to take care of me? Please don't."

"I'm not your dietitian, but you've got to draw the line someplace," Jesse said.

"Heaven forbid," Jeanette said. "Chaga? If you were my dietitian, I'd have to shoot you."

CHAPTER NINETEEN

They drove slowly past the boatyard in the dark, looking for a way in. There was a chain-link fence running along the road and the gate they had driven through that afternoon was padlocked. On a second pass, Jeanette pointed and said, "There."

A billionaire's motor yacht was tied up in the nearest slip to the road. It was so long that its stern extended beyond the end of the fence. No lights were on inside.

"If it's unoccupied, we can go around the fence, make it onto the bow, back up to the dock, and go from there."

"And if it's occupied?" asked Jesse. "How well do you swim?"

"Very well," Jeanette said.

They parked off the road to wait.

"I wish one of us smoked," Jeanette said. "In the movies people sitting in a car waiting for something always smoke."

"I never smoked," Jesse said.

He turned on the radio. Country music. He turned it off again.

They sat in silence.

At 12:40 they moved. They left the car along the edge of the road on a gravel patch in front of a warehouse, a block past the boatyard, and walked back to where the motor yacht was tied off. Jesse went first, moving around the edge of the fence.

People with this much money should find better uses for it, thought Jeanette. No one needed a boat this size. Given her experience with a little johnboat when she was a kid, Simon's lobster boat later, and witnessing vacationing yachters, she knew that the happiness that could be derived from a boat was inversely proportional to its size. She slipped behind the fence and caught up as Jesse made a quick, graceful leap onto the bow of the boat, landing almost silently. The boat dipped from the impact and set off a small ripple in the black water.

"Your hands," he whispered to her, and she contemplated the five feet between the edge of the water where she was standing and the bow. It was not a leap she could make, not anymore.

"Trust fall," Jesse said. She looked at him quizzically.

"Reach up as high as you can and fall straight back toward me. I'll catch you."

"You're kidding," she said.

"If a bunch of middle managers at Amazon can do it, so can you. They call it team building."

Jeanette turned away from him and stood as close to the water as she could get, thinking, If I don't crack my head open on the side of the boat this could work.

She took in a breath, raised her arms, closed her eyes, and let go. She felt his hands grip her under her arms as she fell backward, and he hoisted her onboard. They did not speak. Keeping footsteps light, they hopped off the yacht, onto the dock inside the boatyard, and approached the *Jeanette*.

A light flipped on inside the yacht and they froze. In a moment a man with a flashlight emerged from the cabin and began moving to the bow. Jesse urged the two of them behind a post and then pulled Jeanette down behind a plywood life vest storage cabinet that was located halfway down the dock. Peering around the edge, she could see a second figure, a woman in a robe, emerge from the cabin door, waiting fretfully for a report. She reached behind her and flipped on lights, illuminating the entire boat. A billionaire's money pit, but a beautiful one. The man was dressed in boxer shorts and a T-shirt that failed to conceal a substantial belly. What hair he had was a wiry bird's nest on top of his head. The woman was less distinguishable but looked younger, rail thin, and composed by comparison. Always the way, thought Jeanette.

The fat man shone his light all around the bow, looking for evidence of any kind. Apparently, he found none.

"Musta been some big fucking bird," he said. "Or some damn thing."

"Should we call the police?" his companion asked. Their voices bounced off the water.

"Not calling the cops on a pelican," he said. "Let's go back to bed."

No one had seen a pelican in Rhode Island in decades, but neither Jesse nor Jeanette cared to comment. They stayed where they were until the couple retreated to the cabin and turned out the lights. It was quiet again.

They resumed their trek to the *Jeanette*. When they reached the boat, Jesse climbed on board and held his hand out to Jeanette. She stepped lightly on board.

He moved quickly to the live well and tipped up the lid as she shined the light from her phone on the rim of screws that went all the way around the perimeter. He unscrewed them one by one, placing each one into her open palm. When the last one was out, he took a small jackknife from his pocket and pried up the edges of the well. It popped out easily and he lifted it out of place.

The piece they had removed resembled a deep white tray, about three feet wide and six feet long, certainly large enough to hold quite a few pounds of elvers or a dozen or so lobsters, but not as deep as it should be. The real well dropped all the way to the deck. It might have held two hundred pounds of lobsters or more. Jesse took the tape measure from his other pocket and measured the depth of the false one he had just prized out of place and compared it to the real one.

"Eleven inches," he said quietly. "There was eleven inches of something beneath the eels."

"Something he wanted to keep dry," she said, now whispering. She pointed to the underside of the tray he had removed. A rubber seal ran around it.

"Okay, put it back."

"No way," said Jeanette. "It's a souvenir. Besides, we're gonna need it."

"You're gonna get yourself killed," said Jesse.

"Maybe," Jeanette replied. "Maybe not."

Jesse looked at her with curiosity. He drove the screws back into place without replacing the tray, closed the lid, and the two of them retreated, Jeanette carrying the false-bottomed live well in her arms.

"We can't make it across that yacht a second time," he whispered.

"I can swim," Jeanette informed him. "I told you."

"You'd be soaked the whole ride back," Jesse said.

She stepped halfway down a ladder off the dock, and slipped the live well into the water.

"Boat ride," she said. "Get in."

"The two of us will swamp that thing," he said.

With graceful dispatch he removed all his clothes, including his underwear, socks, and shoes. Jeanette averted her eyes. Jesse bundled his clothes into a neat pile and flipped them silently into the floating live well. Then he slipped silently into the water and steadied the thing against the dock.

"You get in," he said. "I'll help you keep your balance in the water."

Jeanette let herself down, hoping her weight wouldn't plunge the makeshift boat too deep into the water. It was close. Jeanette's knee was barking at her. Still, she balanced herself well enough.

Naked, kicking, he guided her ashore. He paused to look longingly at the hull of the billionaire's fancy toy boat.

"Wish I had my brace and bit," he said. "This yacht could benefit from a few good-sized holes in the hull."

"Next time," Jeanette said.

They clambered up the bank beyond the marina fence. Jesse jostled the live well into the back of Jeanette's Subaru, dressed leaning against the car, and slipped into the passenger seat. Jeanette got into the driver's seat.

"What do you think he was carrying under the well?" Jesse asked as she drove. "Pills? Guns?"

"Where would he be carrying them to? In a lobster boat?"

"Canada," Jesse said. "Canada has gun laws, fireworks restrictions, and all of that. And they don't have the same taxes on cigarettes."

"Fireworks? Cigarettes? What's the margin on smuggled cigarettes? I bet he couldn't fit more than a hundred cartons in there, and it's a lot of fuel to get to Nova Scotia."

"Pills, maybe?"

"It doesn't feel like him," Jeanette said.

"Well, then, elvers and what?" Jesse asked.

"I don't know. But if we live long enough maybe we'll find out."

"I intend to live," Jesse said. "At least for a while."

"I'm not taking anything for granted," Jeanette said. "But I intend to find out."

***

Lester Birdwell heard back from his contacts at the DMV and the state comptroller's office late Friday. He called Tommy B. and told him what he'd learned—that there was no Maine driver's license bearing Bennett Tyson's name, and that the one Big Otis had collected was a convincing forgery.

"Otis didn't like to to slam into the guy's Mustang on purpose. He fancies himself a pretty good driver."

"He's perfect at ten miles an hour on a John Deere," Tommy B. said. "I wouldn't vouch for anything beyond that."

"Well, the license is a phony. No one named Bennett Tyson has paid state or real estate taxes in Maine in the last five years."

That was all Birdwell knew. And, of course, the ballot initiative was going well but was in need of support.

"So, if he doesn't exist, who is he?"

"I don't know."

"Well, we can talk about your initiative once you figure out Bennett Tyson's story," Tommy B. said. "That's the guy I want."

"Tommy, I've done my part, and made a good faith effort on your behalf. Now I think it is only fair if you do yours. For the fishing people of Maine."

"It ain't the thought that counts," Tommy B. growled. Lester Birdwell opened his mouth to respond but there was a click on the line and Tommy B. was gone.

THE LOBSTER

When the lobster first met Simon King, Simon was still married to Jeanette and the lobster was six inches long. The lobster had spent the morning of their first meeting inside a wire cage with a mesh bag containing the heads of three Acadian redfish. He had shared the cage and the redfish heads with a peekytoe crab that came and went through the funnel-shaped entrance every half hour to attend to some important business on the seafloor. At one point a massive four-pound female lobster with a notched tail entered the cage, and the crab and the small lobster cowered in the corner while she greedily pinched and shoveled bits of redfish head into her scissored mouth, acting as though her two companions were not even there. Her large claws, used for hunting and fighting, lay idle while the little pincers at the end of her front feet tore off little morsels. Then, for no apparent reason, she left. The crab and the small lobster waited for a few minutes, then slowly returned to the bag of heads.

When the cage abruptly levitated, the crab ran from one side to the other, then back again, and then folded itself still in the corner to wait it out. The lobster flipped its tail and shot backward toward the funnel but missed, and then having felt the solidity of the wire wall, lay flat against the floor, claws raised, till the piercing light and dry air was all around him.

A yellow rubber-gloved hand reached in, removed the crab, and tossed it overboard as the peekytoe craze had not yet begun. The yellow-gloved hand returned and grabbed the lobster by the carapace. The lobster extended his claws and reached as high up and out as possible, tempting the aggressor's poor judgment, as though to say, "Stick some part of you in here. I dare you." For a very short moment, the lobster and the bearded man eyed each other.

"Catch ya later," Simon said as he tossed the lobster back into the water. The lobster, snapping its tail for propulsion, jetted down, down, down till it reached the bottom and backed under a piece of stone ledge edged by urchins. Its descent was followed by the *plop*, *plop*, and *plop* of the three old redfish heads slapping the water and drifting down with clouds of rotted fish bits billowing around them.

The lobster spent a good deal of time in wire cages on the seafloor. Not because it was trapped, but because in these cages there were bound to be mesh bags filled with things that delight and nourish a lobster. Not only heads of Acadian redfish but also herring, delicious oily bunker, and even, on especially lucky days, the heads of small tuna or freshwater carp, which, although they had been frozen, were very appealing and exotic to a Maine lobster.

The lobster came and went through the funneled opening as it pleased. All the lobsters did. The crabs too. On occasion, the lobster happened to be in a trap when it levitated. The lobster never got used to it, and each time it would flip its tail to jet backward, smash the cage wall, and then hunker down on the floor. Sometimes the glove was yellow. Sometimes it was blue. But after the light and the dryness, there was always a glove. And a face. And then *plop*—back into the water.

It was Tom Hinchcliffe's sternman who first put a lobster gauge on it. The lobster was five years old then and had been picked out of the water and dropped back in nearly fifty times already. Six of those times Simon had done it, as the lobster tended to live where Simon set his traps. It happened to nearly all the lobsters. But this time was different. The blue glove grabbed it and then, instead of plopping it back into the water, another hand placed an aluminum gauge on its back. It flinched and stretched its claws. Its carapace did not fill the gap in the gauge. The gap in the gauge was three and one quarter inches on one side and five inches on the other. A lobster with a carapace between these two measurements, so long as it had no eggs on display and no notched tail—the cut having been made by a lobsterman who had previously observed eggs on her underside—was legal to harvest. Below these measurements, it was a juvenile, and off-limits.

In this instance, Tom Hinchcliffe was not thrilled to see the sternman, his wife's niece, use the gauge. "Getcha eye for it," he said quietly but annoyed. To gauge a lobster that was only three inches at the carapace was to fail at one's job. Three and an eighth maybe, but this lobster was clearly a full quarter inch too small.

The lobster went back in the water.

A year later, the lobster met the conservation warden. It was on Simon's boat. The lobster had been eating herring when the levitation threw it into a panic. There was the light and the dryness. Then the yellow glove. Then the gauge on its back, which had a bit of wiggle room. And then, after a brief pause, the gloved hand tossed him not into the ocean, but into a tank with three dozen other lobsters. This was different. The lobster tucked itself into a corner against the sides of some of his neighbors and waited, feeling the oddly slick white floor and eyeing the walls of the tank and the other lobsters. Every now and then, another lobster would plop into the tank and scoot to the edge. Two hours later, Simon grumbled as a green boat with siren lights atop the center console approached. But he was perfectly pleasant as the warden climbed on board.

"Mornin', Officer."

"Mornin', Simon."

They talked about the weather and the big tides that had come with the new moon while she checked the lobsters in the well with her own gauge. She reached in with a blue glove, picked up a lobster, put the gauge on its back, and then plopped the lobster back into the tank. About one in ten were too small. These she threw back into the ocean, taking a little money out of Simon's pocket each time. And each time, Simon winced. She reached in and picked up the lobster that had been tossed back so many times. She felt the gauge click as she wiggled it, feeling space between the carapace and the gauge's slot. And then she tossed it back in the drink once again. Later she wished Simon a good day, hopped in her boat, untied, and motored off. Fines were not issued for a few lobsters slightly under size, so long as the lobsterman wasn't overdoing it. Notched females were a no-no. But exactly what constituted three and one quarter inches was arguably a judgment call, and everyone made mistakes sometimes. The visit was routine. But it made all the difference in the world to the lobster—for a time.

About one year later the lobster met Simon for the last time. The lobster had been eating bits of flesh from the head of a small tuna. It weighed one and a half pounds. Much of this weight was gained from the fish heads that Simon and others had purchased as bait from the co-op. Its carapace measured a full three and one-half inches. Simon didn't bother to use the gauge.

*
* *

Back at the lobster co-op prices rose, and after a long detour in a holding area protected by the bay, the lobster was moved to a bulk tank with nine thousand other lobsters. Its claws were held closed with thick white rubber bands. All the lobsters had matching rubber bands on which were printed in red ink *Taste of Maine!*

When the shot was fired, a muted thud reverberated underwater, and nine thousand lobsters flinched all at once. After pulling back, they all began reaching out with their antennae to learn what it meant.

A loud splash followed moments later. The disruption to the water sent lobsters scattering, creating a ripple effect as they retreated in a wave of concentric ovals. Then the water calmed. From the epicenter a cloud of maroon billowed and spread. Antennae waved and reached. Olfactory intelligence drifted through the tank. Scissor mouths bubbled and clicked. Then there was a slow, massive, tentative but persistent approach. The lobsters crowded toward the billowing center.

CHAPTER TWENTY

Jeanette caught about four hours of sleep after she and Jesse returned from Wakefield, and she awoke groggy and with a headache. She showered and dressed and was about to head downstairs for a late coffee when she saw Lottie Pride walking down the driveway with a gaudy bouquet in her hands. The lupines had bloomed early in spring, tall, showy pink-purple flowers, crowding out everything in their vicinity with lush color and a kind of determined, priapic pride. They spread across the untended open meadows creating blankets of color and massing along the roadsides. Lottie was clutching a dozen of them. She had no hand in flower arrangement, but these would look good almost no matter what you did to them.

Jeanette watched her from a window, thinking how incongruous Lottie looked with flowers.

She opened the front door and Lottie thrust them into her hands unceremoniously.

"I got a call from Augusta Friday," she said. "I wanted to thank you for calling the governor's office. They want me to testify. I came by yesterday, but you were gone. Thought I'd try again today."

Jeanette took a step back, confused. "Testify? That's good. And thank you for the flowers. But I haven't called anyone. Not yet." She went to get a vase and turned on the water in the sink. "You did it on your own."

"Really? I may keep the damn flowers. I can't believe they called me back."

"I can. You worked hard for it. It's the least they could do," Jeanette said.

"Probably that's why they did it. By the way, you do know your truck is running?"

Jeanette turned off the water.

"Running? Can't be. I have the keys in my bag."

Lottie shrugged. "I noticed it when I parked."

A look of trouble crossed Jeanette's face.

"Come with me?"

"Of course," Lottie said.

Jeanette plunged the flowers carelessly into the vase, grabbed the keys, and the two women hiked up the short incline to the parking area where the Mister Softee truck was humming evenly. No one was in the driver's seat. Jeanette opened the door and looked in. The plastic panels around the ignition had been broken away and the power wires and ignition wires had been pulled from beneath the dashboard, clipped, and jerry-rigged together with black electrical tape. The refrigeration unit was turned to freezing—a setting Jeanette never used.

"What?" Lottie asked.

"Trouble," Jeanette said. "Some kind of trouble. Hot-wired."

She pulled her head back out of the truck and looked around.

"Trouble where?"

Jeanette made her way to the rear of the truck and Lottie followed. She unlatched the swinging back doors but didn't have to pull them open. The body that pushed its way out at them was freezing, but not frozen. It was a man, or had been a man, and someone had lifted it into the truck, bent at the waist facing the front, so that its back and shoulders were pressing at the doors. The weight of it nearly knocked Jeanette off her feet.

It tumbled onto the gravel, a shoe falling off, a black tasseled loafer. Blood had congealed on the man's throat where it had been neatly sliced open, from one carotid artery to the other. The man had bled out and there was enough blood to streak Jeanette's left hand and the sleeve of her blouse as he fell. The left leg of her jeans was darkened all but black with it.

The head looked skyward, but the face could not be seen. Something hairy, slick black like a skunk's coat, was lying across the front of the man's head.

"What is it?" Lottie asked, panting slightly. "What the hell is that?"

Jeanette looked more carefully. "It's a toupee," she said.

The two of them stared in silence at the crumpled figure that had once been somebody—who knew who?

Then Jeanette took a stick from the ground and pushed at the blood-slicked hairpiece, knocking it to the ground. Now there was blood on her shoe. Two dead eyes stared up, still showing surprise, long after the surprise was over. The man had been heavy, nearly bald, with a fringe of short black hair running the rear circumference of the head. Jeanette knew she had never seen the face before. Taped to the man's forehead was a familiar looking piece of brown paper, ripped from a bag and bearing her own handwriting.

Joey,

I brought you a treat. Your favorite. Please get in touch. We have to talk about Simon and the money. Enjoy the sandwich.

Jeanette

"Oh, Jesus," she said quietly.

In the distance the grinding sound of a piece of farm equipment was approaching down the road.

Lottie leaned down and grabbed the man under the armpits and nodded toward his ankles.

"On three!" Lottie commanded. She and Jeanette each grabbed the corpse by the ankles and Lottie counted it off. The body was ungainly, frosty cold, but still soft. Like a steak that had been three-quarters thawed. They dragged it behind the truck, like two trainers lugging an unconscious prizefighter off the mat. Lottie was strong for all her diminutive stature. The sound of the vehicle on the road was gaining on them.

They let the body fall in the brush and stepped out as Big Otis Sumlin, perched on his old green John Deere, came around the bend. Jeanette moved in tight enough so she could hear Lottie's breathing and smell the distinct staleness of cigarette smoke on her clothes. She stuck her bloody right hand in her pocket and kicked some gravel over her shoes. Lottie wiped her hands on the back of her jeans, and slid in front of Jeanette, covering her left side, trying to hide the blood.

"Ladies," Big Otis said cheerfully, waving at the two women standing too close together. Lottie returned the wave reflexively.

"Otis," Jeanette said in as cheerful a voice as she could.

Otis slowed the tractor to a halt.

"Everything okay?" he asked.

"Couldn't be better," Jeanette said, hoping to Christ that he could not see the bloodstains. "You know Lottie Pride? She's one of my best pickers."

"Very pleased to know you," Big Otis said. "We need industrious women."

Lottie nodded. "Doing a little work on the truck," she said. It sounded pathetic.

Big Otis seemed not to notice. He took a step to get off the tractor. "You ladies need help? I'm a good man with a motor."

Lottie held up her hand. Jeanette was frozen in place.

"All done," Lottie said. "Just tightening the last bolt."

"Women fixing trucks," Otis said. "What won't they think of next?"

He reversed directions and reseated himself on the pillow that covered the broad metal seat of the John Deere.

"Well, I got miles to go. Rain coming." He slipped the old tractor back into gear. It lurched into motion; in a moment, he was gone.

The two women stood, nailed to the ground, until the sound faded, then slipped behind the truck.

"What do you think he saw?" Lottie asked.

"Blind as a bat," Jeanette said reassuringly. But she wasn't sure it was true. Just the other day, she had told Jesse that the man missed nothing.

"The next one might not be," Lottie said. "Move him back in the truck. Now."

"We should call the police," Jeanette said.

Lottie stepped back and looked at Jeanette.

"So they can find a blood-soaked lady crab picker with a corpse on the ground? And both of our fingerprints all over it?"

Lottie bent and grabbed the man's armpits again.

"On three," she said. But she didn't count. They hoisted the body back into the truck.

Jeanette, out of breath, ripped the brown paper note off the dead man's forehead and stuck it in her pocket. Together they forced the doors closed. Jeanette latched them and moved toward the truck's cab, but Lottie put a hand on her shoulder.

"Me," Lottie said. "You stay here. Clean up. Call me later."

Jeanette again moved toward the cab, but this time Lottie stepped in front of her and stopped her cold.

"Me," she said again. "You're not taking any chances. Take a bath instead. Burn your clothes. Shoes into the reach. I'm telling you."

She stepped around Jeanette and got into the truck, which was still humming calmly.

"Keys," Lottie stuck out her hand. Jeanette gave them to her.

"Where are you going?" she asked as Lottie slipped into first gear.

"Jesse," Lottie said.

"Wait, Jesse?" Jeanette said. "I thought you said you didn't know him."

"I said I didn't know an indigenous person named Jesse Ed Davis," Lottie said. "Danny Nearinsky and I were in fifth grade together."

She peeled away, leaving a neat black quarter moon on the road. Jeanette, trying to sort through it—the unknown dead man and the complete confusion about who Danny Nearinsky might be—heard the snap of shattering plastic from under one of the rear tires as Lottie pulled out. When the truck disappeared, she looked on the ground. There was a mangled black name tag lying in the gravel. She picked it up and turned it over. The black plastic had splintered, but the name was still legible on the front in raised gold plastic letters: MICKEY KEEGAN—IT'S A MIRACLE.

***

Jeanette let herself into the house and placed Mickey Keegan's name tag on the kitchen counter. Then she retrieved the note on brown paper she had left for Joey. "We need to talk about Simon and the money." She saw now that they must have taken the note to mean that she was a part of it, whatever it was.

She looked down at her clothes and saw Mickey Keegan's smeared blood darkening her blouse and pants. She took a short, sharp intake of breath and instantly the room began to spin. She held on to the counter to keep her balance, but something was taking over. Her throat tightened; her mouth went dry.

She stumbled upstairs and climbed into the shower fully clothed, turned on the cold water, and let it pour down on her, on her clothes, on Mickey Keegan's blood. She saw it swirl around the drain and recalled seeing such a thing before—*Psycho*, at the summer drive-in down by the co-op, where they showed old movies once a week. She tried to speak out loud, but words wouldn't come—her voice was gone. She stripped off the clothes, left them in the tub as she scrubbed herself until she was rubbed raw.

Wrapped in a terry cloth robe she raced dizzily to the bedroom where she threw herself on the bed seeing the vision of crabs crawling all over her, and then just the blackness her closed eyes afforded. She tried to breathe, and felt she couldn't, even though she knew breath was entering and exiting. Eventually, and she couldn't tell how it happened, she was asleep. When she awakened not twenty minutes later, she thought, I must bleach the clothes properly, but it was hard to get up off the bed.

After she had begun the heavy stain cycle in the machine, she moved down the dock, her shoes in a mesh bait bag along with a decent-sized rock. She climbed into her boat, started the motor, and went full throttle to the middle of the reach. She dropped the bait bag into the water and watched as it slowly sank. As it faded into the dark water, she thought about calling Toland for help. The boat rocked listlessly. The shoes were gone. But she continued to stare into the darkness. How could she ask him to keep this to himself? He had taken an oath. And if it didn't ruin his career, it would eat him up inside. Protect the young, she thought. She'd failed at it before.

She spun the boat around and motored home. Finally, she sat again at the kitchen counter. She fished around in the junk drawer and pulled out a half-burned purple candle that had been there for years. She lit the wick and melted the bottom, fastening it to a saucer from the drainboard.

"A prayer for you, Mickey Keegan," she said, bowing slightly to the flame. "I am so sorry."

She watched the low, burning candle.

"I'm sorry we never met face-to-face." And she leaned in to blow it out but stopped herself. She picked up the note she had left for Joey and held it to the flame. The acrid, pleasant smell of waxy smoke and burning paper filled her nostrils.

"Goodbye, Joey," she added. Then she made a drink and stood at the counter. There was a knock at the door, and she felt the panic surge in her. She peeked out the window and was relieved to see Lottie there, pacing, smoking. She unlocked the door and let her in.

"I'm sorry it took a while," Lottie said. "I had to stop for cigarettes."

"Are you okay?"

"Recovering," Lottie answered, dousing the burned-down cigarette with the kitchen faucet and going to the stove to light up another. She circled into the room and dropped into a chair in the dining area. "I've done a lot of things for a lot of causes, but I've never delivered a dead body before."

"Thanks. I don't know what I would have done."

"Jesse has the truck, by the way. He seemed to know what to do with it. You want to tell me what this is all about? Who was that man with the toupee?"

Jeanette explained the trip with Jesse to Wakefield. Lottie shook her head bleakly.

"So," she said, "a dead man in your truck. And a psychopath on the island. We're in a spot."

"I'm glad to hear you say 'we,'" Jeanette replied. "But you don't need to do more than you've already done. You didn't sign up for any of this."

"I did not, it's true. In fact, I warned you."

"I had a panic attack," Jeanette admitted, "The whole nine yards. It's been years. I took a shower with my clothes on."

"Tobacco is good for that," Lottie said. "It calms you down."

Jeanette shook her head sadly. She didn't know how to smoke.

"For now, just sit with it," Lottie said. "Jesse will be back. Just have to wait."

"Jesse. Jesse. So you did know him? What did you call him—Danny something?"

Lottie looked away and set the cigarette down on the saucer that now lived on the end table. A plume of smoke twisted across her face.

"I shouldn't have done that," she said. "Not at that moment."

"I don't understand."

"I didn't know how to handle it."

"Didn't I ask you—"

"You did. You asked me if I knew a tribal member named Jesse Ed Davis and I said no. But that's not his name and I didn't know why you wanted to know, and so I . . . I was . . . guarded. And he's not Native."

"Wait. What? He's not Native?" Jeanette demanded. "How could that be?"

"The thing is, you and I, we didn't really know each other much yet," Lottie said, ignoring the question. "And you were talking to the guy in the red Mustang. I didn't know your angle. I'm sorry. I shouldn't have let it go so long."

Jeanette sighed. "You're right. You shouldn't have. What else do I need to know that I don't know already? Who is he?"

"Daniel Nearinsky," Lottie said. "His parents founded that commune over on Cape Herrington."

"The lunatics who pick up our crab guts for fertilizer?" Jeanette asked. "Isn't it some kind of a cult?"

"Some people say that," Lottie said. "Either way, Danny never wanted to be one of them. Not even as a kid. So, he invented himself. Can you blame him?"

Jeanette stood up and walked toward the front door, moving slowly. She opened it and looked out into the darkness. There was not much moon, and no sound from the reach. No breeze either. Calm everywhere—the water, the air. She closed the door and turned back to Lottie.

"I actually wish he was here now. Pissed as I am."

"I'll stay," Lottie said.

"You don't look much like a bodyguard," Jeanette replied. "No offense."

Lottie took the last long drag and exhaled smoke through her nose toward the fireplace.

"A woman killed Custer," she said.

"I beg your pardon?"

"Buffalo Calf Road Woman. She was Cheyenne. And when he was dead, she spiked his ears with an awl so he would be a better listener in the afterlife. Then she wore his sword for the rest of her life."

Jeanette looked at Lottie and waved her hand at the smoke in between them.

"I'm not her."

"You might be more like her than you know. You're molting. Like a lobster. Or a crab."

"Just because I'm the crab lady doesn't mean . . ."

"Tarantulas do it too. Probably painful; once you've shed the old shell, you've got none until the new one hardens around you."

"Soft-shells. Shedders," Jeanette said.

"You can be eaten alive. But when the new shell does harden, you've got space to grow inside it. And the new one is harder than the old one."

Jeanette stood up and went to the mirror. She looked at her reflection. She'd lost weight, had no appetite, and needed her hair cut, but somehow it seemed to her that Lottie had a point. She tried to picture Buffalo Calf Road Woman standing over Custer's dead body, jamming an awl through his ears and into his brain. She didn't feel ready for that.

"I don't know," she said. "I just know the minute I understood what had happened to Joey Pizio I knew what I needed to do."

"Well," Lottie said. "You need to be listening to that."

Lottie stubbed out her menthol and examined the filter end.

"I've always wondered," she pondered, "whether Buffalo Calf Road Woman took any personal pleasure in driving stakes into Custer's head. I've always chosen to believe that she found it very satisfying."

"Maybe," Jeanette postulated. "But maybe she just needed to get the job done."

CHAPTER TWENTY-ONE

Lynne Framer was at the lobster co-op when it opened on Monday morning. Her husband, Barton, had returned that week to their rental to check up on the progress of their home under construction. It was going well, but then on Saturday they'd had a fight about flooring—reclaimed heartwood pine versus pre-stained larch. After a bottle of merlot and some half-hearted makeup sex, they were ready to celebrate with a lobster dinner, but the co-op closed on Saturday at three thirty. Lynne had driven out to the dock and couldn't believe that a place that thrived on tourism and needed her goddamn dollars would not be selling lobster on a Saturday evening. Or on Sunday. But Monday morning they were open. The idea that the lobster co-op was a co-op for fishermen, not weekenders, had never occurred to her.

"I'm glad you're finally open. Two please," she said to a wiry man in rubber overalls. "One and a half pounds."

"Yes, ma'am," he said cheerfully and picked up a double thick paper bag, white with blue-and-red lobster images on it. *Taste of Maine!* was printed on the side. He put on a thick blue glove and walked toward the bulk tanks. They didn't get a lot of retail customers.

Lynne followed. The lobsters were clustered thickly in one section of the tank, like ants covering a pile of spilled honey. He reached in and picked up a lobster from the edge of the mass, shook it once, and dropped it in the bag. Then he reached in and grabbed the lobster that had first met Simon nine years ago. It was at the center of the great mass of lobsters. The lobster flipped its tail and raised up its banded claws. Lynne Framer noticed that there was a shred of denim hanging from its front leg pincer, but she didn't care. She wanted her lobsters. The man in the rubber overalls dropped it in the bag with its companion. Four still eyes peered into the moist darkness.

The man weighed the bag on the scale at the far end of the tanks, swiped Lynne Framer's credit card in the machine next to the scale, and handed her the bag, the card, and the receipt.

As she walked back to her car, he paused and looked back at the wriggling mass of lobsters. He had never seen them cluster like this before and wondered what it was about. As the car door closed, he picked up a broomstick with a nail in it that they used to move packed crates of lobster around in the tank. He poked the broomstick into the mass of lobsters, and they scooted just out of the way of the wood. He saw a little bit of blue fabric waving in the water. The back end of the nail hooked on to something soft but heavy at the bottom of the tank, and he pulled it till it rolled over. The lobsters dispersed, revealing what little was left of their prize. The clothes had been shredded by thousands of little scissor mouths, and much of the flesh was gone as well. The frenzy had been indiscriminate. Not all that much of Bennett Tyson remained.

*
* *

Big Otis had gotten the call at a little after eleven in the morning. This was not something that could be made to go away. An oxy addict who can be said to have died on a creek bed was one thing. An unmistakable gunshot victim in a lobster tank at the co-op, no matter how little of him was left, was quite another. It was not lost on him that this was the guy with the bad driver's license. Big Otis wondered if he should call ex-governor Birdwell and consult but sat on the impulse. He heard his own father's voice in his ear: "Don't stir it, it'll stink." Words to live by. He'd said it to Little Otis a hundred times if he'd said it once. But it was a little late for that. The story would be on every TV screen up and down the coast by midafternoon.

The workers at the co-op had gathered quickly around the tank when the body was discovered. After a short discussion and a vote by acclamation, they had packed most of the nine thousand lobsters in crates and loaded them onto the first truck that arrived. No one in New York or Boston needed to know what the lobsters had been feeding on. Lobsters will eat anything, including each other, so what difference did it make? By the time they called the police there were about eight hundred lobsters left in the tank with Tyson's remains—just enough to have done the damage, not enough to cut too deeply into the weekly take when, inevitably, they would be destroyed or released.

Toland excused himself for a moment after the body had been identified and called Jeanette.

"I gotta be quick," he said. "It's a circus over here. But you need to know this. Bennett Tyson is dead."

"What? Are you sure?"

"Dead as the last nail in a coffin. They found him in with the lobsters, all et up. Not clear yet what happened, but it seems he was shot first."

Jeanette was silent.

"Jeanette?"

"I'm here."

"Okay. Are the women working up at the crab shack?"

"Should be," Jeanette said. "I haven't been. Lottie's here with me."

"Well, get the two of you up there where you'll have some more company—and some witnesses. I may be a while. I'll stay in touch."

At the crab shack, where Patsy and Amelia were hard at work, Lottie took her seat silently. Jeanette followed. It had been only a little over twenty-four hours since the discovery of Mickey Keegan's corpse, and now Bennett Tyson?

"Where's the truck?" Patsy asked as Jeanette settled at the table.

"Muffler," Jeanette said. She began to pick. Busy hands, she thought. Manual therapy.

* * *

At the end of the preliminary investigation, which took until well after the sun was down, Toland thought to check the day's receipts, and he found that Lynne Framer, the woman he had taken in after Joey Pizio's death, had been the first and only retail customer of the day. He shook his head sadly and turned to his partner.

"Guess she's not gonna fall in love with the island," he said. "We better pay a visit."

Back at the Framer's rental house, the lobsters went into the pot alive. Thirteen minutes later, they came out. The exact time of death would have been hard to certify.

Lynne loved lobster but had always felt bad about boiling them alive. This time was especially hard for some reason. She had waited so long for them and now felt so guilty. Barton was amused by the strange combination of appetite and shame and felt himself stirring as he watched her. Maybe it would be hotter tonight than last.

As they sat down, the doorbell rang, and Barton rose to see who it was. Lynne could not wait though—the melted butter might get cold. She plucked a piece of lobster meat out of the elbow below the claw and greedily swallowed it, as Barton greeted two police officers with some apprehension.

Lynne looked down and noticed, at the end of one of the lobster's small legs, close to its mouth, the little pincer clutching at something flat and translucent. She picked at it with curiosity. Its curved edge was oddly familiar. As Toland and Bert stepped into the living room, she prized it out of the little pincer at the end of the lobster's leg and held it up to the lit candle that she had put on the table in hopes of a romantic atmosphere. She stared at it and her breath stopped. Beyond a doubt, it was a human thumbnail, yellowing and bitten down, flesh still clinging to its underside. She dropped it onto her plate and saw the rubber band securing the lobster's large claw and the brightly printed message there: *Taste of Maine!*

She ran to the bathroom and threw up.

*
* *

Lester Birdwell had had the same impulse as Big Otis—to call and find out what the old man knew. But, like Big Otis, he sat on it. Instead, he put in a call to Tommy B., who was sitting down to a dinner of leftover McRibs and mashed potatoes.

"Tommy," he said. "What the hell happened down there?"

"Hell if I know, Governor. Guy got eaten by hungry lobsters—that's a new one on me."

"I thought someone shot him and threw him into the lobster tank."

"I heard that too," said Tommy B. "Hard to believe."

"Only one man I know with a pistol," said Birdwell. "I saw it on my desk."

"Stop kiddin' around," said Tommy B. "That damn thing hasn't shot anything in years except rats. Nothing I like more than shooting rats at sunset."

"This guy was kind of a rat," Birdwell said. "Bad driver's license and all."

"Not that kind of rat! The ones with fur and a skinny little tail. That's the ones I shoot. I don't shoot people, even the ones I don't 'specially like. Lucky for you."

Birdwell took a breath. Just for effect. Then, sensing that he had knocked Tommy B. just far enough off balance, he turned on the voice he once reserved for campaign conversations with widows and mothers cradling babies in arms.

"Tommy, Tommy," he said. "I don't think you did this. I would never imply that to anyone. But just the same . . . I would like to see every man working in your syndicate put a signature on the petition for the ballot initiative. It's good for them, God knows. And it'll keep away the competition—we'll be too powerful to challenge. When it passes, I'll be worth my ten percent. I do want my ten percent now. I mean, you wanted Bennett Tyson gone, you asked me for help, and he's gone. Maybe I shot him."

"You couldn't aim good enough to blow your own brains out," Tommy B. said. Then, after a pause, he continued. "You'll get your signatures."

Tommy B. pushed the little red button on his iPhone and dropped it into his pocket.

"Son of a bitch is gonna get his ten percent, too," he said to his dinner.

***

A little after nine that evening a pair of headlights reflected off the front windows of the house and the sound of a truck engine woke Jeanette, who was dozing on the sofa. Lottie was in her usual chair, having declined to go home. They looked at each other and froze.

"Mister Softee," Jeanette said and got up to open the front door for Jesse Ed Davis.

"Citizens," he said. "Got her all clean. Lottie Pride, what are you doing here?"

"Standing guard, I guess," Lottie said. "In my sleep."

Jesse moved to the kitchen and lit the burner on the stove. "Chaga?"

"Did you hear?" Jeanette asked. "The lobster tank?"

"The whole world did. May we assume that Thurston Harney is on a killing spree—for reasons not entirely understood?"

"We may," Lottie said.

"What did you do with Mickey Keegan?" Jeanette asked.

Jesse began to heat the water in the pot.

"An innocent man dies," he said, "for no reason at all. It happens all the time. And there's no death, really. It's just the transference. One collection of organic matter is placed in the earth and becomes sustenance for other, less complex collections of organic matter who will one day go through the same process and give themselves up. Only humans think of it as death."

"No matter how we think of it, we all still try to avoid it. The porcupine ran as fast as he could."

"Fair."

"So could you cut the crap and tell me what you did with the body?"

"There are sacred burial grounds in numerous places in this historic state," he said. "And then there are places that are very close to the sacred burial grounds. They are not sacred and not frequently visited because no one seems to know where they are."

"And?"

"And there are very good chemical solvents; their existence will ultimately hasten the extinction of the human race, but sometimes they are necessary for cleansing blood and other substances from people's working vehicles."

"And?"

Jesse reached above the stove and took three mugs for the Chaga.

"Say something. Jesse! For God's sake."

"Here are your keys," Jesse said, placing them on the kitchen counter.

"Typical Nearinsky," Lottie said. "Man of mystery."

Jeanette closed her eyes and breathed deeply. "That's right. Nearinsky," she said. "Lottie tells me your name is Daniel Nearinsky. And you're not Native," Jeanette said.

Jesse nodded slowly, taking them both in. "I never have claimed to be."

"You sure *acted* the part!"

Lottie snorted to suppress a laugh. She and Jesse exchanged a glance.

"What? Am I crazy or something?" Jeanette asked.

"No, no. Not crazy. Maybe a little racist."

"Definitely racist," Lottie chimed in.

"I just thought . . ."

"Lots of white people see some guy," Jesse cut her off. "He tells the truth, he's able to sit still, has good posture. And he's got long dark hair and olive skin and a big nose. They think he's Indigenous. If a

Passamaquoddy kid grew up and became a Hollywood agent, everyone would be shocked to find out he wasn't Jewish."

"Also could be racist," Lottie said, sipping at the Chaga Jesse had brought to her. "Or antisemitic, maybe?"

"I was thirteen," he continued. "I had a naming ceremony instead of a bar mitzvah."

"Why would you do that?" Jeanette asked.

"Contrary to what you might have heard, growing up the Jewish child of communist vegetarians in rural Maine isn't all it's cracked up to be."

CHAPTER TWENTY-TWO

The lobster co-op was unlit except for an all-night flood that was aimed down at the parking lot, spilling out onto the water, where the lobster fleet bobbed in eerie silence. As Jesse and Jeanette approached the parking lot, he asked if she'd gotten any response from her call and text to Simon.

"Crickets," she said.

He nodded. "And Officer Toland Bates?" he asked. "What does he know about Mickey Keegan?"

"Nothing," said Jeanette.

Jesse nodded again as they pulled into a parking space where the lobstermen left their trucks.

"Wise move," Jesse said. "I'll come in with you. You don't want to be alone in there."

"It's better if you stay," Jeanette said. "Keep an eye on what's happening out here. You see something, text me."

"Okay," Jesse said. "Don't linger."

Standing outside, in the nighttime salt air coming off the harbor, she somehow felt stronger. In the house, she had begun to feel like a trapped animal, on the receiving end of whatever came. Out here in the open, it was as if the tide had shifted. She was not afraid, although it occurred to her that perhaps a wiser woman would be. Maybe her new shell was hardening. But something had snapped. She was done waiting and seeing.

She made her way to the shack where, during business hours, Billy Willig kept watch over the dock and the co-op. She slipped inside, pulling on a pair of latex gloves she had taken from the first aid kit at the crab shack. She used the light from her phone to look around. There were three keys hanging on hooks inside the door. She took them all. It was quiet on the water, and her eyes had adjusted; the half moon and the stars would be sufficient. She killed the light, made her way from the shack to the exterior stairway, climbed quickly, and tried the keys. The second one let her in. The place was eerily cavernous when empty and dark. She didn't need the keys for Tyson's office; as she suspected, yellow tape was plastered across the wide-open door. The disassembled pieces of Tyson's dead bolt had been neatly left on a side table by the police. She slipped under the yellow tape.

Once inside she turned her phone light back on and went to the cheap metal filing cabinet in the corner—three drawers. They were stuffed haphazardly with file folders in something resembling alphabetical order. Simon King was in the middle drawer.

She removed it and opened it on Tyson's desk. Invoices, some expenses for fuel and supplies. Handwritten notes, each note with a date, tabulating something. She recognized the handwriting, which she had not seen in years, except for his signature on the occasional alimony check. Another pang. Some other handwritten notes were scribbled in the margin. Question marks and calculations. Maybe in Tyson's hand. A penciled-in circle was drawn around a single name on the page: *Elmer Swetman*. She hunted for anything that would point to some other kind of merchandise besides eels but found nothing. She was beginning to turn pages, sure that it would be somewhere, when she heard the ping on her phone and simultaneously saw the red-and-blue revolving lights on the road—a cruiser approaching. Jesse had messaged her:

Cops arriving.

She turned off the light on her phone and cleared the desk, grabbing Simon's file. The cop car turned in at the driveway and came down the hill to the parking lot. Jeanette watched it idling, thankful that Jesse's truck was just one of a half dozen that were always parked in the lot overnight. In the dark, she made her way back to the file cabinet, closed all three drawers, and crawled into the space under the desk, pushing the rolling chair out of the way. She crossed herself, though she would never be able to explain why. Evangelical guilt from her youth in Christian summer camp, maybe. But it was a Catholic gesture. Still, best to be on the safe side. She quickly texted Jesse back:

Think I'm secure. Watch for me.

Two policemen came up the stairs and swung open the unlocked door to the offices. They shone flashlights around the large, empty room.

"Open door must have set off the alarm," one of them said. "Billy didn't lock up."

"Every village needs its idiot. I'll write it up," said the other. "Likely the wind blew it in."

"Best check the offices," said the first one.

Office doors opened, then closed, footsteps getting closer. She held her breath. Then the door to Tyson's office opened and one of them was in the room. A flashlight lamped around, the beam reflecting off the glass door. She could see heavy shoes on the floor through the gap in the legs of the desk. Be silent. Just don't be here now, she thought. Let Ram Dass figure that one out. Then there was a light on her face.

"Ma'am?" It was said quietly, almost decorously.

The cop got down on one knee and peered under the desk. Jeanette took a sharp intake of breath. She was face-to-face with Toland Bates. She held a finger to her lips. Toland stared at her, his face a picture of confusion. But after a moment he stood again, left the room, and shut the door behind him.

"Clean as a whistle," he said. "Dunno what it was."

She waited until the two had departed and she heard the car take off. It took her quite a time before she could unlock her right knee and extract herself from beneath the desk. She made her way back to the truck.

"You waited long enough," Jesse said.

"Isn't that what you've been trying to teach me? Stillness? Patience?"

"I expected to see you led out of there in zip ties."

"Toland covered for me."

Back home, her heart still pounding, she considered pouring a brandy, but there was work to be done. She heated up the Chaga instead, added some maple syrup and half-and-half, and opened the Simon King folder on the kitchen counter, trying to make sense of Simon's cramped handwriting. Each page had a list of names and locations, small towns up the coast, and the amounts paid to various eelers for various weights. According to the sheets, when they did all the calculations of ounces to pounds and rounded out the funds disbursed, Simon was paying a dozen or so eelers $2,500 for every pound of elvers. It all seemed in order. There was nothing indicating that the business was anything but elvers. It didn't make any sense. She looked again at the name with the penciled circle around it: *Elmer Swetman*. Next to it, Tyson, or someone, had written *Only a hundred*.

"That's something," Jeanette said.

Jesse nodded. There were other tabulations she could make no sense of. She had no idea what it meant, but maybe Elmer Swetman—whoever he was—might.

***

The two FBI agents had grilled Otis Sumlin Jr. for just over two hours before they drove off in their black car. They had not been impressed, and the chief was in a foul mood when Toland Bates stepped into his office.

"You wanted to see me?" he asked.

"Not especially," Little Otis said, "but I'm lookin' at you."

Toland stood silently.

"What do you know about a man named Thurston Harney?"

"Just what I told you before all this happened, Chief. Bert gave him a speeding ticket, Wisconsin plates, the car smelled like Roundup. Pizio died with Roundup in him. With all due respect, sir, you didn't want to hear it."

"With all due respect," Little Otis repeated, skeptically. "He's our man now, and the Feds want to 'assist.'" He uttered the word with complete contempt. "You ever know them to 'assist' without making a mess of everything they put their hands on?"

Toland remained silent. He hadn't known the Feds to do anything at all on Caterpillar Island ever before, and doubted the chief had either. Besides that, it seemed to him that the chief had done most of the screwing up unassisted.

"Get on the computer and find out what you can about the guy."

"Well, he done a stretch in Waupun," Toland offered. "That's a penitentiary in Wisconsin. Manslaughter. Could be murder—I don't know how they do plea bargaining out there. Never been."

"How do you know even that much?"

"I looked it up in the system back when, sir."

"You showed initiative."

"Yessir," Toland said.

"Never do that, you hear me? Unless I tell you to."

"Yessir."

"Now I want you to show some initiative here."

"Yessir."

"If it ain't broke, you ain't lookin' hard enough. And send Bert Gantry in. Feels like I've got a force full of fools, starting with him."

Toland nodded, thinking to himself, Fish stink from the head.

* * *

At eight A.M.—almost three hours into his day—Keith Fulbright closed the door to the shipping container where he kept his tools, crossed the creek, walking on exposed rocks, and knocked on Jeanette King's door. She jumped, whipped her head around, and was deeply relieved to see Keith's face peering in the window next to the door. In the few days since the discovery of Bennett Tyson's body—or what was left of it—every unexpected sound caused her body to jolt in one way or another. Her fearlessness at the co-op seemed a long way away.

"Coming," she shouted, getting up from the sofa, where she and Toland were sharing a morning coffee. She had thanked Toland more than once for ignoring her looting of Bennett Tyson's office and had been trying to explain the confusing data she had found in Simon's papers. Sensing her anxious state, he had spent the night on her sofa.

Keith smiled when he saw them.

"Word's all over the island," he said to Jeanette. "You've been keeping company with two young men. Do they know about each other?"

Toland looked down, embarrassed.

"Very funny," Jeanette said. "They've been looking out for me since Joey died. And now this with the lobster tank . . . I've just been on edge and living alone . . . you know."

"Usually a pretty quiet island," Keith said. "Been ungodly noisy so far this spring. Officer Bates, you must be earning a lot of overtime."

"Not sure it's worth it," said Toland. "I'm pretty worn down. What happened to your hand there?"

Keith held up his left hand. It was bandaged in a way that allowed only his thumb and pinky to move.

"That's the damnedest thing," Keith replied. "I's riding on my mower Sunday morning, caught my wedding ring on a bird feeder, and pulled the darn thing right off."

"Your ring?"

"Not hardly. The finger."

Jeanette grabbed the edge of the sofa.

"You lost your finger?"

"Can't say I did. It was right there in the lawn. Easy to find since I just trimmed it. The lawn, that is."

"Good Lord," Jeanette said. "I hope they were able to reattach it. They can do miracles now, I know."

"They can. Well, they said they could. Insurance would cover it too. But then they said no using my hand for six weeks. And then physical therapy for another three months to get it to work right. I told the doctor never mind. You can keep it. I don't have three months. I'm sixty-eight. Don't know how much longer I'm gonna be able to climb a ladder. Gotta get back to work."

"But Keith—"

"It's okay," Keith said. "It's not like it was a thumb or anything."

"But . . ."

"Never mind the finger. I just come to tell you—the Framers have gone off and fled. I'm building a house for nobody."

"They're gone?"

"Spooked," said Keith. "If I was a summer person I'd be spooked too. A lot of these people here, they don't like them's from away, but I do. I count on them."

"I don't mind them generally," Jeanette said.

"Well, you sell crabmeat to them. And you're one of them."

"I am not. Born and bred in Maine."

"They say your parents come from New Hampshire," Keith said.

"Four and a half miles from the state line!" she protested.

Keith shrugged. "That means away to folks here. I mean, if a cat gives birth in the oven, it don't mean the kittens is biscuits."

"I consider myself a biscuit," Jeanette said.

"Have it how you like it," Keith said. "The Framers say they're gonna buy a ski chalet in Vermont. He says to me, 'Vermont and Maine, what's the difference?' I like to hit him in the head with a shovel when he said that, but he was talking to me on the phone. We'll work out a deal soon as I'm not mad at him."

"Keith! We'll be neighbors."

"I already got a house," said Keith. "Lived there since forever, and I like it. Caroline likes it. But if you know anyone who wants to buy a half-built house . . ."

"I'll keep an eye out," Jeanette said.

***

That afternoon, Toland found himself called to a conference room at the police department in Bangor. There was no place as big on the island or even in Brockton. There were a half dozen Federal men, and the entire police force from Brockton itself, and the island. Even so, the table was only half full, and spring flies were using it as a landing strip. Over the years there had been enough spilled sweet coffee so that the residue interested them. Toland snatched one out of the air successfully, but the rest continued to buzz and hum.

The Fed at the top of the table stood up and the room quieted down—except for the flies.

"This will get to local outlets and social quickly, so I wanted all of you to be aware of the information we've received. Thurston Harney is dead. His rental car was found still aflame outside the county zoo, in Wauwatosa, west of Milwaukee. Firefighters doused it at three A.M. this morning, Harney was found inside. The metal Amex card in his wallet ID'd him. In case there are any media inquiries, I'm handing out a statement to each of you and you are to keep your comments to what's in the statement. That is all."

The core of officers nodded gravely as the Fed took a stack of papers from his briefcase and started to hand them down the line. Toland waited his turn.

"If there are no questions, you all can get back to work," The Fed said. Toland read the statement. He needed to get out of there and call Jeanette.

CHAPTER TWENTY-THREE

He reached Jeanette from the car on the way back from the meeting.

"Who in the world wanted Thurston Harney dead?" Jeanette wondered aloud.

"Probably lots of people. I mean, you and me to start. And Jesse."

"But who in—where did you say?"

"Wauwatosa. It's a good question," Toland said.

"Why though?"

"Must have made someone real mad, I guess. Maybe someone was close to Tyson? Anyway, it's good for you they're both gone."

Jeanette had her first full night's sleep in weeks. The next morning, she got in the car and headed north along the coast. It was a cloudless day, and the news of Thurston Harney's demise combined with bright sun and blue sky burned off some of the residual dread that had settled around her. There was something to be said for just putting some distance between herself and her surroundings.

Elmer Swetman lived in a mud-brown single-wide, not far from the water on the edge of a town called Billington. It was the southernmost spot on what appeared to be Simon's route along the coast in search of unlicensed elver trappers. The poor, dilapidated hamlet had a general store, a street lined with unpainted saltbox houses and trailers, untended yards, and a pair of churches that flanked the store. According to the ledger that Jeanette had taken from Tyson's office, Simon was paying Elmer Swetman at the rate of $2,500 a pound for his catch, though Swetman had only a few ounces to offer at a time. Sometimes only an ounce, for which he would receive $156.25.

Swetman had dogs, which made Jeanette's approach to the front door noisy. They were chained up but began to howl like banshees as soon as she got out of the car to make her way across the small yard, which was littered with outboard motor parts and rusting red gas cans. The dogs were so fearsomely noisy that the door of the mobile home opened before she reached it and a stooped man, about seventy, Jeanette guessed, appeared in a sleeveless undershirt, canvas slacks the same muddy brown as the outer walls of the place, and bare feet. What there was of his hair hung over his forehead, and he wore a pair of glasses too big for his desiccated face.

"Help you?" he asked, his jaw working on a slug of tobacco.

"Looking for Simon King," she said.

"You too," he said without affect.

"I beg your pardon?"

"I had something for him," Swetman said, "but I couldn't keep 'em."

"Elvers," Jeanette said.

"I'm not saying anything," Swetman said. "I don't know who you are or what you want."

He gestured inside where she could hear the TV blasting away at too high a level. Swetman was no doubt losing his hearing as well as his hair, and God knows what else.

"I'm missing my programs," he said. "What do you want with Simon King?"

"I'm his wife," she said. "Just looking to find him."

"Can't help you there," he said. "Going back to my programs."

He turned and began to walk back inside; she followed him uninvited. The screen door slapped shut, but he didn't seem to notice she was inside. The place stank of sour sweat, wet dog fur, and musty clothes, and there was no light except for what the TV's shifting images threw on the wall.

"Mr. Swetman," she said. He ignored her. Or didn't hear her. "Mr. Swetman," she repeated, practically shouting. He turned and looked at her, apparently unsurprised that she had invited herself in.

"Last fella came to see me," he said. "He bought me lunch, at least. And a supply of Captain Morgan's spiced, kept me for a week or two. That's sippin' rum, you know. Not like some of these. Got some flavors to it."

"I could manage that," Jeanette said, "if you'll talk to me."

Swetman looked at her for a long time, and finally went to turn on a table lamp to get a better view. He squinted at her and flicked off the TV from the remote in his hand.

"Married to Simon King," he said. "Might not be much fun."

"It had its moments," she replied. "Why don't you come out with me? Get a little fresh air. Show me where the liquor store is."

Swetman looked toward the kitchenette at one end of the place.

"Well," he said, "I could maybe use a refill. Maybe something to eat. Money's kinda tight since your man took off on me."

"That makes two of us," she said. "Maybe we can help each other."

"I'll need to put on some shoes."

First stop was Rooster's Liquor and Convenience, where Elmer Swetman picked out a plastic handle of Captain Morgan's spiced rum and carried it to the cash register.

"I don't know why they call the place Rooster's," he said. "Ain't seen a rooster in Billington since I was half grown. Nor a hen, neither."

At the register he had the cashier add a half dozen nip bottles of Fireball Cinnamon Whisky and Jeanette paid while Swetman carried his loot to the car. Then he directed her to a Shell station down the highway where he bought a bucket of fried chicken from the attached convenience mart, which he carried to a picnic table behind the place. The chicken was dry and oily, but Jeanette dug in with what she hoped looked like enthusiasm. Swetman had transferred a few of the nip bottles of Fireball to the pocket of his canvas pants and set them on the table in front of him. He took three and pushed a fourth at Jeanette.

"You paid," he said.

She smiled, twisted open the tiny bottle and slugged it, feeling the burn all the way down her gullet where it hit the chicken at the bottom. It was not a pleasant feeling. But gaining trust was important.

"So," she said. "You sold Simon elvers."

"'Nother fella came by here some time ago, wanted the same information." She tried not to look interested. "I told him what I'll tell you. The man had a nice boat. Swept in once a week regular, paid me a hundred dollars an ounce. I tried to have a few ounces at least, but you know fishing—you never know what you'll get. And setting the traps, well—it's hard on the knees. My knees anyway. Ain't what they were."

"A hundred dollars an ounce," she said, nodding blandly. Only a hundred. That's not what the margin note in the ledger said. It was easy to figure. If the ledger said $156.25 an ounce, it meant Simon was stealing a little more than a third of the money that Bennett Tyson was fronting him to buy elvers. Week in and week out.

She looked across at Elmer Swetman, who was wrestling with a chicken wing that had got stuck in the gap where a couple of his teeth were missing, and her heart sank. Stealing it from Tyson was one thing, but stiffing this poor, dying specimen of a man? A man who took what he could get from the man in the nice boat. The *Jeanette*.

Swetman managed to wrestle the chicken wing into his mouth.

"Good?" Jeanette asked.

Swetman shrugged. "It'll make a turd," he said, and polished off the third nip bottle.

"Do you want some water?" Jeanette asked. "You could probably use some water."

"I got what I need," Swetman said, now sounding a little more expansive and woozy. "But you need to eat more chicken. You're all skin and bones."

She tried to smile. Elmer Swetman was all skin and bones. She took a drumstick, hoping the dark meat might be less dry.

"Did the price go up or down ever?" She worked hard, trying to swallow. Her hope had been misplaced. The drumstick meat was like rope.

"For the last three years it was a hundred dollars. I heard about folks getting more last year, but Simon's the only one buying here."

"This other guy who came by asking," Jeanette said, and let it dangle there.

"Drove a fancy red car. Expensive sunglasses. Very important fella. At least to himself it seemed like he was. What else you need to know?" Swetman asked.

"What else don't I know that I should?"

"He asked me about the price too. Asked me a whole lot of questions. God's truth, I don't get to talk to a lot of folks these days. It's mostly me and my programs, a little fishing, talking to the dogs, and whatever I can get to eat and drink. You ever have those sardines in a can? That's good eatin' with some Triscuits. You can make a meal out of that. You wouldn't want to drive me to the general store, would you?"

"Sure," Jeanette said. "I'm buying."

Fifty-six dollars an ounce, she thought. That would have kept this man in Triscuits and canned fish all summer. Of course, there would be dog food to consider, but still.

***

As Jeanette was treating Elmer Swetman to spiced rum and chicken wings, Jesse Ed Davis received the call he'd been waiting for. Kat Rutherford wanted to know if she could come see him.

"We can meet," Jesse said. "But there's a third party who needs to be there."

When Jeanette had returned from her trip up the coast, Jesse briefed her on his visit to the meeting about the ballot initiative, and the call from Kat Rutherford.

"Birdwell's behind it is my guess," he said. "She wants to come see me. It can't be a coincidence—Tyson in the lobster tank, Thurston dies in the rental car, and then the phone rings. I told her I'd meet her if you'd be there."

"Then I'll be there," Jeanette said. "Have you ever been to a little town called Billington?"

"There's a good spot for chanterelles there. Behind the old grange building."

She shook her head.

"I drove up there and met one of Simon's suppliers. Simon was shorting him every week and the guy didn't even know it. He thought he was getting a fair price. I had to buy him a chicken dinner from a gas station and a bottle of Captain Morgan's to get him to talk. And a bunch of Fireball nips. Then he made me eat. And drink. And now I feel like I swallowed a safe."

***

They met the next afternoon in a sports bar in Brockton. It was two P.M. Jeanette had her customary gin and tonic. Jesse ordered a Lone Pine. Kat looked up at the mirrored surface behind the bar and read the special cocktails of the day.

"What's a Fat Ass in a Glass?" she asked the bartender who had come over to take their order.

"Same as a Sombrero," he replied.

"A Biddeford Martini," Jesse added.

Kat looked at him quizzically.

"Allen's Coffee Brandy and cream—about half-and-half."

She shook her head.

"What about the Burnt Trailer?"

"Allen's and Moxie," Jeanette explained.

"One to one," the bartender confirmed.

Kat sighed and asked if he could make her a rye old-fashioned. The bartender went to look it up in a book.

"I work for Governor Birdwell," she said as they waited for their drinks.

"The ex-governor," Jeanette said.

"He still likes to be called Governor Birdwell," she said.

"I'm sure he does," Jesse said.

"He likes a little elegance in his office. He was looking for an assistant. And I'm the great-great-granddaughter of Rutherford B. Hayes, who was president of the United States, which gives him a little history to hang on to."

Jesse looked at the ceiling for a moment.

"I think you're not," he said. "I doubt the arithmetic even works."

"Maybe I missed a generation," Kat replied. "Great-great-great?"

"Maybe," Jesse said. "But I don't think so."

"At least you thought about it," Kat said. "Everyone else just believes it."

"That doesn't surprise me," Jesse said.

"So, Ms. Rutherford," Jeanette interjected. "You decided to reach out." She looked at Kat Rutherford, waiting.

"That night when Jesse came up to me in the parking lot he said, 'I'm your friend in this.' I remember the phrase exactly. I didn't need a friend then. But a few things happened. I thought maybe we could become friends now."

"The man in the lobster tank," Jesse said.

"And the one in the car fire," Jeanette added.

Kat shifted in her chair. The drinks arrived. The bartender put the old-fashioned in front of Kat and she grimaced a little—it had a big, unwelcome sprig of mint sticking out of it. She picked it out, placed it on a napkin, took a large slug, and looked over at Jesse and Jeanette.

"I have information," she said. "I thought maybe you could use it."

"For what?"

"The ballot initiative and the man in the lobster tank. They're connected. And connected to some powerful people."

"I don't doubt it," Jeanette said.

"You don't doubt it, but you can't prove it," Kat said. "I think I can." She finished her drink in one more solid gulp and lifted her glass to the bartender.

"No mint this time please," she said, pleasantly. "Thanks just the same."

"There's a picture of it in the book," the bartender said, a trace of apology in his voice, as he stepped away to the other end of the bar.

"No self-confidence," Kat said to Jesse and Jeanette.

"But you've got quite a bit," said Jesse.

"Look, I think the governor is getting funding for this initiative from an international corporation, which is illegal. And I think it's all connected to the dead man in the lobster tank. And maybe the burnt man in the car too. Because the international corporation is in the elver-buying business and the man in the tank was the competition. I have it all on my phone."

"Your phone?" asked Jeanette.

"I record the meetings on my phone. The boss is too self-involved to even notice."

Jeanette looked at Kat Rutherford carefully. "I'm impressed," she said. Kat tipped her drink glass in acknowledgment.

"Why would you do that?" Jeanette asked.

"If the governor's head was served to me on a plate, I wouldn't weep. Or eat it," Kat Rutherford said bitterly. "But if he went down, at least I'd have my life back."

"We'd all like our lives back," Jeanette said.

"But I'm actually going to need to build a new one. Ten thousand dollars would be a start."

Jesse frowned.

"Money?" Jeanette said, looking over at Jesse with annoyance.

"So you've got something on Birdwell and Bennett Tyson, you want us to pay for it—if it's so terrible, why not blackmail the boss?" Jesse asked.

"Believe me, it's crossed my mind. But I'd rather see him go down than buy me off and get to stay up."

"Ten thousand dollars," Jeanette scoffed. "What do you even have them saying?"

Kat recounted what she had learned.

"Innuendo," Jesse said. "Suggestions."

"What do you want them saying?" Kat asked with annoyance. "'Ahem, I'd like to initiate an illegal international conspiracy, and have someone shoot a poacher and feed him to lobsters'? People don't talk that way in an office. Not even the governor."

"Ex," Jeanette said with annoyance.

"If we were going to pay you for this information, we need proof there's a real link," Jesse said. "A smoking gun."

Jeanette turned on Jesse. "You'd really consider paying this woman?"

"No compromise in defense of Mother Earth." Jesse shrugged.

"Sounds like the definition of compromise to me."

"Listen," Kat interrupted, clearly uncomfortable being talked about. "I can make sure it will work. Think about it." She placed a business card on the bar. "You know how to reach me." She emptied her second drink, picked up the mint sprig between her thumb and forefinger, tossed it into the empty glass like a dart. She stood to leave. "But don't think too long."

CHAPTER TWENTY-FOUR

Jeanette took herself to Bea's Hive of Beauty for her usual shift the next day. She spent a good part of the afternoon thinking about Kat Rutherford, the Korean connection, and the ex-governor. After she'd done her last dye job, she asked Bea Wilbur for a favor. Bea owned the place, and was not only a cutter and stylist, but a makeup and makeover adviser—the only one in Brockton. Jeanette declined to have her hair colored, but she did buy the rest of the package—foundation, powder, blush, eye shadow, and even a little lipstick. Bea spoke lovingly of her own accomplishments as she applied the masks and moisturizers one after another. Jeanette felt like she was being pampered and tortured all at once. But you had to dress for the occasion. The big money lived in Compton Harbor.

"You look ten years younger," Bea practically squealed at the end of the session. Jeanette elected not to smack her.

She had not worn makeup in years; she had sworn off it long before Simon left. She hated it, it took time, and there didn't seem to be any point. Tearing it out of the budget hadn't hurt either. Typically, she felt she had all the strength she needed without it. But today, maybe it would help.

When it was all done, she soaked her hands, taking advantage of the heated paraffin wax bath that was usually reserved for clients, checked herself in the mirror, stuck her tongue out at the tarted-up image that looked back at her, and departed. She drove to Compton Harbor and up the long winding road, past the mansion-sized cottages soon to be fully occupied for the summer by the descendants of the elite. She turned in at Sung Ho Han's driveway. She had never actually met the man or seen the view from on high.

Sung Ho's manservant–cum–boat captain Blake met her at the door.

"Whom shall I say is calling?" he asked.

"Tell him it's his former competition," Jeanette said.

The young man looked puzzled. She shrugged at him.

"Either he'll come down or he won't," she said.

Alone in the room, she looked around and spied a starkly framed lithograph on the wall that appeared to be an artistic rendering of a page of S&H Green Stamps. Rising and walking to it, she saw the signature at the bottom: *Warhol.* Very American. It brought up some resentment in her mind. Her grandmother had collected Green Stamps every time she went to the supermarket, pasted them into books, and redeemed them for several important kitchen gadgets, including a Waring blender that now sat in Jeanette's own kitchen. It annoyed her that the most famous of all hip downtown New York culture heroes had taken it into his head to make fun of the things people once lived by, painting them and pretending they were art. Campbell Soup, Brillo, and now this. It fortified her in her burgeoning and somehow pleasurable hostility toward her host.

Sung Ho appeared moments later, his untucked charcoal chambray shirt perfectly draped on his lean frame. He looked impervious to all things. He held out a hand and led her into the cavernous living room.

"You're welcome here," he said, "but do I know you?"

"I'm the crab lady," Jeanette said. "I used to drive elvers for Bennett Tyson."

"Ah," said Sung Ho. "Please. Come in. Can I offer you a Moxie?"

"Moxie?"

"The official soft drink of Maine. As you no doubt know."

"I do know. But it isn't very subtle of you."

"What do you mean by subtle?" Sung Ho asked, cocking his head quizzically. Most guests in his grand house treated him with some level of deference and pretended, at least, to appreciate the ways in which he might be striving to fit in.

"Imagine this," Jeanette explained. "I'm working in Seoul, and you come to my place for a meeting, and, because I want to fit in, the first thing I do is I offer you a snack of kimchi." Sung Ho's brow furrowed in thought. "And dog," she continued.

Sung Ho frowned.

"That is culturally insensitive," he said calmly. "Why is eating dog something every American cannot seem to avoid thinking about when thinking about Koreans? I do not eat dog."

"I wouldn't mind if you did. I pick crabs for a living. And I eat them. Somewhere, someone's probably got one as a pet. It's all relative. But I don't drink Moxie."

"It is an acquired taste," he admitted.

"If I were drinking something for the taste, I'd have a chocolate milkshake. Gin is a taste worth acquiring."

"Gin I like very much," Sung Ho said.

"So, we have something in common besides eels," Jeanette said.

Sung Ho paused and cocked his head sideways again. "Can I offer you a gin and tonic?"

"Please. Beefeater if you have it. No lime. No fruit. And not much tonic either."

It was after six. Sung Ho nodded at Blake, who scuttled off to where Jeanette imagined a kitchen might be.

"Truthfully," Sung Ho continued, "I am relieved to not be participating in a Moxie charade. It is somehow both too bitter and too sweet at once. But it is only my intention to honor the local culture. This place can be, frankly, very closed to outsiders. Koreans in Korea are no different, by the way. In any case, I would much more enjoy a gin and tonic. And an honest conversation. To that end, I must tell you, I was sorry to hear about your boss."

"Thank you," Jeanette said. "But he wasn't really my boss. We had a deal. I would have thought his demise would make things easier for you."

"Me? First of all, it was an awful thing. I didn't know the man, but it was really tragic. And I'm sorry. And it certainly doesn't make things easier for me—or harder. I work for Bando International. We buy from licensed eel fishermen and ship to Seoul from Bangor. Mr. Tyson, rumor has it, was buying and selling on the black market. He meant nothing to my business. I was just sorry to hear what happened."

The drinks arrived—an unadorned gin and tonic for Jeanette and another with a small wedge of lime for Sung Ho, who sipped it and sighed with satisfaction. Jeanette stirred hers once with her index finger and took a decent slug.

"Well," Jeanette said. "That's a relief. He had his eye on you. And your business." She watched Sung Ho closely. "I thought maybe you'd had him killed."

Sung Ho put down his drink and looked her in the eye.

"I don't take kindly to that accusation," he said. "If that's what it is. I don't know who you are, but I would be extremely cautious if I were you. Any suggestion to anyone else that Bando, or me, or any of us were involved in this would be—"

"Inadvisable," Jeanette said. The first buzz was hitting her.

"To say the least. And actionable."

"Actionable like a car fire in Wisconsin?" Jeanette saw creases appear across his forehead. It's a start, she thought. She took another drink.

"Well," she said, "somebody wanted Bennett Tyson dead. It wasn't a domestic dispute I don't think—not right next to a lobster tank."

"My good woman, why on earth do you think I would be involved in this? Why are you even asking me about it?"

"Bennett Tyson was quickly becoming your biggest competitor, with a buyer in Changwon called Kang Brothers. He had two associates that I know of. One was named Joey Pizio. He was killed. Probably tortured and killed. The other was my ex-husband. He's not been seen in almost a month. Disappeared. And then there was me—I was driving the eels. But then Mr. Tyson himself was killed. Two dead, one disappeared. And then, the man who killed Mr. Tyson goes back to Wisconsin and gets killed himself. Small comfort. That leaves only me—the last woman standing. Again, small comfort. I think I'm entitled to find out what I can. Wouldn't you want to do that?"

Sung Ho was silent for a moment. Taking it in. "I didn't know. I am sorry. That must be very traumatic. And yes, I might want to find out," he said, finally. "I *would* want to find out. And, again, I'm sorry for what must be a very unsettling set of circumstances that you find yourself enduring. But I would not be quick to suspect a highly respected international corporation with branches in thirty-two countries of stooping to the killing of an unimportant elver scofflaw in coastal Maine, nor of his associates. It doesn't make any sense."

"Okay. Well, I guess I'm relieved to hear that. Though I'd like to know what's going on. Any ideas?"

"None whatsoever," Sung Ho responded, eyeing her with some hesitancy. "I'm sorry. I truly know nothing about this."

Jeanette stood and walked to one of the windows that overlooked the water.

"I've never seen a place like this," she said. "A view like this. All from eels, is that right?"

"Not really," Sung Ho said. "Originally built, bought, and paid for by dry goods, a century ago. Profits well invested in things like railroads. Then private banking and money management. And yes, now eels."

"What's the going rate?" Jeanette asked. "As long as I'm here I thought I'd ask."

"For elvers? This is proprietary information, as you can imagine." He seemed almost relaxed now, on familiar turf.

"Not for eels. I already know what you pay for eels," she shot back. "What's the going rate for a ballot initiative?"

Sung Ho started, and then stared at Jeanette. He slowly opened his mouth to speak but Jeanette cut him off.

"You are funding it, I gather."

"This is an absurd conjecture," Sung Ho stammered. He was out of smooth answers.

"Not too absurd. It would probably double your profits. Bando would like that, and they'd like you for it. Though I don't think foreign corporations are supposed to fund ballot initiatives. And I don't think voters would like it either if they found out."

"This is the second groundless accusation you have made against me in the course of one gin and tonic," Sung Ho responded, regaining his footing. "Are you driven by racial animus? Many in the state are."

"I don't believe I'm one of them." Jeanette smiled. "There was a time when this country welcomed foreigners with open arms."

Jeanette felt like she had a fish on the line. Not played out but starting to weave a bit aimlessly.

"Personally, I say you are welcome here. Open arms. But you know, the Native people welcomed foreigners," she said, tightening the drag a bit. "They were the original elver fishermen. It didn't work out well for them. And after that, people fought their way in, prospered, and then tried to slam the door behind them—not exactly the same thing."

"I don't want to fight about immigration history," Sung Ho said. "Or any government policy. We abide by the laws and regulations of the state, such as they are. They change from time to time. If Question Two appears on the ballot and passes, we may benefit. If it doesn't, we will continue as we have, and still prosper." He said it almost as though he was reading from a press release.

"That sounds very agnostic of you." Again, she watched him closely. "But I'm curious about how you and Lester Birdwell know each other. And Gary Kell, who took your trucks off the road and then left his job to head up the initiative for Question Two."

At Lester Birdwell's name, Sung Ho closed his eyes, and as she mentioned Kell and the trucks and Question Two, they opened and darted around the room as though looking for a way out. Sung Ho's jaw began to work but at first, no words came out. "You presume too much," he finally said, weakly.

"Well," she replied, "I'm drinking gin, not Moxie, and in vino veritas, as they say."

"I'm afraid I have no Latin," Sung Ho said flatly. "And you are, frankly, out of your depth."

"I'm licensed in scuba," she responded.

"Blake?" Sung Ho called. The young man appeared instantly. Apparently, he was a bouncer in addition to whatever else he was.

"You may show this lovely lady out."

Jeanette held up her hand and Blake hesitated.

"It's all right," she said calmly. "I won't bite anyone."

"Blake."

She drained her drink and held out the empty glass in her hand. Blake stepped forward and took it.

"No need to get excited," Jeanette said. "Sorry I disturbed your evening. I appreciate the drink and the view. I'll be going."

***

Less than an hour after Jeanette left the hilltop in Compton Harbor, Sung Ho Han had Lester Birdwell on the phone.

"We need to talk," he said. "In person."

Birdwell was already at home, with a Scotch and bitters in his hand and a masseuse waiting for him in the bedroom.

"Okay. How is tomorrow afternoon? I'm free after two."

"Right now would be best."

"Now?" he asked. "I've got things to attend to."

"It won't be a long conversation," Sung Ho said.

Birdwell sighed, but Sung Ho sounded serious.

"Where's this meeting supposed to take place?"

"My car is a half block north of the front door of your house," Sung Ho said.

"How will I know which is your car?"

Sung Ho closed his eyes in frustration. "It is the only Mercedes-Maybach on your block."

He rang off without waiting for a response. Birdwell drained his drink, normally a sipping matter. Then he went into the bedroom, where the masseuse was filing her nails in a bathrobe, under which she appeared to be naked.

"I'll pay you for an extra hour," Birdwell said. "Just got one little thing to take care of."

She did not so much as look up at him. "I've got a client at nine thirty," she said.

***

"We have a problem," Sung Ho said as Birdwell took in the interior of the Mercedes.

"You should see my car," he said. "Red leather, trimmed in black. I think you'd like it."

Sung Ho ignored him. "You know, I assume, of Mr. Bennett Tyson, and his recent discovery in the lobster tank?"

"What of it?" Birdwell asked, nervousness mixing with annoyance.

"A local woman named Jeanette King came to see me. First, she gently accused me of killing Mr. Tyson, then, when she realized that was ridiculous, she told me she feared for her life and seemed to be asking for help. And she started asking about the ballot initiative—the funding specifically. She mentioned you and Mr. Kell by name. She seemed to imply that she knew we were behind it. I don't know what she's intending to do."

"I never heard of her," said Birdwell. Sung Ho's even tone was getting on his nerves.

"I just wanted you to know," said Sung Ho, "that she may make trouble in some way. If she does, Bando won't be tied to any of this. The money flowing to fund the initiative will vanish if we sense it jeopardizing our reputation. My reputation. You need to take on this situation, calm things down, make this go away. Quietly. With extreme discretion. You've got connections, you know people. Put it to bed. Quickly. Don't do anything rash."

"I never do anything rash," Birdwell said, annoyed, but doing his best to cover it. "I'm honored that you came to me."

Sung Ho's demeanor changed. He suddenly seemed pleased.

"Don't be honored," he said, smiling deeply. "Just be helpful."

CHAPTER TWENTY-FIVE

The next day Lottie Pride came into the crab shack early. She found Jeanette already picking. They greeted each other and Lottie went to work in silent concentration.

"I've got something to tell you," Jeanette said. "I went to see Sung Ho Han at the end of the day."

"You what? You drove up there?"

"He got very uncomfortable when I pressed him about the initiative," Jeanette said.

"Wait. I can't believe you went there."

"I was thinking about Custer. So, thanks for that."

"What happened?" Lottie put down her crab knife and the half-picked carcass that she had been manipulating in her hand.

"You should have seen his face when I asked him about the initiative."

"I wish I could have."

"He denied everything," Jeanette said.

"I bet he did. Personally, I consider him a war criminal."

"You might be right," Jeanette replied.

The door to the crab shack opened and Patsy Hinchcliffe pushed her way in, followed by Amelia.

"Morning," Patsy said. "Busy little beavers, up early, catching the worm." The conversation died.

Jeanette and Lottie worked and watched as Patsy rattled on contentedly, knocking off one crab after another, leaving Jeanette in the dust. Lottie kept her head down.

"All over the TV," Patsy said. "Lobsters take revenge. Lobster bites man, man bites dust. Like to see Big Otis cover this one up. Even a town supervisor don't have that much power."

"That horse left the barn," said Lottie "Guy who did it burned up in a car in Wisconsin."

"Little Otis'll try to convince the TV people that the man in the lobster tank died peacefully in his sleep. Blood everywhere."

"Please," Jeanette said. "My stomach."

For a moment the only sound in the shack was the quiet clacking of the knives. Then Patsy said, "I don't know, though. He and his father done it with Tom."

"Who done what?" Lottie asked.

"Big Otis. And Little. When Tom Hinchcliffe died. He was my husband's first cousin. We all grew up together."

"I didn't know that," Jeanette said.

"I said died, I should've said kilt. No way Tom Hinchcliffe gets stuck in his own rigging without some help. Been on the water since he was littler than a lobster himself."

Jeanette put down her knife and the little shelled carcass in her hand.

"He was . . . what?" Jeanette was sure she had heard right, but she wanted more. And Patsy didn't usually need prompting.

"You can imagine," said Patsy, "Big Otis don't want publicity on the island. So that'll never come to light. But it has to be so."

The other two women had not so much as looked up. And Patsy was still working, her large fingers moving with the supple dexterity that Jeanette had envied for years. Apparently, they'd heard all this before in one form or another. Outlandish rumor was one of Patsy's usual stomping grounds. Conspiracy theories kept her entertained, and TV was full of them. She might as well have a few of her own. No doubt Bennett Tyson's death was at the top of her list for this season's entertainment.

"Tom had a heart condition, I'll give you that," Patsy said. "All I'm saying is that whoever done it knew he had a heart condition, which, of course, everybody knew. You know how it is—you fart on this island and everybody in town opens their windows just to clear the air."

Jeanette waited. Simon had known Tom Hinchcliffe, and she had met him a few times. She had heard that Tom had a bad heart and was too stubborn to carry a sternman with him anymore. It had never occurred to her, or anyone as far as she knew, that foul play was involved.

"Ladies, I'm sorry," she said. "I just am not feeling well." It was a bad excuse, but the truth was worse. She was feeling the beginnings of a clutching in her gut again. And sweat began to break out.

"Don't tell me we're gonna talk about cramps again or hot flashes or whatever they are," said Amelia. "I'd rather talk politics. And you know I don't talk politics."

It came. The wave, worse than before. Jeanette took one deep breath, couldn't take another. Her head got light, and then she was physically dizzy and couldn't feel her feet planted on the ground. She groaned once, uncontrollably, and pitched forward onto the table covered with tiny bits of crab exoskeleton into a deep purple-and-black void.

***

The hospital room was in Augusta. Jeanette opened her eyes having no idea how she had gotten there. But she recognized where she was. All hospital rooms look alike. She knew them well, and there were no rooms she hated or dreaded more. They were where you landed after they had dismantled you. She had sworn she'd never see the inside of one again, not voluntarily, and a rage rose up inside her as her eyes darted around the room.

She looked above her bed to the left, following the cursed tube that was secured to her forearm. She was on an IV drip but nothing more complicated than that, unless there were meds in the bag. Then she looked across the room. There was a policeman sitting in one of the two vinyl-upholstered chairs and a man in a cheap black suit in the other. The clash of colors between the cop's navy blue and the aquamarine of the chair's upholstery should have been enough to bring her fully alert, but she had no idea who these men were, and fully alert wasn't a place she wanted to be. She was alone and unprotected.

"Gentlemen?" she said weakly.

"Jeanette King?" asked the plainclothes one.

"That's right," she said. "At least I think that's right."

"I'm Detective Barnes, from the Rhode Island State Police," he said, flashing a badge quickly. "This is Officer Bolton."

Stay groggy, she said to herself. Groggy.

"Rhode Island?" Her voice was timorous and soft. "Aren't we in Maine?"

"We are," said Detective Barnes. "But it's a little matter of some suspicious happenings in Wakefield. The boatyard there. We'd never approach you in the hospital, except we need a little help."

Jeanette shook her head slowly.

"I don't understand," she managed to say.

"Man gone missing," said Officer Bolton. "Man by the name of Mickey Keegan."

"I'm afraid I still don't understand."

"I'll take it from here," the plainclothes one said to Bolton, who promptly clammed up. "A man named Mickey Keegan, who owned and operated Miracle Boats in Wakefield, Rhode Island, has disappeared, foul play suspected."

He waited. Jeanette waited.

"But," she said finally, "aren't we in Maine?"

"Seems he was selling a boat," Barnes said. "Last person on his list for the day was a woman named Lynne Framer."

"Lynne Framer?" asked Jeanette.

"According to our investigation she has an address right next door to you. But when we swung by, the place was still under construction."

"Lynne Framer," Jeanette said again. "I think they have multiple homes—the Virgin Islands, Colorado, or something like that, I'm sorry. I'm just so groggy."

"Of course," said the plainclothes cop, Barnes. "The thing is—it seems your husband owns a boat that was for sale down there. It has your name on the stern. *Jeanette.*"

"Husband?" Jeanette asked, sounding bewildered. "I have no husband—I lost him years ago."

"We were hoping you could tell us where he is."

"I lost him," she repeated. "Didn't I say that?"

"We understand. If I show you a picture of someone, you think you could tell me if you know who he is?"

"It would be a miracle," she said dreamily.

"It is a picture of a man we saw by the marina."

"I thought you said Lynne Framer. That's a woman. They might want a boat. Summer people, you know?"

Barnes rose stiffly, trying not to show his irritation, and signaled to Bolton, who produced a photograph from a leather folder that had been lying on his lap. Jeanette stared. It was blurry, like a single frame from a movie. A well-built man stood with an upside down fake live well covering his head. Aside from the live well, he was stark naked.

"Who's that?" she asked, looking away and toward the window.

"That's what we'd like to know. Thought maybe you'd seen him around with Mrs. Framer. You know, around the house or something."

Jeanette just shook her head, which she then let fall back on the pillow.

"He's only wearing a box. On his head. Why would a man with a box on his head spend time at my neighbor's construction site?"

"We don't know what that means," Barnes said.

"I don't know what you're saying. Aren't we in Maine?"

"I'm sorry if you found it distasteful," Barnes said.

"He looks good to me," she said. "He does." She was grateful that Jesse wasn't standing guard over her in the hospital.

"Excuse me, what's going on here?"

The voice came from Lottie Pride, who had just poked her head in the door, and, seeing the cops, had pushed her way in with authority.

"Can I help you, gentlemen?"

"I'm sorry," the plainclothes cop said. "Who are you?"

"A friend." Seeing them unimpressed, she added, "I'm also Ms. King's attorney," with an emphatic thrust of her hand at the cop who took it and shook it warily.

"You're not questioning my client without an attorney present?" Lottie asked. "When she's under sedation?"

"These men have been very kind," Jeanette said. "Lottie, really. They just need information."

"You *need* to respect the law," Lottie said. "You know she's sedated. Inadmissible. Do you have a warrant?"

"Now stop that, Lottie," Jeanette said, slurring her words slightly. "Please."

"We're only here for help," said Barnes. "It's not any kind of a formal proceeding, Miss . . ."

"Pride. Lottie Pride."

"She's too knocked out to help anyhow," Bolton, the uniformed one, said.

Detective Barnes put a card into Lottie's hand and gestured for Bolton to rise. He then turned to Jeanette. "Thanks for trying, Ms. King. We really do appreciate it."

He nodded and touched her blanket, and he and Bolton departed.

Lottie stood in the doorway watching them go, and then moved to the window to watch their car drive away. Then she turned to Jeanette.

"Can you move?" she asked.

"I'm fine," Jeanette said, suddenly sounding completely clear. "But they didn't need to know that. What am I doing here?"

"You collapsed," Lottie said. "Patsy called the ambulance, and I rode in it with you. I called Jesse, told him to guard the house. We're in Augusta. You were bleeding internally—I guess the pain finally got to be too much so you passed out. You woke up long enough to get into a pissing match with the guys wheeling the gurney in and the docs put you on something that knocked you out cold."

"Well," Jeanette said, "it's gone now. Get me out of here."

"What was that all about? With the cops."

"Wakefield."

Lottie reached into her purse and pulled out a Band-Aid. As she detached the IV from Jeanette's arm and fixed the Band-Aid in place on Jeanette's wrist, Jeanette said, "Rhode Island State Police today, Maine State Police tomorrow. This isn't going away." Lottie patted the Band-Aid to make sure it was properly secured. "Okay?" Jeanette nodded. "Okay," she repeated, this time not as a question. "Your clothes have gotta be in that little closet."

"You make a good lawyer," Jeanette said, "especially for a crab picker. I'm grateful." She began to dress.

"We do what we have to," Lottie replied. "I make a pretty good doctor too. Or at least I talked to one of them. I'm also your next of kin, by the way."

"Nothing surprises me," Jeanette said, pulling on clothes as quickly as she could. Her balance was off, and her gut still gnawed at her.

"No cigarettes—"

"I don't smoke," Jeanette said.

"I do," Lottie replied. "But not in your house anymore. Secondhand smoke. No more gin, no more tonic, no more Sara Lee, not many more cheeseburgers. And no stress, if you know what that means. That's what they told me, and I wanted to be the one to tell you. This is serious. They might even take a piece of your intestine if you'll agree to let them."

Jeanette stopped doing up the buttons on her denim shirt and looked at Lottie, suddenly alert and angry.

"Those bastards are never cutting me open again. Is that clear? I just want it to be clear."

"Stay in focus," Lottie replied. She kept a weather eye on the corridor as the occasional nurse or doctor moved back and forth. Then it was empty, and Lottie gestured to Jeanette to move.

"We don't have much time," Lottie said.

"Less every day."

CHAPTER TWENTY-SIX

Jeanette was at the picnic table outside the crab shack at lunchtime the next day, with a banana in her left hand. She peeled it halfway down and forced a bite into her mouth. "God, I hate bananas," she said, swallowing. The three other women laughed. She was now supposed to be subsisting on bananas, apple sauce, white rice, toast, and chicken broth. It didn't seem funny to her. But she actually felt better, which made her depressed.

"Jeanette," Amelia said, "you're sure you're feeling up to working?"

"We'll see if I cut my finger off," Jeanette said, smiling.

Now, as they sat at the picnic table, Jeanette pushed the remains of the banana, half peeled, into the trash with the crab shells. There was no way she could face consuming the rest.

"I never could stand bananas myself," said Patsy, wiping mustard and mayo off her chin with a paper napkin. She had an Italian sub from the Bread & Butter Mart. Jeanette wanted to kill her. But when an enormous, impeccably kept yellow pickup truck pulled up to the front of the shack Patsy put down the sandwich and blanched.

"What's he doing here?" she asked as Tommy B. Donovan got out of his prized vehicle carrying a small cardboard box. "Not here to buy crabmeat."

"Who is he?" Amelia asked.

"That's Tommy B. Donovan," Patsy said.

"The biggest of all eel thieves. Used to sit on the Fisheries Committee," said Lottie Pride.

"His kind doesn't belong on any committee," Patsy hissed in a whisper.

Tommy B. ambled up to the picnic table and stood in front of the four women, rocking slightly on his heels.

"Ladies," he said. "Nice day."

"Tommy," Patsy said, her voice in neutral.

"Miss Jeanette King. I've been hearing your name. Pleasure to finally make your acquaintance. Tom Donovan. People call me Tommy B."

"Good to meet you, Tommy B.," Jeanette said, remembering him crushing the porcupine with a Louisville Slugger, trying to put the thought out of her mind. "What brings you here?"

"Wonder if I could have a word with you," he said to Jeanette, "if it don't spoil your lunch plans."

The other women packed up quickly. Lottie Pride was the last to go. She gave Tommy B. a genuinely hostile stare before she left. The Eel King.

"I appreciate it," Tommy B. said, ignoring her as he remained standing, staring awkwardly at Jeanette. "Hear you been sick," he said. "I brought you some cookies."

"I only wish I could eat them," she said, looking down at the cardboard box neatly tied with red-and-white baker's twine. He must have gone all the way to DiCapo's in Bangor, she thought.

"Come to offer my condolences," he said.

"Condolences?"

"That fella you were working for. Hell of a way to die. Kinda gruesome."

"You could say that," Jeanette replied. "Thank you, but we weren't close personally."

Jeanette looked at Tommy B., wondering what in the world he was actually doing here.

"I don't think he gave you much competition," she said.

"Well, he was planning to. Wonder what's happened to his business. I thought maybe we could work on that together," Tommy B. said, musing, or seeming to muse.

"I was just the delivery woman. Mainly I'm the crab lady." She gestured to the shack.

"Well, you knew him. So I wondered. The thing is, we're licensed to trap and sell. I was thinking if this initiative goes through, we could maybe kinda grandfather them in under our license—whoever he was buying from. He done it illegally. I could make it legal. Maybe you could manage it. Bigger profit margin than crabs."

Jeanette smelled trouble. Tommy B. knew how to set nets for trapping elvers. Maybe for people too.

"I wish I could help you," she said. "But I don't know. I just picked up the harvest at the co-op and drove it. I don't really know much about it."

The man shifted awkwardly from foot to foot. He had to want something more than he was asking for. And he thought he could get it for the price of a box of cookies. She waited.

"I understand you been up to see an acquaintance of mine—Korean fella lives in Compton Harbor."

"Who told you that?"

"Doesn't matter who told me—I just don't think it was the smartest thing you coulda done, but I guess you were upset. Hell, I'd be upset if my business took a hit. Specially that kind of hit. What was Tyson paying you to drive them elvers?"

"Why would you want to know that?" Jeanette asked.

"Well, I'm just guessing you could make more if you work with me. There's real money in it. But you won't work with me if you keep sticking your nose in. I'm telling you for your own good. It can get, well, how do I say, kinda expensive."

She stared at him. What was it the doctor had said about stress?

"See, these big men, like this Sung Ho fella, they don't want folks like us—I mean you and me—coming around with all kinds of wild ideas, you know what I mean? It could change your life. Not in a good way."

"Are you threatening me?" Jeanette asked. "The Eel King threatening the Crab Lady?"

"I would never. I'm strictly talking upside. You could go from being a crab lady to being a crab countess or something. Crab queen. Hell, I'm a king."

"Thanks for the opportunity," she replied.

"Look," Tommy B. said. "Mainly I just wanted to say I'm sorry about what happened to you. And I was worried about you. It's better not to bother people we all depend on. Annoying them can even be dangerous."

"That doesn't sound like upside."

"Well, it ain't. But I wanted to bring you those cookies. Sorry you can't have 'em. I wouldn't worry though. Patsy can knock 'em off in one sitting."

He laughed and walked back to the truck, leaving the box of cookies on the table. Jeanette watched him go. He pulled the truck back onto the paved road and sped away, dual tires spitting gravel behind them in a dramatic display of masculinity.

Back in the crab shack, the women were picking.

"What was that about?" Patsy asked.

"I'm not sure," Jeanette replied. "He brought these cookies. Said he was worried about me." She put them down on some fresh newspaper on the crab table. She cut the string with the curved blade of the crab knife, opened the box, and pushed it toward the center of the table.

"I can't have these," she said. "You all take them."

"We don't eat those kind of cookies," Patsy said, and she swept the box across her work surface and onto the floor where they spilled into a crumbly mess. The other three looked up at her and for once, all of them stopped picking. The table was littered with crab bodies in various states of dismemberment. The floor was littered with Italian cookie fragments. No one moved.

"What's going on, Patsy?" Jeanette asked.

Patsy snorted. "Man never did a nice thing for no one in his life without gettin' something twice as nice back. I swear that's the man killed Tom Hinchcliffe, and I don't want his damn cookies . . ."

"Pretty brash of you to say that about the man," said Lottie.

"When Tom started with those elvers," Patsy said, "selling them under the table, bang. He was dead. Knotted in his own rigging. Now it might could've been something else. I only know what the good Lord allows me to know. But I'm not stupid. Tommy B. thinks he owns the water—at least any water that's got glass eels in it."

⁂

When Jeanette got back to the house she put on a pot of rice and sat down. She placed a call. Toland Bates picked up on the third ring

"Your favorite cousin just paid me a visit," she said.

There was a pause on the other end of the line. Then Toland asked, "You okay?"

"He brought me cookies."

"You can't eat those. What, is he trying to kill you?"

"He actually might be. Not yet though. And not with cookies."

"We need to figure out who killed Thurston Harney," Toland said, "or this is never gonna end."

"You want to come over and talk about it?"

"Not today," Toland said. "I'm in Wauwatosa."

"Wawa what?"

"It's in Wisconsin."

CHAPTER TWENTY-SEVEN

Toland arrived at the Wauwatosa Police Chief's office, identified himself as a police officer from the state of Maine, and asked to see the chief on an urgent matter. He was ushered into the office, which was furnished entirely in state-issued materials, circa 1970, which needed dusting. Chief Owen Crothers greeted Toland with little more than a professional nod. He was a thick man with a bullet head that he apparently shaved each morning.

"How can I help?" he asked, sounding like he didn't much want to.

"You've got a case," Toland said. "Related to a case in Maine. Man named Thurston Harney. Died in a burning car some days ago."

"I remember," said Crothers impatiently. "Not an everyday occurrence."

"We believe he killed someone in Maine not long before."

"Wouldn't surprise me. He was familiar to us."

"Spent time in Waupun."

"Yes, he did."

"We've got some concern that the perp who killed him—"

"Did us a favor," Chief Crothers interrupted.

"Well yes, but we are concerned the perp may actually be in Maine, or connected to Maine, and thought we might be able to coordinate some."

"And you drove all the way out here for that? Ever hear of email? Or the telephone?"

Toland paused. "The thing is," he said, "I got a mother lives out here, in Grafton. She's not well, I feared I might not see her again, so I kinda combined business with pleasure, not that it was a pleasure, exactly. Your mother living?"

"She is," said Crothers. "Alive and well, may God bless her every day."

"And may she stay that way many more years," Toland said, removing his hat. "May God bless you both."

He had no idea what windows might open, but it was the best shot he had. People in the Midwest were supposed to be friendly. And maybe very religious. He had no clue really.

"I'm sorry about yours," the chief said. He reached out and shook Toland's hand across the desk. "May God bless her, and you for caring for her."

Toland looked down at his shoes and tried to conjure up a tear, thinking about his actual mother, long dead in Maine. It's now or never, he thought. He kept his head lowered and plunged on.

"She didn't recognize me," he said, his voice cracking. "Came all this way, and she didn't even know me."

"I'm sorry, truly sorry, son." Chief Crothers seemed a little shaken up himself. "But you know the Lord will provide for her."

"God bless you for saying that," Toland said. "It's a comfort." It crossed his mind that if God were on duty this morning, He might not appreciate the complete fabrication. But, then, maybe He would.

Or She would. Perhaps God was on his side. Especially when it came to Joey Pizio, Jeanette, the eels.

He raised his head and spoke to Crothers.

"We live in a quiet community. A God-fearing community. The idea that this may be connected to our little island doesn't sit well with me, and I feel a moral obligation to do all I can to right it." The best lies, he had learned, contained some truth.

"Well, I can appreciate your concern, and your commitment. But if there is concern that this man was killed by someone who crossed state lines, why wouldn't the FBI be assisting?"

"Well, that's the thing. I mean, they've made an appearance, but, and I hope you'll excuse me for saying this, have you ever known them to 'assist' without making a mess of everything they put their hands on?" Perhaps, Toland thought, this was a sentiment shared by police chiefs everywhere.

Crothers smiled knowingly.

"I appreciate your initiative son. Your commitment to family. And, frankly, your well-placed distrust of the federal government. Not to mention your moral compass. How can I help?"

"May I ask you some questions? And maybe look over the case files, any witness statements?"

"I am an open book, son."

Toland began to probe. Crothers peered into his computer screen and began to type.

"Thurston Harney," Crothers said, "did eight years in Waupun and was released about three years ago. Second-degree murder."

"Seems like a short sentence," Toland said. "Murder?"

Crothers tapped some more.

"Seems the man he murdered might have been worse than he was. He was in and out twice before that. When bad people kill other bad people, juries don't seem to care much. And I imagine the man who set him on fire in that car thought it was arguably God's work; he was likely no better. Looks like they gave Harney fifteen to twenty and he served eight."

"Do you happen to know where this killing that got Harney the twenty years took place?"

"Looks like Waukesha," Crothers said. "Outside Milwaukee."

"Wauwatosa, Waupun, Waukesha," said Toland. "Lotta tribes. Like Maine."

"They were everywhere back in the day," Crothers said, "before we run 'em off. Kept the names."

Toland continued to probe. He hoped the story of his dying mother had been enough to keep any doubts Chief Crothers might have about his road trip at bay. The truth was that he knew that no one in either the Maine or the Wisconsin police forces would give much of a damn who had set fire to Thurston Harney—a career criminal, just as good dead as alive. But whoever it was may have also been behind killing Joey Pizio and even Bennett Tyson. Maybe his cousin, Tommy B., maybe the Koreans in competition with each other. He couldn't let it go. After all, Little Otis *had* asked him to take initiative. So, he had driven thirteen hundred miles to dig. There had to be answers. But so far he had come up empty. According to Crothers, no one had noticed a yellow pickup truck. No Maine license plates had been recorded coming or going through any tolls before or after the event except his own. There had been no mention of Koreans. There was, plainly, nothing to go on at all. It seemed that whoever had killed Thurston Harney was not only as sadistic as Harney had been, but as meticulous.

"I am sorry, son. But I promise, if any new information emerges, you'll be the first to know," Crothers told him.

"Bless you," Toland said. He handed Crothers his card. "The cell phone is best. I'll go back to mother and wait."

***

The Milwaukee public library had PDFs of old microfilm going back to the Harding administration. The local paper had been around at least since 1917 and had given Thurston Harney's previous murder conviction full play. He had bludgeoned a business partner to death in a dispute over the proceeds from an insurance fraud. A simple pistol shot would have done the trick. No one would miss either of them. What gave the trial interest was Harney's apparent enthusiasm for mayhem. A woman, likely a prostitute, testified against him, claiming that he had chained her to a radiator against her will. Toland was struck by that part—against her will. It had never occurred to him that there might be a woman somewhere who might consent to being chained to a radiator. It was a strange world. The other item of interest was a sidebar about Harney's reputation as a men's fashion aficionado. An odd duck, Toland thought.

There was also a mug shot. Thurston Harney did not look entirely human. His nose was flattened, and his facial skin was stretched across his cheeks, but his cheekbones seemed not to exist. He looked like a man whose skin was made of plastic wrap pulled tight and fastened at the back of his neck. Toland took a picture with his iPhone and was about to head back to the motel when he had a thought. He began scrolling back through the microfiche, searching for a different kind of article, one that might explain one other thing. It took about ten minutes on the search engine to find the headline:

PRINCETON BOY DISFIGURED AS
TRACTOR TIRE EXPLODES

Young Thurston Harney, according to the story, had dreamed of becoming a surgeon. But on his return from his freshman year on a full scholarship at Princeton he had taken a summer job at Waukesha Truck Repair and Maintenance. Toland imagined it didn't suit his collegiate tastes, but no doubt he still needed to earn some money to try to keep up with his classmates.

Before his scheduled return to the Ivy League, he'd been leaning over a new tractor tire that he had just mounted on a used rim. The article speculated that although he could not get the bead of the tire to seat properly inside the rim he must have kept pumping air. The bead burst over the rim flange and the tire exploded into Thurston Harney's face. A coworker had described to the reporter how the force had catapulted young Harney into the air. He landed on the concrete floor of the repair shop unconscious, his face a flap, attached at the hairline. His survival, as of the date of the article, was uncertain.

Toland read the account and was shaken. He imagined that Thurston Harney had never seen Princeton again and was perhaps lucky to have seen anything. Having your face and your ambitions ripped from you in one violent explosion could run a man to anger, he thought. Maybe lifelong anger. Maybe a lifelong taste for revenge.

Jeanette had called Lottie early that morning.

"Listen, I have to live a different life, like you said. And I don't know if I can, and I don't know that I won't be shot and tossed into a lobster tank before I even get the chance to try, but can you come help me pour perfectly good alcohol down the drain?"

She preferred to let Lottie do the tonic pouring while she collected the gin bottles and arranged them on the counter like a set of bowling pins. It was a kind of altar, she supposed. Saying goodbye.

When Lottie arrived, she looked at the collection and said, "Let's not pour it. Let's donate it to the Clamdigger."

"I don't think that's legal," Jeanette said. "Aren't you supposed to have a license?"

"Like an eeler?" Lottie asked. "You think Zach will complain?"

"We could leave it on the doorstep wrapped in swaddling clothes," said Jeanette. "Whatever they are."

Lottie smiled. "Sounds like a plan. Let's get to it."

They had emptied all but one of the half-used tonic bottles from the fridge into the sink when Toland Bates arrived, looking like a ghost.

"Toland," Jeanette said. "I thought you were in Wisconsin," Jeanette said.

"I think part of me still is," he said. "Mind if I use the sofa?"

He had driven through the night, stopping every three or four hours for a hamburger and coffee. He had a particular fondness for hamburgers. He had weathered a traffic jam maneuvering around Chicago, watched the sun set in his rearview mirror as he skirted Lake Erie, and saw it rise again over the Atlantic, north of Yarmouth. By the time he reached the island it was almost lunchtime. He had taken a couple short naps at rest stops and was certainly in need of another.

He was asleep in two minutes, his peaked cop hat shading his eyes and face. Snores emerged from underneath it.

"Peace," said Jeanette. "It's wonderful."

They packed up the gin and a bottle of brandy in an old wooden crab trap that Jeanette had found on the road some years before, wrapping it in a moth-eaten wool blanket that she had saved. Jeanette penned a short note:

> *Please take care of our babies and give them a good home.*

The plan was to drop it off at the back door behind the kitchen of the Clamdigger and leave it at that.

Lottie had also discovered three Sara Lee cakes in the freezer, which she tucked neatly around the edges of the trap.

"Those are for Zach personally," Jeanette said.

The two of them sat down to lunch at about one. It was Jeanette's third meal of the day: Chicken of the Sea, mixed with some Kraft low-fat mayo on white toast. There would be three more before she was done, each of them as small and repellent as this one. She was supposed to be on the diet for ten days, and this marked day five. She was ready to start carving notches into the kitchen cabinet.

Lottie reached into a sack she had planted on the counter and extracted a half-pint carton, which she placed on the table in front of Jeanette.

"Coconut water," she said. "Part of the new regime."

Jeanette looked at it with a skeptical eye, unscrewed the cap, and took a swig. She looked like she was swallowing kerosene.

"Tastes like the sweat from the inside of a baby's fist," she said.

"You're welcome."

As they were doing the dishes, Toland awakened and sat up on the sofa, looking over the back of it at them. His hair was tousled, and he squinted in the light. Jeanette smiled. He looked like a five-year-old done with his afternoon nap after a busy morning. For a moment she was reminded that grief also lived here, inside her always. But for the moment she decided she was going to concentrate on the loss of the gin instead. Good to have coping mechanisms.

"What are you two women up to?" Toland asked.

"The real question," Jeanette said, "is what have you been up to? You went to Wauwatosa, Wisconsin?"

"Trying to figure out who killed Thurston Harney. What the link is."

"Did you?"

"You would'a been the first to know."

***

It was just after full dark when Jeanette and Lottie drove up to the back door of the Clamdigger. They kept the headlights off for the last fifty yards or so. No point in being detected at this point. The rain had been falling all day, and the gravel parking lot was swirling with mud. Water pelted down on their heads as they carried the loaded crab trap to the granite slab step at the back door. A single light burned above, and a small porch canopy covered the step, keeping it dry enough so that there was at least some possibility that Jeanette's note would not be rendered illegible by the downpour. They maneuvered the crab trap into position and turned back to the car. A flashlight caught and froze them. It was a powerful light, coming from the bushes at the edge of the gravel lot. Someone was approaching but they were too blinded by the beam to see who. They did not move. There was no escape. In a moment the light went out and a figure approached. When it got close enough to the back door to be seen, Jeanette began to breathe again.

"Jesus," she said.

Jesse Ed Davis stepped into the light and turned off the torch.

"If you're gonna shoot me, shoot me. Don't scare me to death," Jeanette said.

"I followed your car," Jesse said. "What the hell are you two up to?"

"Never a dull moment," Lottie said. "Can we get out of the rain? There's such a thing as pneumonia."

"I was down at the co-op just before the rain started. Just looking around," Jesse said.

"Please," said Lottie, "inside the car, please?"

"And?" Jeannette asked.

"The boat's back. The *Jeanette*. Tied up at its mooring, bobbing in the current. Simon's back on the island."

CHAPTER TWENTY-EIGHT

The following evening Jeanette motored over to the co-op in her dinghy just as the sun was setting. She tied up at a dock below the parking lot and hopped out. Lottie was waiting for her in her car. The *Jeanette* was on its mooring. The fake live well was under a tarp in the dinghy. They worked their way back to the Clamdigger where Zach the bartender greeted Jeanette happily, though he was distressed to discover that Jeanette did not want her martini, and Lottie only needed water.

"Designated driver," Jeanette said.

"Both of you?" Zach asked. "Dunno as we've had one in here before, much less two." Jeanette ordered a haddock and chips. Lottie rolled her eyes.

"Could be my last meal," Jeanette said. "I'll eat what I want."

"You think he came back because he heard about Tyson?" Lottie asked.

"Stands to reason," Jeanette said. "And probably Thurston Harney too. He thinks he's safe."

"You don't think Simon killed Thurston Harney?" Lottie asked.

"Simon's a schemer; he's not a murderer."

The conversation plunged on, but Jeanette's mind was elsewhere. She was about to see Simon, who was alive and, as far as she knew, physically unharmed. She wanted to wring his neck. And she wanted to keep him safe. It was as though he was a small child who had wandered off and gotten lost, only to return hours later, bedraggled, scared, and in need of a mother's warmth. When little Liam had done the same, she had spent hours in a panic-stricken search, only to find him at sunset, toddling down the driveway in tears. She was elated, relieved, and furious at the sight of him. And full of love. It was a long time ago. But, as time had shown, her ability to keep him safe was temporary. What would happen this time with her man-child ex-husband? She could not imagine.

It was full dark by the time they had paid the bill and made it back to the co-op. In the inky sky, the stars were competing for attention. There was a crescent moon. In the harbor the boats looked like a ghost fleet. There was no one about, and no sound but the water lapping peacefully at the riprap bank along the end of the pier closest to the land. Out in the harbor, the fleet of boats lay in darkness. If Simon was back, whether he was aggregating elvers or lobstering, he'd be on the boat just before first light as he had been for his whole life. You could set your watch by it.

"You sure you want to do this?" Lottie asked.

"No. But I'm sure I'm doing it."

They walked in silence to the dock, where the dinghy rose and fell in the water. They climbed in, and Jeanette untied them. Lottie rowed in a smooth and practiced rhythm out through the fleet of lobster boats, as Jeanette directed her to the *Jeanette*.

The dinghy bumped up against the hull and its namesake stood up to clamber aboard.

Lottie unsheathed the false live well from its tarp and stood it on end; it reached the rail of the larger boat, and Jeanette pulled it on board.

"Wish me luck," she said.

"Good luck," Lottie replied. "I'll see you in the morning." She turned the dinghy back toward the dock.

Jeanette watched her go, oars barely breaking the water, moving in near silence. When she lost the dinghy in the dark, she turned and wrestled the fake live well onto the cover of the real one, stood back, and admired her handiwork. The well was perfectly lined up atop its former host. Jeanette turned toward the cabin and began to let herself down inside, where it was black dark. She hit her head hard, having forgotten the dimensions of the stairwell she used to know by heart. She cursed out loud, just like she did the first time she had hit her head there. Then she cursed Simon silently. For creating this mess. For being a schemer. And finally, for not calling her when he got back to town. She tapped the flashlight app on her phone and the tiny beam allowed her to find the easiest way into the bunk. She aimed the light around her and down to the floor, plotting the quietest way to get herself back on her feet, and then lay back and put the little light away.

She put her head back but found that sleep wouldn't come. Instead, she was seemingly in a state of suspended animation. The slow roll of the water did not play nicely with the aftereffects of the haddock. Music ran through her head, old country-western tunes from the beginning of her marriage. She'd made love in this bunk—how many years before—while Travis Tritt and Shania Twain scratched their way through a blinkered radio speaker that was hooked up to the boat's battery. Finally, the third time Pam Tillis's "Mi Vida Loca" began streaming through her brain, she drifted off, remembering what it was like to have another body there and feeling the chill of it gone. She was bedeviled by dreams; she was somewhere in the Caribbean. The fish were impossibly large and colorful, and she drifted among them with a tank on her back, filled with astonishing pleasure at the sight of them. In the middle distance a boy was swimming toward her, unprotected by mask or tank or regulator, just a boy who appeared to live in the water. When she began to swim toward him, he turned and fled. And then he simply disappeared. She turned back and the fish were gone too. She was in an empty ocean.

At a little after four thirty, she jolted awake. Something had bumped up against the side of the *Jeanette*. She pulled her feet onto the floorboards and waited, sitting at the edge of the bunk. There wasn't enough headroom to stand up straight, making this the easiest position in which to remain still. She was shaking off the dream. Then someone heaved himself on board, and the boat bobbed slightly in the water with the weight of him. Simon, she hoped.

Jeanette started to step toward the stairs that led to the deck when she heard a long scraping noise from above and froze. Something was coming on board, something being dragged up from a dinghy. Better to let it settle, she thought. There was just enough light peeking through the hatch for her to see legs leaning toward the rail as a man hauled whatever it was onto the deck. It landed on the boat with a thud. Then his body turned and stopped. He was facing the fake live well, silent and still. She waited.

"What the goddamn hell . . ." he said finally. Simon's voice. But it trailed off. She could hear the bewilderment and knew it would shift into something else in a moment—fear. Or rage. She took the three steps swiftly and her head was near enough to detect the familiar smell of him before he sensed her presence. His head turned quickly. The face, to the degree she could make it out in the first light of dawn, was a mask of uncertainty.

"Hello, Simon," she said.

Simon stared at Jeanette in the predawn. Then his eyes moved between her face and the false-bottom live well; his jaw moved. He was chewing something. Gum, or more probably tobacco. But he couldn't seem to speak. His hair looked grayer and his body thicker than the last time she had seen him, but she wasn't sure. His face was red from the sun, and he hadn't shaved in a couple days. He had not been expecting company.

"I haven't been on the boat in a while," she said. "Lots of memories. When'd you get the new windows? Bomar. Impressive."

"Jeanette. What are you doing here?"

He looked at her, then again at the well, and then at the thing he had dragged onto the boat. She followed his eyes there. Propped up against the rail was an identical copy. She saw it and halfway laughed.

"You got yourself a new one," she said. "At least we know you're still in business. We just don't know what business."

"Lobsters."

"Bullshit."

"Eels," he said.

"Eels I know. What else?"

"Who's we?"

She climbed fully up from the hold and stood on the deck face-to-face with him.

"How are you, Simon? Where'd you run off to? Why? What are you doing back here? Why the hell haven't you returned any of my calls? Or texts?"

"Where'd you get my live well?" he asked.

"We're trading hostages?" she asked. "Friend of mine and I took it off the boat in Rhode Island. That's where we met the man who killed your salesman, Mickey Keegan. He was trying to get to you. I warned you off going back there. Your turn."

"I guess I should say thank you," he said.

"You should, but that's not an answer. Jesus, Simon, we were married more than twenty years. I'm entitled to some information."

For a moment they looked at each other.

He pushed the first fake live well back toward the stern—far enough to make some space—and sat down on the lid of the actual one. There was something abrupt about his movement. She suddenly regretted not looking inside the well when she first boarded the boat and had a chance. Too late now. She sat down next to him. They had sat this way before a lot of years ago. It should have meant something to her now, but for all the nostalgia in her dreams and the smell and look of the boat when she was on it alone, and even the scent of Simon himself, which had once had the power to arouse, now it all meant nothing.

"Not much to tell," Simon began. "I got a call from the boatyard, saying they sold the boat, but to pay me I needed to come back and sign some damn thing. I grabbed my keys and then you called."

"But you didn't pick up."

"I wasn't in a talking mood really."

"You never were."

"But then I saw the text. And I listened to the message. And I didn't go."

"You didn't respond either. Left me to worry myself sick about you."

"Sorry. I'm bad with the thumbs. Christ, you know that, Jeanette. I don't manage to text."

"Simon. What have you gotten yourself into?"

"Why do you care?" he asked.

"You didn't kill Tom Hinchcliffe by any chance?"

Simon bounded onto his feet in a rage.

"And leave him tangled in his rigging?" she added.

"How the hell dare you accuse me of any such a thing? Tom Hinchliffe was a friend of mine. I never did no one no harm in my whole goddamn life. Not him, not anyone else."

The speech was barely long enough for her to also bounce up off the live well and flip up the lid. The hydraulics kicked in and the lid tilted up toward the stern. Just enough to see deep into it. The two of them looked down at the same time.

Inside the live well, stacked as neatly as they would be in a vault, were packet upon packet of hundred-dollar bills. Tidy, dry, and plentiful.

"Jesus," she said. "Never harmed anyone in your life. Tell it to Elmer Swetman."

"Elmer Swetman?"

"For starters. And every other deadbeat eeler you've been stealing from for how many years?"

Jeanette waited, but Simon did not reply. She understood that he was calculating how much to say, if anything. She was on the point of demanding that he speak when the sun peeked above the horizon out on the water and the two of them cast their gaze out to sea. A color wheel began to transform the tint of the lobster fleet, the water and the wooded granite islands that dotted the bay. It was an ever-evolving display. The view was so striking, pink blush and ginger orange banking off the mirrored surface of the water and beginning to light up the morning, that they both remained quiet. In the unexpected silence she was registering, for the first time in a long time, how fortunate she was to be living in Maine, by the water, in a world of lobster boats, stone, and pine. She wondered if Simon was thinking the same.

The boat barely rocked, a placid unchanging rhythm accompanied by the sound of water lapping against the hull. The moment couldn't last long, but it was worth stretching it as far as it would go. Answers could wait that long.

The world is charged with the grandeur of God—the first line of a poem she had been forced to memorize at Christian summer camp more than forty years earlier. It was surely charged with grandeur, she thought. She wasn't at all convinced of the source. But it was something to see.

"Sometimes a thing is almost too good to be true," Simon said, finally.

"The sunrise," she said.

"Not the sunrise," he replied. "The money."

"Okay," she said impatiently. "The money. Let's talk about that." But as she said it her heart died a little. When it comes right down to it, she thought, he's been blessed with the emotional capacity of a dog tick. It was what it was. Damn.

"I never thought I'd see anything like it in my life," he said. "And I earned every penny. That's all I'm gonna say."

Jeanette nodded, beginning to put it together.

"But Joey Pizio found out you had it."

Simon looked at her, frustration playing across his features. Jeanette smiled. He's annoyed that I can think, she thought.

"We had an arrangement," he said.

"A simple one," she said. "He knew you were stealing from your suppliers—so he got his little piece. Until they killed him. Tortured and killed him. Liam's old Little League teammate."

"They what?"

"So, you didn't know that."

"Jesus," Simon said. "He just wanted in. I let him in. He needed it for pills. Everyone needs fucking pills. Or girls. Or both. Everybody needs something. But to torture that kid . . ." he trailed off.

"Everybody needs something," she repeated. "You needed a boatful of money. For what?" Simon shook his head.

"I been talking to Jack Strudwick, down in the Keys."

"Who?"

"You don't remember? From the TV show. You never were listening."

"The sleazeball with the *Treasure Hunt* show?"

"Jack Strudwick found the goddamn *Elena Belle*. In a hundred and fifty feet of water off the Dominican Republic with a million dollars in coins and jewelry. But he's gettin' on in years. He wants a partner. I know boats. I know the water."

"And I know Jack Strudwick," Jeanette said. "He's the guy who went to jail for tax evasion and once for something else, I don't remember. I read all about him."

"Well, he got a raw deal. And now he's building up again and he wants me to join him. He says there's a Spanish galleon that sunk off the Dry Tortugas in 1622, and he's onto it. But he needs some capital and a captain who knows currents, and . . ."

"Jesus, Simon, this is worse than the lobster skylight. It's a scam."

"Don't start with the skylights again. That was a good idea."

"You know he's gonna steal the money you stole. Or at the very best, he'll burn through it all with you, chasing some fantasy."

Simon chewed in silence. Jeanette waited.

"The guy's got his own museum, you know?" he said, finally. "I'd like to be someone like that—before I die. Can you even understand that?"

Jeanette nodded. She'd always understood it somehow. She'd just never said a thing about it.

"Well," she said, "you might not have much more time before that happens. Is that what you were doing in front of the house, in the reach, in the dark every Wednesday? Trying to be someone? Meeting a kid who got tortured to death? What were you doing there?"

"It wasn't supposed to go like that. It was a job. I loaded up the elvers and met Joey in the reach. He paid me, took the boat, and delivered the load to Bennett. I took my Whaler back to the dock, and eventually the *Jeanette* would show up at my mooring with a cooler full of cash for next week's eel shopping. That was the deal."

"And Bennett never suspected you were skimming?" Jeanette said.

Simon paused and opened and closed his eyes a couple times.

"This spring. Once," he said. "He let it go, but it got me a little nervous."

"It should have."

"That wasn't the big thing though. One morning, maybe two weeks later, somebody threw me out of the boat," he said. "For no damn reason that I could figure. Some big guy, a stranger, hiding right where you were just hiding—in the hold. Stormed up the stairs and pitched me into the drink."

Jesse.

"Dried myself off and hightailed it out of here. Okay—I got the message. They're onto me. I've got cash, more than I'll need. And yeah, I skimmed some. It was fair considering what everyone else was making. So, I put the boat up for sale, bought a car in Rhode Island, and drove back up into Aroostook County to lay low for a bit. Potato country. Just keeping it simple. Didn't know if I'd ever come back. It's a godforsaken wilderness up there, I have to tell you. You can't hardly get anything to eat. Poutine. Jesus. How'd you get the fake well off my boat?"

"A Phillips head screwdriver," she said. "I had help from a friend—the guy who threw you out of the boat. Jesse Ed Davis. He wanted to know what was going on with the elvers, because that's the kind of thing he actually cares about . . ."

"The guy who threw me off the boat's a friend of yours?" Simon cut her off, his voice rising in the dawn light. "You're fucking a goddamn environmentalist?" His voice boomed, echoing off the water. It was a sound she'd heard a hundred times too many in the past, a sound that promised physical violence could follow at any moment, though it never had yet.

Still, when he got like this, there was no talking him out of anything. Simon would only see the world one way: his way. She turned contrite.

"He's not my boyfriend, Simon," she said, her voice quite suddenly demure. "He's just a friend. And I've just been scared is all. I don't want anything to happen to you. Or to me. And if you want to go into business with Jack Strudwick, well, that's your business." She put her hand on his shoulder, gently. His nostrils unflared, and he softened.

"I have a good feeling about this thing with Jack."

"Okay," she said. "Okay. I bet it'll work this time. Just promise me you won't let them hurt you. Or me."

"Don't be silly. Of course I won't. The bad guy's already gone." Now he was comforting her. "You're just spooked is all," he said.

"If you say so. God. I'm tired. I need to go home and sleep and not think about all this. Pull your dinghy up here and get me back to the dock and I'll leave you alone, okay? But call me back next time. I worry about you."

"Okay," he said, smiling for the first time. "I'll call." He went to the rail to drag the dinghy up to the *Jeanette*'s hull. "Truth is, now that I have a little more financial stability, I was considering maybe you and me could try getting back together. You always liked the Keys. There's diving and such."

"Oh, Simon," she said, "it might be a little late for that, honey."

As he leaned over the rail to catch the dinghy's bowline, she backed away, got herself into a crouch, and then lunged, grabbed his shins from behind, and upended him. He barked as he went over the rail. She heard him hit the water and was glad he had missed the dinghy. She didn't want to kill him or break his back.

She stepped to the steering console and flipped up the seat pillow. There was the key, where Simon had always kept it, clipped to the same buoy-shaped Styrofoam fob it had been connected to since the day he bought the boat.

She started the engine and moved swiftly to the bow to uncinch the mooring line from its cleat.

Simon was screaming at her from the water, but she knew he could make it into his own dinghy. She had to move quickly to make sure he didn't end up back in the *Jeanette*, or even under it, where the prop might tear him apart. She gunned the engine and headed away.

The *Jeanette* plowed out of the harbor toward the lighthouse on the point. She didn't look back. Scanning the dashboard, she saw the GPS recorder was on and she moved to kill it, but then stopped herself. Let it go, she thought. Could be useful.

She navigated toward open water and took out her phone. Jesse picked up on the first ring.

"Get a big bag," she said. "Bring it to the dock. Just make sure Simon's gone. Take my dinghy and meet me behind the lighthouse."

CHAPTER TWENTY-NINE

Jesse found the *Jeanette* bobbing in the chop behind the lighthouse with Jeanette at the helm. On board, Jesse stared at the money in the well.

"Plunder" was all he said. He opened the duffel bag he had grabbed from his truck and began transferring the packets of bills into it, silent and methodical. As he worked, Jeanette told him what she had learned on the boat with Simon.

The bow rose on the crest of a wave and slammed down into the water, sending a torrent of white, salty spray across the console windshield.

"He was my husband," she said to Jesse as he worked. "He's also a fool. Steal money from criminals to invest in a treasure hunt. Jesus."

"It's not his money," Jesse said. "The money is for the elvers."

They rode in silence except for the full-throttle whine of the engine and the whipping of the wind, out of the bay and into rougher water, out where the halibut fishermen ventured during the season. For a half hour Jesse took them in a wide loop, followed by gulls and the occasional egret. They were in deep water when Jesse turned to Jeanette.

"Where to, captain?"

"Little Piglet," she said. Jesse looked at her quizzically.

"There's an old stone foundation on the north side where Simon and I used to take a sunset picnic sometimes in the summer. When we were kids. Otherwise, nothing there."

"Little Piglet?"

"It's shaped like one," Jeanette said.

"A piglet is already little," Jesse said. "The GPS recorder's still on. Is that gonna be a problem?"

"That's good," Jeanette replied. "We'll need to leave a trail."

"What are you thinking?" Jesse asked.

"I'm thinking everyone thinks you're an 'Indian,'" Jeanette said. "Why shouldn't we help Simon make the same mistake?"

"How?" Jesse said.

"Don't get smart with me."

* * *

It took them the better part of an hour to get there.

The island was small and isolated, a stone shoreline with stands of spruce and cedar and the occasional white birch competing for daylight. No more than two acres altogether. It lay northeast of the chain of similarly unoccupied upheavals of land that dotted the bay with the open ocean on the other side. Why anyone would have wanted to own it, much less live on it, was beyond Jeanette's imagination. Its gravel beach was a nice place to sit for an hour or so in good weather, but that was about it. A good nor'easter in cold weather would likely polish off any human life that dared to brave it. Yet there was a remnant of human occupancy still standing.

They anchored the *Jeanette* and took the dinghy to the gravel beach. Low branches from an old, gnarled oak tree hung over the beach, hollowed with age. Behind it was an old stone hut. It was roofless, the walls were crumbling, and a pale silvery lichen, growing from the fissures in the rock, had taken over much of the surface. Moss hung from the trees and covered the ground as well, blankets of yellow, lime, and bottle green and gray jostling for space in the dappled light that the overstory let in. There was no doorway, only a dark opening in the stone leading to an unseen interior. Jesse hopped out of the dinghy, bounded up the beach, and looked inside. He returned to the water's edge, where Jeanette was holding the dinghy against a rock wall just off the shore. There was an old iron ring that had been pounded in decades before, rusted but still sturdy. Jeanette tied off the boat.

"The hut's safe," Jesse said. "Come on."

Rust-eaten iron pipes stuck up from what was left of the hut's floor, the remains of some sort of plumbing or drainage system. Jeanette admired the smell, the damp pungent perfume of humus and mineral-rich water that trickled down the walls, the salt air. Their voices echoed off the stones as they spoke quietly for some time.

"You're willing to do this?" Jeanette asked. They had talked about it on the boat.

Jesse nodded. "It's a good plan."

"You'll be okay here on your own?" Jeanette asked. "You're sure?"

"There'll be a good moon tonight," Jesse said. "And a low tide. I like a raw bar."

Jeanette nodded. "If you say so." Then a thought crossed her mind. "Give me twelve hundred fifty dollars."

"Jeanette, we can't go and just spend this money. It's not our money either."

"It's for the elvers," she said, reaching into the duffel.

She climbed into the dinghy and Jesse untied it from the old iron mooring ring in the granite. After stashing the money in a bait bag she found snagged in the floorboards, she rowed out to the *Jeanette*, secured the dinghy to the stern rail, and headed back to the mainland. She anchored the boat near the mouth of the Orleans River, close enough to where Tommy B. had his eeling operation set up. Someone would find it there and alert Simon. She left the key and, musing on how things would play out on Little Piglet, she motored around the end of the island and brought the dinghy back to her own dock. It was late for lunch, and she was supposed to eat.

※

Jesse saw the *Jeanette* approaching Little Piglet at about eleven the next morning. He rekindled the fire that he had built on the gravel beach the night before and sat cross-legged in front of it, under the hollowed-out oak, on a little pillow he had made by folding the duffel bag in thirds. Simon anchored the boat about a hundred yards from shore and clambered into his dinghy, starting up the outboard and motoring to the beach. Jesse remained still and impassive. Simon pulled the little boat up onto the gravel and looked at Jesse with some surprise.

"We meet again," he said.

"So we do," said Jesse. "Please remain quiet. I'm just concluding the offering."

"Offering?"

Jesse held up his hand and intoned, as if to the gods, the phrase that he'd been turning over in his mind—one that might sound vaguely spiritual. He wasn't going to waste an actual Native ceremonial chant on this event. Bill Penny wouldn't have allowed it. And Simon wouldn't know the difference.

"Change in the ocean," he chanted in a keening monotone, "change in the deep blue sea. Change in the mountain, change in the land . . ."

He faded into an indistinct hum. The song was a relic from Taj Mahal's first album, on which the original Jesse Ed Davis had played a particularly effective guitar lick. Jesse couldn't remember the whole lyric, but a few strands would do. He thought it best to leave out the line about changing his woman, and so he faded his hum into a couple animalistic grunts and lowered his hand, beckoning Simon toward him. He stirred the dying fire with a stick as Simon walked over. When the two men were within a yard of each other, Simon pulled a pistol from his pocket and aimed it at Jesse's face. With a deliberate slowness he pulled back the hammer. Jesse stirred once more, placed the stick across his lap, and raised his eyes to meet Simon's.

"How can I help?" Jesse asked.

"Surprised I found you?" Simon asked.

Jesse didn't answer. Nor did he move.

"You and your girlfriend left the GPS recorder on. Didn't take me long. Funny. You and her have one trick between you. It's a good thing I can swim."

"It was a safe assumption," Jesse said.

"Where's my money?"

"It wasn't yours," Jesse replied. "And it wasn't mine. I made an offering, so that we all might be forgiven. It took almost all night."

He stirred the fire. The charred corner of a hundred-dollar bill came to the surface, ruined but still distinctly identifiable.

"You did what?" Simon asked.

Jesse poked at the bill, and the fire consumed it, sending up a brief yellow spit into the air.

"I should kill you," Simon hissed.

"Perhaps you will," Jesse said. "I don't think it would solve your problems. And it might create more. But perhaps you will anyhow."

Reluctantly, Simon lowered the gun, but didn't put it away.

"Four hundred and eighty thousand dollars gone up in smoke? It don't make no sense."

"Just paper," Jesse said. "Pieces of paper. From a tree. From a printing press. That's all."

Simon stood above Jesse, breathing heavily. Jesse remained still, as always. Simon took the stick from Jesse's hand; Jesse did not protest. He watched as Simon poked at the fire. Currency, all but completely consumed, stirred in and around the embers. Useless. When he'd had enough, Simon tossed the stick on top of the fire and watched it ignite.

"Who the hell do you think you are?" Simon asked. "And who the hell are you?"

"My ambition is for those two questions to have the same answer," Jesse said.

"Who burns up money?"

"The first money was massive circular carved rocks. Did you know that? Granite doughnuts carved by Pacific Islanders. The wealthy would use them as currency to buy land, stock, rights. A boat that was carrying one, sent as payment for an island, not unlike this island, foundered and sank in a sudden summer tempest. The chiefs agreed that the stone's ownership could still be accounted for and recorded, even if it sat on the bottom of the ocean. The payment was accepted. And banking was invented."

Simon's face had grown darker. He took a step toward Jesse and gestured with the gun for Jesse to stand. Jesse did not move.

"Carved rocks," he said. "You trying to tell me something?"

"Only this. If the money is rightfully yours, you still have it. The only thing missing is the paper representation of it. You have only to convince the authorities."

"Goddammit," Simon said. "You offered my money up to your native gods in a fucking bonfire? And you want me to explain that to the authorities so they can give it back?"

"If it was rightly yours, they'd understand. But I don't think it was."

"Fuck them. And fuck you. You burnt it, you owe it back to me. Time for a second offering to make it right. What do you have to offer me?"

"Raw bar?" Jesse asked, presenting a flat stone with a dozen oysters, clams, and mussels nestled on some seaweed.

"Disgusting," Simon seethed. He kicked the stone out of Jesse's hands and the shellfish scattered across the gravel. He stormed down to the water, climbed in his dingy, and motored back to the *Jeanette*. Jesse rescued a mussel, picked some flecks of gravel out of it, slurped it down, and toasted Simon, who yelled back to shore: "You can swim home."

CHAPTER THIRTY

"Let's start at the end," Little Otis, the police chief, said to Toland Bates. The chief kept his hat on even when he was behind his desk, largely to mask a receding hairline. He was smaller than his father, and softer, but the family resemblance was unmistakable—the receding chin, the watery blue eyes, and the unkempt eyebrows.

"Hand over your weapon, your badge, and change into your street clothes, and then get back in here."

The police station was overheated and Otis Sumlin Jr.'s office seemed smaller and more cramped than ever.

"What's this now?" Toland asked.

"Just do it."

Toland did as he was told, leaving his gun and badge on the chief's desk and his uniform in his locker outside. When he returned, the gun and badge were nowhere to be seen.

Toland stood in front of the chief's desk, shifting his weight from foot to foot.

"You've been recommended for a promotion," the chief said, and raised the tangle of his eyebrows.

Toland swallowed hard. "Well, that's very nice."

"So, I'm putting you on unpaid administrative leave."

"I'm not sure I follow, sir."

"Chief Crothers called me all the way from Wisconsin. Seems you left a nice impression on him. 'Sincere, God-fearing, committed.' You took some real initiative."

"You did ask me to take initiative, sir." Toland's mind flashed on the moment when he had given Chief Crothers his card. He'd told the guy to call the cell number. Too late now.

"You'll talk when I tell you to talk," Little Otis said. "The chief told me how concerned he was for your blessed mother as well." Toland looked down at his feet. "She's dead, Toland. You forgot that? You used your own dead mother as bait for your fishing expedition."

Toland simply stood stock-still.

"Well, you did say . . ."

"I asked you to take initiative, not dishonor your dead mother. But once Thurston Harney turned up burnt to a crisp, I didn't keep asking for initiative then, did I?"

"You didn't ask me to stop taking initiative, sir."

"I sure as hell didn't ask you to put on your uniform and go to another state pretending to represent our department, did I?"

Toland rubbed the palm of his hand over his forehead and feathered his fingers through his hair. This was serious.

"So let me ask you one more question," the chief practically barked.

Toland stood and waited.

"What on God's green earth made you think you should go and do this, on your own, without any kind of departmental authorization? Why didn't you come to me?"

"Well, sir," Toland began, but the word *sir* stuck in his throat and he started again. "I tried to tell you. All the way through. First, you said, 'It's an overdose. Don't stir it, it'll stink.' And then, you said it was an accidental house fire. 'Don't stir it, it'll stink.' Then Thurston Harney is dead. 'Don't stir it, it'll stink.' But somebody killed Thurston Harney, and it might be somebody from here. It was already stinking. And you didn't want to smell it. I mean, I know you don't want me looking, but I have to. I think this might go all the way up to the top."

"You saying my father is involved in this? My papa is about as involved as your mama."

"My mother's dead!" Toland said, raising his voice for the first time. "You can say anything you want about me. But keep your mouth off my mother—she died at forty-two. She wasn't half Big Otis's age and never done nothing bad to nobody."

"Well then, why are you driving to Wauwatosa to tell the chief of police that she's senile?"

Toland fumed.

"It's the fish head that stinks! The both of you just want it quiet and peaceful. Like father, like son. Big Otis and Little Otis. Serving and protecting yourselves."

The chief lurched up from behind his desk and lifted a hand as if he might strike Toland across the face. Then he put it down and smiled.

"By the time this is over," he said, "you'll be lucky to get a lifetime appointment as game warden."

"Yes, sir." Toland said. Game warden sounded good.

***

Jeanette had just hung up the phone and was slipping Kat Rutherford's business card back into the binder clip with the other business cards in the junk drawer when she saw Toland pull up to her house. Jeanette nursed a cup of Chaga while Toland drank water. He wasn't in uniform. He explained why as he began to pace the room, letting all the news sink in.

"The only good thing," Toland said to her, "is I can call him Little Otis to his face from now on."

"Oh, honey," Jeanette said. "I think I did this to you. I'm so sorry. I never should have dragged you into this."

"Did it all by myself," Toland said. "I'm full-grown and don't regret a thing about it."

"Little Otis Sumlin should be ashamed of himself," she said. "Just lost his best man. Now he's got the department he wants, the damn fool."

Toland shrugged.

"You'll be reinstated," Jeanette insisted. "Isn't there a review board or something— can't you bring an official arbitration?"

Toland stopped and refilled his glass.

"I don't know," he said, "I might kinda prefer calling him Little Otis."

Toland sat down across from her, calmer now. "It feels kinda weird though—not having a job to do."

"I've got a job you can do," Jeanette said.

"What's that?"

"Pay a visit to Sung Ho Han."

***

Winding up the narrow road in Compton Harbor, Toland Bates felt himself, almost involuntarily, getting into character. He had borrowed a badge and a wallet from Bert's locker, one that he could flip open to flash credentials.

He was dressed in street clothes with a plaid jacket, thin black tie, and a smart-looking green felt Tyrolean he had found at the L.L. Bean outlet store in Brockton on the way. Somehow, he couldn't picture conducting police business without a hat on his head.

A brief rain had blown away and a cool May day was offering stiff breezes. When midsummer came, the reach would fill up with the sailboats of the summer people on a day like this. As he turned into Sung Ho's driveway, he could see a US flag and a Maine State flag whipping back and forth from a flagpole in the front yard.

Blake the houseboy blanched at the sight of the badge and scurried off to find his master. Toland looked around the living room, duly noting that the water could be seen from windows on both long walls—ocean on one side, bay on the other. It all seemed impossibly rich. Sung Ho's flower garden was not yet in full bloom, but it was immaculately laid out. Dahlias and daylilies were poking up through the soil and would be undulating in the breeze soon enough.

"Dang," Toland said aloud as Sung Ho descended the stairs.

"Officer," he said, extending a hand without even asking to see the credentials. Toland was vaguely disappointed. Alarming unimportant blond boys like Blake seemed like pretty small potatoes.

"Detective," Toland corrected his host. "Detective Crothers. Thank you for seeing me."

"Of course," Sung Ho said, gesturing to a chair.

"Nothing to be concerned about," Toland said. "I'm just looking for some help."

"You might have called," Sung Ho said.

Toland shrugged. "Protocol," he said. Sung Ho nodded. Neither of them had any idea what was meant. "We've got a problem. We thought you might have some information."

"If I do, it's yours."

"You do business with this eeler named . . ." Toland consulted a small pad that he took from his breast pocket. The pages were blank. He was starting to feel that adrenaline rush that he remembered from Wauwatosa. He wondered if props were something separate from the costume or if they were one and the same. "Thomas B. Donovan?"

"I do," said Sung Ho. "I don't know him well, but we—my company—buys from him and his associates."

"Do you know him well enough to describe his personality?"

"His personality?"

"It seems," Toland said, "that he threatened a woman named . . ." Here he flipped the page of his little notebook a second time. The page flip was an ad-lib. "Jeanette King. Apparently, she had been to see you, and then, a couple days later, this Donovan fellow arrived at her place of business and threatened her. Any idea of how those things might have been connected?"

He put away the notebook.

"Threatened?" Sung Ho asked, his voice betraying a hint of disbelief. Or was it concern? He was a good actor too, Toland thought, but not good enough.

Sung Ho took a quick breath. Assessing a strategy, Toland thought. He waited.

"I don't know anything about that," Sung Ho said finally. "Tommy B. is a blustery sort of fellow; you know these fishermen."

Toland nodded. "I do."

"Well, I don't know what happened, but it's hard to imagine that it was a threat. I don't even know why the two of them would have met. But I can't imagine Mr. Donovan threatening a woman like that."

"Would you tell me why she came to see you?"

"I don't actually know," Sung Ho said. "I've been wondering about it myself. She was frightened. A man she was working with had been killed. A man who was also in the eel business, but not with Bando. Not with my company. An unlicensed fisherman."

Toland nodded sagely. "Do you by any chance know the name of the company this man was selling to—your competitor, so to speak?"

"What does this have to do with Mr. Donovan and Ms. King?" Sung Ho asked.

"That's just what we're trying to find out," Toland said. "Believe me, none of this has anything to do with you. We're just trying to put it together ourselves, the death of Mr."—another quick look at the little notepad—"Tyson. Bennett Tyson. And Mr. Donovan, and this Ms. King, who seemed to be working with Mr. Tyson, but came to see you. It's all a little confusing. We thought you might be able to shed some light."

"If I could, I would," Sung Ho said.

"And then there's another man," Toland said, "Somewhat deformed around the face as if from some accident—name of Thurston Harney. Ever meet Mr. Harney?"

"I don't know who these other people are. Or who they were selling eels to, if that's what they were doing. Bando is the market maker in Korea. Must have been some smaller, fly-by-night outfit. We never worried about them. That is, my company didn't. Did you say deformed around the face?"

"So we've been told. Not important. This other elver buyer—you don't know if they even exist anymore?" Toland said.

"I know nothing about it," Sung Ho said.

Toland nodded again. Then he smiled. "It was worth a try. Thanks for your cooperation."

"May I ask," Sung Ho said, "what this 'competitor' as you call it—what that has to do with my elver supplier and Ms. King?"

"I honestly can't tell you," Toland said. "Just following every thread to see if any of them lead us anywhere. We've been hearing a lot about this elvers ballot initiative." Toland watched Sung Ho, who became visibly uncomfortable. "Seems people are getting quite worked up about it. You just never know when a dot will connect with another dot."

"That is beyond my pay grade," Sung Ho said, a little too humbly. "Up to the people and politicians of Maine. But if I can help your department in any way, please do let me know."

They shook hands at the door. Blake nodded and closed it. Toland went to his car.

Leaving Sung Ho's driveway, he turned toward the water and proceeded about fifty yards, past a gravel turnaround where Jeanette waited in the Subaru. She waited for Toland to pass and turned her ignition key, leaving the car in park, waiting for Sung Ho to start driving. It was not a long wait.

She tailed Sung Ho Han from his ivory tower above the Atlantic north through Mount Desert Island and across Route 1 to the Orleans River, where Tommy B. Donovan had a crew working. Then she pulled up short of the gravel parking area and watched.

Sung Ho's silver Mercedes stood out next to the row of mud-spattered, dinged-up pickups parked along the river, as did the well-dressed man who stepped out of it. He carefully picked his way down the bank where

Tommy B. was talking animatedly to Simon. She thought he must be looking for work with Tommy B.

Sung Ho waited at a fair distance for the conversation to be over. Simon turned and headed down to a small dock on the river where a dinghy was tied up. He hopped on board. Sung Ho approached Tommy B. Their conversation was brief.

Clambering back up the bank, Sung Ho stopped to check his shoes before clicking the unlock button on his key chain and opening the passenger side door of the Mercedes. He reached in and took a pair of clean suede loafers from the seat, trading them gracefully for the muddy pair on his feet. Those he placed in a plastic bag that he extracted from his jacket pocket, stowing them on the floor of the passenger side. The man was always prepared.

The Mercedes backed its way onto the road, and Jeanette put her car in gear. She followed at a safe distance, letting a couple cars pass her as Sung Ho took Route 1 across to Belfast and then turned onto Route 3, heading toward Augusta. A little less than an hour later, Sung Ho pulled into a parking spot in front of Lester Birdwell's office. Jeanette pulled over and typed a quick text to Kat Rutherford:

He's here

***

Sung Ho Han entered Birdwell's outer office unannounced. Kat Rutherford was at her computer, building a massive pro-initiative email blast for registered voters. She had no intention of hitting send; she would print it out and put it on her boss's desk. Let him think it had been spread wide. The initiative was woefully short of signatures and time was running out. She looked up to see Sung Ho standing in front of her desk.

"It's an urgent matter," he said.

After giving Birdwell a heads-up on the phone, she gestured Sung Ho into the inner sanctum, palming her iPhone as she followed.

"Can I offer you water, coffee, anything?" she asked, discreetly slipping the phone behind the vase of flowers that she replaced every three days.

"Thank you, no," Sung Ho said, giving her a strange little salute. She nodded and left the room.

"To what do I owe the pleasure?" Birdwell asked.

"It's hardly a pleasure," Sung Ho told him. "I asked you to handle things in a quiet, civilized way and you instruct Tommy Donovan to go and threaten this Jeanette King person? How does that help matters?"

Birdwell frowned. "I didn't tell him to threaten anyone, I asked him to take care—"

"I asked *you* to take care of it," Sung Ho said. "Discreetly. You put it in the hands of a greedy, hot-tempered elver fisherman?"

"I don't know what to say," said Birdwell, looking injured. "I did what I thought was the best thing to do. If it didn't work out, we'll have to try something else."

Sung Ho stared at Birdwell. Birdwell noticed that his nostrils were actually flaring a bit, something he wasn't sure he had ever seen before in real life. His face reddened with alarm. He had thought Sung Ho the most placid individual he'd ever known, until now.

"*We* are not going to try anything else," said Sung Ho. "There is no *we*. We—you and I—are not associated in any way."

"But the initiative . . ."

"Is dead," Sung Ho said. "The money that has come from Bando to support your efforts has stopped as of this moment. And let's face it, you would have had no money at all without me. But we will never speak of it, not to a living soul. I explained to you at the beginning that we are a very conservative company. Koreans as a rule are perhaps more concerned than Americans with reputation. We actually care how we look to other people. We are not part of this. We were never part of this, and anyone who says anything to the contrary would be making a grave mistake. Do I make myself clear?"

"I don't understand," Birdwell said.

Sung Ho stared at Birdwell in disbelief.

"There was a very famous jazz musician," he said. "This musician was asked to explain what jazz was and replied, 'If you have to ask, you'll never find out.' The only question surrounding this quote is which musician said it. It is attributed to many. None of them came from Maine. I am now saying it to you."

"Honestly," said Birdwell. "I just don't get it."

"That," said Sung Ho, "is the entire point."

He rose, turned, and left, not so much as bidding Kat Rutherford a farewell. When he was gone, she went quietly and deferentially into her boss's office to see if he was all right, or needed anything, but he didn't seem to even hear the question. She didn't repeat it. She simply went to the vase to prop up a couple of the weaker stems of asters and irises that were beginning to droop. They had looked lovely only the day before. She would have to replace the whole thing in the morning.

THE EEL

In the spring of 1996, when Jeanette and Simon were having sex on the mattress in the back of his truck for the first time, neither of them was aware that a massive glass eel migration was happening all around them. In the intervening years, a constellation of setbacks—relentless trapping, climate change leading to changing currents, disease, hydroelectric dams, and perhaps causes that no person could discern—had reduced the migration by 95 percent. No matter how many there were, they were worth something. The scarcer they became, the more valuable they were to those who netted them.

One glass eel was no different from another. They were indistinguishable to human eyes. But on a dark night, the spring after Liam died, one would distinguish itself. It was one of three swimming low and to the right as Tommy B.'s seine diverted all the other elvers approaching the creek mouth. The others were carried by the net up and into a live well, then by a cargo plane to a factory farm in Korea for an eighteen-month detour. Then back across the ocean as unagi, to be served somewhere in the world. Only three elvers slipped by the nets and avoided this fate. Tommy B., who had already begun making more money on eels than anyone he knew could make on lobsters, hadn't noticed the three stragglers. With elvers, you went for the cloud, not the individual.

Of these three, this particular elver was the one that did not get swallowed by a brook trout the next day. And it was also the one that did not get grabbed by a great blue heron a year later, when, against habit, it ventured out into shallow water before it was legitimately dark outside.

This was the one that settled first in the pocket pool in the creek and then, during a wet spring flood, pushed itself up the little trickling tributary, over the wet millstone, into the small pond on the lot where construction on a vacation home had been started, and then stopped. It settled into the pond, apparently for a long stay.

After the divorce, Jeanette got the partially finished house at a discount and finished it herself. The eel had been living in the pond for two years. It was now almost twelve inches long and weighed just under a pound. It ate worms that ventured into the water, mayfly nymphs and caddis larvae, and scavenged on anything that found its way into the pond and died. It was not the only eel in the pond, but it was not social. The eel residents slipped silently by each other in the dark and gave each other space.

Years passed. Jeanette battled family tragedy, cancer, and near bankruptcy and found a means to survive. Unlike the eel, she didn't hunt, yet she lived on crabs captured by others, among other things. They both did what they could.

The evening before Jesse Ed Davis threw Simon into the reach, less than a mile away, the eel caught a whole frog. There had been a small splash, but the pond was back from the house, and Jeanette didn't notice it. The eel was now a thick six pounds. It ate only at night and was clear and confident in its motions. During the day, it lay still in the roots of an undercut bank, digesting, waiting. Its lot was to wait, then to take what it wanted, and to grow. Until one day, it was time.

CHAPTER THIRTY-ONE

The next morning at about ten Jeanette pulled two loosely crumpled plastic drop cloths away from the back of the furnace and retrieved the red tackle box. She carried it upstairs to the kitchen, removed and counted the $8,750 that Joey Pizio had handed to her. She added the $1,250 that she had rescued from Jesse's duffel and placed it back in the box. It seemed like a lot of bills to be handling all at once on a small island where a dollar was a resource to be husbanded carefully. At eleven A.M. she was sitting, apparently idly, on the bench in front of Bea's Hive of Beauty, when Kat approached and joined her, looking weary and a little haggard.

"You look tired," Jeanette said, without further greeting.

"Thanks. You look radiant yourself," Kat replied. Jeanette grunted in acknowledgment. "I'm glad we could make this work," Kat said.

"You got it?"

"I got it all," Kat replied, reaching into her purse and retrieving a thumb drive on a key ring. "Here's your smoking gun." Jeanette reached out her hand for it, but Kat held on to it.

"Just one question," Kat said. What made you change your mind?" Jeanette thought about it, looking up into the new green leaves above them.

"I came into a little money?" Jeanette said, as if it was a question, a trial balloon. Kat smiled.

"And your moral superiority? What became of that?"

"I wish I could tell you. I . . . some combination of self-preservation and needing to make the world right."

"Even at a price?"

"Even at a price."

Kat gave her the thumb drive. "That's why I came to you both in the first place. Make things right."

"And ten thousand dollars," Jeanette said, handing Kat the tackle box. Kat opened it and counted.

"It's not really enough money," Kat said. "Not for what you're getting, not for the risk."

"There's never enough money," Jeanette said. "There are some fishing lures in the box too. Gratis. You know, give a woman ten grand, she'll burn through it in a day. Give a woman spin baits, she'll have fish for a lifetime. That's in the Bible. Or someplace."

Kat shook her head. "Don't worry about me," she said. "I'm self-reliant, to a fault."

She rose, and, without saying goodbye, walked to her car and was gone.

***

Roland Finkle knew enough to pick an unobtrusive corner booth at the Pancake House, which was not crowded in any case. He was drinking a Coke as big as a bait bucket when Lottie Pride slipped into the banquette across from him.

"We met in Mount Chase," she said. "At a town meeting for the elver-fishing initiative. You gave me a card."

Finkle had already sorted that much of the story out just by looking at her. He had attended half a dozen meetings and had met only a couple interesting people in the process.

"What's your name?" he asked.

"My name is Lottie Pride," she said. "I'm from the Center for Indigenous People's Fishing Rights."

"Have I heard of that?" Finkle asked. "C-I-P-F-R? Doesn't sound like it makes much of an acronym."

"Acronyms, shortcut words, nonsense names for big multinationals—that's the property of settlers, not people from a place. It is worth the time to say the name of things."

"Are we on the record?"

"Always," she said. "It is one of the advantages of not being full of shit. These recordings were delivered to the Center for Indigenous People's Fishing Rights by an anonymous ally. The anonymous part is real. The recordings prove what we have been saying for years. Almost six hundred years. It is the ex-governor, the US-based executive from Bando International, an industrial-scale elver fisherman, and a fisheries bureaucrat conspiring to plunder natural resources, pass a special interest ballot initiative using foreign funding, and maybe even kill someone. That last part's a little fuzzy."

"Jesus. How'd you get this?"

Lottie furrowed her brow and exhaled, seeming disappointed in Finkle. "I already told you. It arrived. Anonymous. You're a reporter. Report. The people in the recording are all members of the Association of Cronyist Maine Settlers. Your job is to uncover, and I'm making your job very easy."

"The association of what?"

"ACRONYMS," she said, with an eye roll, and pushed the thumb drive across the table at him.

Roland Finkle looked momentarily confused, then cracked a smile. When he smiled, Lottie looked relieved. He isn't a complete idiot, she thought.

"Once you listen, give me a call."

A cheerful, generously built server in a pale blue uniform approached, her order pad at the ready.

"Can I get you something to start, honey?" she asked.

Lottie looked up at her. "I'm not staying, but you can bring this man another tub of corn syrup."

**

Toland Bates was returning the Tyrolean hat at the L.L. Bean outlet store when his phone began to ring.

"Excuse me," he said to the salesgirl, who looked to be about a sophomore in high school. Hiring the summer help already, he thought. He answered the phone.

"Officer Bates," said a voice he remembered well.

"Chief Crothers. Good to hear from you, sir. How are you?"

"Well, thank you. I'm hoping you are enjoying your new promotion. I put in a good word for you with your chief."

"Thank you for that, sir. That was very generous of you. I'm still waiting to hear how it lands."

"God willing, it will go well for you. Listen, officer I need to tell you something. We've had a disturbing twist over here, and I wanted you to know."

"What's that, sir?"

"The person who died in the car fire is not who we thought."

"How do you mean?" Toland asked, moving to an unoccupied aisle in the store.

"It was Thurston Harney's rental car, and the corpse had Thurston Harney's metal Amex card in what was left of his wallet. So, we made the ID. But the teeth don't match."

"The teeth . . . ?"

"Best as they can figure," Crothers went on, "Harney faked the thing. The body belongs to a homeless gentleman who lived on the streets out in Milwaukee. Least he used to. Most likely Harney picked him up in the car, offered him a meal or whiskey or something, and took it from there. A terrible fate for one of God's creatures. Fortunately, Harney's mamma took him to the dentist, at least till he went off to Princeton."

"Jesus!" Toland exclaimed.

"Well, son." Crothers seemed off put by the Lord's name. "More like Lazarus, but meaner."

"Where is Thurston Harney now?"

"Anybody's guess. But I thought you ought to know," Crothers said.

"Thank you, sir. Of course. If you hear anything else, please do call me. Cell phone is always best."

"Of course. Good luck with the promotion, Officer Bates, and I am glad the Lord brought us together."

"Me too," Toland said, but his mind was racing. He put the Tyrolean hat back on his head and exited the store. He jogged to his car, in a hurry to warn Jeanette, praying that Harney was still in Wisconsin.

As he drove off to the south, a man with a disfigured face stepped out of a rented Ford Explorer, entered the L.L. Bean store, and asked the young girl at the checkout counter to direct him to the men's department.

***

Jeanette was as alarmed as Toland at the news. She met Simon at the dock—the weather was warming.

Simon greeted her with fury.

"That was a hell of a stunt," he said. "Your boyfriend burns up my money. For what, Jeanette?"

"He's not my boyfriend. And we did it to protect you from your fool self."

"I'll tell you what. He needs protecting from me. I'm not the kind of man who—"

"Simon!" She cut him off. "He's coming for you."

"What do you mean? Who?"

She told him about Thurston Harney's resurrection, the call from Toland, the teeth.

"You gotta go back to Aroostook. Or visit your friend Jack Strudwick in Key West. But I'm telling you Thurston Harney's coming back, and you and that money are gonna be his passion."

"The money's on you," Simon replied. "Up in smoke, I didn't do that. You did. Even if I wanted to give it to him, what am I supposed to do—explain how banking got started?"

"Simon, you've got to go."

"To Florida? In a lobster boat?"

"I don't care where, Simon, but if you want to live you need to get gone."

"You really care if I live," Simon said. "That's a comfort at least. I guess it's not quite love."

"If love means I'd prefer not to have you forced to drink weed killer, or to get hog-tied in a car and lit on fire, or eaten by lobsters, then I love you. Just please, hide yourself."

* * *

Roland Finkle's voice on Kat Rutherford's answering machine caused a chill to run down her spine. If the reporter found her this quickly, surely the world would find her almost as soon. He had published his exposé that morning and all hell was bound to break loose. She had listened to the message for a second time when the phone rang again. She dared not pick it up. After the fourth ring the machine clicked on and she heard Lester Birdwell's voice, chipper as usual.

"Honey," he said, "good news! Quick trip to Nassau coming up. Got our own plane this time and I know you'll want to be with me. Some important business to do down there. Mostly sun and sand for you though. You lucky thing," he said cheerfully. Too cheerfully. He left the flight details and rang off. She sat frozen in place for a moment, her breath coming quickly. Then she steadied herself and stood up from the bed.

"Big girl pants," she said to the empty room. "Put 'em on."

She had three letters of recommendation printed on Birdwell's stationery; she had been signing his correspondence for years, so that part was easy. They were already in her laptop case. She had packed some blank letterhead as well, just in case. If she left before dawn, she could be in western New York by the end of tomorrow. She had a cousin in Skaneateles, who had told her that the state house speaker in Albany was looking for someone. Surely he would look forward to meeting the great-great-granddaughter of Rutherford B. Hayes.

CHAPTER THIRTY-TWO

Tommy B. Donovan was just sitting down to dinner with a plate of microwaved mac and cheese in front of him and a glass of Allen's Coffee Brandy in his hand when the knock came on the door. He cursed quietly to himself, abandoned his food, which was still steaming and dotted with splashes of hot pepper sauce, and went to see what was up. Opening the door, he found himself facing a man he had never seen before, dressed in an imitation Polo golf shirt with an L.L. Bean logo on the breast pocket and a pair of pleated corduroys, with a black-and-red plaid guide hat on his head. He looked acutely uncomfortable and stood stock-still with a leather kit bag slung over his shoulder. Kinda early for summer folk, Tommy B. thought. And this one looks like he hasn't decided if he wants to go sailing or hunting or hiking. He had on a pair of boat moccasins to complete the picture. Must be lost, Tommy B. thought. Looking for the golf club or someplace. But there was something about his face that said none of this was truly who he was. In his fine clothes he looked to Tommy B. like a store mannequin man who wasn't quite dead or alive.

"Time to talk," the man said, almost as though it was a question, but not quite.

"Okay," Tommy B. said, not opening the screen door that separated them. "Talk."

"Not here," the man said. "Inside." Tommy B. hesitated. The man continued, "You see," the man said, "I was at the lobster co-op on a certain night, and I have certain information."

For a moment Tommy B. didn't move, didn't speak. Then he opened the screen door and stood back. The strangely dressed man walked calmly into the room and settled into the one upholstered chair in the anteroom without being invited. He set his kit bag carefully on the floor.

"Take a drink," the man said. "Finish your supper. I'm in no hurry."

"Can't eat now," Tommy B. said. "Lost my appetite."

He took the drink down in one good swallow.

The house was sparsely furnished. There was an old rag carpet on the floor and four folding chairs at a Formica table off the kitchen. The mid-century table might have fetched something at a collectibles fair, but nothing else seemed to be worth a dime. For a man who had fought his way to the top of a lucrative business, Tommy B. appeared to be incapable of figuring out how to spend money. The compact man looked around wondering whether there was some other expensive habit involved that you couldn't see—prostitutes or horses or sports betting. Or was Tommy B. simply a man who was born to fight, where the fight is the only pleasure, and the rewards are incidental and useless? He had noticed the immaculately kept yellow truck in the driveway, but how much could a man spend on a truck?

Tommy B. paced a little and put his glass down on an empty knickknack shelf behind him. The shelf was lined with a decade of dust that lifted listlessly off and settled again. The man in the chair nodded to himself. Not even a cleaning lady. Mysterious.

"What'd you want?" Tommy B. finally said.

"Just to talk," the man said. "You don't know me, and I don't know you, but I recognize the truck."

"My pride and joy, you might say."

"Seems to be. I first saw it at the co-op a little while back."

"I'm there sometimes."

"This particular Saturday night you were on your way out. Myself, I was headed there for a meeting. After hours meeting with a fella I was in business with. Or at least he asked me to do a bit of business, which I did. But he hadn't paid me yet. We'd gotten into a bit of a dispute."

"I don't allow nothing like that," Tommy B. said. He backed into the dinette area and took the Allen's Coffee Brandy bottle from the Formica tabletop, moved back to the shelf, and refilled his glass. He did not offer any to his guest. "Cash on the barrelhead, that's the way I do it. No disputes that way."

"Well," said the man in the chair, "it was a little more complicated than that. Seemed there might be a second job, a more lucrative job, but this gentleman, whom I trusted—I'd shared a residence with him for years, back in Wisconsin—he didn't want to pay me for the first part till the second part was complete. We had not come to mutually agreeable terms for the second part. So, we needed to meet in order to work through our differences."

"Well then," Tommy B. said. "Maybe you learned a little lesson. Get the details ironed out first." He lifted his glass in a silent toast and took half of it in a gulp. He was wishing he hadn't left his pistol in the glove box of the truck.

"Sometimes, the details emerge as you go," the man said. "You open a door. Behind it, there is another door. The point is, I was just a few yards from the co-op's driveway when you and that yellow truck came tearing out of there at quite a pace. If I hadn't hit the brake, I would have slammed right into you. Seems like there was someplace you were in a hurry to get to. Or get away from. I wasn't in a hurry, you see—just meeting a fellow, this fellow I was going to talk to. I didn't expect to find him in a tank full of lobsters. But that's where he was. It was quite a surprise."

"I don't know nothing about that," Tommy B. said. "If you don't mind, I'd like to go up and get my teeth." He gestured to the stairway. There was another gun in the drawer of the night table.

"I can understand you plainly," the man said. "If you didn't need your teeth to eat your dinner, you don't need them now."

"Mac and cheese," Tommy B. said with exasperation. "Goes down easy." But it was a lost cause.

"I assume," the man said, "that you had a good motive to shoot him. People usually do."

"I swear to God I don't know nothin' about this. Not a single thing."

The man dipped his head, as if possibly accepting the truth of Tommy B.'s statement, and lowered his hand into the kit bag. When he pulled it back there was a gun in his hand. It looked to Tommy B. like a Glock of some kind, but it was covered with a camouflage skin, so it was hard to tell. Tommy B. didn't care what kind of gun the man had. He was thinking about the two that were out of his reach.

"I've been doing this a long time," the man said. He looked like he was trying to smile, but his face wouldn't cooperate.

Tommy B. swallowed. He wanted to take another slug of his drink but found himself paralyzed by the sight of the gun and by the strange calm that seemed to envelop the man in the chair, not to mention the formality of his talk, which somehow complemented his disfigurement.

"I don't want to shoot you," the man said. "That's not my motive—I don't even know you. But I would like to know why you killed a man who owed me seventy-five thousand dollars and might have been convinced to help me find considerably more. That wasn't thoughtful of you."

"I told you—"

"The obvious reason is that you knew about the money and you have it someplace, but I don't know as I believe that. When I look around your place, I can only conclude that you don't care about anything but your truck. Of course, it can be hard to read a man. Some men collect money the way others collect beer steins. Are you a collector?"

"Mister, I don't know where you come from or what you want, but I'm a fisherman. That's all I am." Tommy B. managed to loosen his arm muscles enough to polish off the contents of his glass.

"I said I didn't want to shoot you," the man said. "I didn't say I wouldn't."

"Can I sit down?"

"By all means. Grab one of those chairs from the dinette. Let's talk."

Tommy B. moved deliberately to the Formica table and lifted his dinner chair, spinning it around and setting it down at a better distance from the other man's firearm. He reached back and took the bottle, cradling it in his lap.

"Seventy-five grand is a lot of money for killing a little punk like Joey Pizio," Tommy B. said as he settled into the chair. "He never saw that much money in his life, even if you added it all up from the minute he was born till the minute he died."

The man shrugged. "He wasn't in my business," he said. "Every business has a price scale. You know that. And every man in the business has a quote. That's my quote. Mr. Tyson and I were looking for some information. I thought maybe I could get it and I had to work hard at it. But that's what I do. Someone had a lot of Mr. Tyson's money. A lot more than seventy-five thousand dollars. I needed to find out who, and where it was kept, in order to earn my fee. That's all."

Tommy B. stared at the man and tried to fathom why he was being allowed to hear this information. If this guy tortured and killed Joey Pizio and don't mind saying so, it can only mean one thing, Tommy thought. The man in the mismatched summer outfit was planning to kill him. He couldn't reach the guns. All he had left was information.

"Bennett Tyson wanted my business," Tommy said. "And I worked hard to build it and wasn't gonna let him near it. I went to the lobster co-op to back him away from it."

"And you accomplished that by shooting him and tossing him in the lobster tank?"

"I had some information," Tommy B. said. "I knew he had a fake driver's license; he wasn't who he said he was, and I'm best friends with the town supervisor, who makes things happen here—or stops them from happening. I was in a good position to have this guy in handcuffs anytime I wanted to, and I knew it. And I needed Tyson to know it. I didn't know nothing about no money."

"Just competition?" the man asked. "Another eel hunter you wanted to be rid of. I heard there was one earlier—last spring. That's what Mr. Tyson told me."

"You're talking about Tom Hinchcliffe? No one knows who killed Tom Hinchcliffe."

"I thought he died of a heart attack."

"So he did," said Tommy B. But a certain energy drain had crept into his voice.

"You just tied him up and left him there."

"I did no such thing."

"He was hunting eels. Mr. Tyson was hunting eels. You don't like people who hunt eels."

"It's called fishing. Or some calls it trapping. It ain't hunting."

"Either way," said the man in the chair. "Fishing, hunting, heart attack, murder—it's all the same to you."

"I didn't want to kill him. I just wanted to back him away," Tommy B. went on. "The thing was, he didn't take it very well. In fact, he did just what you did—pulled a gun. People on this island mainly use guns to hunt deer. Or sometimes bear. But this wasn't a hunting rifle. It was just a handgun. Just like the one you got there. I mean, not exactly, but close enough. And that's the gun that shot him. We got into a scuffle, that's all."

"And you shot him with his own gun."

"Swear to God. I didn't want to. Not why I went there. But what could I do? He attacked me. You look high and low, you'll never find a gun that I own that killed any man. His own gun."

"And the money?"

Tommy B. was about to deny any knowledge of any lost money, because he actually had none, when a thought occurred to him.

"There's a fella," he said. "Fella named Simon King was in business with your partner." The man cocked his head. Tommy B., for a moment, had his attention.

"Bennett Tyson wasn't my partner," the man in the chair said. "He hired me to do a job. Different things."

"Okay. Either way. This King fella disappeared in his boat after Joey died, and then he came back after your partner—sorry, the guy who hired you—landed in the tank. He came by the other day looking to start up again with me. But none of his people got licenses."

"This is interesting," the man in the chair said. "I'm glad I stopped by." He held the gun still in his hand and rocked the chair back on its back legs a little, adjusting his aim as he did so.

"Please continue."

"That's what I got."

The man in the chair leaned forward, and the two front feet of the chair hit the wooden floor. It was a soft knocking sound, but to Tommy B. it sounded like a pistol shot.

"Where did this gun in my hand come from?" the man asked.

"How the hell do I know? Come out of your gunnysack there, that's all I know about it."

"It's a satchel. Do you want to see what else is in the satchel? I don't think you do." He reached down into the kit bag. Leaving his hand inside gripping something. It could have been anything.

"Look, mister, I'm tryin' to help. None of it was planned out this way—I didn't know Tyson owed you or anybody any money. I just figured if I could get him to leave the island my whole problem would go away. When Tyson died—all right, when I shot him—this Simon King fella came back. Beats me. But I'll tell you what. Him coming and going all around Tyson dying makes me think he's got your money—or a way to it, or he took it."

The man, behind the scar tissue, seemed to be thinking.

"Thank you for sharing your theory about Simon King. It is already familiar to me."

Tommy B. stopped. He had played his only ace. He took a moment to catch up.

"Joey Pizio," he said finally, deflating. "Shit."

The man nodded slowly. "Mr. Pizio has given us all the help he's ever going to give. The important thing you've told me is that Mr. King has returned."

"He's back," Tommy B. repeated, brightening slightly. Maybe there was hope.

"Back," the man said. "What does 'back' mean?"

"Hell, I don't know. He's around. Got a house out on Heller Lane, keeps his boat at the co-op. He runs the thing up the coast to buy elvers, I don't know."

"Does he arm himself?"

"He hunts deer. He and a bunch of pals go for bear once a year. Probably has a pistol in his glove box. Everybody does. But I don't think he's carrying all the time."

"Tell me more."

"I don't think I know more."

The man in the chair reached deeper into his sack and Tommy B. held up his hand.

"Hear me out a minute, can ya?" he said. It sounded more like begging than he had hoped it would. "If you want to find him and your money, I'd be glad to help you. I know the people here, and how things work. King wants to work for me. I know how to go about finding him. Good for both of us. Give me a little commission, like you was asking Tyson for."

The man kept the gun perfectly trained on Tommy B.'s chest and pulled a black coil of rope from the sack; he tossed it onto the floor. Then he dipped again and came out with a fixed-blade hunting knife. It had a stunningly beautiful polished birchwood handle. Tommy B. recognized it. Scandinavian. Made by reindeer herders. The Sámi. A puukko, it was called. He had often thought about buying one, but the folding buck knife from Walmart was adequate, so he always talked himself out of it. Now here it was, and he regretted not having bought one when he had the chance; the man propped it on the coil of rope, blade pointed at Tommy B.

"Sharp knife," the man said.

"I envy you that," Tommy B. said.

"I thought it must be the sharpest damn knife in the whole damn world," the man said. "But look at these."

He dipped into the satchel a third time. When his hand emerged, he had four little knives spread between his fingers. They were white, plastic-handled knives that Tommy knew were used for picking crabs. The blades were shaped like a bird's beak. He stared at them.

"All of them sharp," the man said, "but look here."

He held up one of the little knives; the blade had been so frequently sharpened it had become wire thin; the handle was partially melted.

"Sharper than the other four, sharper than the puukko," the man said. "At a fraction of the cost. In the right hands, a person could perform a surgery with a knife like this."

"Hell," Tommy said. "I don't need no commission. I'd do it for the honor of cleaning the place up. I'm born and brought up here. I know things that could help you. What about it?"

"I have a better idea," the man said. "A simple idea. Why don't you call Simon King?"

"On the phone?"

"Well, not like you call a deer. Of course on the phone."

"Now?"

"I'll spell it out," the man said. "Pick up the phone and call Simon King. Tell him you've thought over the idea of him joining you in your work, and that maybe it can all be worked out. But it's gotta be done quick." He looked around the kitchen. "I'll tell you what. Tell him he should come right over and meet you here to talk it through."

Tommy B. eyed the phone.

"If I get him here, you won't shoot me?"

"If you get him here, I promise I won't shoot you," he said. "It's not my style."

CHAPTER THIRTY-THREE

Jeanette's cell phone rang a little after six the next morning.

Simon.

"Dammit, Simon," she barked into the phone. "You know I hate to miss my sleep. What the. . ."

"Jeanette. Thank god." He sounded scared. The reception was bad, his voice crackling in and out. "The guy, he came, took me . . . Little Piglet. You gotta come get me . . . you and your boyfriend."

"He's not my boyfriend," Jeanette said. She heard a dull thud and Simon groaned.

"You gotta get me," he begged. "Take my Whaler. Faster than your boat. I don't wanna die here."

"You want me to come out to Little Piglet with Jesse in your Whaler?"

"Just you two. No cops. No guns. Key's under the floorboard," he said. There was a pause, and Jeanette heard a voice in the background. "He says you better bring all the money too."

"I'm on my way," she said, sitting up in bed, taking it all in. For a moment she was afraid she'd lost him. Then she heard his voice again, farther away from the phone.

"No kidding Jeanette. He gave me . . . two hours."

"I'll come as fast as I can," she said, but the line was dead. She tossed aside the covers and went for her clothes. So much for the morning shower. She called Jesse as she dressed.

"I can pick up Toland," Jesse offered.

"No," she said sharply. "I need him to come in his own car. I'll pick you up and explain later. Be there in ten minutes." She didn't give him time to object.

She was about to call Toland when she saw a text light up on the screen.

Lottie:

> Guess where I'm going? To Augusta, to meet with the goddamn governor of Maine! It's a great day. Just wanted to let you know. I'll check in after.

At least someone was having a good time.

She reached Toland and told him to meet Jesse at the co-op dock where Simon's Whaler was tied up.

"Thurston Harney has Simon," she said. "And thank God you're not a cop anymore—he said no cops, no guns. Just get there. If you beat us to it, look around at the dinghies tied up there. There's bound to be a mess of canvas tarps rolled up in one or two of them. Just take them."

"Steal them?"

"Borrow them. We'll put them back. Then get back in your car and wait for me."

⁎
⁎⁎

Sung Ho Han had called Bando's CEO after reading Roland Finkle's piece in the *Chronicle*. Better to tell Bando than to have Bando tell him. Now he was in the back seat of the silver Mercedes, speeding toward the tiny airport in Bar Harbor with Blake at the wheel. He was to catch a small plane to Boston, and then a jumbo jet to Seoul. He felt certain that he would be, at the very least, reassigned, perhaps to a desk job in a sweltering, tiny office at Bando. Maybe worse. Who knew how many laws had been broken. Sung Ho was trying to prepare himself for whatever was waiting for him 6,800 miles away, across a continent and an ocean.

He left the car with Blake, and they shook hands. It was to be driven back to the cottage and left there until further notice. Perhaps the car, along with the residence, would be up for sale in one tidy package.

Inside the only building at the airport, a flight officer was checking in a passenger who carried only a briefcase and an incongruous straw hat that looked more like a souvenir than any kind of headgear. It was Lester Birdwell. The ex-governor turned around and saw Sung Ho standing behind him. He extended a hand, and Sung Ho looked at it, as though it was an object of curiosity, but not something that he wanted to touch.

"Partner," Birdwell said. "Imagine that. You and me, traveling on the same day." His hand hung in space, then slowly descended.

"Quite the coincidence," Sung Ho said.

"Where you headed?"

"Boston," Sung Ho said. There was no point in giving up anything more.

"Bahamas," Birdwell said. "Chartered my own plane."

"You're traveling light," Sung Ho said.

"You don't need much in the Bahamas," Birdwell said. "I've got friends down there. And my lovely assistant, who should be joining me any minute."

The flight officer handed Birdwell his paperwork and gestured to the glass door that led to the runway.

"You can tell Miss Rutherford I've already boarded," he said.

"Have a good trip, Governor," the man behind the desk replied.

"Thank you, sir," Birdwell said. Then, turning to Sung Ho, he said "Bon voyage. And I'm sorry about the trucks."

He saluted casually and walked out the door onto the tarmac, where a Learjet 45 was waiting. Sung Ho shook his head and presented his passport and boarding pass to the flight officer, who looked it over carefully.

"I'm afraid I can't let you board until the governor is taken care of," he said without expression. "You can take a seat there next to the restrooms."

"I don't understand," Sung Ho said. "He's not even the governor."

"Please be patient, sir," the man said.

Sung Ho frowned. Through the glass door he could see Birdwell navigating the narrow steps of the boarding ramp that dropped down from the fuselage and heaving himself into the plane. The ramp was pulled up. Sung Ho was about to turn away when four black cars raced down the runway and surrounded the Learjet on all four sides. Eight rear doors opened as if synchronized and a man got out of each, all of them dressed in black suits. Eight men, ramrod straight, surrounded the plane, each wearing an identical earpiece.

"What's going on?" Sung Ho asked.

"I'm not at liberty to say," answered the flight officer. "I'm sorry, I'm on my break now. We'll get you boarded as soon as we can."

As he turned to retreat into the office behind the counter, Sung Ho said, "I have a connection in Boston. An international connection."

"You'll make it," the man said. "This won't take long to sort out." He disappeared behind the door of the office.

Sung Ho stood alone and watched with fascination as Lester Birdwell was taken off the plane, led to the car closest to the ramp, and handcuffed. With some difficulty he got himself into the back seat and the car drove away, followed by the others.

* * *

They loaded a snarl of old blue canvas tarps into the back of the Whaler and propped them next to a rolled-up seine that Simon used to catch bait. The key was under the floorboard, as promised.

Jeanette drove the boat at full throttle. Approaching Little Piglet, she could see Thurston Harney standing on the pebbly beach, dressed like a wealthy city dweller lost at sea in a camel-colored cashmere jacket and rep necktie. He stood in front of the gnarled oak, next to the remains of Jesse's fire. The sky was dark and on the move, and Harney's hair was beginning to drip from the rainfall. Charred corners of hundred-dollar bills had been pushed here and there by the last high tide but were clearly visible, tucked into the gravel-strewn seaweed. Harney stared out at the Whaler as it approached. Jeanette, standing at the helm, stared back at him. Jesse moved back and sat on some flattened cardboard bait boxes in front of a crumpled blue tarp and a broken crab pot.

She slowed the engine, threw the boat into neutral, and they bumped up onto the pebble beach.

"Well, hallelujah," Harney said. "The cavalry rides to the rescue."

He pointed his camouflage-covered pistol at Jesse as they stepped off the boat. His dead eyes seemed to be held in place by his taut skin.

"Mickey Keegan," Jeanette said. "Boat salesman."

"Lynne Framer. Bullshit artist." He nodded at Jeanette, as Jesse dug an anchor into the loose rocks on the shore. Harney looked at them both impassively. Finally, he spoke. "Walk," he said. He used the gun to point up toward the remains of the stone shed.

There was a light coming through the door gap in the roofless stone hut, which appeared to Jeanette as a kind of beast from ancient times that had risen from the ocean with its front teeth knocked out. Or an unfinished jack-o'-lantern with only a mouth, through which yellow candlelight was visible.

The rain was spitting now, a squall on the way from the east. She stood behind Jesse as it started to pour.

"Come in for a minute," the man said. "If you want to see the circumstances as they are. They're not good. And I'm getting wet."

The words chilled her blood. Was Simon lying in his own vomit on the floor, already poisoned? Was he sliced open, or lying there with a bullet through his temple? She swallowed hard and followed Jesse into the structure, trailed by the small but solidly built, well-dressed man.

Light beamed from a hissing Coleman carbide camper's lantern that was placed on a stone outcropping at the back of what was left of the building. Simon was lying on the floor, bound and gagged. A piece of duct tape was wrapped entirely around the lower part of his head, closing off his mouth, and his eyes were wide with fear. A long cut on his right cheek, under his eye, oozed blood. He nodded at Jeanette and Jesse, but the eyes didn't change. He was a beaten man. Jeanette, stilled by the sight of her ex-husband tied like an animal about to be butchered, felt her blood pressure drop. She took a slow, deep breath. I'm not letting this psychopathic little shit think I'm some woman who can't take whatever he's dishing out. I'm not going to be that person. I'm just not. I've thought this whole thing through.

"What have you done?" she asked. Her voice sounded flat and far away to her, as if someone else was speaking in a monotone.

"What have I done?" the man asked. "What I haven't done is put a bullet in a woman. Not once. Hate to start today. You this man's wife?"

He gestured to Simon, who nodded again.

"Ex-wife," Jeanette said.

"He talks about you a lot," the man said. "When he's able to talk. Tried to tell me that your boyfriend over there burnt up all my money. Brought me out here on his lobster boat to try to prove it. But that's just a plain falsehood. No one sets fire to that much money. I pointed that out to him, and he said maybe you had it then. You and the Indian are thick as thieves. That's what he said."

The Coleman lamp flared, sputtered, and began to go out. Waterlogged, maybe. As it flared, died, and flared again the shadows on the granite walls danced a crippled jig. The rain was pelting down on all of them, and it had turned chilly. Jeanette's teeth began to chatter, and she tightened her jaw to hold them still.

"He is not my boyfriend." Jeanette said. The words came out strangely through her clenched teeth.

"The point is," Harney said, "I'd heard as much as I could stand from him, so I put him in a condition where I don't have to listen to him anymore. The point is," he repeated, raising his voice slightly, "that a good part of that money is mine. I did a job for it, and I expect to get paid. But all he had for me was this cock-and-bull story about a fire, some kind of 'offering.' I thought maybe I ought to ask you. That's what he suggested—talk to my wife and the man who burned it all—so I had him give you a buzz. Might save his life."

So Simon had given her away. She looked at him, his pitiable condition, and understood that she might have done the same thing in such circumstances. Who knew what anyone would do when life itself depended on it.

"So," Harney said, "You've seen your idiot ex, and he's all right, just a little roughed up. Now it's your turn," he said, turning to Jesse. "You have been accused of arson. It's a federal crime to destroy US currency, but the truth is, I think you're innocent."

"I'm guilty as charged," Jesse responded, gesturing back to the beach, where they had seen the burned remains.

"You're pardoned," Thurston Harney said. "I don't believe it was enough money to worry about."

"The money was ill-gotten, I offered it up as smoke. I burned it up in a traditional manner."

"People don't burn up money like that. They just don't," said the man.

"The first money was circular carved rocks," Jesse began.

"I heard it already. From him. And how you told him. I've heard enough lies and legends for one day," the man said. "Especially a day like this where I'm stranded on a piece of rock out in East Jesus in a goddamn monsoon."

"Little Piglet," Jesse interjected.

"What did you say?"

"The piece of rock is called Little Piglet. Names matter, even if this one was named by a settler who thought the island looked like a small swine. That's the legend. But names. They matter. Maybe it was a foretelling—that one day, a small swine would actually arrive."

"You've got a mouth on you. I hope it opens soon and utters some true words. You'd think a stone cabin would have a roof, at least. This is a one-hundred-percent cashmere jacket."

"You should have brought a poncho," Jesse said. "Be prepared."

"Oh, I'm prepared," the man said, his face very close to Jesse's. "We've established to my satisfaction that you, Big Chief, have lied through your teeth about this sacrifice bullshit. That makes you the first one I'd shoot. But the lady, she'd be sorry. She'd miss you, and she'd end up giving me the money after all, and then she'd be lonely all the rest of her life, so how about a little truth and reconciliation?"

Jesse and Jeanette were silent. The man lunged toward Jesse and stuck the muzzle of the pistol against the carotid artery on the left side of his neck.

"Now would be a good time," he said.

"Down by the shoreline," Jeanette blurted out. "All right?" The man lowered the gun.

"Progress."

"Damn, some people can't keep quiet," Jesse muttered, looking down.

"It's only money," Jeanette said to Jesse. Then she turned to Thurston, "If you want it, it's yours." She sounded breathless. "By the shoreline. We'll show you." The little man looked at her.

"Maybe it is, and maybe you will," he said. "But not yet. I always like to generate a little leverage first. And I've been doing this a long time."

The man turned to Simon, who remained on the floor with his eyes wide.

"You stay here and guard the fort," he said, as he stepped delicately around him.

Turning to Jeanette he said. "You and the Indian are coming with me."

The man lifted his head and swept the hand that wasn't holding the gun toward the doorway, like a head waiter inviting patrons to a table. They stepped back outside.

He kept them ahead of him, leading them to higher ground.

A balsam fir rose fifty feet or more toward the sky, growing out of a wide fissure in the rocky ground. They were in a thick stand of trees now, and the overstory was fighting off the rain, without much success. The man extracted a set of double-locking nylon zip-tie handcuffs from his pocket and handed them to Jeanette. Then he turned to Jesse.

"Put your hands behind your back," he said. "Around the trunk." Jesse backed up against the tree.

"We didn't used to have these," the man said amiably. "These cuffs are 'efficient and easy to use.' That's what it says on Amazon. They have over twelve hundred positive reviews. Just slip them over his wrists and pull."

"Do it," Jesse said, resigned. "Do what he says."

At the foot of the tree there was a handsome leather kit bag, its fine surface now blotched and dark from the rain. As she pulled the cuffs tight, she looked around for help, but saw only the woods, dense and deep.

"I know—" she said, but the man put the pistol in her face, and she went silent.

"I don't want to hear from you," he said. "Not yet. Not a sound."

She nodded. Jesse watched her.

"I had a nice chance to do some exploring once I got your husband taken care of," the man now said to Jeanette. "I knew you'd have a plan, so I made my own plan, which was not to follow yours. There's a lot of resources on this island, trees and the like. Left my bag here so I could grab it when the time came. Left my hands free. Now look at it. Goddamn weather."

He picked up the leather bag and looked at it with disgust.

"Pitiful," he said. "First my jacket, now my tooled leather bag. Goddamn pitiless place, Maine."

He reached into the bag and extracted the birch-handled knife. Now he had the knife in one hand and the pistol in the other.

"Where's my money, Indian?" the man asked.

Before Jesse could speak, the man raised his finger to his lip and quietly hushed him. Jesse looked confused, and then the blade of the birch-handled knife entered his body in the center of his belly. Slowly. Just to the right of his navel, below his rib cage. Jesse shouted in surprise and pain. It was the first time Jeanette ever heard him raise his voice. It was agony that emerged.

"No!" she bleated and lunged at the man, but the pistol met her squarely in the throat.

"You killed him," she said, too shocked and driven by rage to cry.

"No, no. I cut his guts. *Very* painful in the guts. You would know. No arteries though. See how it's oozing, but not squirting? He's got the better part of a day before blood poisoning starts to get him. Then it'll take him a day or two. Two at the most. Sepsis will set in and start to wear out his organs. Miserable way to go. Blood poisoned by your own partially digested shit. You see, I know where to put a knife. I know what I'm doing. Could have been a surgeon."

Jesse moaned and grimaced and stared at the man with hate in his eyes.

"Hurts, doesn't it? But if he gets help soon, it's one thing. Give him twelve hours and his odds go down. Way down."

Jesse's head rocked back, and he gritted his teeth and grunted at the sky. No words, just the sound of a strong man telling the gods how much it hurt. It was an eerie, guttural, birthing, animal sound. Defiance in the face of hopeless odds, and all-consuming pain.

"Now let's finish this while he still has time," the man said to Jeanette.

Jeanette found it impossible to turn away from Jesse. But the man put the gun to her cheek and pushed her head around.

"Take me there," he said.

Her feet stumbled over the roots as she staggered away from Jesse, grabbing at saplings and dead branches to keep her balance. She was no longer really there—just a human body moving. But she knew what to say.

"It's the truth," she said. "We just burned enough to throw off Simon."

"I knew that. Very sneaky. That's what caused me to have to hurt the Indian," the man said. "Your husband can believe that mythological crock if he so chooses. I do not. Anything less than the truth would be a mistake. A fatal mistake. You and the Indian are close. That's what I hear. Time is of the essence now. So, let's save a little time, shall we?"

She led him back to the beach, feeling the tip of the pistol barrel at the back of her neck. The Whaler's bow rested on the gravel beach, tilted off-center. Thurston Harney grabbed her arm and twisted it painfully behind her neck. He spoke into her ear.

"Where is it? Save his life, and maybe I'll let you keep enough cash to buy yourself a new wardrobe. Maybe there'll be enough left over to get your hair done. You look like hell."

Something in Jeanette had had enough.

"I don't pay to get my hair done," she said, trying to find a way to put some space between the two of them. "I cut hair on the weekends at a cheap salon in Ellsworth. I wait tables at night and all week long I pick crabmeat to survive."

"I'm touched," he said. "I'm enjoying this conversation. But I'm starting to get chilled and it's a long way back to shore. And there's a dying man back there. So, I would say now. For real. Where's the goddamn money?"

The man was pressed up against her. "It's in the tree," she said.

"Grows on trees, is that what you're telling me?"

"In the hollow." She gestured to the oak tree, and the deep hole six feet up its trunk. "It's almost half a million."

"Well, show me," the man said, guiding her to it, pressing her between himself and the tree. She could feel him, warm and damp behind her. Jeanette's mind spun.

"Oh, Jesus," she groaned, and clutched her stomach.

"What now?" the man asked, incredulous.

"My gut," she wheezed. Her knees buckled, she slumped down to the ground and lay there whimpering. He looked down at her and shook his head.

"Did you ever see a doctor about that?" the man asked. Jeanette rocked forward and backward and groaned in response.

"Pitiful," he said.

He stepped over her and reached up and into the hollow.

Then Thurston Harney heard four sounds—or was it five? Simultaneous, or it seemed so. A quick slap from behind him, the strange hiss of the air being split, and two quick low thumps. Then, a hard crack, a bat hitting a ball, from just in front of him, coming from the tree. The entire cacophony took less than a quarter of a second.

The sounds didn't appear to make any sense to him until he tried to turn away from the tree and found he couldn't. He was pinned. Slowly, he slipped backward, away from the tree, and watched the rear half of an arrow, fletched with plastic vanes, emerge from his chest, and remain stuck in the tree. The arrow had two blue vanes and one white, all three covered in bright red blood. For the man, the timing was all backward. He saw the arrow, and recognized it for what it was, but only then did he feel himself punched, hard in the back, and the sharp pinch in his chest. He reached up with his left hand and felt just to the left of his sternum where the pinch was. His hand came away warm and wet. And red. His eyes changed from surprise to anger. He snarled, spun around toward the water where the slap had come from, and began to raise his gun. Then he seemed to lose his balance as the pistol clattered onto the rocks. He crumpled to the ground, kicked his legs once like he was running lying down, and then seemed to relax. He lay very still. For the first time, the man smiled.

Jeanette pushed herself up and began to brush herself off.

Toland Bates, crouched down, half hidden by a crumpled blue tarp, peeked over the side of the Whaler. He had notched another arrow. He wore both a life vest and a leafy suit face mask. He looked like he was dressed as a piece of shrubbery that had gone waterskiing.

"You okay?" Toland asked, hopping onto the beach. "Your stomach bad?"

"I'm fine," Jeanette said. "I haven't had stomach trouble since I started drinking Chaga. I just had to find a way to give you a clear shot. He wouldn't give me any space."

"He killed Joey Pizio. He was gonna kill you, and Simon, and Jesse. And I . . . I . . ." He trailed off, processing what he had done.

"You ruined his nice coat," Jeanette said. "Let's go get Jesse."

CHAPTER THIRTY-FOUR

Jesse Ed Davis awakened in the hospital a day and a half later. He had missed most of it, and almost died in the process. When he arrived at the hospital in Brockton, he took six units of packed red blood cells in eight hours. The doctors kept him sedated for another twenty-four. They said he was talking nonsense. Jeanette tried to explain that maybe he was just talking the way he usually did, but in the end, she let it go. He deserved the rest.

She was sitting by his bedside when the door opened and Lottie Pride walked in with a newspaper under her arm.

"Jesse," she said. "You all right?"

"Lottie," Jesse said thickly. "Good of you to come. What's in the news?"

She unfolded the paper from under her arm. The *Portland Press Herald*. "They interviewed me about the Center."

Fisheries Department to Establish Tribal Advisory Council

"They quote me!" Lottie said. "'When it comes to cooking up fisheries management policy, they only let us in the kitchen when they want to put us in the chowder,' said CIPFR Director Lottie Pride. 'Indigenous people were managing the fishery sustainably since before Moses parted the Red Sea.'"

"That's a good line," Jeanette said. "Red Sea and all. Marine reference."

"Man. You're good," Jesse agreed, speaking slowly but deliberately. "What's CIPFR?"

"It's an acronym," she said. His head fell back on the pillow. "And I hate it," she added. "But at least they locked up Birdwell."

"Is this happening?" Jesse asked. "Or is it the morphine? It's a nice dream, anyway."

"It's happening." The voice came from a wraithlike older man who pushed open the door and stepped gingerly into the room.

"You," Jesse said, suddenly more alert.

"They told me you got stabbed in the gut," said the old man. "I'm glad that's all you got."

Jeanette looked up at the man, who was gazing down at Jesse with a smile that caused every inch of his face to break into creases and wrinkles. He looked, she thought, like a tall, gaunt action figure from a space alien movie on TV.

"Hello, young woman," the old man said to Jeanette, extending a hand. "I'm Bill Penny."

***

Big Otis had spent the morning touring Tommy B. Donovan's modest clapboard house, where the body of his friend, the island's most powerful eeler, had been discovered by the neighbor's dogs. Tommy B.'s mouth had been sealed shut with duct tape, and his head had been half severed by an exceptionally sharp blade. The floor was sticky, mostly with his blood, although a bottle of Allen's Coffee Brandy had been knocked over as well. Until they were pulled out of the house by their distraught owner, the dogs were careful to lick around the Allen's.

The rest of the day was taken up with answering questions, first from law enforcement and then from news reporters. Big Otis had tag teamed with Little Otis and tried to keep his son from saying anything foolish. Roland Finkle, who had been hired away by the *Portland Press Herald* after breaking the Bando/Birdwell corruption story, was asking for photos.

Now father and son sat across from each other at dinner, while Big Otis's wife, her arthritic feet swathed in a pair of fur-lined slippers, doled out portions of Dinty Moore beef stew, which she had heated from a can in the pantry. It would be enough for the three of them. To the press and the authorities, Big Otis had not described Tommy B. as a friend. Still, he quietly mourned the loss.

"That fella," Little Otis said, "the one that Toland shot with the arrow. That's the fella what put the other one in the lobster tank. Why'd he cut Tommy B.'s throat?"

"Hard tellin', not knowin'," Big Otis replied. After a moment, he continued. "Tomorrow I'd like for you to grease the fittings on the flail mower. I've got to get back on the road. Things are quite a lot overgrown."

"Dad. I'm not the tractor greaser. I'm the police chief."

"Well, I'm the supervisor. And it needs greasing."

Little Otis nodded.

"How'd it go today?" Big Otis's wife asked the two of them as she settled into her dining room chair.

"Oh, you know," Big Otis said. "Things tend to sort themselves out."

* * *

Keith Fulbright came to the front door of his house just before sunset to find a wizened old man standing on the porch neatly dressed and holding a traditional Passamaquoddy lidded basket, woven from black ash and sweetgrass.

"Help you?" Keith asked. He'd been installing kitchen cabinets all day. His back was stiff, his knees ached, and he was hungry. But it wasn't in his nature to show it.

"Name's Bill Penny. They tell me you've got a house for sale, right on the creek across from Jeanette King, the crab lady."

"I do," said Keith. "Won't be done with her until the end of the fall."

"I'm not in a hurry," Bill Penny said. "Can I talk to you?"

Keith invited Bill Penny into the front room, introduced him to his wife, Caroline, who was standing in the kitchen door wiping her hands on a kelly green print apron with little brown flowers on it. She nodded at the old man and said to her husband, "Dinner's in five minutes. You don't want to keep a lobster stew waiting, now. It'll toughen on you."

With that she backed away, leaving the two men alone.

"Lobster stew," said Penny. "How do you prepare it?"

"Lobster, butter, milk," said Keith. "Same as everyone else. You do anything else to it, it might be good, but it won't be lobster stew. You can put some pepper in it at the table."

Penny nodded. "It's good to have food traditions."

"I wouldn't know about that," Keith said. "That's just the way you make lobster stew."

Penny nodded again.

"The house on the reach," he said. "Is there a price?"

"Hadn't thought about that much, as it's not done," Keith said.

"It would be an all-cash transaction," Penny replied. "And I do mean cash. Three hundred sixty thousand dollars."

"Four hundred work for you?"

"Three eighty would meet in the middle. I'm afraid I couldn't go higher. Cash though," Bill Penny raised his eyebrows and waited.

Keith Fulbright was hoping to get a little more, but he was not unaware of the advantages of a cash transaction or the suddenness with which this would all come upon him and solve a problem. And, besides, his stew wouldn't wait.

The shrill ring of a timer sounded in the kitchen. Caroline appeared in the doorway, wiping her hands on her apron.

"All right."

"Last thing," said Bill Penny.

Keith gestured to the kitchen. "I gotta go," he said.

"Can the shipping container you worked out of be a part of the purchase? Not your tools or anything, just the box."

"Well, it wasn't free."

"Keith, stew is ready."

Bill Penny looked at him waiting for an answer.

"Well, hell, it's just an old shipping container," Keith said. "You're welcome to it."

"Enjoy your dinner." Bill Penny shook Keith's hand. "The basket contains my down payment. We can finish this tomorrow."

* * *

"If it wasn't for the mist I could see your home across the creek from the Center," Bill Penny said to Jeanette.

They were sitting out on her dock, bundled up in the chill of an October night. There was a light burning in the upstairs window of the new house next door, which would now be the headquarters of Center for Indigenous People's Fishing Rights. Lottie Pride lived upstairs and was furiously generating grant proposals. She had accepted an annual salary of $21,500 to run the new Center.

"If you pay me any more than that," she had explained, "I lose my MaineCare insurance."

Bill Penny had helped Keith Fulbright build a diorama in the main room downstairs and had installed a saltwater aquarium. There would soon be two touch pools on the outer deck so that children could handle some of the sea creatures under close supervision. Keith had never built a touch pool but was eager to take it on and thought it was an excellent idea to line each one with the two shallow live wells that had come off the *Jeanette*. They would be labeled *Joey's Pool* and *Liam's Pool*. In the summer months, there would be elvers in the aquarium, and sea cucumbers, starfish, and a couple crabs and small lobsters—their claws banded—in the pools for visitors.

On the dock Bill Penny tapped his pipe on the wide arm of his Adirondack chair to loosen the tobacco.

"Heard anything from Simon?"

"Not for a while now," she said. "Sold the boat to Patsy's husband and migrated to Florida. Like the birds. Treasure hunting."

"The Sunshine State."

"I hope he doesn't migrate back," she said.

"You believe they busted Toland Bates down to game warden?" he asked.

"Well, he went rogue on them," Jeanette said.

"He also shot the worst bad guy they've ever had on the island," Bill Penny said. "Those Sumlins are a piece of work."

"Toland couldn't be happier," Jeanette said. "I think he's found himself."

Behind the house that would soon serve as the Center, there was a metallic grinding. Jesse Ed Davis was installing a chimney and a spark arrestor on the roof of the shipping container. He had salvaged a wood-burning stove from the dump.

"Would it kill that boy to live in a house?" Bill Penny asked.

"It might," Jeanette said.

"I know. But one thing I've learned with all my years, when winter comes, it's good to have a warm place to go to the bathroom."

"The measure of civilization," Jeanette observed.

"Not hardly. But it is convenient. Especially at my age."

"Well, I'd a lot rather have Jesse next door than those people from away," she said. "With the twin Teslas."

Bill Penny nodded and smiled. "You know, you're all from away."

The two of them sat in silence listening to Jesse work, and the water lapping against the dock. Then Bill said, "You've got this light that burns all night at the end of your dock here," he said. "Bad for bugs. Good for bats. Winners and losers."

"I like to feed the bats with the bugs," Jeanette said.

"Don't let what you happen to want disturb so many other creatures. Get a green bulb. I'd like to look across the creek and see that."

DEPARTURE

October rains swelled the pond and the creek. As the pond rose, the moon waned, and the nights became black. The night the new moon came, the rain stopped, the cloud cover was thick, and there were no stars. The tide was high but starting to fall; the eel in the pond felt a pull. Ancient wisdom. It pushed its way up and out of the little beaver pond, into the creek, and slipped down the flow, toward the ocean, swimming with the current. Seven years before that, less than three inches long, with two compatriots, it had slipped past Tommy B. Donovan's nets, not knowing it had ever been in danger, even for a moment. Now it was upward of three feet long, girthy but supple. Something was changing in it. For the last few weeks, its impulse to hunt, even to scavenge, had waned with the moon. Its digestive tract began to shrink; reproductive organs had begun to form in its place. One appetite was being replaced by another.

It passed the spot where, years ago, its traveling companions had been swallowed by the brook trout. It continued downstream. At the mouth of the creek, where it met the salty water, the eel slithered by the spot where it had evaded Tommy B's net. It entered the reach. The light at the end of Jeanette's dock, where Bill Penny sat nursing the dregs of his root beer and talking with Jeanette about moths and bats, illuminated a wide circle on the seafloor. An undulating shadow slipped from the darkness into the light. Jeanette didn't notice. Bill Penny, looking into the illuminated water, nodded to the eel as it passed—a shadowy shooting star. As quickly as it had appeared, it slid back into the darkness and was gone.

There would be no knowing what compelled the eel to abandon life in the pond, initiating a move that, with luck, might lead to offspring it would never know; whether lucky or not, it was a move that would certainly end in death. One could never say of an eel, or of a person, whether the turns that defined the shape of a life were born of volition or of destiny, whether they were driven by will, or by powers beyond understanding. As the eel wove into the sea it would not be possible to distinguish the extent to which its progress was owed to its own exertion or to the current. Forces conspired to carry it south and east.

So it writhed on uninterrupted, weaving with the tide, undulating forward into its future.

ACKNOWLEDGMENTS

Many people contributed to the creation of *The Glass Eel*, including those who live and work in Maine and whose personalities, energies, and attitudes inspired us. Should they pick up the book, they'll (probably) know who they are. We owe a debt of thanks to each of them. Additionally, several people read and commented on early drafts of the book, including Linda and Anna Daisy Viertel, Jesse Adelman, Clara Coleman, and Susan Schulman. Our agents, Robin Straus and Danielle Matta have worked tirelessly on our behalf. Luisa Cruz Smith, our editor at Mysterious Press took great care with us and the book and, as a Native person herself, was particularly thoughtful in reviewing our writing about Native people and Indigenous issues. Our initial editor Maggie Crawford, and then our copyeditor Kathy Strickman provided us with care and wisdom at the beginning and then at the end of the process. The design team and marketing departments supported us far beyond what we could have expected, and we are grateful to all of them. Finally, thanks to our partners, Linda Viertel and Rebecca Parekh, who tolerated and even supported our absence so that together, we could write this book.